Shades of the Past

Shades of the Past

Book Six
The Morcyth Saga

Brian S. Pratt

Shades of the Past
Book Six of The Morcyth Saga
Copyright 2007, 2008 by Brian S. Pratt

Books written by Brian S. Pratt can be obtained either
through the author's official website:
www.briansprattbooks.com
or through any online book retailer.

ISBN-10: 1438276265
EAN-13: 9781438276267

The Morcyth Saga

The Unsuspecting Mage
Fires of Prophecy
Warrior Priest of Dmon-Li
Trail of the Gods
The Star of Morcyth
Shades of the Past
The Mists of Sorrow*
***(Conclusion of The Morcyth Saga)**

The Broken Key

#1- Shepherd's Quest
#2-Hunter of the Horde
#3-Quest's End

Qyaendri Adventure

Ring of the Or'tux

For my Grandma Jessie. As a boy it was always fun to stay with her: picking worms, canasta, and penny slots at Lake Tahoe when no one was looking. Will always love her.

Prologue

The common room of the tavern is packed with the noon meal crowd. Tradesmen and travelers make up most of the Squawking Gooses' clientele. A few farmers are scattered about, those who are in town for one reason or another.

A tirade is in progress over by the bar, a woman is telling her man off in rare form. Apparently she's the wife of the proprietor, the man being the proprietor himself. He looks as though he's taking it with a grain of salt, simply letting her run out of steam while he waits patiently.

A man over to one side sitting at a table near a window has been watching the spectacle from the beginning. He's not sure just what started it but it has at least been a distraction while he awaits the others who are to meet him here. Several hours overdue, his impatience is steadily growing into anger.

No sooner does the woman stop explaining to the man how stupid and ignorant he is, then she turns and stalks through the door leading into the kitchen area. The look on the proprietor's face is one of relief and the man wonders how he puts up with such behavior from a woman. Shaking his head, the man glances out the window. "Finally!" he breathes under his breath as the two men whom he's been waiting for ride up the street toward the inn.

Remaining in his seat, he watches as the men approach and then come to a stop where the other horses are secured to the rail outside. Dismounting, they secure their steeds to the rail and make their way into the inn.

One is rather tall, easily half a head taller than any of the other patrons in the common room. Red haired with a trim beard, he looks as though he's seen his share of conflict if the numerous scars on the exposed portions of his body are any indication. The other man only comes to his shoulders, flaxen hair and carrying himself with confidence. Neither are ones you would want to run into alone in a dark alley.

They pause in the doorway as the tall man takes in the people in the common room. Seeing the one they're to meet he taps his partner on the shoulder and they make their way across the crowded room. When they reach the table where the man waits they take their seats. The man who has been waiting for them says, "About time you guys got here."

"Take it easy," the tall man says. "Took some time to find the numbers you wanted."

"Not to mention the items you requested," the flaxen haired man adds. "Those are hard to come by."

"Did you get them, then?" the man asks.

"Yes," the tall man replies. "We got everything you requested."

"And the men?"

"They're waiting outside of town," flaxen hair says.

"Good," he grunts and then glances around to be sure none of the other patrons are paying attention. Lowering his voice he says, "He lives outside of town. I've kept an eye on the place for the last three days. It looks like we'll have little trouble."

"Thought there was a veritable army there?" tall man asks.

"There was," he replies. "But most everyone pulled out two days ago. All that's left there are two men and one of them only has one leg. There's also a woman and a child but I doubt if they will cause us any problems."

"Is the mage still there?" flaxen hair asks.

Nodding, the man replies, "I saw him doing some strange experiments."

"Are you sure taking on a mage is a good idea," the tall man asks. Usually afraid of nothing, the thought of crossing one who can wield the power makes him uneasy.

"That's why you brought what you did," he says. "Those who I deal with say he has a fortune there in gems. From what they've learned, he has a trader sell them in other towns to avoid drawing unwanted attention to himself."

Grinning, flaxen hair asks, "Didn't work, did it?"

"No," replies the man with an evil grin. "This is going to be the biggest score we've yet made."

"When do we go?" tall man asks.

"Tonight," replies the man. "Once the sun goes down."

Rising up to the sky, it floats gently upon the breeze. Finally, his vision has seen fruition as the rising object continues to gain altitude. Oh sure, he had help but this has been his project from the beginning. Delia found the material, Ezra sewed it together for him in just the right way and James added a suggestion or two that helped.

He always knew this would work, his first attempt was a month ago. Using a small sack made from the light material he managed to get it to rise a little in the air when held aloft over an open flame. When it actually lifted several feet into the air he almost broke down and cried right there. For too long he had endured the snide remarks from others who thought he was crazy. Some even here at The Ranch looked at him odd at times but James never let anyone say a word of derision to him.

Now, a month later, he's trying something a bit more ambitious. Using a much larger balloon, he's hoping to have it rise and stay afloat for a much longer time. The balloon has now floated to the treetops and is becoming dangerously close to being entangled in the upper reaches of a tall pine. "Move...come on," he says as the balloon comes ever closer to the branches. "Rise damn you!" he practically yells just before the edge snags a branch. The balloon lurches to the side and starts deflating.

"Damn!" he yells.

"Not working?" a voice asks from nearby.

Turning, he finds Fifer there walking toward him. Leaning upon a crutch, he hobbles as best he can. Actually, he can get around pretty good with it and even has begun practicing with his sword, though isn't nearly as good as he once was. He lost his leg on the journey to Ironhold last Fall.

"The wind keeps taking it into the trees," he says. "Have to find some way to make it rise faster."

"I'm sure you'll make it work," Fifer says. "Oh, your wife said to tell you dinner is almost ready."

"Thanks," Roland replies. "I just need to get it down before I return. Tell her I will be a few minutes."

"Sure thing," he assures him. Turning his back on Roland, Fifer begins making his way back across the clearing. He grins to himself when he recalls how this clearing came to be.

It was early last winter, shortly after their return from Ironhold. James had been out here working on some experiment or another and had laid waste to a swathe of the forest. By the time the fires died out, almost forty acres had burned. In the middle of the ashes was a clearing several hundred feet across devoid of anything living.

James had come out of it looking the worse for wear. Most of his hair had been singed and he said if he hadn't erected a shield in time, he wouldn't have lived to tell about it. When asked, he didn't go into very much details on what he was doing or why.

After that and during the rest of the winter, things were in high gear. He wasn't told the particulars of what was transpiring and had the feeling no one but James, maybe Illan, knew the whole truth. But from what was going on, he knew James no longer was going to be content with waiting for danger to come to him. He was going to take it to them.

During the early winter months, Delia made many trips to and from The Ranch, much more frequently than she ever had before. The items she was dropping off here didn't make much sense: small, round glass balls with a hole in the top, not to mention the barrels of lantern oil. Didn't make much sense to Fifer.

Once the snows had set in around December, Delia and the pit fighters she uses as guards rolled into The Ranch and stayed. She began training the recruits in the use of slings. To the chagrin of Jiron, his sister Tersa joined the others in learning the use of the sling. James had a slug belt made for each of them, similar in design to the one he uses.

All through the winter, James, Jiron and Illan worked in the workshop. All others were kept out as they did who knows what. Fifer tried to look in through a window once but found it to be covered with a dark cloth to prevent anyone from discovering what was going on inside.

When news came last week that the passes were open to the east, James announced that everyone would be leaving for an extended trip. Didn't say where they were bound but everyone had a good idea, especially after what happened in Ironhold. Each of the recruits was given the option of staying behind or going with him and all opted to go.

Two days before they left, James told each of the recruits to spend what time they wished with their families before they set out.

When the day came to leave, James, Illan and Jiron brought many packs out from the workshop. Bulging with unknown items, they began securing them to the many pack horses he had acquired during the winter, a dozen in all.

Before he left, he told Roland that if he didn't return, The Ranch was his to do with as he saw fit. Then he, along with the recruits, Delia and her guards as well as Illan and the others, rode out the lane and took the road north.

Entering through the back door, Fifer finds Ezra putting the last of the food on the table. Arkie is already sitting in his highchair and perks up when he sees Fifer come in through the door. "Ife," he says in his baby talk. The last month or so he's begun to talk and be somewhat understood.

Giving the boy a smile, he says to Ezra, "He'll be in shortly. His balloon got caught in the tree again."

Shaking her head, she says, "That's the third time in two days."

He takes his seat and is amazed at just how large the table seems now that most everyone is gone. Roland and Ezra still reside in the old house, the new one is for James. It was completed not too long after their return from Ironhold and he quickly took up residence there. But until they know for sure that he's not coming back, he's still the master and that's his house.

A few minutes later, the door opens and Roland enters carrying his balloon. A long jagged hole is apparent from where the tree limb had punctured it. He puts it on the counter and then takes his place at the head of the table. That's his spot now that James is no longer here.

The meal passes quickly, the eaters are no longer in danger of being struck by Arkie's food, Ezra finally got it through to him that throwing one's food is not to be tolerated. Afterwards, they adjourn to the living room where they use to have the nightly gatherings.

With just the few of them here it doesn't have the joviality that it once did. Fifer wouldn't even mind hearing another of Uther and Jorry's fantastical tales. Of course, ever since Delia showed up and stayed, Scar and Potbelly have given them a run for their money. Each night it seemed the two pairs would try to outdo the others in seeing who could tell the most outrageous story. Some were quite good.

Fifer takes his seat on the couch and is immediately attacked by the two puppies James had acquired over the winter. Cyne and Tor, the dogs of Corbin had puppies and he had given James two. One is brown and James began calling him Bandit, the other was black and has the name Shiloh.

"Down boys," he says as they jump upon his lap, tails wagging furiously in their excitement.

"They sure took a liking to you," Roland says from his chair near the fireplace.

Ezra joins them and sets Arkie on the ground. Immediately, the pups jump to the floor and begin to wrestle with him, much to his delight. His squeals of excitement elicit barks and before you know it the front room is a veritable cacophony of noise.

Outside the sky is starting to darken. It still hasn't come to that time of year yet when the sun stays up longer. Ezra begins humming a song they've heard a hundred times before. It's one from her homeland, one that her mother sung to her as a child.

Fifer relaxes, the melody soothing him and he closes his eyes as the music flows over him and through him. Even the play of Arkie and the pups on the floor becomes slightly subdued as each is affected by her voice.

The evening progresses and times of song or stories are intermixed with times of silence. It was during one such time when Bandit's ears suddenly become erect and he leaps to his feet. Fifer notices him looking around for a few seconds before Shiloh starts acting the same way. A growl begins to come from deep within their throats.

Just then, three flaming balls sail through the open window and land near Arkie. The balls are emitting noxious fumes which quickly fill the room.

Crash!

The front door slams open a second later from the force of someone kicking it. Men armed with swords and crossbows race within.

Ezra screams and rushes to grab Arkie from amidst the burning, smoking balls. Neither Fifer nor Roland are armed.

"Stay right where you are!" the leader of the men tells them.

With Arkie in her arms, Ezra moves to stand behind Roland who has come to his feet. Fifer remains seated, his crutch having been knocked to the floor when the dogs had jumped on him.

"What do you want?" Roland asks, fear for his family evident in his voice.

"First we want your gold," the leader says. "Then we want your woman."

In a voice much calmer than the situation would seem to warrant, Roland says, "I advise you to leave while you still can."

"Ha!" a tall man with red hair says. "You can't do anything, mage. Your powers have been taken away."

His head does feel a little fuzzy. Glancing to the smoldering balls lying in the middle of the floor, he realizes what he's talking about. They must emit something that renders mages unable to focus and draw upon their power. Then realization dawns on him. *They think he's James!* If it wasn't for the gravity of the situation he might have laughed.

"Where's the gold!" a short, flaxen haired man demands. Holding a crossbow threateningly, he shouts, "Where is it!"

Roland glances to the window and sees even more bandits looking in. At least four crossbows are aimed at him and the others.

"Well?" the leader asks. "Are you going to tell us or do we start by killing the boy?"

"No!" screams Ezra as she clutches Arkie even tighter to her breast.

Before James left, Roland had expressed concern over just this sort of eventuality. What if someone came in search of James and attacked? With just he and Fifer, they would be taken out fast. So James worked it out and said if ever they were in danger here at The Ranch, Roland was to say a certain word.

Staring at the leader of the bandits, he says the word, "Phantasm!"

"What?" the leader questions. Suddenly from outside, a man's voice cries out in pain and fear. Then more voices are heard as others join their voices with the first. A quick glance to the window shows the men who had been there are there no longer.

A red sphere blossoms to life in the middle of the living room. Bright red with bands of a darker red swirling through its middle, it hovers there for a brief moment.

Screams from outside have turned to high pitched panic as men race away from the house for their lives. Within the house, the remaining bandits stare in nervousness at the sphere hovering before them.

"What trick is this?" demands the leader.

The sphere flashes and a beam of red light strikes the leader in the chest. A cry of agony is torn from his throat as it burns a hole completely through him. As he falls to the floor dead, the other bandits panic and turn to flee from the house. One of the crossbowmen lets fly a bolt at Roland but a red beam flashes out and destroys it before it can reach him.

Three more flashes and three more bandits fall to the floor dead before the rest can leave the house. Fifer retrieves his crutch from off the floor and quickly moves to the window to see what's going on outside. Bandits lie dead on the ground and more flashes can be seen off in the woods as multiple red spheres pursue those still alive. Their screams and cries of pain grow fainter the further they move away from the house. The sphere which had materialized within the house suddenly winks out.

"It's okay," Roland says to Ezra who has her head buried in the crook of his neck. Sobbing, she still clutches Arkie in her hands. He pats her on the back as he tries to calm her.

"What's going on out there?" he asks Fifer.

"I don't think any are getting away," he replies. "Whatever James set up is taking them all out fast."

Bringing her to arms length from him, he looks in her eyes and says soothingly, "It's okay. Take Arkie into our bedroom and shut the door. Fifer and I have work ahead of us this evening."

She nods her head and takes Arkie from the room, the pups follow them.

Fifer turns from the window and says, "It's grown dark out there again. I think it's over."

"Give me a hand to get the dead out of here and buried," Roland says.

"You got it," he replies. Together, they begin hauling the dead out of the house. It takes some doing, but Roland digs a hole out in the woods and Fifer brings the dead over one at a time.

Chapter   One

There's a crispness to the air as the camp makes ready to get underway. High in the mountains as they are, there are still remnants of the winter snow lining the road. When word reached him the pass was clear and should remain so, James immediately mobilized and got underway. Of course as in all things, it snowed in the mountains for twenty four hours the day they left The Ranch but the bulk of the snow had managed to melt away before they arrived.

As the various sections of the camp are broken down and put away, he gets his own equipment and tent ready. Devin has been given the duty of assisting him in the setting up and breaking down of his tent and belongings. Basically, all he's responsible for is what's on his back. Devin takes care of the rest including saddling his horse.

He glances over to where the others are busily packing away those items that were used the night before. The camp has begun to set up in three distinct areas due to the number of people he's brought with him. One area is the 'command area', that would be his tent and Illan's which is in the center of camp. Next is Delia's area where she has her slingers and archers. Finally, Jiron's group sits on the opposite side of the command area where he has the pit fighters, those who had been Delia's caravan guards, and what's left of Miller's band.

"Almost ready sir," Devin tells him as he finishes cinching the straps securing James' saddle to his horse.

"Thank you Devin," he replies.

Illan comes toward him leading his horse, "Shouldn't take much longer before we're ready to ride."

Nodding, James glances to him and says, "Good."

"We might make Illion this evening," he tells him.

"I know," states James.

Illion. That's where Orlander resides, the dealer in stolen goods who swore to kill him after their last encounter. Surprisingly, he didn't make any attempt to make good on his threat of vengeance all winter. James had been sure he would have, so vehemently had he threatened him.

Caleb and Jace have pack horse duty today, the recruits rotate through that duty. Their job is to make sure the pack horses, and there's quite a string of them, are ready to go when everyone else is. Also to ensure they are fed and watered. Some of the items carried in the packs upon them are unknown to most of those traveling with James. He made it clear that it would be unwise and possibly unhealthy for anyone to become overly curious and take a look.

He sees Tersa over with Aleya and Errin where they've finished packing away their belongings and are in the process of saddling their horses. She has a slug belt around her waist, the slots are full of iron slugs and a sling hangs from a clip. At first he was concerned about her decision to join the ranks of Delia's slingers. This was no pleasure excursion they were embarking upon. Though now he's come to except the fact that this is her decision.

Everyone had been told, just prior to their leaving that they were moving to tackle the Empire. James made it clear to them that some, if not all, may not make it back home alive. It filled him with pride when every last one of them chose to come. For some it was payback for what the Empire had done to their homeland. The others saw it as a grand adventure sure to become a bard's saga. Not so James. He knows war to be pain, sorrow, and death. Nothing glorious or wonderful about it, just something which has to be dealt with.

"Would you leave me alone?" Potbelly's voice reaches him from across the camp. He and Illan glance over to see where Scar is standing next to him. What is said by Scar to Potbelly couldn't be made out but Potbelly's face turns into a grimace as Scar turns and walks away.

"I missed their incessant bickering," he says with a grin to Illan.

"Wasn't Jorry and Uther enough for you?" he asks back.

"Almost," he replies.

"Think what we brought with us will do the trick?" Illan asks after a moment's silence.

"I hope so," replies James. "We'll see when we get there."

Of everyone who's accompanying him, Illan knows the most of what is ahead for their group. He's the unofficial general, and except for James, his word is law. After him, James has divided the remainder into two groups. One group is comprised of those utilizing missile weapons under Delia and the other consists of the fighters under Jiron. Miko just sort of hangs out with James.

Miko has begun to mellow out over the summer. Perhaps having the Star in his possession is affecting him, James isn't sure. It was decided that the Star would not be hidden away, rather it rests within a pouch hanging at Miko's hip. Since they're going to war, the healing Miko will be able to do could become invaluable.

When he first came to possess the Star, he healed Fifer of a serious injury which was about to take his life. Since then he's used it twice. Once was for a woman in Trendle who ran afoul of a pack of wolves near the fringe of the forest. There had been rumors of what Miko had done floating around town and since the local priest was away on temple business, they sought him.

Just as happened with Fifer, he prayed to Morcyth, a nimbus surrounded his head, and a glow materialized and healed her.

The second was on James himself. After an experiment went bad, he was covered in burns and wasn't breathing. Miko brought the Star and healed him. He was leery about doing it, the warnings James had said about only those of this world could touch it and live. But as it was this or he dies, he tried it and it worked. His burns healed and he survived.

"We're ready," Jiron says as he rides forward. Delia and her group are climbing into the saddle as well.

James glances over to Caleb and Jace and receives a nod from them saying the pack horses are ready. "Let's go," he says. Leading the way, he returns to the road from where they made camp and begins the descent through Dragon's Pass down into Madoc.

The sun is low on the horizon when James begins walking through the streets of Illion, the people he passes are in a state of agitation. Worry over what the Empire will do and whether they will move in this direction has them all on edge. Many are already evacuating, over the winter they heard the tales of what the Empire's forces are like from the few refugees who managed to make it out. None want to experience the horror of what they heard.

Though there is fear and worry, the people still must continue about their daily routines, those who aren't fleeing that is. Many are still upon the street, some returning from shopping, others trying to learn the latest word from the south. Off to one side, James spies a group of kids playing some game as they race around. Grinning to himself, he's glad they are able to find joy while they can. If what he plans works out the way he hopes, these people will have little to fear.

He works his way through to the seedier part of town, over to an area he has been in once before. A burnt out husk of a building is all that remains of what use to be Orlander's tavern. He's surprised it hasn't been torn down yet, you'd think Orlander would have built another in its place.

Glancing around, he tries to locate Orlander or those who may know of his whereabouts. He intends to talk with him to reconcile the situation, heaven knows he has enough who wish him ill.

Ahead near what looks to be an abandoned home are five street thugs just hanging around. He makes his way toward them and they quickly take note of his approach. One disengages from the others and comes forward to meet him.

"Excuse me," James says as he comes to a stop several feet away. "Could you tell me where I might find Orlander?"

"Orlander?" the thug asks. "Why would you want to see him?"

"Got business with him," replies James. "Now, where could I find him?"

"Maybe you should tell us your business first and we'll see if it's worth our while to help you?" At that, the remaining four thugs move to flank James on either side. The one before him pulls out a knife and the others do likewise.

"I really don't want any trouble," James tells them as he starts to back away.

"Then give us your money and you won't have any," the lead thug says as he threatens with his knife.

Sighing, James shakes his head and says, "Have it your way." Suddenly, five shimmering fields spring into being around the five thugs.

"What's this?" questions the lead thug. He puts his hand out toward it and is surprised to encounter resistance. "Hey!" he cries as he begins banging on the field surrounding him. The others react in fear and apprehension as well. "Let us out!" "Help!" their cries echo down the darkened, shadowed street.

James glances first one way and then another to see if anyone is coming to their aid. Amazingly, the few people who had been on the streets have vanished. Turning back to the lead thug, he asks, "Now, where can I find Orlander?"

Panicked eyes stare at him from within the shimmering field. "He's that way," the thug says as he points further down the street.

"Where exactly?" He glances down the street in the direction indicated and only sees more old abandoned buildings in desperate need of repair.

"The old tannery," another of the thugs says. James turns his attention to him as he continues. "It's down two streets on the left. You can't miss it."

"Alright," James says as he begins heading down the street.

"What about us?" another of the thugs cries out. "You can't leave us like this!"

He pauses in the street and turns his attention back to the thugs. "If what you say is true, I'll let you go," he tells them. Then turning his back on them once again, he resumes his way down the street. What he did to them is one of many things he worked on during the winter in anticipation of the spring campaign. He got to thinking that if the protective barrier can keep things away from him, it should be able to be reversed and hold someone in.

Leaving the imprisoned men behind, he makes his way further down the street. The sun's light has all but faded with the coming of night. Shadows are long and lights begin to appear in a few of the buildings which still have occupants.

After passing the first street and coming up to the second, he finds the building the thug told him about. Light spills from one of the windows illuminating several tough looking, well armed men loitering outside. One of the men is carrying a crossbow. Nodding to himself, he heads toward the building.

As he draws near, the men outside become aware of his approach. The man holding the crossbow turns it to bear upon him. "Is Orlander within?" he asks once he's stopped before them.

"Who wants to know?" one man asks. The hilts of two longswords jut out from behind his shoulders and he looks like one who can definitely take care of himself in a fight.

"One who wishes to put to rest a situation between us," James explains.

"What's your name?" two swords asks.

"James," he replies. "I burnt his tavern down last fall."

At that two of the men gasp and two swords nods to another who enters through the door behind him. "Didn't expect you to make yourself so available," he says.

James remains silent as they wait for Orlander's appearance. They don't have long to wait before the door opens and Orlander walks out with a crossbow in hand. Half a dozen others follow him through the door.

"At last!" he says with a gleam in his eye. He raises the crossbow and before James has a chance to say anything, fires. The bolt flies toward him and strikes the all but invisible shield surrounding him. Ricocheting off the shield, it flies toward one of the thugs standing nearby, narrowly missing the man's face.

"What sort of trickery is going on here?" Orlander demands when the bolt fails to find its mark.

"No trickery," explains James. "I simply wish to talk to you."

"Take him boys," Orlander commands and his men pull their swords and attack.

James simply stands there as they run into the barrier surrounding him. After a few moments of fruitless attack, he asks, "Can we talk now or do you wish to continue?"

Orlander motions for his men to back off as he looks at James with a calculating look. "You a mage?" he asks.

"Among other things, yes," replies James.

"Why don't you just kill me?" Orlander asks after assimilating what he just said.

"It's not my way," he explains. "I wish to stop further bloodshed on both sides. I came here to see if I can change your mind about seeking my death. During our last encounter things sort of got out of hand and I am here to set things right."

"Out of hand?" Orlander says incredulously. "You stole from me, killed a score of my friends and burnt down my tavern. I'd hardly call that 'out of hand'."

James reaches into his shirt and removes a small sack. Holding it before him, he says, "I have here enough gems to repay you for the stolen items and the destruction of your tavern." He opens the sack and pulls out an uncut ruby half the size of an egg and shows it to him.

Orlander's eyes grow large at the sight of the gem. He licks his lips and says, "Just what do you propose?"

"I give you this sack of gems and you swear to never again seek my destruction," he explains. "Nor will you allow another to seek my destruction should you hear of it."

"What if I refuse?" he asks.

James places the gem back in the sack and says, "Then you don't get the gems and we are at war."

"You seem pretty confident in yourself," Orlander states. He glances around at the men standing with him.

James simply stares at him.

He stands there a moment contemplating the proposal. His eyes flick from James, to the bag and back again. "Very well," he agrees. "We have a deal."

"You swear to never again seek my death?" James asks.

"Yes, I swear it," Orlander replies.

The shimmer of the shield disappears and he hands over the gems.

Orlander reaches out for the sack and then suddenly grabs James' arm. "Kill him!" he cries out.

As soon as Orlander grabs his hand, James drops to the ground.

"Fire!" is heard coming from the shadows on the opposite side of the street. A knife flies from the dark and strikes Orlander in the chest just as two arrows follow, each sinking into his midsection.

Crying out from the pain of the attack, Orlander lets go of James' hand and staggers backward, collapsing in the doorway. His men stand stunned at the sudden change of events. From the shadows across the street, Illan and the other fighters emerge, weapons at the ready.

"Take them!" James orders from where he lies on the ground.

Seeing their leader lying dead across the threshold and the armed men charging, they lose heart and break into a retreat. Arrows and knives fly from the shadows, felling thug after thug. Jiron catches up with one and cuts him down from behind.

"Enough!" Illan's voice rings out, stopping them from pursuing the fleeing men. To Jiron he says, "Secure the area."

"Right," Jiron replies. "Jorry, Uther you take that way," he orders as he points up the street. "Scar, Potbelly down the other. The rest fan out and watch for any who may return." Shorty appears and begins collecting his knives from the fallen thugs just as Aleya and Errin begin gathering what arrows weren't damaged during the attack.

"Told you this was going to happen," Illan says to James as he offers him a hand up.

Taking it, he replies, "I know. I had to try."

"Oh I understand, just knew it wouldn't work," Illan says.

"We got company!" Scar hollers from his position down the street.

A squad of the city guard is coming down the road toward them. The last time he was here, James saw them with Orlander during his pursuit.

He's been fairly sure since then that they were in his pay. How they'll react to his death is anyone's guess.

As the guards approach, everyone moves a little closer together. Jiron and Miko stand before James as Shorty, Errin and Aleya position themselves behind him.

The officer in charge takes in the scene as they approach. A dozen people dead as well as Orlander's corpse lying in the doorway. He motions for his men to stop as he comes forward the last couple feet. "What happened here?" he asks.

"Came to settle a few things with Orlander," James replies. "Things sort of got out of hand."

"Looks like murder if you ask me," the officer says as he eyes James.

Before James can answer, two men approach out of the dark. "It wasn't murder," one of them says.

"That's right," the other affirms. "Heard Orlander order his men to kill him before the fighting started. Orlander started it."

Around them a crowd of people has begun to form as the locals come to see what's happened. Some, upon seeing Orlander's dead body give a cheer.

"Good riddance," one woman says.

"Streets will be safer without him around," another states.

"So you see," James says to the officer, "this was in self defense."

The officer glances around from James to the others with him, as well as the crowd which seems to be for James. Turning his attention back to James he says, "Alright." To his men he says, "Get a crew together and let's clean this up."

"Yes sir," one of his men says.

James bends over and retrieves the sack of gems and puts it into his shirt. The officer notices but says nothing. "Will there be anything more?" he asks.

The officer shakes his head. "No. Since you didn't start it and witnesses say it was self defense, you can go."

"Thank you," he says and to Illan he nods for them to get moving. As James moves away from the building, one woman comes up to him and gives him a hug and kiss before hurrying away.

"Looks like everyone is quite happy Orlander is gone," observes Jiron.

"I can understand why," agrees James. They make their way back down the street the way they had come. Down a couple blocks they come across the men who are still surrounded by the shields, James cancels the spell. One of the men was leaning against the barrier when it disappeared and falls to the ground. Freed, they waste little time in getting as far away from James as possible.

Miko laughs at them as they race down the street.

On the other side of town, they meet up with Delia and the slingers who had stayed with the horses. Devin comes forward with James' horse as they draw near.

"Everything go okay?" she asks.

"About as expected," Jiron says.

"They won't bother us any more," Miko says as he makes a slashing motion across his throat indicating they're all dead.

"Sorry it didn't work out the way you wanted," Delia says.

"So am I," states James, "at least he won't bother me again and the town appears to be quite happy with the outcome."

"Yeah, one girl came and hugged him," Uther says with a guffaw.

"Better not let Meliana hear about that," says Miko.

"I'm sure she would understand," replies James. Meliana has been on his mind of late. Maybe after this business in Madoc is over he'll be able to arrange a visit, either he go there or she here.

Mounting, he says, "Let's head down the road a couple hours before we stop. Don't want any of his men to seek vengeance for tonight's affair." Heading out, he takes the road leading eastward toward the Sea of the Gods. He plans to take the northern route around the Sea seeing as how the Empire controls the southern shore. With any luck, they should reach Pyrtlin by day after tomorrow. It's a major town sitting on the northern shore and they should be able to resupply there.

Chapter Two

The road to Pyrtlin is a fairly straight shot from Illion, heading mostly due southeast. Traffic is heavy as most are fleeing to the safety of the northern kingdom. From what they've managed to learn, the Empire has made probing attacks on Madoc's defenses, both around Lythylla that is situated to the east of the Sea, and the line to the west between the Silver Mountains and the Sea.

The mood of the people is one without hope for a future for their country. The southern half has already been swallowed by the Empire and by all accounts, they mean to take the rest by the time the snows come in winter.

"Think he made it?" Jiron asks James near the end of the first day after leaving Illion.

"Who?" he asks, not sure just who he's talking about.

"Qyrll," Jiron clarifies. Qyrll is a Parvati they met earlier in Cardri where Jiron saved him from an ignoble and dishonorable existence bound to one who used him as a fighter for sport. Though his people are part of the Empire, he and Jiron had become fast friends. Qyrll had decided to travel with them until he could repay the Shynti in kind.

During the battle for the Star in Ironhold, he saved Jiron's life and considered the debt paid. Just before James and the others left for Madoc, he began heading back to his homeland, deep within the Empire.

"Don't see why not," James replies. "Cardri isn't at war with the Empire, and though relations are strained, he isn't considered an enemy. He should be able to just walk across the border with little problems."

"I hope so," he says. Jiron holds an odd position with the Parvatis. He is a Shynti, which is a rare designation they give to only the best and bravest of warriors. It basically makes him one of them.

"With what's coming ahead, you know we are going to have to do battle with Parvatis at some point," James reminds him. The last time they were at Lythylla, the Parvatis were a sizeable force within the Empire's army.

"I know," he replies. He hates to think they may kill friends and relatives of those they met while in the Parvati homeland, but such is the fortunes of war. Though the fact that he was a Shynti worked to their advantage the last time they were in Lythylla, he seriously doubts if it would have the same effect as before.

They ride on until close to dark before setting up camp. With this many, it takes some doing to get everyone in their proper position. Illan was most adamant that each of the groups set their tents together in the same area. But as the journey has progressed, so has the ease with which everyone finds their place. It's almost reached the point of becoming routine.

In the hour before they stopped, they passed one of those traveler's stopovers with an inn. Though most were hoping for the comfort of a bed, it was decided to pass it by. James doesn't want to let on, but he's afraid one of them might talk while among other people. He would like to minimize their contact until the battle is joined. Less chance of a spy or rumor alerting the enemy of their intentions.

A quick meal and then right to sleep, with sentries posted. James, Illan and Delia are no longer part of the sentry routine, they have plenty of others for that role. Mainly it's been the recruits with the old timers here and there keeping an eye on them.

Early the next morning before the sun has even crested the horizon, they're preparing to get underway. By the time the sun shows itself, they are already a mile further down the road.

"Should reach Pyrtlin by this evening if we keep a brisk pace," Illan announces during one of their breaks to rest the horses.

James nods that he heard while watching Delia working with her slingers. During most of their breaks she cycles through them, working with two or three at a time. Right now she has Devin, Orry and Terrance. Devin and Orry have taken to the sling with skill and are continuously improving both their marksmanship and their range. Terrance on the other hand struggles with just getting the bolt to go in the right direction.

"Again," Delia says after all three of their stones find their marks. Two hit dead center the tree a hundred feet away while the third flew wide by a good two yards.

As Terrance sets the next stone in the pocket of his sling, Delia comes over and says, "Stay loose. Never take your eye off the target, not even for an instant." Taking hold of one of his legs, she moves it away from the other. "Keep yourself balanced at all times," she explains to him. "If you become unbalanced while you twirl your sling, the shot will not fly true."

"Yes ma'am," Terrance says as he grits his teeth and takes hold of his sling. Terrance, a younger son of a farmer had been excited when he became part of the new recruits at The Ranch last year. Oh sure, there was a lot he didn't care for, such as the incessant drills and Illan yelling at you when you didn't do it perfectly. But he feels like he's found his place in the world. Farm life had always been pure drudgery to him, unlike his other two brothers who were able to find satisfaction in tending the crops.

Placing his feet just as Delia instructs him, he takes sight of the tree they're currently using for a target. He takes a deep breath to relax and then starts twirling the sling over his head. All the others have managed to achieve the whining noise when the sling reaches a certain speed. Try as he might, he just can't seem to get it.

"Just relax and let it go when the time is right, not before," Delia says behind him.

He lets the sling twirl another second before sensing the time was right and releases the stone. The sling opens up and the stone flies rapidly toward the tree. He holds his breath as he watches the stone arc through the air only to fly a foot to the right of his intended target.

"Damn!" he curses under his breath.

Delia pats him on the back and says, "Better. You keep yourself balanced at all times and keep practicing and you'll get it." When he turns to look at her, she adds, "Four more tries then we've got to go."

"Yes, ma'am," he says and then reaches down for another stone.

Delia turns to the two others and says, "Four more."

"We heard," Devin replies.

Leaving her trainees to their practice, she walks over to where Illan and James are standing, watching her.

"How are they doing?" Illan asks as she approaches.

"Better," she says. "I just wish we had more time to practice."

Thunk! Thunk!...............Poof!

At the sound of the stones hitting the target, they turn to watch just as Terrance lets fly. His stone again flies wide, this time by a good four feet.

Delia sighs, "He's simply not getting it."

"He'll be good enough for what I want him to do," James assures her.

"I hope so," she says. "In an actual battle it might be better to have him watch the horses."

"We'll see," Illan says. "He definitely has the determination."

They watch the next pass, and again he misses the target, this time by only a narrow margin. He turns to see them watching and James gives him a thumb's up. Grinning, he bends over to pick up another stone.

When they began their practices on the road, they complained about not using the slugs in their belts. Delia had explained that she wanted them used to different sizes and weights. "What are you going to do in the heat of battle when all your slugs are used up?" she asked them. After that there was no more complaining.

"Time to go," Illan says after the slingers have sent their final volley toward the tree. Out of the four tries, Terrance had managed to strike the tree once.

"Alright!" Delia hollers to her slingers. "Time to go!"

It takes but a minute for everyone to return to the saddle and begin heading down the road. The rest of that day, with the sun shining overhead in a cloudless sky, they make good time and reach Pyrtlin before nightfall.

Finding a suitable spot outside of town, they set up camp. Once all is settled in for the night, James turns to Delia and says, "Take a couple of your slingers and see about buying some rations."

"Not a problem," she says. Raising her voice, she hollers, "Moyil, Jace and Caleb, bring your packs, we're going into town."

Devin comes to James and says, "Your tent is all set up."

"Thanks Devin," he replies.

Delia picks up her own pack as well as several others and with the boys in tow, heads into town. Being a trader, she is the logical choice for this particular duty.

As she heads into town, James walks over to his tent. "You lyin' piece of horse dung!" Scar's voice reaches him from where the fighters are bivouacked. He glances over to where his voice came from and sees him standing with hands on hips facing Uther. He pauses a moment to see what's going on.

"I ain't lyin'!" Uther insists. "We really were asked by the High Lord of Jearinan to go on a hunting trip with him. You see, it was after we had rescued his daughter from…"

James shakes his head and continues on to his tent. *Will that ever end?* He has no clue where Jearinan is or if there is even a high lord. Someday he's going to investigate some of their outrageous claims, just to see if they are in fact true.

As he enters his tent, their bickering continues. At least it's good natured, neither takes the insults and accusations of the other seriously. James assumes it's just part of the fun. Inside he finds his cot already put together but not much else. The first night Devin was assigned as his helper, he had practically unpacked everything he brought with him. It took almost two hours before everything was repacked securely. From that point on, he told Devin to only put up the tent and cot, that if he wanted something more, he would get it himself.

Lying down on his cot, he passes the time until dinner has been prepared by thinking of what lies ahead. He seems to have ample time to do nothing but think lately. Since he's the one in charge of this expedition, no one is letting him do anything. He supposes they would even delegate someone to wipe his butt if he let them. Well, perhaps not that but he's been removed from cooking detail, sentry duty and all the other daily little chores which must be done. All he has to do is get on his horse in the morning and off at night.

He has a fair idea of how to convince the Empire to leave Madoc. With any luck it will actually work. First order of business is getting Pytherian and the Ruling Council of Madoc to agree to reconstruct the High Temple of Morcyth on the exact spot where it had resided before. That shouldn't be too hard, if the agreement was to expel the Empire from the borders of Madoc.

The last time he was within the city of Lythylla, Councilman Rillian who was a member of the Ruling Council had worked with the Empire to open the gates for their army. Little love is lost between the councilman and James. He knows that should he still be a member, he will work to prevent any agreement against the Empire to come to fruition.

That is but one hurdle, the other is what the Empire may throw at him once he joins the fray. Aside from the mages and the priests of Dmon-Li which play a prominent part in their forces, there could be more of those creatures he faced in the pass on the way to Ironhold last fall. With any luck, there won't be all that many of those available or even something worse. He does have some ideas on how to deal with them should they show up again.

He must have dozed off for he's startled awake when Miko sticks his head in the tent to say, "Dinner's ready."

"Be right there," he says as he sits up. The interior of the tent is dark, the sun must have gone down already. Miko holds the flap open for him while he gets up and makes his way outside.

From the entrance to his tent, he has a commanding view of the Sea as it stretches eastward to the horizon. A few boats are still upon its surface, the lights from their lanterns visible in the deepening gloom of twilight as they make their way home.

"Is Delia back yet?" he asks.

"Not yet," replies Miko. "Illan said if she wasn't back soon he was going to send someone to find her.

"She should have been back by now," he says worried. He spies Illan over to the side near the campfire getting a plate of food from Nerrin who pulled cook duty this evening. Son of an innkeeper, he tends to cook better than most and pulls it more often than the others. Miko they won't allow to perform this particular duty. Uther said he tried to poison them all the last time. James had to admit the stuff he put in that concoction he called stew didn't go well together.

Walking over, he accepts a plate from Nerrin and walks with Illan off to the side. "She's not back yet?" he asks.

Shaking his head, Illan replies, "No, she's not. Give her another half hour and we'll send Scar and Potbelly to find her."

"Alright," he agrees, concern in his voice.

Jiron is eating with his sister Tersa near the slingers' area, Aleya and Errin are with them as well. Those four tend to be together more than the others. A bond has grown between Aleya and Errin, and it seems Tersa has begun to join their group. Perhaps because they're the only girls among all the men. Delia, though a woman as well, is in a position of authority which puts her at some distance from them.

"Finally!" Miko exclaims from the side of the camp closest to Pyrtlin.

James looks up to see Delia returning with the three lads in tow. The packs they're carrying are bulging from the food they acquired. He finishes the last of his food quickly and hands his tray back to Nerrin on his way over to greet her. "We were getting worried about you," he says.

"Now don't be fretting," she says. "I ran into someone I knew from back before the City fell and we got to talking."

Behind her James sees Moyil grinning and gesturing with his hand, moving the fingers to the thumb over and over while mouthing 'yackity

yackity yackity'. She glances over her shoulder at him and he stops, all the while putting on an innocent face. James can't help but smile.

She must have caught what he was doing out of the corner of her eye because her lips curl into a slight frown. Turning back to James, she says, "We bought as much as we could carry. The prices are more than we thought, things around here are scarce. If we succeed, I may start trading between Cardri and Madoc. There's a profit to be made here." Despite having put her trading career on hold for the time being, she still sees things as a trader would.

"I'm sure there is," he says.

Turning back to her helpers, she says, "Moyil, if you would be so kind as to help me distribute these among the packhorses before you eat, I would greatly appreciate it."

"But I'm hungry," he complains. He looks to James for help.

"Don't look at me," he says.

Crestfallen and starving, he takes the packs from Jace and Caleb and proceeds over to where the horses are tied.

Delia flashes James a grin and follows him over. Maybe he'll think twice before making fun of her behind her back again.

After everyone, including Moyil who received a scant portion due to his lateness in reaching the cook pot, finishes eating they come together at the center fire pit near the center of camp. There they continue in the tradition James had established back at The Ranch where stories are told and songs are sung.

Tonight Scar and Potbelly are in rare form as they relate a tale of how back at the City of Light when they were but young teens they became entangled in a struggle between two elements trying to wrest control of the less than savory aspects. According to them, they stumbled across an assassination plot of one faction who was targeting the leader of the other.

By means both devious and bordering on the unbelievable, they saved the man, won his trust and had the chance to become his lieutenants in the organization he was creating, but instead passed it over in favor of the fight pits which they had heard about and were interested in joining.

"I don't seem to recall anything like that going on," Jiron says as they finally wind down. You can say a lot about their stories, but dull and uneventful are not among them.

"Of course not," Scar says. "This was before we met."

"That's right," adds Potbelly. "It's not like events concerning this sort of thing are talked about. These sorts of people don't take kindly to their affairs becoming public knowledge."

"That was the biggest piece of trash I ever heard!" Jorry says from where he sits across the fire from the pair. Uther nods in agreement.

"True or not," Illan says as he gets to his feet, "it's time for us to turn in. We still have many days ahead of us before we reach Lythylla."

As everyone but those pulling sentry duty begins turning in, the two pairs eye each other with silent intensity. It seems a rivalry has begun between them and things, not to mention tales, are bound to get more outlandish.

James heads for his tent and can hear Uther say to Jorry, in a voice loud enough to be heard by everyone, "You'd think if they were going to make up a story, they should at least make it entertaining." Rolling his eyes heavenward, he enters his tent and gets ready for bed.

Lying upon the cot, he stares at the roof of his tent as a smile plays across his face. *If nothing else, at least things won't get boring.*

The grass covered rolling hills extend ahead of him until they disappear in the horizon. A beautiful day, sun high in a crystal blue sky, the odd fluffy white cloud drifting by. The scent of wildflowers is borne upon the breeze as it brings a welcoming coolness to the heat of the day.

Small animals race by as he walks, seemingly completely unconcerned by his passing. A deer, or something very similar actually comes right up to him. He reaches out his hand and it allows him to stroke its neck before darting off.

A sense of peace and tranquility fills him as he walks through the grass. He doesn't walk long before the sound of a carnival reaches him. Scanning the horizon, he can see the top of the Ferris wheel behind a hill off to his right. Intrigued, he turns in that direction and hurries along.

Topping the rise behind which the carnival hides, he sees a sight he's seen played out many times before. Whenever spring and summer come, so did the carnivals and fairs. This one is just like all the others, carnies working the crowds, enticing them to either buy or play one of the overpriced games.

A smile comes to him as he walks down the hill. The sights, the smells, all remind him of home. Off to one side he sees his favorite amusement park treat in all the world. Cotton Candy. Oh man does he love that. Of course it has to be the pink variety, none other is nearly as good. Reaching into his pocket for money, he realizes he didn't bring any. All that he produces is a single ride ticket, good for any of the rides. Saddened by being unable to buy the cotton candy, he still walks his way through the midway enjoying the sights and sounds.

It suddenly occurs to him that he is the only one there other than the carnies. He stops in his tracks and gazes around but no one other than himself is there. At least he'll not have to wait in line to use his ticket.

As he walks along, he looks at all the different rides available to him. Of course there's the roller coaster, the funhouse and the inevitable carousel. What would a carnival be without one of those?

"One ticket!" cries out the carnie in charge of the carousel. "One ticket is all it takes."

Shaking his head, James says, "No thanks." Moving on he comes across the bumper cars, he likes them but by himself they would be little fun. Then comes other rides, one by one, all of which he doesn't have any interest in. Most of them are the kind that tends to make you throw up by spinning around and around.

Continuing to pass from one ride to the next, he suddenly catches out of the corner of his eyes a flash of blonde hair moving in the aisle on the other side of the rides. Turning to look closer, he sees a girl roughly in her teens moving along going the opposite way.

"Hey!" he hollers to her but she fails to respond. Moving quickly, he passes between two rides and enters the aisle in which he saw her. Looking down the direction she went, he sees her getting into a boat.

"Wait!" he calls to her. Why he needs to reach her isn't clear, just that he must. Breaking into a run, he hurries toward the ride she's about to enter. It's the Tunnel of Love.

A large single story building sits atop a stream. Several boats are lined up behind her and a carnie is just finishing securing her in and then throws the lever. Her boat begins to float with the current and moves to enter the opening.

James starts to get into the next boat but the carnie stops him, "Ticket please." Reaching into his pocket he discovers the ticket is gone. "I've got to follow her!" he cries.

"You can't get on without a ticket," the carnie states.

Not knowing what else to do, he stands there and watches as she disappears into the Tunnel of Love.

"Sir?" a voice says, bringing him back to consciousness.

Opening his eyes, he glances over to the tent flap and sees Devin there. "What?" he asks.

"Illan says we need to be on the road soon," he replies.

"Alright," James tells him and then lies back as the tent flap closes again. Trying to catch the fleeting remnants of the dream, he begins to be unable to recall the details. Sighing, he gets up and starts getting dressed. The one thing about the dream he recalls is that the girl was in some way familiar. Why, he's not sure.

By the time he's dressed and leaves his tent, the memory or the dream has faded completely and all he's left with is a feeling of having lost something.

Chapter   Three

In less than an hour they're up and on their way. The sun rising over the Sea creates a truly dazzling display as the waves upon its surface sparkle in the early morning light. Leaving the city of Pyrtlin behind, they take the east road along the northern shore of the Sea.

Not long after Pyrtlin disappears behind them, they come to a crossroads where they can either continue along the shore to the east or take the road to the north. They continue along to the east.

"We should arrive at Shore Town sometime before the evening meal," Illan explains to James. "There we'll need to take the northeast road out of town."

"Wouldn't it be quicker to stay next to the Sea?" questions Jiron.

Shaking his head, Illan says, "There's a mountain range on the eastern shore of the Sea which we will have to ride around." To the east they see the peaks of the mountains silhouetted against the sky in the distance.

"How long will it take us to reach Lythylla?" James asks.

"A week or so," he answers.

The rest of the day passes fairly quickly and just as Illan predicted, they reach Shore Town shortly before the evening meal. They find an out of the way inn where they stop to have a bite to eat. Having been on the road for many days and eating their own cooking makes them all long for a real meal.

The mood here in Shore Town isn't nearly as harried and anxious like what they found back in Pyrtlin. Probably due to the fact that before they're going to be attacked by the Empire, other cities will have to fall first. Everywhere there are signs of preparations being readied in the event the Empire makes it this far.

From where they sit having their meal in the inn, they watch a group of boys who are put through drills, similar in nature to those Illan had the recruits doing back at The Ranch. When James asks a local at a nearby table about the drills, he's told that Madoc has called for a levy. All able bodied men and older boys are required to present themselves for training in the defense of Madoc.

"Look at that," Caleb says as he watches the lads. "They don't even know how to hold a sword." Others offer their observation as to the boys' lack of skill.

Illan turns to them and says, "You weren't much better before I got a hold of you." He then winks to James and gives him a grin.

A quick meal of roast duck, bread and ale and then they're off. They travel several more hours, putting as much road behind them as possible before they decide to call it a day and make camp.

The next day and a half finds them reaching the northern edge of the mountains and skirting along the foothills before coming to a town known as Raider's Doom. It sits on the banks of a river flowing from the north where two main roads intersect. Illan tells them that after they cross the river they'll turn southward and follow the eastern side of the mountains until they come to an end. From there it's only a day to Lythylla.

Raider's Doom is a quiet, little town, not nearly the metropolis one would expect to sit on the convergence of two main arteries. Not a small town to be sure, but the people there have a quiet calm about them that's been lacking in the other towns they've passed through. It almost seems as if they are not concerned about the war coming in their direction.

"They don't seem to care about what's going on to the south," Uther states as they pass through.

Kids playing in the street, ladies taking their time in their daily routines, no one seems worried or concerned about what the future might hold.

"Hope they can stay that way for a long time," James replies. He hopes someday every town could have that same carefree attitude.

"How did the town get a name like Raider's Doom anyway?" Devin asks from the rear.

Before Illan has a chance to explains, Scar pipes up and says, "You see, a century ago, there was this band of raiders…" For the next twenty minutes, he regales everyone with a tale of raiders and a trap laid by the local villagers. How the raiders were slaughtered to the last man. "…and that's why it's called Raider's Doom. Since that day, so the story goes, no raider has ever been seen in the area."

From somewhere in the back, in a voice barely heard, James hears Uther ask Jorry, "You know how you can tell when he's lyin'?"

"How?" Jorry asks.

"His lips move," explains Uther. At that, laughter breaks out up and down the line.

Before Scar has a chance to begin an argument, Illan announces loudly, "No, it's true. It actually happened the way he said."

Scar turns to look at Uther with a smug expression and then turns back to the road.

The road continues to follow the river and they are able to make good time. Other travelers pass them coming from the south from time to time, those fleeing the coming of the Empire. Seems no one has any confidence that Madoc and the alliance will be able to hold the Empire when they finally make their move.

Near the end of the day, the road begins angling more to the southeast and away from the river as it continues in a more southwesterly direction. Not long after leaving the banks of the river, they come to a junction where a smaller, little used road branches off and moves to follow the river.

"If you take that road," Illan explains, "it will take you to Serene Lake." He turns in the saddle and glances to James. "I know you have an interest in things of nature. On the far side of the lake, Thunder Falls roars its way into the Sea."

"Thunder Falls?" he asks.

"Largest damn waterfall I've ever seen," he explains. "If you stand near its base, the sound seems to vibrate through to your very soul. Quite an experience."

James would like nothing better than to take an excursion to see this wonder of nature. But time is pressing and they need to reach Lythylla before the Empire begins the attack. "Maybe another time," he says wistfully. Glancing at the fading light, he says, "Perhaps this would be a good time to make camp for the evening."

"As good as any," agrees Illan.

They move off the road and set up camp near the banks of the river for easy access to the water. The mountains rise just to the west, casting deep and long shadows in the sun's final light of the day. Another couple days and they should arrive at Lythylla, then things will become interesting.

Just as twilight sets in, the sound of dogs barking can be heard coming from the direction of the road to Serene Lake. In the gloom, six figures appear and are soon revealed to be local farmers, one of whom is in the lead with two dogs on leashes.

They all come to their feet when it looks as if they're heading straight for them. James moves to meet them as they enter the campfire's light. "Have you seen two small children?" the man in the lead asks.

"No," replies James. "You are the first we've encountered. Are they lost?"

Nodding, the man says, "Since day before yesterday. They are my children," he continues, a sad and worried look upon his face. "They are a wild pair but they've never been away this long."

The dogs sniff around, as if trying to find the scent. James notices the man holds a shirt in his hand, one too small for him to wear. Indicating the shirt, he asks, "Is that one of theirs?"

The man glances at the shirt and nods. "My son's," he replies. "Been using it for the dogs to get the scent, but so far they haven't picked up the trail."

James glances first to Jiron and then to Miko. Miko has a serious expression on his face and nods his head. He knows what James is thinking. Holding his hand out, he says, "If you give me the shirt, I can help you find them."

Looking suspiciously at him, he asks, "How are you going to do that?"

"I'm a mage," he says and instantly the farmers become less friendly. Again the reputation of those who do power in this world has begun to turn others against him. "I can help, I've done it before."

One of the men takes a closer look at him and asks, "Is your name James?"

Surprised, he replies, "Yes it is."

The man grabs the father of the lost children by the shoulder and begins whispering in his ear, the others with them move closer to hear. After a minute of whispers passing back and forth, they turn as one to face him.

Holding the shirt out, the father says, "Heard of you. They say you helped out Lord Pytherian last year and prevented the Empire from taking Lythylla."

"True," he admits as he takes the shirt. He glances around and spies Devin not too far off. "Go get my mirror," he tells him.

Devin nods and rushes to his tent.

While he waits for Devin, James says, "We'll find them for you."

Hope comes to the man's eyes and a slight tear as well. It's clear to see how much he cares for and misses his children. James decides he's a good man. Devin returns shortly with his mirror.

He holds the shirt in one hand while resting the mirror atop it with the other. Concentrating on finding the one who last wore this shirt, he lets the magic loose. The image in the mirror begins to shift and then turns completely black.

A gasp is heard from the father as he asks, "Are they dead?"

James glances around at the fading light and says, "It may be they are simply in an area with no light, like a cave or something." Canceling the spell, he hands the mirror back to Devin.

The shirt has long sleeves. Taking hold of one of the sleeves halfway down from the shoulder, he again concentrates on the owner of this shirt, willing the sleeve to point the way. After letting the magic flow, the sleeve begins moving and points to the east, not directly following the road, rather more toward the mountains. "They're that way."

"You sure?" the father asks.

"If James says they're that way," Jiron speaks out, "you can believe they are."

To Illan, James says, "Stay here with the others and watch the camp." Then to Jiron and Miko he says, "You two come with me." Once Jiron and Miko nod, he turns to the father and says, "Now, let's go find your kids."

Moving away from camp, he follows the direction the sleeve is indicating. Behind him he can hear whispers from the farmers, what they are saying isn't clear.

"Think they're alive?" asks Jiron. The father grows silent as he awaits James' answer.

"Don't know," he replies. "This will just lead us to them. We'll have to wait until we get there to find out."

As they move from the light of the campfire, James' orb springs to life and hovers above and slightly behind his head. The farmers gasp in shock and fear at first, but then Miko and Jiron calm them down with assurances it will do no harm.

The interactions between the others are lost to James as he concentrates on maintaining the spell and keeping his footing in the tangled undergrowth. They travel for half an hour before the ground grows steeper. The loose rocks upon the surface make footing more and more difficult as the incline grows. At one point, James stumbles while lost in concentration and only Jiron's quick reflexes kept him from falling backward down the slope.

"Careful," he says as James regains his balance.

"Trying to be," he replies. As he begins moving again, he takes more care to keep stable footing.

The night continues to deepen and after another hour, the moon makes its appearance, adding its light to that of the orb. "I don't think he knows where they are," he hears one farmer say behind him.

"Quiet!" the father says to the other. "If you don't want to continue, I'll understand. But I'll follow him to the edge of Coryntia's domain if it will get my children back." Coryntia of course being the Hooded Lady, she whose domain lies between the living and the dead.

Suddenly the dogs begin barking. "They've got the scent!" the father cries out.

James releases the spell and allows the father to take the lead.

"Come on boys!" he cries excitedly to his dogs. "Find em."

The dogs pull on their leashes, practically dragging the father along. The others follow right behind. Yowling, the dogs come to a game trail and turn to follow the scent. "What would they be doing this far up the mountain?" their father asks to no one in particular.

They follow the dogs down the game trail for a hundred yards until the dogs abruptly turn into the woods to the right. Moving further up the mountain, they travel for several more minutes through the trees and undergrowth before a darkness appears in the side of the mountain before them. It's a cave and the dogs are moving to enter its maw.

When the farmer reaches the entrance, he pauses and hollers into the opening, "Barric, Aria!" He pauses a moment to listen for his children's response before handing the dog's leash to another. When no answer is forthcoming, he enters the cave.

James hurries along behind, the light from his orb revealing that the cave continues fifteen feet into the side of the mountain before it narrows dramatically. Everyone else follows except the man with the dogs, he remains at the entrance.

"Barric, Aria!" the father again shouts. The only replies are faint echoes coming from further inside.

The far side of the cave narrows to an opening barely three feet across and four high. Looks as if the mountain had shifted in ages past, creating the opening. Water oozes from the sides, collecting in the depressions along the ground.

The father moves to enter the opening first but Jiron puts a hand on his shoulder and says, "You better let us go first, we've done this sort of thing before."

He looks as if he's about to object but then nods and backs up to allow Jiron to move first, then James. Miko follows next followed by the farmer and the others who have accompanied him on his search.

"What would they be doing in here?" Miko asks as he enters through the opening. Having to hunch over due to the narrowness of the opening, he steps through.

From behind the father's voice comes, "They're rather an adventurous pair. Barric's the worst and his sister will follow him anywhere."

The tunnel they find themselves in is moving down a gradual slope, the floor of the tunnel is uneven to say the least. The further they advance down it, the more water is collected upon the floor. At one point the pools of water begin to turn into a small stream flowing along the base of the tunnel.

"Barric, Aria!" cries the father again, but only silence returns. Worried, he continues following behind James and Jiron.

The tunnel they're moving through comes to an abrupt end at a steep, downward shaft descending into darkness. The water flowing along the bottom of the passage goes over the edge and can be heard as it cascades down into the darkness below. As soon as Jiron and James both reach the edge, the father sees them stop and asks, "What's wrong?"

"The way continues down a deep shaft," James explains. The shaft is even narrower than the tunnel which they've been following, barely two, maybe three feet in diameter. The sides are rough and afford many handholds which could be used in climbing down.

Upon reaching the shaft, the father looks down into the depths with dread. "Barric, Aria!" he shouts into the opening. After a moment's silence, from below comes a barely heard female's voice, "Father!"

"That's Aria!" he exclaims, hope springing to life. "Are you okay?" he shouts down.

"I think Barric's dead," she says with a sob.

Miko comes to the fore and asks Jiron, "Do you still have that rope?"

He nods as he lifts his shirt to show the coil of rope secured around his waist.

"Let me have it," he says and ties one end around his middle after Jiron hands it to him. "Hold on tight and don't let go," he tells him as he moves to the edge of the shaft.

"What are you doing?" James asks as he places a hand on his arm.

"What I have to," he says. Removing James' restraining hand, he starts climbing down the shaft. To Aria below he says, "Hold on, I'm coming." Handhold to handhold he works his way down.

James comes to help Jiron in maintaining supportive tension on the rope as Miko slowly makes his way down. After he passes into the darkness, a white light suddenly springs into being and they are able to see him as he continues working his way down.

"Where did that come from?" Jiron asks James when the light appears. There isn't any source for the light that they can make out, it just seems to be there.

"I'm not sure, maybe from the Star," he says. Jiron nods his head in understanding.

Miko continues to work his way down the shaft, the water cascading around him soon has him drenched. At one point a rock gives way and he begins sliding uncontrollably to the bottom but is stopped by the rope. Jiron and James hold the rope steady until he has a chance to regain his foothold.

When the light appeared he was slightly surprised, not knowing where it came from. It bothered him at first, but then the light brought him peace and a sense of purpose. Giving it no more thought, he continued working his way down, one handhold at a time.

Before Jiron's rope is completely played out, he reaches a cavern. Fortunately, the shaft enters the cavern against one wall and he's able to work his way down the wall to the bottom. A large pool of water sits directly beneath the opening forcing him to work his way laterally along the wall in order to reach the edge of the pool.

"Father?" a girl's voice comes from further into the cavern.

Miko reaches the edge of the pool and comes to stand on the cavern's floor. Looking into the cavern, he sees a young girl of about sixteen sitting twenty feet away. Cradled in her lap is the head of a young man of about eighteen. Around the lad's head a cloth has been tied as well as two other bandages, one on his leg and another around his chest. His clothing in those areas is soaked with blood "No, I'm not your father," he says as he unties the rope from around him and goes over to them. Looking up the shaft, he hollers, "I'm down and I found them!"

"Who are you?" she asks.

"You can call me Miko," he replies.

"Is she okay?" her father's voice comes from above.

Miko glances to her and sees her nod her head. "I think so, give me a minute." Coming closer, he kneels down beside her to examine her brother. Next to her on the rock he can see what's left of three candles which she must have had with her when this all happened.

"Where is the light coming from?" she asks him, a little bit of fear edging into her voice.

As he puts his ear to her brother's chest, he replies, "That's kind of hard to explain." He then puts a finger to his lips indicating for her to keep quiet and she nods her head. Trying to tune out the background noises such as the water cascading down the shaft into the pool, her breathing and the sound of his own heartbeat, he listens for the boy's.

Lub...dub.

Very faint, but his heartbeat is there. "He's alive," he says. "But his life is leaving him."

"Oh, Barric!" she cries, holding her brother tighter.

Miko reaches into his pouch and produces the Star of Morcyth. The light within the cavern suddenly increases tenfold as its brilliance shines forth.

"What's happening?" her father hollers down from above when the light from the Star reaches them.

Ignoring his question, Miko holds aloft the Star in his right hand and lays his other upon Barric's chest. Aria looks in awe at him as he closes his eyes and his lips begin to move silently.

No sooner do his lips begin to move than a glow surrounds him and extends toward her brother. Gasping in shock, she begins to recoil from the approaching glow but then her fears melt away as a calmness comes over her.

As the glow continues to envelope both Miko and her brother, she sees her father emerge through the opening in the ceiling. "Father!" she whispers urgently, glad to have him again with her.

Coming to stand on the floor of the cavern by the pool, he turns to see his son enveloped by the Star's glow. Rushing over, afraid of what may be happening to his son, he makes to push Miko away.

"No father," his daughter says, holding up a hand. "He's alive." She nods to Miko and adds, "I think he's a priest."

Looking down at his son, blood soaked and for all the world looking as if he's already passed to the other side, he holds little hope for his survival.

Others begin entering through the opening, first James and then Jiron who has left the rope in the hands of two of the other farmers. They make their way over to the others and arrive just as Barric's chest begins to rise and fall on its own.

"He's breathing!" his father exclaims. Looking to his daughter, he can see his hope and joy reflected in her eyes.

Another few minutes and the glow suddenly disappears, the only light now in the cavern is that of James' orb. Barric's eyes flutter open and he looks around at those standing around him.

Miko gets to his feet and returns the Star to its pouch. "How can I ever repay you?" the father says to Miko as his son begins to sit up.

"There is nothing to repay," he tells him.

James comes and pats him on the back, "Good job."

"Thanks," he replies. Then to the boy's father he says, "He should be okay now, but will need many days of rest before he'll fully recover."

"What temple do you belong to?" the father asks. "I would like to go and give my thanks and make an offering."

Miko looks surprised and glances to James. James just shrugs and allows Miko to handle this on his own. Turning back to the father, he says, "I don't really belong to any temple. The healing of your son was done by the power of the god Morcyth."

"Morcyth?" the father asks. "Don't think I know of him, but tonight I shall pray to him and offer my thanks for the life of my son."

"Maybe we need to start thinking about getting everyone out of here," Jiron suggests.

"Yes," the father agrees. He offers his son a hand and helps him to his feet. Barric has to lean heavily upon his father as his legs have very little strength left.

Lifting his hand to his forehead, Barric scratches and the cloth covering his head falls away. His sister gasps when she sees the pink line where a jagged tear had been but a day before. "It's healed!" she exclaims.

"Of course it's healed," her father says. "That's what priests do."

At that, Miko turns to James and silently mouths, *'Priest?'*

James simply grins and pats him on the back.

Using the rope, they help the brother and sister up to the top first, then the father. James climbs up next and Jiron follows last. They make their way along the sloping passage, the father and another farmer helping Barric along. At the opening, the two dogs greet Barric and Aria with barks and attempts to jump on them but the farmer holding their leash keeps them at a distance.

On the way back down the mountain, Aria explains that this cave is a favorite of theirs. They've been here many times before but this time while descending the shaft, Barric slipped and fell.

"Why didn't you come get help?" her father asks.

"I'm sorry," she says. "But I didn't want him to die all alone and in the dark." Then she lays her head on his shoulder and begins to release the pent up worry and sorrow she's been feeling since that fateful fall. Her sobs last quite awhile, almost lasting until they reach the camp where Illan and the others are waiting.

Most everyone is still awake, worried about what was going on. Devin hears them coming and calls out, "They're back."

As Illan comes forward, he sees the two kids walking with them, Aria clutched to her father and Barric supported between two of the farmers. "Good work," he says to James with a smile.

James turns to the father and says, "You are all welcome to share our fire this night."

Shaking his head, he replies, "Thank you, but no. Our farm is but an hour away and I think it would be best to return and put him to bed. Their mother is beside herself with worry too and I would hate to extend her misery any longer than I have to."

"I understand," James says. Extending his hand, he adds, "Good luck to you."

Taking it, the father says, "You too." Then to Miko he comes over, extends his hand but then reconsiders and gives him a hug. "Thank you so much for my son," he says softly. When he releases Miko from the embrace, tears can be seen at the corners of his eyes. At that, he and the others turn and make their way back down the road toward their home.

Chapter   Four

"So what happened?" Illan asks after the villagers leave. Everyone gathers around as James, Jiron and Miko take turns relating the events as transpired upon and within the mountain. When Miko comes to the part where he heals Barric and is named priest by the father, he falls quiet.

"What's the matter?" Yern asks him.

"I…I don't think I am a priest," he says. "Just because I have the Star doesn't make me one." He looks to James and asks, "Does it?"

James takes a long look at him while he contemplates the answer. The shade of the dead priest of Morcyth had stipulated the glow only manifests for priests of Morcyth and the glow manifested for Miko. Did that make him a priest? Finally he says, "I think by the broadest definition of a priest, you are. A priest calls upon his god and things happen, such as when you use the Star to heal people."

"But, I don't feel like a priest," he says, slightly scared. "You once named me a warrior priest of Dmon-Li. Now am I a priest of Morcyth? Am I both?"

"Maybe simply being in possession of the Star enables him to tap into the god's power without actually being a priest," Scar says. "In fact, Potbelly and I once ran into…"

James stops him with a wave and says, "Not now."

Becoming quiet, Scar glances around and sees that no one was paying him much attention anyway.

To Miko, James says, "If you are, you are. There's not a whole lot you can do about it right now." He takes in Miko's demeanor and asks, "Does it bother you to be so named?"

After a moment's thought, he shakes his head. "No," he says. "A name is just that, a name. I have made no vows of priesthood so I can't consider myself one."

"These are the sort of things other priests should discuss with you," Illan says. Then to all those gathered he adds, "But the night is waning and if we are to get any rest before heading out in the morning, we best turn in now."

"You're right," James says and they break up, each heading to their tents except those currently on watch.

Miko walks with James and asks quietly, "Do you really think I am a priest?"

"Yes, Miko," he admits. "In one way or another, I do."

They walk the rest of the way in silence until James' tent is before them. Pausing before the entrance, Miko says goodnight too. As he moves toward his tent, a smile comes to him and he absentmindedly rubs the Star where it rests in the pouch.

The following morning, with the sun breaking through fluffy, white clouds, they get underway with James and Illan in the lead. The group continues down the road as it meanders its way through the foothills, never straying very far from the mountains.

Refugees from the south stream past in intermittent groups, those fleeing the impending conflict when the Empire makes its push for Lythylla and the north. The few they do speak to tell them the Empire has already made probing attacks on the defenders at Lythylla but have yet to commit their entire force. One man tells them that before he left, the force outside the walls of Lythylla had grown to over five thousand with more arriving every day.

"Grim news indeed," Illan comments to James after the man continues on.

Nodding, James hopes what he brought can win the day against so many. He had thought to face perhaps a thousand, maybe two. *But five thousand?* "We can but do our best," he says with more confidence than he feels. The outcome will primarily depend upon how many mages they have. If but one or two, he should be fine. They have yet to put more than that with any force he's encountered so far and it isn't like they're expecting him to show up or anything.

The end of the day finds them approaching a small town nestled in a small valley in the hills. "Yeln," Illion tells them as the town comes into view. They set up camp south of town in the lee of a hill.

While preparations are underway to set up the tents and get the horses settled in, a family is seen traveling from the south. Illan takes notice of them with keen interest and says to James, "Be right back."

James nods his head and watches Illan move to intercept them. When he's crossed half the distance, an older gentleman disengages himself from the others and moves quickly to meet him. "Looks like he knows them," he says.

Miko comes over and stands with him as he watches the two men. When they come together, they exchange a hearty handshake and then stand there in conversation for several minutes.

The man's family leaves the road and joins the two men. A woman places her hand on Illan's shoulder and he gives her a hug. Suddenly, Illan releases her and stands erect. A few more words are exchanged before he turns and returns to where they have all but finished settling in. Behind him, the family returns to the road and continues making their way north, eventually entering Yeln.

As Illan approaches, they begin to take note of the expression on his face. Many of the recruits have been on the receiving end of that expression through some infraction or other they had the misfortune to make during their training. All hope never to see it directed at them for it means dire consequences. The fact that he's wearing it now can only be bad.

James and Miko make their way to him and James asks, "What's wrong?"

When he nears them he comes to a stop. In a voice quivering in rage, he says, "My wife is dead."

"What?" exclaims Miko.

"How?" asks James. He glances over his shoulder and sees Devin already has his tent ready for him. Turning back to Illan he says, "Let's go to my tent and you can explain."

Illan nods and stalks forward toward James' tent. On the way James catches Jiron and Delia's eye and indicates for them to come along as well.

Devin comes forward, sees the expression on Illan's face and stops in his tracks. His heart begins beating again when he realizes it's not directed at him. He glances to James who says, "Make sure we're not disturbed for anything."

Nodding silently, Devin moves to the tent flap and holds it open for them to enter. Once they're all in, he closes it and takes position outside.

"What's going on?" Delia asks as she looks to James.

He nods to Illan and remains silent. All eyes turn to Illan as he stands there in silence for a full minute. Then in a voice cracking with sorrow and anger, he explains. "My wife is dead. Our son and his family taken. Everything my family has is gone!"

Delia gasps and Miko asks, "How?"

Illan turns his gaze to James and says, "Things have gone ill in Seastar."

Seastar. The last time they were in Seastar, they had freed a captain from jail in order to reach the far side of the Sea in short order. "It's not because of the captain is it?" he asks.

Nodding, Illan replies, "Yes it is. Remember that man whom the captain hit, Lord Faetherton?" When James nods, he continues. "Seems he found out who it was that took the captain from the jail, nothing stays hidden in a small town. From what my friend said, it didn't take him long to extract his revenge on the only ones available."

"Your family," says James in sorrow.

Illan nods. "That's right. Through means legal and foul, he ousted Harlan from the Magistrate's office and basically took over the town. From then it was fairly easy for him to jail my wife, my son and his family. He then took our lands and all our possessions as reparations for taking the captain."

"How could he get away with all this?" Jiron asks, not believing what he's hearing. "Shouldn't the guards or even the townsfolk have done something?"

"With the war going on, all able bodied men are down south," he explains. "There was no one left to stand against him but old men and young boys. He's acquired a score or so of toughs who keep the people in line and none now dare gainsay his wishes."

"Did he kill your wife?" Delia asks.

"Not directly, no," he replies. "She languished in jail, as has my whole family, through the winter. She caught pneumonia and died. My son and his family are still being held."

"Then what are we waiting for?" announces Jiron. Everyone turns to look at the murder in his eyes. "Seems we have some justice to dispense!"

"I agree," says James, Delia and Miko both nod in agreement. "We can't let this continue." To Illan he says, "We're with you, just tell us what you want to do."

"I thank you all," he says and then marches from the tent. "Jorry! Uther!" he hollers in the tone of voice all have come to know and at times fear.

"Yes sir?" Jorry replies as he and Uther come running. The others move closer to see what's going on.

"I've got some work for you two," he says.

Late the following afternoon, Illan along with everyone else but Jorry and Uther, approach the outskirts of Seastar. The mood of the group is somber, the story of what happened to his family has been told to each and every member of their group. They are saddened by his loss while at the same time angered at the man who is behind it.

Jorry and Uther were sent ahead last night to scout the town. They were supposed to have met them on the road this morning but have yet to make an appearance.

"Do you think anything happened to them?" Jiron asks.

"Hope not," replies Illan. He thought he would be feeling anger and rage at this point, but all that goes through his mind are the memories of his Alaina. They first met when he was but a lad and had just entered service with Madoc's army. He was on leave and had journeyed to Seastar for no better reason than that he had never been there.

Riding through town, he saw a flash of auburn hair and a friendly smile and was smitten forevermore. Their son arrived three years after their wedding, the only child to have survived. There were two other pregnancies after that but one had been stillborn and the last, a girl, had died before reaching a year.

Memories of their time together wash over him as he passes through the first of the buildings. People upon the street see him riding into town and stop in their tracks. Several call to him but he ignores everyone, intent on his memories.

He leads the group through town and at first James thought he was heading for the magistrate's office. But instead, leads them through town to the north and into the hills. Not far out of town an estate appears ahead of them, a grand estate with a large stone fence surrounding it. The manor house in the distance stands three stories tall and the road leading through the front gate to the house is cobblestone.

"Is this where you live?" Miko asks once it's become clear he means to go there.

Illan nods, "My family has lived here for six generations."

Half a mile from the gates of the estate, two men emerge from the surrounding trees. James sees it's Jorry and Uther.

"Well?" Illan asks once they've come near.

"Two guards stand at the gates," Uther tells him.

"Not sure how many are inside but we've seen four men enter and two leave," Jorry explains.

"Grab your horses," Illan says and kicks his horse to move toward the gate. They hurry into the trees and reemerge shortly riding their horses, then fall in line with the others.

He rides without hesitation and is shortly approaching the gate. The two men standing guard move to stand before the gate and one steps forward. Holding his hand up indicating for them to stop, he says, "No one is allowed to enter."

"On whose authority?" Illan asks, bringing his horse to a stop, scant inches from the man.

"By authority of Lord Faetherton," he replies.

Illan glares down at the man and asks, "Is this Faetherton here?"

"*Lord* Faetherton is currently in town," the man explains.

Illan glances to Jiron next to him and says, "Open the gate for me."

"Sure," Jiron replies. Hoping down from his horse, he moves toward the gate.

The man steps in front of him and actually puts his hand on Jiron's chest. "I said, no one is allowed to enter."

Jiron pauses only a moment before his takes the man's wrist and twists it painfully. With his other hand, he grabs the man by the back of the neck and throws him out of his way. He resumes his progress toward the gate and the other guard draws his sword, moving to bar his way.

"I wouldn't do that," a woman's voice says in the stillness. The guard glances to the others and sees Aleya with arrow knocked and aimed straight at him.

Jiron comes to him and takes his sword.

"Scar, Shorty," Illan says, "tie them up please." They immediately dismount and remove rope from their saddle bags.

Outnumbered, the guards remain docile while they're being tied. "How many more of you are there?" Illan asks.

One guard remains stoically silent but the other says, "Five."

"Shut up!" the other guard orders.

"What should we do with them?" James asks.

Illan glances at him and says, "No reason to kill them. It's not with them that I have a quarrel." He glances at the two men sitting on the ground and adds, "At least not yet." To Scar and Shorty he says, "You two stay here and keep an eye on them. Let us know if anyone comes."

"You got it," Scar assures him.

Jiron pulls the bar and draws the gate open. He pushes it so it swings around and slams into the inner wall where it remains. Returning to his horse, he joins the others as they move toward the manor house.

The inner grounds have been meticulously kept. Off to one side is a flowering garden of magnificent beauty. Stone paths work their way through the blossoms and two benches can be seen where people could take their ease while enjoying the beauty surrounding them. The sight of the gardens brings sadness to Illan. His Alaina had loved them and spent many sunny days among them. A smile comes to him when he remembers his son as a boy and how he once played in her flowers, ruining many young plants. Her anger at him was fierce but he never really learned to stay out of her plants.

As they move down the cobblestone road, the front door opens and a man emerges. Dressed finely with an air of command, he watches them approach. "How dare you forcibly enter Lord Faetherton's estate?" From windows on the second and third floor, three men have crossbows aimed at them.

"This is my house and I have no need to explain myself to you," Illan tells the man as he looks down at him from the back of his horse. "Tell those men with the crossbows to lower their weapons or we'll kill you all, right here, right now."

The man stands there a moment assessing the situation. That was definitely not the response he was expecting. Since coming here to Seastar, he's heard rumors of this Illan for this is who must be before him. Some of the rumors he didn't give much credence to. It only takes him a moment to decide he's woefully outnumbered and hollers up to the others, "Lower your weapons."

"And tell them to leave my house," he says.

"Everyone, out!" the man yells. The three men covering them with crossbows from above leave the windows and come join the man in front of Illan.

"Where's the other guy?" James asks.

"There is no other," he tells them.

"We were told to expect five here," Illan explains. "So where is he?"

"I assure you," the man says, his nervousness rising, "there is no one else here."

"Jiron, take Yern and Potbelly and search the house," he says.

Dismounting, Jiron says "You got it." With Yern and Potbelly beside him, he makes his way to the front door.

Raising his voice loudly, the man says, "I assure you, there is no one inside this house!"

Jiron pushes him out of the way and enters through the front door, the other two right behind.

"Miko, tie them up," Illan says.

Getting down from his horse, Miko removes a coil of rope and begins securing the hands and feet of the four men.

"Lord Faetherton will not take too kindly to this intrusion," the man warns Illan as Miko ties his hands behind his back.

"No, I suppose not," he replies. "And as far as Faetherton is concerned, where might I find him?" When the man fails to respond, he says, "No matter. I'll find him in due course."

Suddenly, from the back of the house, the sound of a horse reaches them just before a man appears riding hard toward the gate. "Don't let him leave!" orders Illan.

Aleya and Errin turn in the saddle and draw back their arrows. After taking aim, they let their arrows fly but the rider dodges and the arrows fly wide. A whine begins to be heard as several slingers twirl their slings before letting their slugs fly toward the fleeing man. One manages to strike him in the side and almost knocks him off his horse but he somehow keeps his balance.

"Shorty!" Jiron yells as he races from the back of the house.

At the gate, Shorty and Scar have been observing the events transpiring by the manor house. When they see the man racing toward them, Scar moves to close the gate while Shorty takes position in the road. Shorty removes a throwing knife and throws, catching the horse in the chest.

The horse stumbles and crashes to the ground, throwing the man several feet where he lands hard. Shorty runs over with another of his knives in hand but slows when he sees the man is not moving. As he draws close, he finds that the man broke his neck when he struck the ground.

Turning to the others at the manor house, he yells, "He's dead!"

"Get him and his horse out of the road and behind the wall," Illan hollers back to him.

Shorty nods and then he and Scar begin the gruesome job of dragging the dead man and horse to the wall.

"Who was that?" Illan asks, turning back to the man before him.

"Nobody," he replies.

Illan eyes him a moment and then dismounts. To Caleb he says, "Go tell Shorty and Scar to continue keeping watch and to shut the gate." When he runs off to do as bid, Illan turns to Nerrin and Moyil. "Go down there and bring the two guards back here with the others."

"Yes sir," Nerrin says and then they begin running down to the gate.

"Delia, take our prisoners around back and keep an eye on them," he tells her. "Don't want them seen should anyone approach."

"Right," she replies and then gets her slingers to escort the prisoners to the rear of the house.

Illan gives James a glance then enters the house with James, Jiron and Miko right behind.

The front room looks just like any other lady's drawing room with couches where visitors can rest and so forth. He makes his way deeper into the house, passing a side corridor and several doors before coming to what looks to have at one time been a strong wooden door. Axes or something had chopped away at it until a hole was wide enough for a man to enter.

"What's in there?" Jiron asks.

"Some of the more important items my family holds dear," he explains as he stops before it. Reaching into his pocket, he produces a key and inserts it into the lock. Turning it, he unlocks the door and swings the broken door open.

"Shouldn't we go get your son and his family out of jail?" questions Miko.

"All in good time," he replies. "They've been there for months, another hour won't do them any more harm." Entering through the door, he takes the stairs down to the basement.

Signs of looting are everywhere. Shelves smashed, boxes and chests opened if not outright destroyed. "They took everything!" exclaims James.

Illan turns to him and asks, "Can we have some light?" An orb springs to life on the palm of James' hand, flooding the basement with light. He glances to the others and says, "They didn't take everything."

He moves to the far wall where two chests stand smashed open. "Give me a hand," he says and the others move to help him slide the chests away from the wall. Once they've been moved back four or five feet, he leaves the chest where it sits and returns to the wall. He simultaneously presses four bricks and a soft 'click' can be heard.

Another brick looks to have been damaged at one time, a jagged hole, barely an inch in diameter sits just off center. Illan inserts his finger into the hole and then pulls. The wall swings open to reveal another room on the far side.

Indicating the smashed chests and boxes in the outer room he says, "In case of thieves, we kept some of our money and treasures out here, those we were willing to lose. The important items lay in this room."

Several chests sit undisturbed against one wall. Many weapons of master craftsmanship are displayed upon the walls. Other items, including statuettes and figurines are situated upon various shelves lining the room.

"Magnificent," James says as he comes into the room.

"Why did we come in here?" Jiron asks. "I mean, we have plenty of coins and gems."

"That's not why we're here," Illan says as he crosses through the room and comes to the far wall. He again removes a key and slides it in a crack between two bricks and turns it. Pulling on the key, he opens yet another secret door.

When the door opens, James hears Jiron gasp when he sees what lies on the other side. Looking within, he finds a breast plate, a helm, a shield, a sword, and a banner, all bearing the same insignia. A black bird of prey in flight poised to strike, upon a red heraldic field. Behind the hawk are two crossed swords.

"You're the Black Hawk?" Jiron asks with a trace of awe in his voice.

Nodding, Illan says, "I was." He begins removing his old sword belt from around his waist and casts it aside. Stepping within the room, he takes the sword belt with the Black Hawk insignia and straps it on.

"Black Hawk?" questions James.

"The Black Hawk was a ruthless leader during the War of Barrowman's Field," explains Jiron. Glancing to Illan, he says in a subdued voice, "Said to have committed all manner of atrocities upon the enemy."

"I heard that the Black Hawk once put an entire village to the sword as an example," Miko says.

Illan continues putting on his accouterments bearing his insignia without commenting.

"What supposedly happened to this Black Hawk?" questions James all the while watching Illan.

"None knew for sure," replies Jiron. "Some thought he had been killed while others claim he went to a far land in search of more blood."

James looks to Illan as he puts on the last item, the helm. "Illan?" he asks.

Turning back toward the others, he stands there in all his glory. From head to toe he looks like a hero out of the sagas. "It's true I'm sorry to say," he says. "When the war was over, I put Black Hawk away and became Illan. I had enough blood and death to last a lifetime. We did what needed to be done to stop the Empire, though I'm not proud of it."

"My Alaina knew and some close friends," he explains. "There are others from my men who came to live here with me, many joined the regular army. It was a bad time and one which I wished to put behind me."

"So why come here and don your old armor?" asks James.

"My Alaina is gone. There will be those who remember the Black Hawk, both here in Madoc and within the Empire, which may be to our advantage. It was a name to strike terror in the enemy, and it may serve us with what's to come."

He walks away from the room, leaving the banner behind. "Aren't you taking the banner?" Miko asks.

Shaking his head, he says, "No." He glances to James and says, "Now let's go find my son." Securing the secret door behind which the banner lies, he then takes them from the treasure room and closes the secret door. With their help, he puts the chests back in front of the hidden door and takes a moment to hide the fact they were ever moved. When he at last is satisfied, he turns and heads back up the stairs.

Chapter Five

When Illan comes out of the manor house, whatever conversation the others were engaged in comes to an abrupt halt when they see what he's wearing. Murmurs of 'Black Hawk' and other awed exclamations are heard as each comes to understand just what they are seeing.

Some of the recruits, having come from Cardri, are not familiar with the significance of the emblem he's wearing. The others quickly fill them in.

James comes out behind him and says, "We camp here this evening. Delia, you're going to be in charge for awhile. We have some business in town to take care of."

"Very well," she says.

Illan steps down off the porch and comes to where Moyil is holding his horse for him. Moyil's eyes widen as he draws near. Without saying a word, Illan takes the reins from him and mounts.

To those gathered around, James says, "We're going to rescue his son. Jiron and his group will join us. Delia, you and your slingers will remain here to look after the prisoners until our return."

The recruits look upset at not being allowed to accompany them, but realize there is little use in protesting. Those who are leaving with Illan and James mount up and follow them down the lane to the gate.

As they near the gate, Shorty and Scar see him riding toward them in his new armor. "I knew it!" exclaims Shorty with a holler.

"I can't believe this," Scar says somewhat at a loss for words, for once.

When Illan draws close, Shorty stands there with a grin on his face and says, "I knew there was something about you."

"You did, did you?" Illan replies from the back of his horse. "You two stay here and watch the gate." Without any further explanations, he continues through the gate and heads into town.

As Potbelly passes Scar he says, "Things should be more interesting from here on out."

"You got that right," agrees Scar.

Once past the gate, James drops back a little bit and rides between Uther and Jorry. To them he asks, "So what's the full story behind the Black Hawk?"

On the way into town, they fill him in on the details.

About twenty five years ago, the Empire made a push into Madoc in an attempt to swallow up a section of fertile farmland to feed its growing populace. The army was sent to expel them back to the Empire but the fighting raged for many years until a sort of stalemate was achieved.

Unfortunately for Madoc, that stalemate happened to be where the Empire had decided to stop anyway. A portion of the lands now held by the Empire was known as Barrowman's Field and thus the name for the war.

Some believe that the Ruling Council in Madoc decided to create a band of men whose job was to destroy as much of the Empire as they could to force them to draw off some of their forces defending the area known as Barrowman's Field.

The Black Hawk was in charge of that band. Black Hawk and his raiders somehow got through their lines and then it began. The destruction of town after town, some say they slaughtered every last man, woman, and child. They're also rumored to have salted the fields so nothing would grow.

Whatever the real truth is, it worked. The cry from its citizens forced the Empire to pull forces from the border to deal with the Black Hawk which allowed Madoc's army to push them out.

Black Hawk's band supposedly destroyed over twenty villages and small towns, all the while staying one step ahead of their forces. They even managed to avoid direct confrontation with their mages, how no one's ever been able to find out.

Sometime after the end of the War of Barrowman's Field, Black Hawk disbanded his men and was never heard from again.

"Many thought he had died," Uther says, winding the tale to a close.
"But now he's back," James says.

"That's right," agrees Jorry. "But what that's going to mean is anyone's guess."

"Thanks," James tells them as he moves to rejoin Illan at the fore.

"Sure," replies Uther.

Coming abreast of Illan, he glances over to his friend aghast at the things they just told him. He knows Illan must have heard all that was said, he definitely was close enough to have overheard the conversation.

"Did you do all those things?" James asks him.

He rides in silence for a minute before replying. "Yes, to a point," he finally says. "We did destroy towns and villages, sow fields with salt and other acts of destruction. But the wanton deaths of innocents? No, we never did that. Unfortunately, in the fog of war, innocents were killed and for that I shall always feel remorse. But we did what we had to do."

James digests that for a moment then asks, "Why didn't you resume your role as Black Hawk when the Empire first attacked last summer?"

Illan glances to him and then says, "I'm getting old. Sure, I thought about it but my Alaina counseled me against it. Said it would bring back too many bad things. But I couldn't simply stand by and do nothing so I went south to see what I could do."

"I left home before the fall of the City of Light. I hated to leave my Alaina, we both knew it was unlikely we would ever see each other again. She understood and sent me with her best wishes. My son offered to accompany me but I told him to stay and take care of his family." He pauses and then says with a catch in his voice, "It seems that's all I have left now."

They ride in silence for awhile before he gets his emotions under control and is able to continue. "By the time I reached the City, the Empire had already encircled it and I thought it would take months before it fell. Then the following morning to my disbelief, it was over. I worked my way to Lythylla and joined with Miller and his band, seemed like the logical thing to do at the time. The rest you know."

He always knew there was something about Illan. Always an air of command about him and in a crisis always knew what to do and took charge. Now it all makes sense. "After we rescue your son, what do you plan to do? Now that Black Hawk has returned."

"Nothing has changed," he says. "I'm still your man and will stand by you till the end."

"Thank you for that," James tells him.

Illan simply nods in reply.

By this time, Seastar appears ahead of them in the road. The sun now just dropping below the horizon, the lights of town begin to wink into life. "Where do you think we'll find him?"

"My son will be in the jail," he says. Then adds, "I hope."

"No, I mean Lord Faetherton," clarifies James.

"Who knows?" he says. "Though I don't plan to leave until I deal with him." He glances to James and is relieved to see him nod agreement.

Entering the outskirts, they make their way between the buildings, finally coming into an area lit by an oil streetlamp. When Illan rides into the light, his armor blazes forth and gasps are heard from those nearby on the street.

"Black Hawk!" "He's returned!" and other exclamations are heard in an increasing number as more and more people gather round.

"Sir!" a middle aged man exclaims as he comes from a nearby tavern.

Illan pauses in the street and turns toward the man. "We ride," he says. "Brook's Hollow at dawn. Spread the word."

With a whoop, the man turns and races down the street.

As they progress through town, that scene replays three more times. Each time all Illan says is, "We ride, Brook's Hollow at dawn, spread the word." The crowd gathering around them grows as they progress further into town.

When the press of people becomes too great, Illan brings them to a halt. At that, the street grows quiet. "Please return to your homes," he tells them and then takes off his helm, revealing his features to all.

"Illan?" some people ask in shock. Still others stand in dumbstruck amazement. Never before had anyone known who Black Hawk had been. But once they knew, it didn't take them long to realize where he's going. All knew of what Lord Faetherton had done and where his family lies.

"They're in the jail Illan," one man cries out.

Illan nods and says, "Thank you. Now you should all return to your homes." He glances around at the faces he's known all his life. Some he's watched grow to adulthood.

Still shaking their heads in wonder, they begin to disperse.

Sighing, Illan replaces his helm and glances to James. Then he resumes riding toward the jail. Before they reach it, they see lined up before the front door, thirty or more men, ten of whom have crossbows. Standing before them is a man dressed regally and can only be Lord Faetherton. Illan approaches and stops a good twenty feet from him.

"I've come for my son," he announces.

"Your time is past, Black Hawk," Lord Faetherton says derisively. "You and those with you are under arrest for the illegal release of a prisoner."

"I don't think so," Jiron says.

"If you don't remove your weapons, we will be forced to fire," he says.

"If you don't drop your weapons and stand aside, I will kill each and everyone who stands against me!" Illan says with utter conviction.

From his vantage point behind Illan, James watches Faetherton's men begin to shift in their ranks. Each has grown up with the tales of Black Hawk and the viciousness with which he pursues his enemies. Several crossbows actually dip to the ground as the men holding them begin to reconsider supporting Lord Faetherton in the face of Black Hawk's rage.

Lord Faetherton raises his hand and all can see it is not entirely steady as it shakes with the nervousness he's feeling. "When I lower my hand," he says loudly, "my men will fire. Remove your weapons and prepare to be taken into custody.

"When your hand falls," Illan says as he begins edging his horse forward, "everyone dies."

Suddenly from out of the dark to the right of the jail, a dozen horsemen appear. One of them is carrying a battle torn flag bearing the Black Hawk insignia. The rider in the fore says, "Thought you might be here."

"Ceadric!" exclaims Illan.

"Your orders sir?" Ceadric asks.

"When his hand falls, kill them all," he says.

"Yes sir," Ceadric replies and turns toward where Faetherton and his guards stand before the jail. The 'whisking of swords' can be heard as Ceadric and his men draw their weapons.

Hearing that, Faetherton glances from one force to the other and judges his chances. Behind him, some of his men have already judged their chances of survival to be slim at best. Two crossbowmen and three guards break ranks and high tail it out of there.

Standing there in indecision, Faetherton licks his lips and his arm remains up.

To the men blocking the entrance to the jail, Illan says, "Drop your weapons now." When they hesitate, he adds, "I'll not ask a second time."

A second later, the clatter of weapons hitting the ground can be heard as, to a man, they all drop their weapons. Faetherton brings his hand down slowly. Illan glances to Ceadric and says, "Take them inside and lock them away until I decide what to do with them."

"Yes sir," Ceadric replies and then gets his men moving to collect the prisoners.

Illan dismounts and walks toward the jail. James follows suit and tells the rest to stay with the horses.

Faetherton stands there as Illan approaches, still maintaining an air of superiority. "You'll not get away with this!" he states. "I am the magistrate here. You are all branded outlaws."

When Ceadric and the others with him hear that they all break into laughter. "Shut up," one says when they pass by. Another spits at him and it lands on the front of his shirt.

"Now, let's go inside milord," Illan says with a slight derogatory emphasis on 'milord'. Propelling him forward, they move toward the door into the jail.

Along the edge of the streets, the townsfolk have gathered to watch the events unfold. They knew Illan's family is being kept inside and was hoping to see Faetherton's blood spilled, there's little love for the man among the populace. When they see him being pushed through the door and into the jail, a cheer erupts.

Inside the jail, Illan has him move through the door to the holding cells in the back, James follows along behind.

When Illan enters the holding cell area, he sees his son and family all in one cell and comes to a stop. His son looks emaciated and his daughter-in-law and children don't look much better. They must have been given the barest minimum of food to keep them alive. James remembers him from their previous visit as a guard outside the magistrate's office. What he sees there in the cell barely resembles the man he once was.

Illan stops there in the hallway and stares at his son. A rage begins to develop at the way he and his family have been treated. He reaches up and removes his helm.

"Father!" his son exclaims when the helm comes off. His wife looks up from where she's holding their two children and a smile comes to her thin face.

"Alric," Illan says. To Faetherton he says, "Let them out."

Giving Illan a glare, he moves to the cell and removes a key from his belt. Inserting it into the lock, he opens the door. Alric pushes the door open and comes to greet his father. "Father," he says as he gives him a hug. "Mother's dead."

"I know," he replies. "Let's get you and your family out of here then we'll deal with that.

Just then, Ceadric and his men enter with the other guards and proceed to put them into the cells. To Ceadric, Illan says, "Take my son and his family home."

"Yes sir," he says and once the prisoners are securely within the cells, he and his men help them out of the jail.

Once they've left and he is alone with James and Faetherton, Illan turns to Faetherton and asks, "Where's my wife?"

"She's dead," he says with some small satisfaction.

Illan strikes out and connects with Faetherton's jaw, sending him flying backward off his feet to land on his back. "I know that," he replies. "Where is she buried?"

"Over in the cemetery," one of the guards in the cell tells him.

Turning to the guard, Illan asks, "Where?"

"Let me out and I'll show you," he says.

Taking the key, Illan opens the cell door and lets the man out. "If I show you, can I be allowed to leave?" the guard asks.

Illan glances at him and then nods his head.

"This way," the guards says and begins walking to the back door.

Illan replaces his helm on his head and says, "You too, milord." Picking Faetherton from off the floor, he propels him to follow the guard.

James follows them out the back and they turn down the alley to the right. Coming to where the alley opens onto the street, the guard turns to the left and begins moving away from the jail. "Be right back," James says as he turns to head back to the front of the jail to get the others.

"Tell Ceadric to gather the men and bring them to Brook's Hollow at dawn," Illan tells him.

"Okay," he replies then hurries to the front of the jail. He finds Alric and his family are already mounted and Ceadric was about to take them home.

To Ceadric he says, "Illan wants you to gather the men and have them at Brook's Hollow by dawn."

"Do you know what he's planning to do?" Ceadric asks him.

"Yes," he replies and when Ceadric looks askance at him for more information, remains quiet.

"As you will," he says. Turning to his men he raises his voice and says, "The Hawk wants us at Brook's Hollow at dawn." Then he kicks his horse and they ride away down the street, with cries and whoops, his men follow.

James gets into his saddle as Jiron asks, "What's going on?"

"Seems we're going to have company," he explains. "Right now we need to catch up with Illan, he's on the way to the cemetery to find his wife."

"Right," Jiron says and they get moving.

Illan's group hasn't progressed all that far down the street by the time James and the others arrive. They remain behind them as they wind through the streets toward the far side of town where the cemetery is located.

When they get there, Illan has Jorry and Uther keep an eye on Faetherton while he and the guard proceed into the cemetery. They all watch Illan as he and the guard make their way through the headstones and crypts, toward the last resting place of his beloved Alaina. About midway through the cemetery, they come to a stop and Illan falls to his knees.

It looks as if the guard says something to him and then Illan replies. The guard then begins walking away from where Illan is kneeling beside his wife's grave.

"Should we stop him?" Jiron asks James indicating the guard.

Shaking his head he says, "No. Illan told him he could leave if he showed him where his wife was buried."

The guard glances toward them and by the time he's reached the edge of the graveyard has broken into a run and looks to be fleeing for his life. "Guess he felt there might be a change of heart," offers Miko.

"Looks that way," agrees Jiron. Turning to James he says, "How long should we wait?"

"As long as he needs," he says quietly.

Faetherton stands there quietly for several minutes. Then when Illan isn't making any move to leave he says, "You know you all are in a lot of trouble."

Jiron laughs, "I suppose."

"So?" Yern says.

"If you let me go I'll go easy on you when the time comes," he says.

"I doubt if you'll live that long," Uther says.

"Are you threatening me?" he says offended.

Uther looks at him and nods over to where Illan is returning, "I'm not the one you should be worried about."

Faetherton turns to see Illan stalking from the graveyard wearing a grim expression. The color drains from his face as he sees Illan's hand resting on the pommel of his sword.

Illan comes to stand before Faetherton, the others gathered around. "I charge you with the death of my wife, the wrongful imprisonment of my son and his family. I also charge you with the illegal seizure of power here in Seastar. How do you plead?"

Faetherton gasps when he hears that. "How do I plead?" he replies indignantly. "Who are you to make charges against me? You, who killed with reckless abandon many years ago. You hold no authority here."

"Is there anyone here who has anything to say on this man's behalf?" he asks. A silence hangs in the air as he looks to each in turn, finally settling on James, of everyone there, he's the most likely to voice an objection. To the surprise of all, he shakes his head.

"So be it," he says and draws his sword.

"Wait!" Faetherton cries, the doom of the moment finally becoming real to him. He tries to make a break for it but Jorry and Uther grab him and drag him back. Forcing him to his knees, they hold him there to face Illan's judgment.

"You are found guilty, the sentence is death!" he says as he lashes out and severs his head from his body. Jorry and Uther quickly back away to avoid being sprayed by the blood as it fountains from his neck.

"Battlefield justice," Potbelly says.

Wiping his sword on the dead man's clothes, Illan says, "Let's go." Moving to his horse, he mounts and leads them back through town and to his estate. As they leave, James glances back to the dead man and shudders.

Arriving at the estate, they find two of Ceadric's men standing watch in front by the gate. They come to attention when he arrives and one opens the gate to allow them through. Up at the manor house everyone's in a flurry of activity.

As they leave the gate behind them and make their way toward the house, word begins to spread of their return and all activity ceases. The front door to the house is open and before they arrive, Ceadric, Delia and the others come out to greet them.

"Are they settled in?" Illan asks Ceadric.

"Yes sir," he replies. "They're in the dining room having a bite to eat, they were all quite famished. I have riders out to gather those who will have time to reach Brook's Hollow by dawn."

"Good," he says as he dismounts. Caleb and Moyil come forward to take their horses. Illan moves into the house.

James signals for Delia, Jiron and Miko to follow him and he takes them from the bustle surrounding the manor house to an area where they can have some privacy. "I guess you realize things have changed slightly?" he asks.

"You could say that," Jiron replies.

"Poor man," Delia says, saddened by Illan's loss. Then an angry look comes to her as she says, "Those children were on Coryntia's doorstep. Any longer and none of them would have survived."

James nods in agreement. "Illan took care of Lord Faetherton."

"He's dead," adds Jiron.

"Good," she says. "I don't usually wish ill of another, but this was reprehensible."

"I agree," states James. "Our small band is now practically an army."

Delia looks questioningly at him and Jiron explains. "It's Illan. As Black Hawk, he commanded a sizeable force of men, men it would seem who are still loyal to him. Tomorrow at Brook's Hollow, wherever that is, we'll see just how much our group has grown."

"Do you think he'll revert to his old ways?" she asks.

"I don't know," replies James. "He said he still follows me. If I don't ask him to, he will likely continue on as he has been. Only this time with an army at his back."

"With what we have coming ahead, that can only be a good thing," interjects Miko.

Silence fills the air as James glances from one to the other. "I was hoping to have a small band which may remain unnoticed and easily escape. If I take an army into battle, what chance do we have of that?"

"Good point," says Jiron.

"So what do you plan to do?" Miko asks.

"Play it by ear," he tells them. "As a wise man once said, 'No battle plan ever lasts past the first fall of the sword.' Already the plans I've made are undergoing change." He glances over to the dozen or so men beginning to set up camp on Illan's front lawn. "More men can't be a bad thing, can it?"

Jiron laughs, "Hardly. Have you actually looked at these guys? They're battle hardened veterans who are no strangers to war. A better bunch of men you couldn't ask for. True, they're getting on in age, but not so much that it will hinder them."

Nodding, James says, "Perhaps you're right." Already, plans and strategies for how he'll use these men in the upcoming battles are beginning to take shape. "Yes, perhaps you are right." Smiling, he takes them back to the manor house.

Chapter Six

The following morning, Illan takes his leave of Alric and his family. He and his son were up talking through the night about his wife, their future and more inconsequential matters. He offered to leave some men behind for protection, but Alric assured him that with Lord Faetherton out of the picture, he had little to fear.

Alric had been surprised when he learned of Illan's past, that his father was the feared and renowned Black Hawk of legend. In a way hurt that his father never entrusted that knowledge with him, but understanding the motivations behind it. All Illan had to say was that it was his mother's wish he was never to learn, told him all he needed to know.

James and the others, including Ceadric and his men, wait on horseback out front while he finishes his goodbyes. Moyil stands holding the reins to his horse until he appears. At last, he comes through the door, his two grandkids holding onto him, begging him not to go. In the short time he's known them, they grew awfully fond of him. Alric's wife finally has to take charge and disengage them from him.

"You be careful now," his son cautions.

Taking the reins from Moyil, Illan mounts and then turns toward his son. "I will. You take care of my grandkids and I'll be back when I can."

"I will father," he says. His wife stands there with a sad smile as she holds onto the kids to prevent them from charging forward.

He gives her a wave and salutes his grandkids, which gets them even more excited. Then he turns and begins making his way down the lane to the gate. "Goodbye grampa," the boy hollers. He turns in his saddle and waves one more time before turning back.

As they leave the gate and the manor house behind, Illan rides in silence. Memories come to him unbidden of his life here and the family he has left. He glances over to Ceadric and sees him smiling. "What are you smiling about?" he asks.

Ceadric grins at him and says, "I never in my life thought the ruthless Black Hawk would ever be called 'grampa'." At that he chuckles as does many of the others who overheard the exchange.

"We all get old," he replies, "if we're lucky."

In the fore of the column ride James and Illan with Ceadric and Jiron just behind them. The rest follow along at the rear. They ride toward town and when they get there, James is surprised at how many of the townsfolk have turned out. Seems rumors have been circulating about the events of the night before, that Illan is actually Black Hawk and that he's going to thump the Empire just as he did before.

"Illan!" he hears from those in the street. "Is it true you're going to take on the Empire again?"

"Looks that way," he replies.

"Give 'em hell!" another shouts out.

"That's the plan," he exclaims and a cheer erupts from the onlookers.

They work their way through town and the people steadily fall behind until finally dropping out of sight. He takes them along a dirt road which he says will lead to Brook's Hollow. Before they even get there, the smell of wood smoke reaches them.

Along the way, several riders come up from behind, those just now arriving in answer to Illan's call. When they reach the group, they fall in behind with the rest of Black Hawk's men.

What awaits them at Brook's Hollow is even more than what Illan expected. Five hundred men at least await them there. The majority are those who served with him before, but many brought their sons along to follow his banner. The banner bearing Black Hawk's insignia stands proudly in the center of the assembled men, blowing proudly in the breeze.

"I didn't realize there were that many left," Illan says in amazement.

Ceadric comes up next to him. "More may be on the way, it's hard to know for sure."

James looks out over the mass of men and can only look on in awe. Never had he thought he would have such a force of men for what he plans to do. This may work out after all.

A tall rider, well over six feet tall with gray peppering his black hair, comes forward from the men awaiting them and comes to a stop before

Illan. "Sir!" he says with a salute. After Illan returns the salute, the man says, "All are ready. Each has three days of supplies and is eager to go."

"Thank you, Captain," Illan tells him. To those riding with him, he says, "Stay here a moment." Moving forward alone, he addresses those in the Hollow. Raising his voice to carry to the farthest man he says, "Madoc has been victimized again by the Empire. Again, Black Hawk's Raiders are summoned to show them the error of their ways."

A whoop and holler erupts from the men and he's forced to pause a moment until they've quieted back down enough so they'll be able to hear him. "Our goal is simple. Drive them out or die to the last man!" Again, a cheer erupts, oaths are sworn and the men rattle their swords in their sheathes.

When again the Hollow is quiet, Illan hollers out, "This time, I do not lead." A murmur runs through the men at that. He holds up his hand for quiet. When he has it, he motions James to come forward and stand next to him. Once he's there, Illan turns back to the assembled men and says, "This is James, a mage of fearsome power who leads this company. I have sworn him my support for the trials ahead. If you follow me, you follow him." He glances around at the assembled faces and then says, "What say you? Will you follow?"

To a man they yell, "Yes!" The sound of their voices rings out across the hills.

"Then, let's go teach the Empire a lesson they'll never forget!" he hollers and turns around to face the direction they just came from. To Ceadric he says, "Just as before, you're my second. Keep the chain of command the same as it was before."

"Aye sir," he says and then moves toward those waiting in the Hollow.

"Inspiring," James says as they get underway to return to town.

Illan gives him a grin and replies, "It's expected. Something for them to tell their grandkids about."

"I think some of them already have their grandkids with them," Uther observes from behind.

"Well if you think about it," Jorry begins, "that wouldn't make them all that old even if they did. Suppose they had their first child when they were sixteen and then…"

All the way into town, they hear Uther and Jorry argue the possibilities and circumstances about age, grandkids and the men's worthiness in battle. Finally, Illan turns on them and tells them to stop, that it was getting on his nerves. They actually had the temerity to look offended that he said what he did. In any event, it got them to stop.

Once they reach town, James thought they would have taken the road back the way they had come. But Illan instead takes them to the southeast, cross country. "Why are we going this way?" he asks him.

"The road adds another couple hours," he explains. "This way we should reach the walls of Lythylla before night."

Their column stretches back half a mile. At the fore ride Illan and James. Behind them rides Ceadric with a score of men as well as Jiron and Miko. The man who brought the Black Hawk banner rides within that group, the flag proudly flapping in the breeze.

Next comes Delia with the rest who set out from The Ranch as well as all their pack horses. James didn't want them trailing along at the end, felt what they were carrying was too important to take the risk.

At the end ride the men who flocked to Illan's call.

The mood of the various groups is for the most part expectant and hopeful. The group from The Ranch feels better now that they have a band of battle hardened men accompanying them.

As they ride, more men from Illan's old force come and join their ranks. At one point after they stop briefly for the noon meal, they encounter a patrol out of Lythylla.

When the officer in charge of the patrol sees the banner bearing the Black Hawk he breaks into a gallop and races toward them, his men following close behind.

Before he has a chance to make any sort of declaration, Illan hollers, "What's the news from Lythylla?" He then brings his horse to a halt which signals the column behind him to stop as well.

The officer hesitates a moment before replying, his eyes moving from the banner, to Illan in his Black Hawk attire and then the column of men stretching behind him. His men come to a stop behind him, murmurs are heard as they come to understand who it is before them. "The Empire has yet to attack," he explains. "So far they've been satisfied with probing attacks."

"What strength do they have?"

"Last word was close to ten thousand," he replies. "Looks like they've committed most of their reserves in taking Lythylla." When Illan doesn't reply, he asks, "Do you mean to go there then?"

"I do," he says.

At that an excited murmur again comes from the officer's men.

"From here to the city is clear of enemy patrols and agents," the officer tells him.

"Thank you," he says and then gets his horse moving again. As they leave the patrol behind, James hears "Black Hawk!" and other exclamations as the officer's men can no longer control themselves in their jubilation. If anyone can save Madoc in its time of need, it's him.

James had come to the decision before this all began to leave the interaction with other military people to Illan. He understands the subtle nuances to get what needs done far better than he does. In those instances, he stays back and lets him have his way, confident he will do nothing to compromise their objective.

They reach the walls of Lythylla two hours after leaving the patrol behind. During that time, they encounter another three patrols, all telling them the same. Each time they continue on, leaving behind men whose hope for the future has been rekindled.

When the walls appear ahead of them, so does the river. They're able to take in the defenses of the enemy which have sprung up over the winter. Nothing major, simply a wooden palisade stretching to the horizon several hundred feet from the river's edge. Enemy patrols are seen in the area between the palisade and the water. From their vantage point, it's impossible to see what lies on the other side of the palisade.

"Should we ride closer and let them see who it is that's come to join the fight?" asks Ceadric. The revelation that Black Hawk has joined the fray would definitely send ripples of uncertainty and perhaps a little bit of fear through the soldiers.

Illan shakes his head and says, "No. Now is not the time."

"They'll know before too much longer," Jiron says from his position behind them.

"When they do, they do," he says and the tone of his voice tells them this conversation is over.

As they draw close to the north gate, they find it shut tight. Previously, it had been left open allowing refugees the opportunity to escape the coming conflict. By this time though, anyone who was going to flee would already have done so.

A crowd gathers along the wall over the gate as word spreads of the approaching force. When they're finally able to see the Black Hawk banner flying in the wind, a cheer goes up from the defenders.

As they come within a couple hundred feet of the gate, it begins to swing open and six men ride out to meet them. In the center of the group is none other than Lord Pytherian himself. His aide Henri rides beside him as well as four other military officers.

"Greetings Black Hawk," Lord Pytherian says as the two parties come together and stop.

"Milord," Illan replies back.

"It's been awhile," he says.

A chuckle can be heard from the helm. "You could say that," he replies.

Lord Pytherian finally glances at the others riding with the famed Black Hawk and his eyes widen when he discovers James there beside him. "As I live and breathe," he says. "Am I glad to see you."

"Sounds like you are about to have your hands full," he says. "Good to see you again milord."

"You too, James," he replies and then turns his attention back to Illan.

"There are many things which we need to discuss," Illan tells him.

"Indeed," he replies as he turns back toward the city.

Across the river, soldiers of the Empire are taking a most interested look at the new arrivals. From their vantage point across the river, it's hard to tell whether or not they have made out the banner. From the lack of excitement, James figures they haven't yet done so.

At the gate, soldiers and civilians who have stayed behind to aid in Lythylla's defense gather to greet the new arrivals. Shouts of "Black Hawk" and other exclamations greet them as they enter the city. The way they're greeting him, you would think Illan was a returning conquering hero. Thinking back on the tales of his exploits, it may not be far from the truth.

James takes a good look at the walls of the city as they continue along. Several catapults are stationed evenly across the wall facing the river which will be able to rain stone and fire upon those attempting to breach the walls. He almost feels sorry for the enemy. Almost.

Lord Pytherian brings them to a plaza close to the castle area that had at one time been an open air market. Now the stalls lie closed and the whole area is deserted. "Your men can have this area while you're here," he tells them.

To Ceadric, Illan says, "Get the men settled in and wait for our return."

"Aye sir," he says and then begins barking orders as he does as bidden.

To Delia and Jiron, James says, "You better stay here too. Stay close to the others and watch for strangers. You never know."

"You got it," Jiron tells him.

In the center of the plaza is a statue of a rearing horse. The man with the Black Hawk banner goes to it and manages to secure the banner there so it will fly free with the breeze. Illan looks at it for a moment and then turns to go with James as Lord Pytherian takes them to the castle.

"What's the situation?" asks Illan.

"Let's talk about that inside," he replies.

Illan looks to James with worry. Not wishing to talk about it in public can only be a bad sign. James nods his head in understanding.

After they enter the gates leading to the castle area, they make their way across the courtyard. At the castle entrance they dismount and then pass through the gates leading into the castle proper. The pages in the hallway, as well as the men-at-arms all stop in stunned silence when they see Black Hawk among them.

The men accompanying Lord Pytherian continue to walk with him. They reach a pair of double doors and Henri opens one for his lord and waits while they all file through. Once the last one is in, he enters as well and closes it.

Within the room is a large table with a map laid out across its top. Upon closer examination, it's revealed to be a map of the surrounding countryside with figures sitting upon it. It's a map detailing the positions of the enemy's forces on the far side of the river.

Lord Pytherian takes the chair at the head of the table, James and Illan sit across from him. The others take the remaining chairs while Henri remains standing behind his lord.

Indicating the other men there with them, he says, "These are the leaders of our forces. Whatever you have to say to me you can say to them."

Illan glances to James who gives him the go ahead to talk. "Milord, we did not come to place our forces at your disposal," he says. "We, rather James here, has a proposition for you."

"A proposition?" asks Lord Pytherian. Two of the other members of the group visibly frown at the statement.

"Yes," replies Illan.

One member of the group, a gray haired man with ribbons and medals adorning his uniform asks, "And what is this proposition?"

Illan glances to James who stands. "It's simple," he tells them. "I would like your help in constructing a building."

Shocked to say the least, this was the last thing they expected to hear. "A building?" another of the men asks.

"Are we to waste our time hearing this balderdash?" still another says.

"In return," James continues, ignoring the outbursts, "we will drive the Empire out of Madoc."

The man with the medals and ribbons breaks out laughing, the others look angry at being played for fools. "Are you serious?" he asks.

"Completely," he replies.

"You and that band you brought in will drive out the forces which the alliance has only been able to slow?" one man asks. "I hardly doubt that young man."

Lord Pytherian has remained quiet and thoughtful throughout. He remembers the feats James and his band did during the summer when the Empire all but broke through the gates. Also, rumors have reached him of other events concerning him, things which hardly seem credible.

"What building do you require and where is it to be built?" he asks.

The general with medals and ribbons turns to Lord Pytherian and asks, "You can't be taking him serious?"

"Absolutely," he assures him. "For a couple reasons. One, Black Hawk here would hardly tie his fortune with a losing enterprise. And two, I've seen what he can do. For those of you who don't know who he is, this is the mage James."

Eyes widen in surprise at that. He hardly looks the magical type. "This is the James we have been hearing so much about?" one asks.

"That's right," replies Lord Pytherian. "The one who rescued me, who saved the forces from annihilation to the south last summer, and who turned the tide after the Empire broke through the gates. If he says he can do it, we should at least give him the benefit of the doubt."

"I want a temple built in the City of Light," he explains. "It has to be built on its previous site, no other."

"But that's currently in the hands of the Empire," one man says. "And by all reports, they've strengthened the garrison there and have all but rebuilt its outer wall. How do you propose to do that?"

"How is my business," he tells them. "If I can do this, will you rebuild the temple?"

Lord Pytherian looks at each of the assembled military leaders in turn. He can see their doubt and has to admit, he has his own as well. "Yes," he finally says. "If you drive the Empire from Madoc, then we will build your temple."

"What have we got to lose?" the youngest of those gathered states. "Either he does it and a temple would be a small price to pay, or he doesn't and we're out no troops."

"When do you propose to begin?" medals and ribbons asks.

Illan glances to James and says, "Why don't I stay here and get an idea of what we're up against. You go on back and I'll meet up with you later."

"Very well," he says. Getting to his feet, he gives Lord Pytherian a slight bow and says, "Good to meet you again, milord."

"You too James," he replies. "We'll talk more about this later."

James nods and then turns to leave the room. Out in the hall, he shuts the door and makes his way out of the castle and to the plaza where the others have set up camp. When he gets there, he finds Jiron and Delia have already set up their tents, Devin having just completed putting up his.

"Are we on?" Jiron asks.

Nodding, James says, "Yes. Illan's still up there with Lord Pytherian going over the layout of the enemy, troop numbers, that sort of stuff."

"When do we begin?" asks Miko. The others from The Ranch gather around to hear his answer.

"Time for some payback!" exclaims Stig. Stig was one of those from the fight pits in the City of Light and lost many friends when the City fell.

"We'll be able to determine our course of action once Illan returns," he says. "Until then, we should relax as best we can and get some rest. Once this all begins we may not have the opportunity for awhile."

"Your tent is ready," Devin says coming up to him.

"Thank you," he replies. "I'm going to rest until he gets back. Let me know the instant he does."

"I will sir," Devin assures him.

Walking over to his tent, he sees Ceadric already has his men bivouacked and a mess already established. Entering his tent, he closes the flap and then lies down on his cot. He feels bad he's one of the few who has one. The others insisted saying most of what's to come will rest upon him and that he needs his rest. Comfort always being important to him, he didn't argue the point too hard.

Lying down, he lets the cares of the day drift away as he succumbs to sleep.

The smell of summer is in the air. All around him the flowers are in bloom and the tall grass is like the ocean as the refreshing breeze forms waves of bending stalks. The rolling hills are alive with animals both small and large, birds take flight and fill the air with their song.

He stops in his tracks when a familiar sound comes to him, the music of a calliope. Excited, he hurries toward it and finds a carnival nestled in among the hills. The tall Ferris wheel stands majestically in the center with other rides extending outward from it like spokes inside a wheel.

As he hurries down the hill, the smell of scones and funnel cakes reaches him and his stomach growls. Aside from cotton candy, those are the other two musts at any carnival or fair.

Walking forward to purchase a funnel cake, he can almost taste the powder sugar. Sure, they're extremely messy and he usually ends up coated in the white confectionary powder, but he doesn't care. It's all part of the fair experience. Reaching into his back pocket for his wallet, he's shocked to find he's left it behind.

Standing there with mouth watering and a feeling of extreme disappointment, he can only look at the freshly made funnel cake on display before him. It takes an almost insurmountable force of will to turn away, but he manages it. Dejected, he walks away.

Refusing to let his lack of funds ruin his day he puts it out of his mind and walks through the carnival. Strangely enough, it seems as if except for the carnies, he's the only one there. Glancing from ride to ride, he sees that though they're in motion and functioning, no one is riding them. Decidedly strange.

He reaches into his front pocket and withdraws a ride ticket, how he came to possess it he hasn't a clue. But when fortune smiles upon you, don't ask questions. Each ride boasts a sign signifying a single ticket is all that's required to ride.

It's hard to choose a single ride from so many. He walks along gazing first one way and then another, trying to make up his mind. Suddenly, out of the corner of his eye, he catches a glimpse of a golden haired girl.

When he turns to look, he sees her moving away from him quickly down a side aisle, her flowing golden hair bouncing with each step. Surprised and pleased to find another person here besides himself, he rushes after her. Something about her strikes a chord of remembrance, but what it is eludes him.

"Wait a minute!" he hollers, hoping she will pause long enough for him to reach her. But she fails to respond to his plea in any way and continues toward a ride at the edge of the carnival.

No matter how fast he runs, he's unable to close the distance before she reaches the ride. It's the Tunnel of Love. She hands her ride ticket over to the carnie and gets in one of the boats which will take her through the entrance.

"Hold that boat!" he yells, trying to increase his speed. Then he watches in frustration as the boat carrying the girl leaves the loading dock and sails upon the water toward the entrance to the ride.

He reaches the loading dock and the carnie asks, "Ticket?"

Holding out his hand, he realizes his ticket is no longer there. Looking around in anxiety, he discovers the ticket lying on the ground back the way he had come. He runs toward it just as a gust of wind picks it up and blows it still further away. Running, he finally reaches the ticket and grasps hold of it.

Turning back to the Tunnel of Love, he sees the boat bearing the golden haired girl has just passed through the entrance. He hurries back to the loading dock and gives the carnie his ticket.

"Step carefully please," the carnie says as he takes the ticket and motions for him to step into the first boat.

Moving into the boat quickly, he takes his seat. The carnie pulls the lever releasing the boat and he begins drifting along with the current toward the entrance. He peers inside but is unable to make out the boat bearing the golden haired girl, or anything else for that matter.

Upon reaching the entrance, he's able to see inside a little and upon the right side of the tunnel is a large, heart shaped picture with two white lights shining forth. As he passes through the entrance, he's able to see the golden haired girl far ahead of him.

"Excuse me sir."

Feeling as if he's being wrenched awake, he yells, "No!" He glances around and sees Devin standing there at the tent flap, a worried expression upon his face. The dream begins to slip away though he tries to retain the memory.

"Are you okay sir?" asks Devin.

Trying to recall what it was that was so important, all he's left with is a feeling of loss. Looking to Devin, he says, "Yeah." Sitting up, he puts his head in his hands and feels the last vestige of the dream slip from him.

"Illan's returned," he tells him.

"Thank you," he replies.

Devin then steps back and closes the tent flap, leaving him alone once more.

Sitting there in the darkened tent, he tries to recall the dream and why he had cried out but the memory is gone. Shaking his head, he gets to his feet and leaves his tent.

Chapter   Seven

Stepping from his tent he finds Illan surrounded by the others, telling them in part what he's learned. When he sees James exit, he ceases his conversation and moves toward him. "We should talk in your tent."

Coming to a stop, James nods his head and then returns inside. He's followed in by Delia, Jiron, Miko and Ceadric. Illan pauses a moment at the tent's entrance and says to Devin, "See that we're not disturbed."

"Yes sir," he replies as Illan enters the tent.

They're crammed inside the small tent which had never been intended to include so many at one time. "We're going to have to get you a larger tent," Jiron says with a grin.

"Feel sorry for poor Devin if we do," jokes Miko.

"Enough of that," Illan says. "There's much to talk about." When he has everyone's attention, he continues. "From the reports gathered today, it would seem we face anywhere from fifteen to twenty thousand troops."

James' face falls and Delia gasps.

"Can we handle that many?" Jiron asks.

They all look to James and the doubt crossing his face tells them he doesn't think so. "So many," he says. "I never thought to have to face so many right away."

As James sinks into silence, Illan says, "Their siege equipment arrived sometime today. Lord Pytherian suspects an attack either late this evening or first thing tomorrow morning. They have a dozen catapults and mobile bridges they plan to use to ford the river in different places during the assault."

"Where are they kept?" James asks.

"The latest reports put them sitting at the rear of their lines," he says. "A thousand or so troops are stationed in the area."

"Is there any word whether they have a mage with them?" Miko asks.

"None have been spotted, but that doesn't mean they aren't there," he replies. To James he asks, "Have you felt anything?"

Shaking his head, he says, "Nothing. If there is one, he's not doing anything that I would be able to detect."

"Could you find out?" asks Delia.

"Not without alerting him to my presence," he says. "And that may prompt an immediate attack." After a moment of thought he asks, "If we took out their siege equipment, would that delay their assault?"

"It would have to," interjects Ceadric. They all turn to gaze at him as he continues. "The catapults they could probably do without, but those bridges they'll absolutely have to have in order to cross the river and would be integral to their battle plan."

James nods his head and remains quiet as he considers different tactics.

"Lord Pytherian said he would keep us apprised of any change in the enemy camp," Illan says after a few moments.

"Just blast them," suggests Miko. "Do that thing you did outside the City of Light. From what Jiron and the others told me, it took out most of their army."

"That would only work if they have a mage," he replies. "It may come to that. But keep in mind, I haven't worked on the finer points of that spell and the consequences may prove disastrous for all."

"What do you mean?" Delia asks.

How can he explain it to them? What in their experience would compare with the detonation of an atomic bomb? From the description Jiron supplied him with of the explosion, it resembled an a-bomb more than anything else. There didn't seem to be any radiation fallout from that blast, but he would just assume not tempt fate a second time.

"I can't really explain it," he tells them. "Just take it on faith that it isn't something that I'm willing to do unless there are no other alternatives."

"Very well," Miko says, obviously disappointed.

After a moment's consideration, he says, "Here's what we do…"

Once James lays down what he plans to do. The others offer their expert advice and together they work out a strategy which should work. Ceadric selects fifty of his most battle hardened and skilled fighters for the mission. Together with Delia and the slingers, Errin and Aleya, and all the other fighters from The Ranch but Jiron, they make their way through the darkened city on horseback and exit through the north gate.

Each slinger has upon their back a pack that has been carried by pack horse all the way from The Ranch. None have yet been told what is contained within. Aleya and Errin have a dozen specially modified arrows in their quiver along with another containing regular arrows behind their saddles. Delia, after she and James spent a few minutes near one of the pack horses, returned with two small pouches secured to her belt.

Once they pass through the gates, they edge away from the river so as not to reveal their presence to the enemy sentries posted on the other side. An hour later finds them coming to the section of the river which Lord Pytherian's people said would have the least likelihood of having patrols. Here the river runs deep and swift making any attempt to cross extremely dangerous.

"What do we do now?" Yern asks her quietly.

"We wait," Delia replies. She turns her gaze to the glow of the enemy's camp in the distance and hopes this works.

"Ready?" Jiron asks him.

"No," he replies. "I never will be for this sort of thing." Hanging from his belt are several small pouches. When Jiron glances at them in question he says, "Just in case." Jiron nods his head and they get going.

He and James are making their way through the streets of Lythylla toward the gate which faces across the river to the enemy camp. In Jiron's hand is a ten foot pole with a white flag. Lord Pytherian assured him that this is the accepted custom when one wishes to speak with an enemy without fear of attack. To be honest, James about laughed when they told him that. He couldn't believe that on two different worlds, the same method would be used to initiate a parley.

Illan walks beside them as they approach the gates. When they reach them, he says, "We'll stand by to open them quickly should the need arise." Henri, Lord Pytherian's aide is there to facilitate the opening of the gate should it become necessary.

Behind them, the remainder of Ceadric's men ride. James didn't feel they were necessary, but Illan insisted saying it was best to be prepared for all contingencies.

At the gates James nods to Henri who shouts to a man stationed along the wall above the gates, "Is it clear?"

"Yes, sir!" the man replies.

"Open the gates!" he hollers to those in the gatehouse.

With a clack and a creak, the gates begin opening. They part just enough to allow the two men to walk through. "Good luck," Illan says before they begin moving out to face the enemy.

"Thanks," replies Jiron. James is frankly too nervous to make much of a reply.

"Let's go," he says and steps through the gate. Jiron follows a half step behind with the flag raised high.

As they make their way the short distance to the edge of the bridge, the gate swings closed behind them, shutting with a deep thud. Before them, they see activity arising from the enemy encampment.

The gate of the palisade is open and troops are beginning to spill forth. Soldiers, crossbowmen and a company of Parvati's take their position on either side of the gate, leaving an avenue through which James and Jiron can pass.

Crossing the bridge takes a large amount of will to force his legs to make the journey across to the other side. "What idiot came up with this idea?" he exclaims under his breath. "He should be shot."

Jiron chuckles as he says, "You did."

Once past the bridge, they have to cross several hundred feet before reaching the enemy's lines. When they reach the halfway point, a single individual exits the palisade's gate and moves to intercept them.

"Doesn't look like anyone of much importance," observes Jiron.

"Maybe not," he says. "Probably wants to see what we want before deciding if it's worth being taken before the commander of their army."

The man is undeniably a soldier, and by the looks of his armor and the insignia upon it, one of high rank. When the two parties are five feet apart, both sides come to a halt. As the bearer of the white flag, it's customary for James to make the first declaration.

"We wish to parley with the leader of the host," he states.

"Are you giving your surrender?" the soldier asks.

"No," James replies. When the man looks questioningly at him, he adds, "Rather to discuss the removal of the Empire's forces from within Madoc's borders and the cessation of hostilities between the two nations."

The man looks in absolute disbelief at him. "Take your foolish notions away before we kill you!" he exclaims, his disbelief turning into annoyance at being bothered by such stupidity.

"You would violate the sanctity of the Flag of Truce?" he asks.

"The Flag does not grant you immunity indefinitely," the man explains. "Only so long as the talk is in progress and a short time afterward to allow you to return to your side."

"I am not leaving until I speak with the leader of the Empire's forces," James insists.

"Go back," the man says. "This talk is at an end." Turning his back on James and Jiron, he begins walking back to his line.

"What should we do now?" Jiron asks quietly once the man has passed beyond where he could overhear the question.

James glances to him and says, "We wait."

"But they'll attack shortly," he tells him. "He as much as promised that."

"I know," he replies. "We need them to."

He and Jiron stay standing there before the assembled soldiers of the Empire. The man who had talked with them stops when he reaches their ranks and turns to observe James and Jiron still standing there.

"How long do you expect them to give us?" James asks.

"Don't know," he replies. "But the longer it takes, the more time Delia and the others will have to get into position.

Five minutes go by before the man runs out of patience. A command is given and the crossbowmen move to the fore and take aim on the two men standing alone before them. "I guess time has run out," observes Jiron.

"It would seem so," he replies. "I hope this works."

"So do I," admits Jiron quietly.

Another command and the crossbowmen release their volley of bolts toward the pair. The soldiers watch in amazement as the two men stand their ground despite the bolts flying toward them. Just before the bolts connect, a shimmering shield springs to life surrounding them. The bolts are deflected to the side.

A gasp ensues from the gathered soldiers as they realize a mage stands before them. Another command and a second volley speeds toward them. Just as the first had, the second volley strikes the shield and is deflected away.

From the defenders manning Lythylla's wall behind them, a cheer erupts and James glances backward to see the battlement from one end to the other packed tight with observers. Seems the entire garrison and most of the civilians are up there to observe the encounter.

"My turn," James says, more to himself than anything else. He brings his hands close together and then slowly brings them apart. A myriad of small red orbs flow outwards from between his hands toward the enemy soldiers. The orbs dance and zoom all the while emitting white sparks that sizzle through the air.

Moving quickly, the orbs soon near the assembled Empire soldiers. Before the orbs have a chance to reach them, panic erupts within their ranks and the men begin moving quickly back through the gate to avoid the oncoming orbs. Another cheer erupts from the defenders atop the walls, as well as a little bit of laughter.

As the orbs reach the fleeing men, they begin zinging them with small shocks. Each one doing little harm, but extremely irritating. "Are they going to kill them?" asks Jiron.

"Hardly," James says with a grin. "It's just to get their attention."

"I think it did that," he agrees.

Suddenly, James causes a starburst of immense proportions to spring into being overhead, bathing the entire countryside in light. It begins descending toward the enemy camp and before it has a chance to descend very far, James feels the tingling sensation which always accompanies another doing magic. Then just as quickly as the glowing orb appears, it winks out.

He turns to Jiron and says, "I guess that ends the question of whether or not they have a mage with them. They do."

Jiron nods his head in understanding. The orbs don't last very long once they encounter the soldiers and quickly dissipate.

Then, from within the palisade, the man who had greeted them before once more makes an appearance. James maintains his shield around himself and Jiron as they await his approach.

The man stops several feet from the edge of the shimmering field and says, "The commander has agreed to your proposal for a meeting."

"Thought he might," James tells the man.

"Are we to be granted safe passage?" asks Jiron.

"Of course," he replies. "Feel free to lower your shield at any time should you so desire."

Jiron snorts at the idea and James says, "If it's all the same, I would just as soon not."

Shrugging the man says, "Suit yourself. If you'll follow me?"

As they move to follow the man, Jiron lets go the pole bearing the white flag letting it fall to the ground. No point in carrying that any longer, both he and James know they'll not be let go so easily. The man pauses but a moment when the pole hits the ground, then casts a quick glance at the flag lying in the dirt before he resumes his progress toward the palisade.

James follows along behind, Jiron at his side. When at last they pass through the gate, it shuts behind them.

"That's the signal," Delia says when the starburst lights the sky. She sees Ceadric nod and then opens one of the pouches hanging at her belt. Taking out a round object, she places it in her sling and moves to the edge of the river.

The moonlight overhead gives her barely enough light to see the far bank as she takes position. Winding the sling over her head for a second, she let's the object go and it's soon lost in the darkness. Holding her breath, as does everyone else there for if it goes into the water their plans are ruined, she silently prays there isn't a splash.

A second and then two passes without the telltale splash indicating the object went into the water. "Good job," Shorty says from his position further back.

Everyone visibly relaxes, the success of what they do here at the river is paramount if they are to accomplish their mission. She reaches in and takes out another crystal which had been in with the object she just sent to the other side.

'You only have a count of one hundred before they lose power,' James told her when he gave her the pouch. 'Fifty for the way across and fifty for the way back.'

With James' words on her mind, she takes the crystal to the river's edge. She sets it down three feet from the water and then returns to the others. Mounting her horse, she says quietly to the others gathered there, "We must cross swiftly if we are to be able to return this way."

"We understand," Ceadric says. The other's nods are barely perceptible in the moonlight.

"Very well," she says and then edges her horse toward the water. When she gets there, she recalls the words James told her would activate the spell embedded within the two crystals. The object she had sent to the other side was a clay encased crystal, so encased to have enough weight to make the journey to the other side. Without the clay, the crystal would have been too light to make it.

"Golden Gate," she whispers. The crystal on the ground before them flares briefly, an answering one can be seen on the opposite side of the river. Then, a shimmering 'bridge' forms between the two sides, ten feet wide and reminiscent of the shields she has seen James use to protect himself from arrows.

"Let's hurry," she says as she kicks her horse into motion. She begins silently counting, *one…two…three…* as her horse steps upon the shimmering surface. Worried that her horse's hoof might sink through, she braces herself. But her horse steps upon the bridge and quickly passes across to the other side.

Thirteen…fourteen…fifteen… she sits there as the others hurry across, two at a time. As the last one reaches the far shore, she reaches forty-five and says the word to cancel the spell to save its power for their return crossing, "Earthquake." When James had told her the words of command she commented about how they didn't relate to a bridge at all. He had chuckled and said they referred to a city back home, San Francisco. That a famous bridge there was called the Golden Gate and the place was prone to earthquakes which destroy bridges.

With the utterance of 'Earthquake', the shimmering bridge disappears and the crystals grow dark. Getting down from her horse, she removes another crystal from one of the pouches and places it in roughly the spot where the bridge crystal lies on this side of the river. This crystal will light the way when the word 'Beacon' is uttered in its vicinity. Without it, they would be hard pressed to find the exact spot where the bridge lies in the dark.

Mounting back onto her horse, she turns to Ceadric and says, "Now for the catapults."

He gives her a nod and they quietly make their way to the lights of the enemy camp in the distance. The rear of the encampment is a couple miles away and they ride quickly toward it in silence.

As they near, they're able to see the makeup of the enemy's forces as well as the layout of the camp. Behind the palisade is a large open area, currently crammed with soldiers, most likely congregating there because of James. Delia worries for him but sees that his plan is working.

The massive light explosion in the sky earlier has drawn most of the forces away from the rear of the encampment where the siege engines lie. There is still a presence there, but they should be able to handle them.

Twenty catapults and ten long bridges sit at the rear of the encampment. Each of the bridges has a protective covering built over them that will shield the attackers from any arrows fired from the walls by the defenders. The top of the covering is reinforced with leather that looks as if it may have been treated to withstand fire.

When they've ridden as close as they dare, Delia and the slingers dismount from their horses as well as Errin and Aleya. Ten of Ceadric's men, those who had brought bows, dismount as well. Ceadric and the rest wait there with the horses. Should problems arise, they'll come quickly to the rescue.

Campfires dot the area around the catapults, giving Delia and her group ample light for targeting. From behind her, she hears Moyil quip, "Nice of them to light the area for us."

"You know it," answers Terrance.

"Quiet! Both of you!" she whispers firmly.

If it was broad daylight there would be no way in which they could possibly get away with this. No cover with which to speak of, all of the trees in the area have been cut down either for the palisade wall or the soldier's campfires. They feel rather exposed there in the moonlight, and if the soldier's attention wasn't riveted on the events transpiring by the main encampment, they most likely would have already been discovered.

They make their way quickly and quietly toward the siege equipment, stepping lightly to remain unheard. As shadows in the night, they close the distance until they are within range of their slings. Delia brings them to a halt and gathers them in a close huddle as she talks to them. Ceadric's archers keep watch around them.

She takes out one of the glass spheres contained within her pack and holds it up before them. "These are filled with oil," she explains. "Hit each of the catapults with three." Then glancing to Aleya and Errin she says, "Once they're covered in oil, light those arrows James gave you and set the oil afire."

They nod their heads in understanding.

"Start with the bridges," she says. "Just as we practiced, space yourselves and begin with the one at the far right and work to the left. Be quick, we won't have much time." When she sees they understand her, she says, "Get in position." Then she moves to Hedry, the man in charge of the archers. "You ready?" she asks.

In the moonlight, she can see him give her a grin as he says, "Whenever you are."

Turning back to her slingers, she sees they've already moved into position with a gap of five feet between them. Each slinger's sack containing the glass oil bombs as James calls them sits before them on the ground. Coming up behind Terrance, she lays her hand on his shoulder and says, "Take your time and aim for the center. They're big, so if you're off a little, you should still be able to hit it."

Terrance glances over his shoulder and says, "I hope so."

Behind them, three of Hedry's men place their shields together upright on the ground to form a small wall. Behind that wall, one of Hedry's men gets a fire going. Next to it, Aleya and Errin remove the specially prepared arrows and place them on the ground next to them. After a moment, a small glow can be seen coming from behind the shields, the majority of the light is being blocked.

Seeing that all is in readiness, she whispers, "Ready!" Taking an oil bomb out of the sack before her, she sets it into the cup of her sling. "Fire at will," she says and then begins to twirl her sling over her head. Beside her up and down the line, the others take an oil bomb and set it in their sling.

Hedry's men take position behind the slingers, alert for any enemy soldier that may be in the area. When Hedry was told what they planned to do, he thought it was madness. Surely the catapults and bridges would have guards and scouts in the area in case Madoc's forces tried just this sort of maneuver. Illan had told him the likelihood of there being enemy sentries behind their lines would be remote. The part of the stream they crossed is impassable except by boat so the chances were good they would be able to sneak right up to them before any knew they were there. And so far, he'd been right.

Delia lets the oil bomb fly and watches as it flies into the opening of one of the bridges, striking the interior. As the bomb shatters, oil is splayed all over the sides and the floor. Before the first bomb shatters, the second is already in her sling.

Next to her, Terrance has loosed his first bomb and out of the corner of her eye, she sees it strike the bridge next to the one she's working on. A satisfied, "Yes!" is heard and she grins.

The first couple of bombs strike the bridges before the enemy even realizes something is amiss. Hedry watches as one soldier who stands near a bridge under attack turns as the second bomb strikes. The man calls out to another soldier nearby as he moves closer just as the third bomb strikes.

When the bomb shatters right before him, he staggers backward in shock, oil splattering his armor. Just then, an arrow from one of Hedry's archers flies from the dark and takes him through the chest. The soldier stumbles backward and collapses. Several enemy soldiers see him fall and the arrow sticking out of his chest.

A cry erupts and at that, arrows start flying out of the dark as Hedry's archers begin taking out the enemy soldiers quickly. Their cry raises the alarm and soon the entire rear flank turns from where they've been watching the area near the palisade and rushes to the defense of their siege equipment.

"Now Errin!" Delia cries.

Behind her, Errin and Aleya each take up one of the specially treated arrows and dip the tip in the fire behind the shields. Each arrow has an oil soaked rag tied just behind the arrowhead which ignites quickly. Taking but a moment to aim, they fire at the oil coated bridges.

Two arcs of fire soar through the air, each striking adjacent bridges. When the flaming arrows sink into the oil soaked wood, the oil bursts into flames. Using one arrow per bridge, they soon have all the bridges aflame and begin on the catapults.

Delia has moved onto her first catapult by the time the first bridge erupts in flame. The slingers continue peppering the remainder of the catapults as bridge after bridge begins to burn.

The enemy soldiers at first didn't see from which direction the attack had originated. But when the flaming arrows began to appear, one soldier gives out with a cry and they surge forward.

Arrows fly from Hedry's archers as the soldiers race past the fires to close with them. Some stop and attempt to put out the fires, those that do are the first to be targeted by the archers. The bridges must burn.

Ceadric draws his sword and says to the men mounted behind him, "For Madoc and Black Hawk!"

With battle cries filling the night, the horsemen charge forward and close with the enemy foot soldiers before they have a chance to reach Delia and her group. Riding them down, the battle hardened men lay about them with their swords, felling men left and right.

More soldiers stream into the area, racing to put out the fires consuming the siege equipment, but arrows continuously knock them backward.

Before the last few catapults have been struck by the bombs, a not so distant horn sounds from out of the darkness to the right and another answers from the left. *It's a trap!*

Chapter   Eight

On the far side of the palisade, James and Jiron are led across an open area toward a large tent bearing the Empire's flag. Now on the other side, they can see just what awaits them in the coming battle, should battle there be. A sea of tents fan out for over a mile. Men are virtually everywhere but most are congregating in the area just behind the palisade, armed and ready for battle. The camp is immense.

The rear of the palisade has a walkway near the top to afford crossbowmen a place to stand while they rain bolts down upon anyone foolish enough to attack. Numerous wagons, horses and the usual accompaniment for an army in the field are present as well.

Around them, the soldiers stand in hushed silence as he's led through their ranks. Jiron's right hand stays on the hilt of his knife where it still rests in its scabbard. Walking beside James, he tries to take in as much information about the layout and makeup of this army as he can. Such information could be useful when they return to Lythylla.

As they near what has to be the command tent, two guards stationed at either side of the entrance come to attention as the man leading them passes through. The tingling sensation of magic grows as James makes to enter. Not so much that another is increasing what they are already doing, rather that he's coming into closer proximity to it.

"There's magic inside, stay close," he says in a whisper to Jiron before entering.

A table has been erected within the tent, large enough to accommodate a dozen men. More guards are stationed within the room as well as two crossbowmen. What he sees seated at the table stops him in his tracks. At the head of the table sits a warrior priest of Dmon-Li. To his right is an officer and to his left a man in robes, obviously a mage. He can hear Jiron's slight intake of surprise when he, too, comes to realize what they are facing.

Stiffening his backbone, James takes another three steps into the tent before coming to a stop.

The warrior priest looks him up and down, sizing him up. Completely encased in armor except for his helm which sits on a stand behind him, the man makes an imposing sight. Shoulder length black hair with dark, piercing eyes that seem to bore to James' very soul gives him a foreboding feel.

"We've met before," the warrior priest replies.

Surprised, James says, "I don't think I've had the pleasure." This man doesn't look like Abula-Mazki, but who knows when you're dealing with the gods.

"Almost had you outside of Kern, but was balked by the commander of Cardri's forces," the warrior priest replies. "Almost came to war, but we decided upon discretion at that time." After Saragon when he and Jiron were coming through Mountainside, they were set upon by a warrior priest that hounded them all the way into Cardri. This must be him.

The warrior priest's intense gaze continues to bore into James as he says, "You wished this meeting. Why?"

His confidence is somewhat dampened by the knowledge of facing off against a warrior priest and he hesitates. Suddenly what he came here to say sounds weak and stupid. "I came here to tell you the time of the Empire's occupation of Madoc is at an end. Your forces must return back behind the original border."

The officer beside the warrior priest barks out in cruel laughter. "Madoc is all but ours now," he says. "We are not about to simply hand it back."

James glances to each of the three behind the table as he considers how to get the heck out of there. He hadn't planned on a warrior priest, a mage maybe, but not one of those. "You have until the sun rises to make up your minds," he says, stalling for time. He knows what they'll say, he just needs this to last until Delia and the others make it across the river.

Coming to his feet, the warrior priest says, "You needn't wait until the morning for our reply." A sudden spike in the tingling sensation and a blast of energy strikes the shield as the warrior priest gives his reply.

The force of the blast bowls them over and they're flung from the tent. Still encased within the protective shield, James and Jiron get to their feet as the warrior priest and the mage emerge from the tent.

"Brace yourself," James says as the tingling spikes yet again.

A ball of flame flies toward them and strikes the shield. Rather than being deflected, it settles upon the shield and begins eating it away. The temperature inside is increasing rapidly, James and Jiron begin perspiring. Nothing but flame can be seen all around them. Whatever is transpiring on the other side of the shield remains unknown.

James can tell the integrity of the shield won't last much longer under the flame's attack. He says, "I'm going to give you a crystal. Once you have it, step away from me and say 'Shield'. It will form a protective shield similar to mine around you." He opens one of the pouches and hands him a crystal with a deep crimson glow. Before he gives it to him, he adds, "It will only last about ten minutes, less if you are targeted magically."

Jiron takes the crystal and nods. Stepping back, he says, "Shield!" and a shimmering shield springs up around him.

Reaching into another pouch James removes several other crystals, each glowing a deep crimson. Holding two in each hand, he concentrates and then let's the magic from each of the crystals flow through him in one massive surge.

Whoom!

The shield surrounding them explodes outwards in a gigantic explosion. Soldiers, tents, and everything else in the vicinity gets lifted up and thrown backward several yards. Those who were closest to the blast lie unmoving upon the ground.

The warrior priest is knocked backward by the unexpected blow, the mage fares even worse. The fiery mass coating the outer side of the shield is blasted outward. The caustic mass flies in every direction, striking men, tents, wagons, etc, including the mage. When it hits, it begins burning and eating away at the flesh. The mage cries out as his flesh is consumed by the fiery mass and is soon lying on the ground, the remnants of his body smoking.

Fires break out all over this section of the camp wherever the fiery mass comes to land. Even the palisade is burning, some of the hellish fire having been thrown that far.

James tosses the now shattered, empty crystals to the ground as another shield springs up around him. Going on the offensive, he lets loose the power…

Crumph! Crumph! Crumph!

...and the ground between him and the warrior priest erupts, throwing dirt and dust into the air.

Once the warrior priest's vision is obscured, James pulls out two crystals and says, "Activate. Countdown twenty." Turning to Jiron he says, "Let's get the hell out of here!"

He tosses them to the ground behind them as they turn to race back toward the palisade. Soldiers are already moving to extinguish the fires burning there before they have a chance to catch. They take no more than two steps when he again feels the tingling sensation spike. "Dodge!" he yells.

Bolting to the right, James feels the sizzle as another fireball shoots past right where they had been a moment earlier. "Keep going," he says to Jiron. "Whatever you do, don't look back!"

Just as the tingling sensation spikes again, the countdown reaches zero.

Schtk! Boom!

A blinding white light blossoms behind them and the force of the blast knocks them forward to the ground. Heat and sound accompanies the wall of force and it feels as if their being broiled alive but then it passes by.

"Damn!" Jiron says as he gets back to his feet. "What did you do?"

"Explain later," replies James. He glances over to the palisade and sees there are still about a thousand men between here and there. Behind him, all traces of magic have disappeared. Hopefully he got the warrior priest with that but he finds that rather unlikely. If Abula-Mazki can survive a mountain falling down on him, this one will probably survive as well.

The pouches at his waist are nearly empty. He actually hasn't used much of his own power as yet. Like he told Jiron back when they first met, if he has time to prepare, he doesn't get tired. And he's had all winter to prepare.

They make a break for the gate in the palisade, bolts rain down upon them but each is protected in their own protective shield. Jiron only has another eight minutes or so and then he'll be at their mercy. Before they reach the leading edge of soldiers, James removes one of the two remaining crystals and throws it ahead of him toward the approaching troops.

"Down!" he yells to Jiron.

Jiron sees him fall to the ground and drops as well.

The crystal flies through the air and hits the ground just in front of the troops. Suddenly, a dozen soldiers drop to the ground as the crystal leeches a hundredfold. A fraction of a second later, six red beams like lasers shoot out from the crystal, at an upward angle reminiscent of search lights. They slice through whatever it touches and then the beams rotate forty-five degrees. A cry erupts all over the field of battle as men are cut in two, literally sliced apart by the beams. Then after the beams come to rest, they blink out.

Boom!

The crystal explodes in a deafening roar, leaving a four foot crater where it had lain.

"Come on!" cries James as he gets to his feet. The number of soldiers between them and the gate has been reduced by almost two thirds, the rest are fleeing for their lives after witnessing the devastating attack.

"James, the gate is closed," hollers Jiron.

Looking toward the palisade, he sees the gate standing closed. "See if you can open it," he says as the tingling sensation again comes to him. Glancing back, he sees the warrior priest coming fast, whatever damage the massive explosion earlier had done to him is no longer apparent.

Turning to face the warrior priest, he lets loose the magic…

Crumph! Crumph! Crumph!

…but it doesn't even faze the man. As the ground erupts around him he continues moving quickly toward him, seemingly unaffected by the blasts. When he spies James there before him and the sea of dead behind, a hellish grin comes to him. Raising his hands over his head, he speaks words which are painful to hear.

Each word seems to go through him like a knife. Standing there before the warrior priest, James instinctively covers his ears as the words continue to set his mind and nerves afire.

Then from around him, among the dead a black mist begins to arise, the sight of which brings a horror which nigh on paralyses him. As the warrior priest continues speaking the words, the mist coalesces in many different areas among the dead.

Through strength of will alone, he manages to get his feet once more moving toward the palisade. Ahead of him he sees that Jiron is still some distance from it as he, too is overcome by what is transpiring around him.

Step by step, he progresses toward the gate in the palisade. Not very far from him is one of the points where the black mist is coalescing. It starts to take on a distinct shape of a bipedal humanoid roughly three foot in height. When the warrior priest utters the last word, the form solidifies and a pair of red eyes stare out from the black, demonic head.

To James' horror, the head turns in his direction and the mouth twists into a malignant grin. The lips pull back to reveal a row of jagged pointed teeth. A quick glance reveals numerous of these creatures are upon the battlefield, each point where the black mist coalesced now contains one. Then suddenly they're in motion.

James lashes out with the power at the one closest to him and has the satisfaction of seeing it lifted off its feet and thrown backward a dozen yards. The lethargy he experienced while the warrior priest was casting his spell ends and he's able to once again race toward the gate where Jiron is attempting to lift the bar keeping it closed.

A cry that sends a shiver down his spine pierces the night from behind and he glances over his shoulder to see another of the hell spawn running awkwardly to catch him. Again he lashes out with the power and the creature is thrown backward.

Turning his attention to the gate in the palisade, he sees Jiron with his back to it, knives flying as he battles two of the creatures. The shimmering of the shield surrounding him has disappeared, the power within the crystal having been depleted. Behind Jiron, he sees the bar keeping the gate secured has been removed.

More of those creatures race toward him and Jiron. Each time one gets close to him, he blasts it back with magic. Jiron is now facing three and is at least holding his own, the creatures shy away from the touch of the cold iron of his blades.

Cries from the creatures sound throughout the battlefield. James casts a glance around him and sees dozens of the creatures closing rapidly. He's not going to make the gate before he'll be swarmed by them. Not too far ahead of him, Jiron has his back to the gate and is holding off five now, his knives moving so fast they're but a blur.

The last hundred feet between them is quickly filling with more of the creatures. He blasts out with his magic and ten are flung away only to have the space immediately filled by others. Unable to hold them at bay any longer, he throws up a protective barrier just as one creature leaps over the heads of his fellows and smashes into it. The contact of the creature causes an immediate increase in the amount of power required to keep the barrier in effect, just as the touch of those creatures back in the pass on the way to Ironhold had.

Must be similar in nature, though there's nothing of fire about these creatures. Within the barrier, James concentrates to maintain the barrier against the onslaught. His forward motion stopped as more and more of the creatures bar his way. They're packed in so tightly around him that some are beginning to stand on the shoulders of their fellows, creating a wall of creatures on the outer side of the barrier.

The magic of the warrior priest has been absent since the appearance of these creatures which has James worried. Of course it could be that the summoning of these creatures took all he had. He fervently hopes so.

Jiron can no longer be seen through the press of creatures, they have worked themselves three high around his barrier and their combined effect is draining the magic from him in growing quantities. He's not sure just how much longer he'll be able to hold it.

Miko is among those upon the battlements keeping an eye on the enemy camp. James has been inside now for some time. He had laughed along with the others when the enemy soldiers were scattered by those small spheres that flashed and zapped. Though now he's begun to worry. It's been many minutes since they were escorted in through the palisade to meet with the commander.

He glances down to the courtyard below where Illan and the rest of his men sit on their horses awaiting the signal to come to James' aid should the need arise. When Illan looks up at him, he shrugs. Turning to look back at the enemy camp, he prays they're alright.

Then from the heart of the enemy camp, a flash of red and then a moment later a massive explosion rips through the night. Fire seems to be thrown in every direction.

"What happened?" Illan hollers up at him.

Miko turns his head to face him and says, "A large explosion in the camp. Looks like James is giving them what for."

Schtk! Boom!

A massive white light accompanies an intense explosion from the same area as the earlier one. The concussion of the blast is such that those on the battlements can feel it roll past them. Miko strains to see what's going on but the whole area is one mass of moving bodies and can't make out where James and Jiron are.

When beams of red light shoot out into the night, he turns and descends the steps three at a time to the courtyard below. When he hits the bottom, he races to Illan. "We need to go, now!" he hollers as he gets into the saddle.

"The catapults are on fire!" they hear the cry from someone on the wall.

"Good," Miko hears Illan grunt beside him.

From atop the wall, Henri's voice hollers, "Open the gate!"

From behind them, they hear one of Illan's men say, "Black Hawk flies again!"

When the gates open, the cry goes up, "For Madoc and Black Hawk!"

Illan kicks his horse and they race forward across the bridge toward the palisade. The area between the bridge and the palisade is devoid of enemies. Riding hard, they close the distance quickly.

Intent on the gate before him, Miko is suddenly struck with a feeling of unease. Exactly what the cause is he's not sure. The closer to the gate he rides the stronger the feeling becomes. By the time their party nears the closed gate, the feeling of unease has grown to one of immediate urgency.

"We've got to get to the other side!" he hollers to Illan.

"Stephen, Ison, open the gates," Illan hollers. As two riders dismount and rush to the gate, he glances at the empty wall above them. *Where are the crossbowmen?*

One of the men behind him says, "I hope the gates aren't locked."

"Could be a problem," another replies.

Miko sits in his saddle with growing trepidation as the two men reach the gate. Grabbing hold of the crack between them, they pull hard and to everyone's amazement, begin to swing open.

Before the gates swing open more than a foot, Miko kicks his horse into a gallop and races forward.

"Miko!" cries out Illan. "Let's go," he tells his men and they race after him.

When Miko reaches the gate, he almost rides over Jiron. He takes one look at the creatures battling him and he realizes this is the source of the ill feeling. A blinding white light erupts and he's surprised to find the Star of Morcyth in his hand. He hadn't even been aware he took it out.

"Miko!" Jiron cries when he rides past him into the swarming mass of creatures.

Unknown words begin issuing forth from Miko as the light from the Star burns the creatures around him and begins forcing them back.

"James is out there somewhere," Jiron hollers to him.

He looks around and sees what looks like a pile of the creatures. The shimmering light from James' shield can be seen in brief glimpses under the undulating mass of creatures covering it.

Behind him, the unmistakable sound of swords striking flesh can be heard as Black Hawk's Raiders wade into the creatures. Pushing his way forward through the creatures, he draws closer to James. Where the light from the Star touches the creatures, smoke begins to issue.

The words continue to come forth, words of unknown origin and meaning. Now close enough to the pile atop James' barrier that the light from the Star strikes them, they begin to fall away. He looks in relief as he sees James with one knee on the ground, an intense look of concentration on his face as he works to maintain the barrier.

Around him, the battle is drawing to a close. The creatures continue the attack even though the Star burns them. They don't come close to Miko and the Star, instead they rush toward Illan and the others where they are cut down by the cold iron blades of expert swordsmen.

"James!" Miko hollers as he comes to a stop next to the barrier. The creatures surrounding James have been driven off by the Star.

Opening his eyes, he looks up to see a rider on horseback, a blinding sun held aloft in his hand. At first he doesn't realize it's Miko, but then recognition comes. Getting to his feet, he glances around and when he finds the creatures out of the immediate vicinity, cancels his shield.

"Thank goodness you showed up," he says coming to stand beside his horse. "Don't know how much longer I could have withstood them." He staggers slightly as a momentary wave of dizziness hits him.

Reaching down a hand to steady him, Miko says, "Come on, we need to get you back to Lythylla."

"Did you find Jiron?" he asks as he takes the hand and swings up behind him once his head clears.

"Yes," replies Miko. Indicating the fighting going on by the gate, he adds, "He's back there with Illan and the rest." He turns his horse and with the Star held aloft, rides back to where the battle still rages.

The number of creatures has been significantly reduced, Illan and the rest are finishing taking care of the last few. Several of his men have fallen to the creatures, but both he and Jiron have survived with but minor injuries.

They arrive just as the last one falls. Illan glances to James and then the sea of dead bodies. "You never do anything halfway do you?" he asks.

"No," he replies a touch sad. He hates the killing as much as anything, but what else can he do but allow them to kill him?

Off in the distance the glow from where the siege equipment burns is visible. "Looks like Delia and her crew managed to take them out."

With no more of the creatures to worry about, the light from the Star goes out and Miko puts it back into his pouch. He glances to Illan, "Guess we won't have to worry about an attack for awhile."

Just then, horns are heard and they see coming from out of the dark the rest of the Empire's forces, at least eight thousand strong. Another blast from the horns and they begin moving toward them.

"Back to the city!" Illan cries. One of his men has Jiron behind him on the horse and they race toward Lythylla.

Before they move through the gate of the palisade, James glances backward and scans the battlefield for the warrior priest. All he finds is the oncoming soldiers and the dead, there's no sign of him. Then they're through to the other side and racing toward the gates of Lythylla.

When those on the battlements see them ride through the palisade, a cheer erupts and the gates swing open. The pursuing Empire soldiers stop at the palisade when they realize James and the others will reach the safety of the walls before they'll have a chance to catch them.

Cries of 'Madoc!' and 'Black Hawk!' resound as they make their way through the gates. Lord Pytherian as well as the other leaders who were present during their initial meeting are there to greet them.

"Unbelievable!" one of the men says. "I heard rumors of what you can do, but I had no idea."

Illan pulls up to a stop and asks, "Any word from Delia and Ceadric?"

Shaking his head, Lord Pytherian replies, "Not yet. We have riders out in that area and men on the walls looking for them."

James swings down from behind Illan. "I hope she's alright," he says.

Chapter Nine

"Retreat!" Ceadric yells to his men. The press of soldiers is too great for them to break away effectively. Arrows begin flying from Hedry's men, taking out those pressing Ceadric and giving them a chance to disengage.

The two forces that so recently made their appearance are closing fast. Most are foot though the force to their right has a contingent of cavalry as well. Delia scrambles to get her people back to their horses quickly.

"But there are three catapults that are still serviceable," Orry states. The rest of the siege equipment is burning out of control despite the efforts of the soldiers that have made it to them.

"Leave them!" she hollers. When they broke off the attack, each grabbed their pack with what oil bombs they had left. James was most explicit in that they must remove all the evidence they can. Of course the shattered remains may give them some clue as to what happened anyway but why help them any more than they have to.

Ceadric and his men, now fewer by half a score, join them as they swing into the saddle. "Back to the river!" Delia hollers. Each realizes the way they came across is the only avenue left if they are to survive.

As they break into a gallop leaving the burning siege equipment behind them, the enemy forces begin forming an arc. "They're going to drive us to the river and annihilate us against its banks," Yern shouts.

"Not if we can find where we came across," Delia hollers back. Two miles to the river with soldiers bent on their destruction behind them, they push their horses to the limit. They manage to maintain a constant distance between them and the cavalry coming up behind. The foot soldiers begin to fall behind.

After several minutes of riding, the river appears before them. "Beacon!" Delia hollers and a half mile away to the right, a light appears.

"There it is!" Devin exclaims.

Unfortunately, the force to their right has already passed the beacon which now lies behind their lines.

"What should we do?" Uther asks.

"Ride through them and kill them all!" Jorry yells with a touch of bloodlust in his voice.

"Ceadric," she says. When she has his attention she says, "Fall back. Let me ahead." She takes the lead and leads them on while maintaining a fast pace. From her remaining pouch she pulls one of the two crystals contained within. She moves to set it into her sling when her horse suddenly leaps to avoid an obstacle on the ground and the crystal falls from her hand.

"No!" she cries as the crystal hits the ground. She removes the remaining crystal from her pouch then gets it set into the sling just as...

Ka-Boom!

...the crystal which dropped on the ground explodes in a great eruption, throwing rocks and dirt into the air. Fortunately all their riders had passed the area before the explosion. The concussion wave from the explosion causes a few of the horses to stumble but they manage to correct themselves quickly and continue on.

With the last crystal in her sling, she winds it up and lets it loose toward the approaching cavalry between them and the beacon. "Stop!" she cries to the others and they quickly bring their horses to a halt. Hitting the ground, it lands a good twenty feet in front of the leading edge of attackers.

The approaching cavalry comes toward them rapidly and passes over the crystal lying on the ground.

Ka-Boom!

Horses and men go flying in another massive explosion. "Now!" she cries. "Ride hard!" Kicking her horse in the flanks, she gets it back to a gallop and races through the dead and dying.

Ceadric comes along beside her as they clear the area devastated by the explosion. Before them, no more than a hundred yards away, the glowing crystal beckons.

In the moonlight from above, they see the foot soldiers that had fallen behind the cavalry moving toward them at a run. A third is moving toward the glowing crystal by the bank of the river.

"We'll hold them off," Ceadric tells her. "You get your people across."

"But once we start, there's only a limited time before the bridge will disappear," she replies.

"Just do it!" he yells. Then to his men he hollers, "For Black Hawk!"

A cry erupts from his men as they break off from Delia and her band to engage the enemy. "They'll be killed!" Shorty exclaims.

"Let's move," she tells him. She veers to move directly to the light in the distance. It isn't long before the sound of Ceadric and his men engage the foot soldiers heading for the beacon.

Upon reaching the light, she says, "Golden Gate." The shimmering bridge once more springs into being. "Now hurry across," she tells the others. "It won't last very long."

As the others move to cross, she takes Devin by the arm and asks, "Can you swim?"

Halting his horse, he turns to her and replies, "Yes, why?"

"I need you to do something," she says.

Leading his men against the enemy, Ceadric realizes this will probably be his last fight. Sword falling, he takes out another soldier and quickly brings it back around to block the hack from another.

He needs to slow the advance of these soldiers to allow Delia a chance to activate the crystal and get across. With any luck, he and his men will be able to disengage and make it across as well.

They stall the enemy for several minutes then he glances back to the river. Seeing Delia and her group beginning to cross he hollers, "To the river!" As one, his men break off and race for the river. Several were unable to disengage successfully and were cut down before they could get away. Using the light ahead as a guide they race for their lives, which may very well be the price if they fail to make it in time.

As the light draws closer, he sees young Devin standing there with the light held aloft in his hand. He's waving them to hurry as he shouts, "Twelve...eleven...ten..."

Ceadric hears him coming ever closer to one and pushes his men even faster. The first rider hits the bridge as Devin says, 'Six'. On the far side of the bridge Delia and her band are lined along the banks with slings in hand, her two archers are there as well with arrows knocked and ready. At 'Four' Ceadric's horse races onto the bridge. As Devin reaches 'Two', the last of his men hit the bridge and begin to cross.

The last five are still over the water as Devin says, 'One'. A second later the bridge disappears. Men cry out and horses scream as they fall into the river below.

Once the bridge disappears, Devin moves to collect the bridge crystal lying on his side then places them in a pocket. A noise behind him causes him to turn just as enemy soldiers appear out of the dark before him. Turning back to the river, he races for the water and before he jumps from the shore into its raging depths, he hears Delia holler, "Now!"

Slings twirl and bowstrings twang as the enemy begins falling behind him. As closely as the soldiers are packed together, if a slug thrown by a sling misses one it's sure to hit another, either to the side or behind. Hedry's archers move into position with her slingers once they've dismounted and together rain a devastating volley of deadly projectiles and missiles across the river.

"Get the men out of the river!" cries Ceadric to the rest of his men. Moving to the edge, they work to get the men and horses struggling against the current to their side safely. Of the five men in the river, only four manage to reach the shore, none of the horses make it.

"Where's Devin?" Delia asks as she sets another slug to her sling.

"Over here!" she hears him cry from downstream. The river has carried him further away.

One of Ceadric's men cries out, "I'll get him," and then races downstream to retrieve him.

Across the river, the soldiers are falling back now that their prey is beyond their reach. Soon, the hail of arrows and slugs ceases as the enemy moves out of range.

"What's the damage?" Ceadric's voice rings out.

"Seventeen dead," Hedry replies.

"Your group Delia?" he asks.

"If Devin makes it back then we're all accounted for," she replies.

"Everyone back away from the river," he says. "Let's not give them anything more to look at."

As everyone begins moving away, Delia goes to the bank and retrieves the second bridge crystal. When she bends over to collect it, she's surprised to see it's broken in two. Picking up both halves, she puts them into her pouch. Mounting up, she joins the others.

A few minutes later, the man who rode to Devin's aid returns with him and the fifth of the men caught upon the bridge when it fell. Both have been battered by the current, but otherwise are unhurt.

"Let's return," Ceadric says.

"We did it!" exclaims Orry.

They turn to watch the siege equipment across the water burn as they make their way toward the lights of Lythylla in the distance. Soldiers of the Empire are silhouetted by the flames as they work to put out the fires. The remaining three are being pulled away quickly to avoid any possibility of the fires moving to them.

Their group feels much lighter with the seventeen men they left on the other side. They talk in quiet hushed tones until Scar's voice rises from where he and the others ride further back. "...no, seriously. It was on a trip me and Potbelly took across the Sea to one of the northern towns. Beset by pirates, we..."

They continue on toward Lythylla as Scar relates the events of an ill fated voyage that cost the lives of everyone on board but himself and Potbelly. Seems the way they managed to escape death was to hide in the bilge compartment below the hold until the pirates left. Of course the fact the pirates torched the ship to hide all evidence, and that they escaped by prying a board loose from the side with two spoons didn't do much for the credibility of the story. Believable or not, it occupies their time until the walls of Lythylla come into view ahead of them.

The gates open as they approach and the men manning the battlements give out with a cheer as they pass through. Illan, James, as well as Lord Pytherian and his adjutants are there to greet them.

Ceadric pulls slightly ahead as the two groups meet and says, "All but three of the siege equipment are aflame. We lost seventeen."

Illan nods his head. "Good work."

"Will want a thorough debriefing about the enemy's layout and forces," Lord Pytherian says.

"From what I could tell, they still have a sizeable army out there," Ceadric tells him. "We were almost caught between two attacking forces. Would have been slaughtered there at the bank of the river if that bridge hadn't appeared."

"From the report James has already given us," Lord Pytherian says, "there were more men than previous reports indicated. But at least their initial assault should be stalled while they regroup."

"Best not to give them that time milord," James interjects.

"What do you mean?" he asks.

"I mean, tomorrow morning, we go on the offensive once again," he explains.

"Do you think that's wise?" he questions. "You and your people have barely come from a battle and you plan to throw them into another?"

"Yes milord," he says. "I plan to do just that."

"Best we talk about this in a more private location," Lord Pytherian says.

"I agree," responds James. He moves to Delia and asks, "Everyone make it?"

"All of our people survived," she assures him. Then she lowers her voice as she adds, "The crystals worked perfectly, we brought them all back."

"Excellent," he says.

"Best we return to camp and get what rest we can before the morrow," Illan suggests.

"I couldn't agree more." He follows Illan and Lord Pytherian as they turn back and enter through the gates with the rest right behind.

They work their way through town, most of the population is turned out to look upon the ones who dealt the Empire such a blow. Cheers and other salutations greet them as they make their way through the streets.

During their ride through the streets, Delia fills him in on what happened and how her people acquitted themselves in battle. He then gives her a brief rundown of what happened out by the palisade and what he observed of the enemies forces.

"Looks like we'll have our hands full tomorrow," she says.

"I'm going to see if we can't have support from Madoc's forces," he tells her.

"It would be in their best interest," she says.

"We'll see," he says.

At the plaza where their camp is set up, Lord Pytherian and his party take their leave. A meeting with Illan and James is scheduled to begin in an hour to work out the plans for the following morning. The others set about getting a bite to eat and then turning in, everyone that is but the leaders. They gather for an impromptu meeting before James and Illan leave for their meeting at the castle.

They meet in James' tent. Ceadric, Delia, and Jiron make sure their people are settled in before they join James, Illan, and Miko in his tent. Before the last three join them, Illan turns to Miko and asks, "Just what happened out there?"

"What do you mean?" he replies.

"I mean, the Star shone bright and you were speaking in a language I didn't understand," he clarifies.

Shrugging, Miko says, "I don't know. When the gate opened and I saw Jiron by the gate battling those creatures, the Star was in my hand and the words were coming out." He glances to the others there before adding, "I didn't know what I was saying."

"Whatever it was," Illan says, "it worked."

James gazes at Miko for a moment, can see the concern in his eyes. "I don't think it's anything to worry about," he says, allaying his fears. "It must have come from Morcyth in some way." He sits for a moment thinking before continuing. "My guess would be that the warrior priest summoned them from somewhere that is in direct opposition to Morcyth and that's why it had the effect upon them that it did."

"Warrior priest?" asks Illan.

James nods his head gravely then turns his attention back to Miko.

"Sort of like your medallion back in that underground complex in the swamp?" Miko asks.

"Precisely," he replies with a nod. "Seems Dmon-Li's priests not only have the ability to control beings from the plane of fire but also to summon demons, for lack of a better term."

"How is it that it works for me?" he asks.

"I don't know. Perhaps because it has no choice if it is to spread its influence upon this world."

Just then the tent flap opens and the other three come inside. As the tent flap closes, James sees Devin there taking his position outside his tent. Once everyone is settled in, he says, "Illan and I will meet with Lord Pytherian shortly. With any luck we'll be able to count on their support in the coming battle."

"If they want to keep Madoc free they better," Ceadric interjects.

"There is a sizable presence here in Lythylla," adds Illan, "not only of Madoc's forces but those of the Alliance." Around the group, a few heads nod in agreement.

"Whatever they decide to do, we still have a battle to fight on the morrow." James glances around the assembled faces and adds, "We have a warrior priest to deal with."

Delia gasps and Jiron nods his head, "Thought so. When I saw those creatures at the gate, I knew something had to be up."

Gesturing to Miko he says, "The Star can deal with those creatures readily enough if they should make another appearance. What I'm concerned with is the sheer numbers we'll be facing. If we can't get help from Madoc, the items I brought along for this campaign may be completely consumed before we're through here."

"You can make more can't you?" Illan asks.

"Sure, if I have a supply of crystals and time," he explains. "But keep in mind it took me all winter to ready what we have. Anything I do on the run will not be as effective."

"So what are we to do?" Jiron asks. "After this, we are going to have many more battles before we're through."

"I know," he says. "I'm not figuring on facing any army head on after this." He looks around at the reaction his words may cause. Illan and Jiron know pretty much what he plans to do so they fail to show any reaction. Ceadric though, he looks confused.

"How can we possibly drive them out if we don't destroy their armies?" he asks.

"By making it difficult for them to keep their troops in Madoc," he explains. "Where I come from, war has been going on for a long time. There are two main things which have to be in place for a nation to send troops into the field."

"The first thing is internal security. If their kingdom has turmoil, then they'll need their troops to maintain order. Also if the people feel the war is harmful that can add to the general unrest. But with the way the Empire's run, the will of the people will probably have minimal effect."

Ceadric nods his head as he begins to understand where this is leading.

"Secondly, you need to be able to support and supply your army. A hungry army, or one whose basic needs are not being met, will be ineffective in combat. Our band isn't big so we can forage for what we need for the most part. As we head into the Empire, we take from the towns we pass."

"What I plan is simply this," he says and then pauses for effect. "When the battle here is over, we immediately head for the Empire. Destroy any and all forces we come across, providing they are no larger than our own. Those we meet as we move into the Empire should be those coming to reinforce the men on the border. With any luck, they'll be smaller bands of a thousand men or less."

Ceadric chuckles at that. When James glances to him he grins and says, "A thousand men being a small band. You sure are confident of yourself."

"With what we have already with us," he replies, "a thousand men shouldn't be too much for us to handle."

"We took out that many earlier this evening," Jiron states.

"Anyway," continues James, "as we progress into the Empire we destroy bridges, war factories, caravans, and anything that may be used to take supplies to the men in Madoc. At some point, they're going to begin pulling forces from elsewhere to come after us. They'll not let us wander at will within their borders."

"Just like the old days," Ceadric says to Illan.

"Only this time, we're not killing civilians," he explains.

"Good," Ceadric states. "Never cared much for that part."

"But they could bring forces from the south to hunt us down," suggests Delia. "They wouldn't necessarily take the soldiers out of Madoc to do that."

"True," agrees James. "But if they do, that leaves them open to rebellion from their less than complacent subject territories not to mention the time it will take for them to travel that far. From what we've gathered, many are itching for the chance to throw off the shackles of the Empire. I'm counting on the Empire not willing to take that risk."

"In short, we make it extremely difficult for them to keep their forces in Madoc by whatever means available." The others nod and Ceadric is actually wearing a grin.

"I like your plan," he states.

"Our key to success is to stay mobile," James continues. "Keep their armies on the move while we take out their infrastructure."

Delia is staring at him in an odd way. "Yes?" he asks.

"You're doing all this simply to have a temple built in the City of Light?" she asks.

"For the most part, yes," he replies. "Also to free Madoc from a fate it doesn't deserve." He nods at Miko and says, "Not to mention payback for what they've already done to us and others. I'd take down the entire place if I could. Slavery is an abomination and I would like nothing better than to see every slaver put to the sword."

"I'm with you on that one," says Jiron.

James glances to Miko, expecting some reaction to that as he was only one present to be subjected to the hell of being a slave, but he remains quiet.

"What I've said here remains just between us. Agreed?" he asks. When everyone gives their agreement, he says, "We've got a hard day ahead of us. I suggest you get what rest you can before morning." To Illan he says, "We better get the meeting with Lord Pytherian over with so we can get a few hours of sleep."

Standing up, Illan nods his head. To Ceadric he says, "Get the men bedded down. We're up with the dawn."

"Yes sir," he says and then leaves the tent. From outside they can hear his voice shouting orders as he does Illan's bidding.

"We'll be back soon," James says as he gets to his feet. To Delia he says, "Have Devin hit the sack too. I won't need him when I return."

"Okay," she tells him.

He glances over to Jiron and says, "Get everyone to sleep. I want everyone up by dawn."

"You got it," he says.

Illan moves to leave his tent and James follows. Outside they find an exhausted Devin and James nods to him as he and Illan head for the castle.

Despite the lateness of the hour, the streets are still full of people. All are simply agog with the latest rumors about the events that transpired earlier in the evening. Few recognize them as they move through the dark streets and they arrive at the castle in short order.

At the gate, a page is waiting for them and takes them to the same conference room they met in earlier. Surprisingly, only Lord Pytherian is there, the other leaders are absent.

"Where's everyone else?" James asks as the page closes the door behind him. Moving to the table, he sits down in a chair across from Lord Pytherian, Illan takes a seat the chair next to his.

"Thought it would be best to meet here in private," he explains.

"There's no trouble is there?" Illan asks.

"I don't know," he replies. "There's been rumors going around of an agent for the Empire within the walls, but so far nothing definite has been uncovered."

"Could just be rumors," says Illan. "Such always happens during a siege."

"Possibly," Lord Pytherian replies, though his expression tells he doesn't believe that.

James then begins to relate the layout of the enemy forces as had been seen by himself and Delia's group. He also tells him of the warrior priest he encountered during his parley. When he tells of the subsequent battle and the killing of the mage, Lord Pytherian strikes the table and with a grin exclaims, "Good!"

"But the warrior priest is still out there," he explains. "Not sure how that will affect tomorrow's battle."

"What do you plan to do?" he asks.

James then gives a brief rundown on what he plans. When he's done, he asks, "Will you and your men be willing to back us up?"

"Plans are already being set in motion to do just that," he answers.

"Excellent," says Illan.

"Once the battle is over," James tells him, "we're going to push into Madoc."

"With any luck we'll draw elements of the various armies currently occupying Madoc into following," Illan says. "If they do, you must be prepared to take advantage of that and press those that remain hard." James and Illan then begin to give him a rundown of their plan once they begin moving into the Empire.

Throughout their narration Lord Pytherian sits and listens occasionally nodding his head at one point or another. When they're finished laying it down, he says, "I may be able to help you with what you plan."

"How?" James asks.

"By the time you're ready to leave, I'll give you a map detailing where various weapon storehouses and other vital complexes to their war effort are located."

"That would prove most beneficial milord," Illan says.

"Any mines located in their northern territory would be helpful too," adds James. When Lord Pytherian glances at him questioningly, he explains. "May be able to collapse them and render them useless for years."

"I'll see what we can do," he says.

"Whatever happened with Councilman Rillian?" asks James.

"He stepped down from the council," Lord Pytherian replies. "Seems those he represents felt that with all the controversy surrounding him it would be best for another to lead." He gives them a grin, "He wasn't too happy about the situation let me tell you. The man who replaced him has so far conducted himself properly. We do have agents on him just in case though."

"That would be a reasonable precaution," agrees James.

"You needn't worry about the former Councilman Rillian," he tells them. "He left when most of the population fled Lythylla some time ago, as did the Council. It would be bad enough to lose Lythylla, but to lose the Council would be disastrous. The people need something to rally around in times such as these."

"So the civilians who are left...?" prompts James.

"Are here to take care of the military," he explains. "Or those just too stubborn to leave despite what may happen. Others are family members of the soldiers who chose to stay rather than be separated."

"I see," James says.

For the next hour they work out the finer points of the battle plan for the morning. Once all is in readiness, Illan and James take their leave. With only a few hours before dawn, they're not going to get much sleep.

On the way back, they find the streets much more deserted than they were before, the people having finally returned to their homes. At the plaza which currently houses their people, James and Illan say their goodnights and each head to their tents. There are a couple of Ceadric's men on guard duty stationed about the area and they nod or salute when they take notice of James or Illan.

His tent stands dark and lonely, Devin having long since turned in as he told Delia to have him do. Opening the tent flap, he enters and lets the flap swing closed behind him. Exhausted beyond measure, he doesn't even undress just collapses on his cot. No sooner does his head hit the pillow than he falls asleep.

Chapter   Ten

"Sir?" When no answer is forthcoming, Devin pokes his head in the tent and finds James lying there on his cot sound asleep. "Sir?" he says again, this time a little louder hoping to wake him without startling him. It's said that to startle a mage out of sleep is fraught with perils.

When he still doesn't respond, Devin moves inside and comes over next to his cot. Placing his hand on James' chest, he says softly while giving a small shake, "James, wake up."

James sits up abruptly and Devin jumps backward in shock at the unexpected movement.

Bloodshot eyes opening, he glances around the tent and sees Devin off to one side, staring at him. "What?" he asks in a voice still sluggish from sleep.

"Illan says sunrise is approaching," he tells him.

Groaning, James lies back down on his cot and places an arm across his face. "Go away," he says. It feels like he just closed his eyes after he returned from the meeting with Lord Pytherian.

"Yes sir," Devin says and backs out of the tent.

He lies there in silence for several minutes and is about ready to slip back to sleep when the tent flap opens again. "Go away Devin," he says, arm still over his face.

When Devin doesn't answer he turns his head toward the tent flap and opens an eye just in time to see a bucket's worth of water come flying through the air toward him. Eyes flying open, he freezes in startlement as the cold water hits him.

"Ahhh!" he cries as he sits up, drenched with water.

"Time to wake up sleepyhead," Jiron says with a chuckle.

James glances toward the flap and sees him there with an empty bucket in his hand. "What did you do that for?" he says accusingly.

"You did tell me to make sure everyone was up by dawn," he explains.

"I did not!" he replies.

"Yes, you did. Now get changed," he insists before leaving the tent.

Clothes soaked and beginning to shiver from the cold water, he gets up and changes into a dry set of clothes. Once he's changed, he takes out his shaving kit and removes what stubble has grown since the last time he shaved. Leaving the old wet clothes on the floor of the tent, he makes his way outside.

The plaza is a flurry of activity as everyone hurries to make ready for the upcoming battle. Food is being prepared, swords sharpened and armor is mended as best it can. Devin comes to him with a bowl of food and a mug of water.

"Thanks," he says with a yawn as he takes it.

"You're welcome," he replies. Off to one side he sees Illan in his full Black Hawk regalia talking to Henri. Eating his food while he walks, James makes his way over.

"…as if they're fortifying their position," Henri is saying.

Illan turns at his approach and says, "The enemy is digging in. Scouts report that more troops have arrived during the night."

"Possibly another couple thousand," Henri interjects. "Lord Pytherian thinks they may have already been on the way before your attack last night and not a response to it."

He looks to Illan and asks, "Will this change our plans any?"

Shaking his head, he replies, "I doubt it. Just make things more interesting."

Henri glances to James and says, "Hope you can pull this off."

"Me too," he agrees. "How far away is dawn?"

"An hour or so," he replies.

"Have Delia meet me over by the baggage once everyone's done eating," he says.

"Very well," replies Illan. Then to Henri he says, "Tell Lord Pytherian we'll be ready at the appointed time."

"Yes sir, Black Hawk," Henri replies. Giving Illan a salute, he turns and makes his way from the plaza back toward the castle.

James runs through in his mind the various preparations he's done in anticipation of the upcoming battle. He fervently hopes the items he brought from The Ranch will work the way he anticipates.

After everyone's finished eating, he meets with the slingers by the tent where his 'special' baggage is being stored during their stay. Usually there's a guard standing out front to keep everyone away, it wouldn't do to have someone meddle in an area that could kill everyone. Today Terrance has that duty.

He steps inside and leaves with a large sack, the contents bulging the sides. Reaching in, he pulls out a small pouch and begins handing one to each. "Don't open it now," he tells them. Each pouch is bound closed with a red twine, all the various pouches and sacks containing his magically imbued crystals are color coated in this manner for easy identification.

When each is holding their pouch, he says, "This will be your initial ammunition. Inside each pouch are three balls of hardened clay. Inside the clay is something, that once it leaves the confines of the sack it is currently within, becomes activated. Once it does, you haven't much time before it goes off."

Caleb holds up his pouch and gives it an apprehensive look. The others' expressions range from worry to excitement.

"So remove one at a time, get it launched toward the enemy, then remove the next and so forth." He returns within the tent. When he exits again, he hands a long bundle to Devin. "Hold onto this until we get out there. I'll need you and Moyil to give me a hand setting it up. It's imperative we get this in position before the enemy launches their attack."

"I thought we were to attack them?" Terrance asks.

James glances at him and replies, "When they see us march out of the gates, I doubt if they'll simply allow us all the time in the world to get ready."

"Yeah, Terry," Jace says as he elbows him in the ribs.

"Alright, sorry," Terrance says.

Holding up her pouch to James Delia asks, "Will these be enough to destroy the enemy?"

"Let's hope so," he says. "I have a few other surprises as well, but I'll be in charge of those." He glances around the assembled group. "When you've exhausted the contents of your pouch, start using the slugs. I trust you've given each an extra supply?"

Delia nods her head and says, "After this they'll each be given three score slugs."

"Good." He glances over to where Illan and the men-at-arms are gathering and sees that they have already mounted and are waiting for them. "Time to go. Get your slugs and let's be on our way."

"Yes, sir," Delia says and then takes her slingers over to another area where the slugs are stored and gives each their supply.

As they leave, James turns back to the tent and goes inside. Many sacks are still contained within, both magical and non. He removes a crystal from one of the sacks and places it on the floor just inside the entrance. Stepping back out of the tent, he says, "Shield." A shimmering barrier springs up around the tent, effectively preventing anyone from gaining access to the items contained within. It will last half a day and unless the battle rages longer than that, they should be back in time to post a guard before it fails.

Satisfied, he turns toward where Devin is waiting with his horse. On Devin's belt, he sees the pouch he gave him already secured there. Slung across his back is a pack, bulging at the bottom from the weight of the slugs Delia gave him.

Taking the reins, James mounts and turns to gaze over the assembled force. Illan's Black Hawk Raiders all but fill the courtyard. Jiron and his fighters are close, as are Delia and her slingers. Errin and Aleya have been assigned to Hedry and his archers for the duration of the battle.

Miko rides forward and comes to a stop next to him.

"Stay close," James tells him. Miko nods in reply.

Glancing at his companion since the beginning of this whole adventure, he can't believe the changes he's gone through. First, losing his youth to the Fire, and now his demeanor is changing yet again. The Star he carries appears to be mellowing him, he's become more serious and confident. His playfulness resurfaces every now and then, but those occurrences are growing less frequent.

"Ready?" he asks Miko.

He gives James a grin and says, "Like you always say, 'No, but I never will be for something like this.'"

James returns his grin and then nods to Illan.

"Move out!" Illan hollers and with James next to him, they leave the plaza. Just behind them comes the rider bearing the flag with the Black Hawk insignia. The sight of the flag gives the men a sense of pride and esprit de corps.

Word must have spread through the night despite their best attempts at secrecy that something was planned for this morning. The streets are lined with people, both soldiers and civilians. Cheers follow them as they progress toward the western gate.

They find the courtyard before the gate crammed with men, the walls are packed tightly with archers. Lord Pytherian stands in the only clear area among the sea of men. Next to him are five men, all five are dressed in matching brown jerkins and pants, each holding a wooden staff. Upon the breast of each is a symbol of a plant encircled by a ring of interwoven leaves superimposed over a gnarled staff.

"Priests of Asran," Illan says.

James nods his head and remembers the slain priests they came across in Asran's temple during their foray into Saragon. "Wonder what they are doing here?"

"We'll soon see," he says.

They bring their force to a stop before Lord Pytherian who gestures to the priest next to him. "Black Hawk, James, I'd like you to meet Brother Willim."

The priest steps forward, nods and says, "Glad to make your acquaintance."

"He and his brothers have come to join the fight against the Empire," Lord Pytherian explains.

"Many of our brethren have died at the hands of the Empire," Brother Willim states. "Asran has sent us to aid in whatever way we may." He indicates his brothers and adds, "We are the Hand of Asran."

Illan clears his throat and then says, "I thought the priests of Asran were nonviolent."

"For the most part that is true," replies Brother Willim. "I and the others you see here are part of an order that fights when necessary to preserve Asran's name. Sometimes a weed must be pulled or a diseased branch removed."

James grins at the symbology he uses in describing the Empire. *Druids, that's what they are.* "We are more than happy to have those of Asran beside us this day," he says. "A great battle lies before us, the first of many before we see the lands of Madoc free again."

The first rays of the morning sun crest the horizon and strike the upper battlements. He dismounts and motions for the other leaders to gather round. Taking out his mirror, he says, "Let's see the layout of their camp before we begin."

They gather round, including Brother Willim, as the image shifts and a bird's eye view of the enemy's camp appears. Crossbowmen line the palisade and the area behind is filled with men. Currently it doesn't look as if they're preparing for battle, they must think none is forthcoming after the night's events.

"That's a lot of men," Jiron says from over his shoulder.

"Yes," agrees Brother Willim.

Once they have a good idea of the composition of their troops, he scrolls the view further away from the camp. As he moves it along the road leading south, they see another force of foot soldiers marching to reinforce the men outside their walls.

"How far away do you think they are?" James asks.

Lord Pytherian says, "Couple hours at the most. If they ran maybe an hour."

After another brief scan in the other directions, they find that the men coming from the south are the only other force on the way. Putting away the mirror, James glances around at the others and says, "We better get this over with before they arrive."

Mounting back upon his horse, he glances around at the sea of faces surrounding him. *Hard to believe a year ago all I was worried about was whether or not I studied hard enough to pass the next test. Now I'm leading an army to battle. Dave would have loved this.*

To Brother Willim he says, "You and your brothers stay near me."

Brother Willim nods and falls in behind. Miko comes to ride next to him as does Illan.

"Let's go," he says and they move to the gates. A clattering of metal announces the locking mechanism has been released and the gates begin to swing open. Off to the side are four small catapults which a crew of Madoc soldiers will bring forth and line up behind them on the far side of the river. During the meeting last night, Lord Pytherian suggested using them to batter down their palisade. Said it would save lives if James' forces could gain the other side quickly.

"We need to quickly get the catapults within range of the palisade and be ready should they launch an assault," he says as he rides through the gates. Moving fast, he breaks his horse into a trot and is soon crossing over the bridge to the far side of the river. The Hand of Asran runs with ease and keeps pace with him.

They make it just past the bridge before the enemy takes notice of them. A flurry of activity is seen on top of the palisade as enemy crossbowmen move into position. The palisade gate swings shut.

"I don't think they're planning on coming forth," Illan says as they reach the point where the catapult's volley will strike the palisade.

James glances to the enemy fortification, shut tight and daunting. "Let's get set up first," he tells him as he dismounts. "Then we'll see what we can do to draw them out."

Illan starts organizing their troops while James takes Devin and Moyil, along with the package Devin's carrying, to an area a dozen yards further toward the palisade. Glancing at the crossbowmen on the walls he hopes they stay put for a few minutes until all is in readiness.

He takes the package and unrolls it on the ground. Within are three six foot staves, each are sharpened on one end. Attached by a leather thong to the other end is a crystal, glowing a deep crimson. One of the staves has a red chord tied to it just beneath the crystal.

Handing Devin and Moyil each a staff, he takes the one with the red chord and moves to center himself before his men. Raising it high, he plunges it into the ground. When he has it secured and not likely to fall over, he says to the other two, "Do the same with yours, ten yards in either direction.

They nod their heads as Devin moves to the right and Moyil moves to the left. Once they reach approximately the specified distance, they turn back and glance to James. When they receive his nod, they drive their staves into the ground. After they're securely within the ground, he and the boys return to where the others are waiting. Some look at him questioningly about the staves but he gives no explanation.

By this time the catapults are in position, a wagon of large stones stands ready by each. He has Jiron and the fighters from The Ranch station themselves just behind the line of staves. Delia and her slingers are placed just behind them. Brother Willim with his brethren move to stand near James. The Black Hawk banner bearer moves to the fore and stands just past the line of staves. At that a cheer erupts from the Black Hawk Raiders who are arrayed to either side at the rear.

James glances back to the walls of Lythylla. The gate stands open and he knows Lord Pytherian has riders and fighters ready to come to their aid should he require it.

"Cowards!" he hears Stig exclaim when the enemy remains behind their palisade.

"It's not cowardice to remain behind a fortification," Illan says loudly. "Why should they meet us in battle when they can defend from a point of strength? It's obvious we're going to attack."

All of the strategies James worked on had one element in common, the enemy was to attack. He's not sure if what he plans will be as effective going up against a foe that is entrenched behind a protective wall.

An idea comes to him and he has Devin ride back into Lythylla. When Illan raises an eyebrow in question he just grins and shrugs. Shortly after he enters the gates, Devin reappears again followed by several wagons full of barrels.

The wagons roll forward and come to a stop by the catapults. "Oil and pitch," James finally says to Illan.

"Going to burn the palisade down?" he asks.

"Doubt if it will do that," he says. "But it will annoy them and give us a smoke screen." He moves to the officer in charge of the catapults and asks, "Can you hit the wall with the barrels?"

The officer turns and gauges the distance to the palisade and replies, "Might. Not sure how they'll fly once released."

"If you can at least get close it will be worthwhile," he tells him.

"Close for sure," he says and then has his men begin loading one barrel at a time into each catapult's cup.

"Fire when you're ready," James tells him.

Once all the catapults have a barrel in their cup, the officer yells, "Loose!"

The lever on each is pulled and the arm launches the barrels toward the palisade. Four fall short while one containing tar manages to hit the wall near the gate. A cheer goes up from the men as the arms of the catapults are once again pulled back in place. Another barrel is placed within the cup and let loose.

James watches the second volley fly overhead when all of a sudden he feels the familiar tingling of magic. Atop the palisade, he spies the warrior priest with arms upraised. When the tingling spikes, a fireball materializes as it flies toward the catapults. About to cast a counter spell, he feels another tingle, this one closer.

Brother Willim throws a small, green object into the air and says a few unintelligible words. The object begins to grow as it races toward the oncoming fireball. It grows at an astounding rate and when it encounters the fireball, engulfs it and drags it to the ground.

"Nice," he hears Jiron say from his position in the front of the group.

The catapults continue their barrage of pitch and oil. James moves to Hedry and asks, "Can one of your archers send a flaming arrow out there?"

"Not a problem," he replies. Turning to his men, he hollers, "Erik, Jorn, send them a present if you would."

Having overheard what James had asked Hedry, they remove a piece of cloth. Tearing off four strips, they tie them tightly just behind the arrowheads of four arrows. With a third person bearing a lit torch, they move forward past the line of staves to get within arrow range.

Another fireball flies from the palisade wall, this time aimed at the archers moving forward, and again Brother Willim brings it down.

The archers finally reach the appropriate distance just as another volley of barrels sails over their heads. By this time the area before the palisade is covered in pitch and oil, some of the barrels having managed to strike the walls of the palisade. The torch bearer lights their arrows and they take aim.

Loosing their arrows, two flaming lines of fire streak through the air on a trajectory to land within the flammable material. Just before they close the distance an unnatural gust of wind knocks them awry and they land a dozen yards short. A tingling sensation ran through him just before the wind materialized, indicating the warrior priest was responsible.

"Damn!" curses James. He watches as they aim and loose the last of their modified arrows. As before, when they're halfway to their target, another gust of wind skews their trajectory and they fall short. The two men and the torch bearer turn about and head back quickly to their lines. A cheer rises from the men manning the palisade.

As another volley of barrels flies overhead, the officer in charge of the catapults says to him, "That's the last of them."

"Start with the rocks then," he tells him.

Nodding, the officer begins having his men fill the catapults with large boulders.

James moves back to where Illan, Ceadric and Jiron are conferring. Jiron looks to him at his approach and asks, "Now what? Looks like we're stymied."

"No, we're not," he replies. He moves to intercept the torchbearer as he rejoins the others. Before he has a chance to extinguish the torch, James takes it from him. Turning toward the enemy, his shimmering shield springs into being and he begins moving forward.

Brother Willim and his fellows fall into line behind him to follow. He glances back and sees them there. "Stay here with the others," he tells them.

"No, we go with you," Brother Willim replies.

Shrugging his shoulders, James continues marching toward the oil and pitch spread across the base of the palisade. A quick look to the palisade shows the warrior priest is no longer there. *Where did he go?*

As James reaches the range of the crossbowmen lining the walls, a volley of bolts flies forward only to be deflected by his shield. Brother Willim and the others are using their staves to knock the bolts from the air before they can reach them. Small bursts of tingling sensations tell James it's not skill alone which is allowing the bolts to be deflected by the staves.

He comes to a stop ten feet from the edge of the oil and pitch. With all his might, he throws the torch forward. As the torch leaves his hand, the gates of the palisade open to reveal the warrior priest.

The torch hits the oil and pitch, igniting a raging inferno. The heat from the flames forces him to back away quickly. The Hand of Asran backs away as well. Suddenly from beside him, he hears Brother Willim gasp.

Returning his gaze to the inferno, he sees four creatures emerging from the flames. Half the size of a horse and looking like a large wolf, these creatures turn their red eyes on James and the priests of Asran. One raises its head and howls then all four spring forward.

Dreading another encounter with these creatures, James backs away quickly. Over the winter, he's worked on various methods to deal with them should he ever encounter them again. He reaches into a small pouch on his belt and removes one of two glowing crystals contained within. Throwing it into the path of the charging creatures, he turns and races away.

Brother Willim and his men turn as well and break into a run.

When the lead creature reaches the crystal, James cries out, "Encase!"

A flash of blue light and the creature becomes encased in a block of ice. The red eyes within begin growing dim as the ice steals the heat, and thus its life, away. The other three bound around the encased creature and continue the pursuit. James tosses down the remaining crystal in their path and a moment later, another of the creatures is immobilized in ice.

"What in god's name are those?" Ceadric cries out.

"James called them hell hounds," replies Jiron. When Ceadric draws his sword and makes to go to his aid, Jiron stops him. "Swords won't harm them," he explains. "This is something James has to handle on his own."

Gazing at the events unfolding before him, Ceadric slams his sword back in its scabbard with a curse.

The fire continues to rage, though it is starting to subside now that the fuel sustaining it is being used up. A portion of the palisade is on fire and they can see men working to put it out before it's destroyed. Black, noxious fumes roll over the battlefield, most of it rolling back over the Empire's forces.

James turns and faces the remaining creatures, the shield around him shimmers in the sunlight. Just as before, the creatures strike at the shield causing a jump in the amount of magic required to maintain the barrier. This time, however, he uses the knowledge gained from the last time he faced these creatures and the shimmer of the shield turns slightly blue. When one of the creatures again raises a paw to touch the barrier, it pulls it back with a yelp as the coldness of the shield burns it.

The creatures pace around the shield as they try to figure a way in. As they pace, the ground under them suddenly erupts as vines rise from the earth to ensnare them. Casting a look to Brother Willim, he sees the Hand standing several yards away, one of the brothers lost in concentration.

"The warrior priest!" another brother says as he points toward the now dying fire. The flames seem to roll back as a path is cleared through the fire. Making his way through the now cleared area walks the warrior priest.

"You take care of the creatures," Brother Willim tells James. "We'll deal with him!"

James nods his head just as the sun overhead is blotted out. Glancing to the sky, he sees a large dark mass approaching from the east. Then the dark mass abruptly descends from the heavens rapidly. At first afraid this may be some ploy of the warrior priest, he's soon to learn it's in fact a large flock of birds. Hundreds, thousands of birds consisting of dozens of species both large and small, dive toward the walls above the palisade and begin attacking the crossbowmen and soldiers lining the top. Pecking, scratching, tearing, they stop the hail of bolts that had begun again once the fire subsided enough for them to see.

Distracted by the sight of the birds, he fails to pay close enough attention to the circling creatures. Before he even realizes, they both simultaneously strike the shield. The abrupt spike in magic required to sustain it takes his breath away. The creatures howl in pain as the cold of the shield burns them, but do not relent. They begin pushing their way through, the acrid smoke coming from where the shield burns them fills the inner area of the shield.

Starting to cough, James is finding it more and more difficult to draw a breath without inhaling the nauseating smoke. He increases still further the amount of power to his shield as he drops its temperature. It drops to a certain point and then ceases to fall any further. Having two creatures of fire forcing their way through must inhibit its ability to become colder.

Each of the creatures has a foreleg inside the shield, their snouts now beginning to press through. James knows he can't prevent them from coming through and when they do, he's toast. *Toast*, he almost chuckles at the pun.

He does have one more ploy to attempt, but to do it he'll have to drop his shield for the required amount of magic he'll need. The problem there is that when he drops his shield, he'll have but a split second before the creatures are upon him. Realizing he has no choice, he closes his eyes and prepares.

The sound of an explosion from outside the shield comes to him but he doesn't allow it to break his concentration. When he's ready, he turns to face one of the creatures, the other is behind him. As he drops his shield he leaps to the side just as two more shields, one around each of the creatures spring into being.

When his protective shield dropped, the creatures were propelled forward by the force they were exerting to breach the barrier. Then a fraction of a second before they struck each other in the middle where James used to be, the shields encasing each spring into life.

The battle between the warrior priest and the Hand of Asran wages behind him but he doesn't let that distract him from the creatures before him. Snarling, biting, scratching, the creatures try to escape their confines. Unlike the shield they tried to breach that had surrounded him, these shields move with them sort of like a hamster in an exercise ball. The magic used to sustain them is much less than when they were trying to breach his protective shield.

Concentrating now on just one of the encased creatures, he decreases the temperature of the shield, which is possible now with the heat of but one creature to contend with. Also, he begins shrinking the shield in around the creature until it is barely able to move. The outer shell of the barrier begins to frost from the coldness within, he can feel the creature struggle mightily to escape and increases the strength and integrity of the shield as he continues collapsing it.

Spots begin to dance in front of his eyes from the struggle to maintain one shield while collapsing the other. His throat dries up and his breathing becomes labored. Behind him, he hears a cry as one of the brothers falls in the battle with the warrior priest, the sound of birds still fills the air.

Now down to the size of a basketball, the shrinking shield finally collapses completely and disappears as the creature dies and vanishes. Turning to the remaining creature, he begins shrinking its confining shield same as the other. This time, with but one shield to maintain, the draw of magic isn't nearly as bad. Still, his inner reserves are all but depleted and the effects upon him are becoming more pronounced.

Headaches and dizziness begin to plague him as the remaining shield continues to implode upon itself, stealing away the life from the creature it contains. Before it disappears, James' legs give out and he drops to the ground, barely catching himself before hitting hard. Almost losing concentration, he lies there on the ground, sending forth the last bits of magic from his reserves as the shield shrinks to the size of a softball and then implodes completely when the life of the creature contained within goes out.

Panting hard, he tries to get to his feet but simply hasn't the strength and passes out.

Leaving James to deal with the creatures, Brother Willim and the rest of the Hand of Asran face off with the warrior priest. Above, the birds have answered their call and are even now diving to distract the crossbowmen on the palisade. In the coming fight with the warrior priest, they can't have their concentration divided with bolts flying at them.

As the warrior priest reaches the edge of the flames, he glances from where James is battling the two remaining creatures and then to Brother Willim and the Hand. Seeing them as the most immediate threat, he turns to face them. From the flames to his right, a veritable meteor shower of fire flies toward the brothers.

In response, the Hand throws seeds in the air and with the power of their god, causes them to grow exponentially. When the meteor shower encounters the tendrils of life, their heat is absorbed by them and few make it as far as where the brothers stand. The few that do are easily avoided.

Ash from the burnt tendrils of life float upon the breeze as vines erupt from the ground under the warrior priest's feet. Twining and twisting, they quickly bind him in a tangle of thick vegetation.

Another brother throws a dark resin which expands greatly into a three foot wide viscous mass which strikes the warrior priest and encases him from the chest up in a sticky, gooey substance.

Taking up their staves, they begin moving toward the entrapped warrior priest.

Bam!

An explosion knocks them backward as the vines and gooey substance is blasted away from him. At the same time, a black miasmic cloud forms before the warrior priest and flows toward them.

Brother Willim raises his hand and a breeze develops to blow the dark cloud away but has no effect. The brother next to him throws a batch of seeds at the black cloud. On their way, the seeds blossom into bright yellow flowers and when they encounter the black cloud, absorb the darkness into them. Turning black, the flowers drop to the ground where they wither and die.

Two brothers have closed with the warrior priest and are laying upon him with their staves. His sword is out and easily blocks their attacks. A swarm of gnats appear in summons to one of the brothers and immediately moves to the warrior priest. They cloud his face and begin working their way into his armor.

Deflecting the staves, the warrior priest seems unaffected by the insects swarming him and crawling within his armor. Suddenly the ground again sprouts vines which work to entangle his legs. Between blows to deflect the staves, his sword strikes down and cuts away the vines holding him.

"Too long has your kind walked the earth," Brother Willim says. "Death is your hallmark."

Around the warrior priest, dozens of dark spheres appear. They begin zooming in and around him as they fly toward the brothers. Each one emits a small burst of energy when they draw near his enemies causing a red welt.

Brother Willim calls out in the language of his god and butterflies fill the air. Giant red and green butterflies begin targeting the black spheres. As each comes into contact with one of the spheres, both the sphere and the butterfly disappear until only a couple butterflies are left.

"Long have we been training to take down one such as you," Brother Willim says. "Our brethren have fallen to yours for far too long. No longer!" He raises his hands to the sky and says, "Now, feel the wrath of the Hand of Asran!"

The staffers fighting him begin to glow with a greenish light as the power of their god infuses them. Striking out, the warrior priest gets inside the guard of one of them and runs him through, eliciting a cry as the man falls away only to be replaced by another.

Again, the ground beneath the warrior priest opens up. This time however, instead of the minor vines from before, these are likened to roots of an old oak tree. Thick, strong and massive, these grasp him in a vice-like grip that quickly immobilizes him. Striking down with his sword, the blade does little more than knick the outer bark.

Legs encased and immobile, his defensive capability is now drastically reduced. Blows from the two staffers land upon him more frequently and with increasing force.

Bam!

An outward explosion attempts to remove the vines from him but only succeeds in loosening them for a brief moment before they tighten once more.

A bright light is suddenly among them as Miko comes with the Star of Morcyth ablaze in his hand. Kneeling down beside the fallen priest of Asran, he begins healing his wound.

Whack!

The end of a staff strikes the warrior priest in the forehead and knocks the helm from his head.

Whack!

A strike to his hand causes his sword to fly through the air.

Whack!

Blood begins to flow from his nose as a staff takes him across the face.

"Now, we finish it!" cries Brother Willim.

The staffers back away from the warrior priest as Brother Willim calls upon his god. The roots holding the warrior priest begin writhing as a cry escapes the man's throat. With a rip and a tear, the roots pull the warrior priest apart as arms and legs come away from the body. One long root wraps itself around the neck and with a quick pull, the head comes away.

As the roots drag the dismembered body of the warrior priest into the ground, a malignant presence can be felt as if some evil spirit walks the battlefield, then is gone. When the last of the warrior priest has been dragged beneath the surface, Brother Willim and the others relax. The flock of birds which had come to their aid begins to disperse as well and men are once again upon the walls.

Coming to his fallen brother, he asks Miko, "Will he live?"

Looking up at him, Miko nods. "Yes. He will need rest for a day or two but he should be alright."

"Praise Asran," one of the brothers says.

Over where James passed out, Jiron has already appeared and is removing him to a place of safety.

A crossbow bolt strikes the ground nearby and Miko who says, "We better get out of here. The battle isn't over yet."

Just then, the gates to the palisade open and the army issues forth with a roar.

Chapter   Eleven

Miko mounts his horse and they hand the injured brother up to him. "Get back behind the line of staffs," he tells them. Turning his horse toward Lythylla, he bolts into a gallop holding tightly onto the injured brother before him.

Brother Willim and the others begin running toward where Illan and the rest are preparing to meet the onslaught of the enemy. As the Hand reaches their lines, Illan says, "Good work there." Brother Willim simply nods his head as he and the other brothers follow Miko on into Lythylla to see about their comrade.

Jiron, leading the horse bearing James, moves through the defenders as they part for him. He soon passes the Brothers and crosses over the bridge into the city. Off to one side of the gates, a soldier waves to him and indicates a nearby guardhouse beside which Miko's horse stands tied to a post. Henri is there and takes his reins as he pulls up alongside Miko's horse.

"Is he alive?" Henri asks, referring to the unconscious James.

"Yes," replies Jiron. "He gets like this every time he does too much magic."

Henri helps him remove James from the horse and together they bring him into the guardhouse. The injured brother is already laid out upon blankets on the floor, a pack has been placed under his head for comfort.

Madoc healers are there and have already begun examining the brother. They place James on a blanket next to him. Jiron takes Miko by the arm and says, "We have to get back to the others."

"Yes, you're right," he says. Then to one of the healers he adds, "Take care of them."

"They'll be fine," the grey haired healer says. "You go do what you have to."

As Jiron and Miko leave the guardhouse, Brother Willim and the rest of the Hand arrive and pass them on their way into the guardhouse. "I think they are in good hands," says Jiron.

"Me too," agrees Miko.

They mount their horses and turn them toward the gate. Jiron pauses but a moment when Lord Pytherian catches his eye from where he's keeping watch on the battle from atop the gate. Nodding to Jiron, he then turns back to the battlefield. The courtyard is filled with every available man, as are the streets leading deeper into the city. The whole Alliance army is waiting for the word to go. It was decided to keep the bulk of their forces within the walls in the hopes of fooling the enemy into launching an attack. If they but knew how many awaited them, they would never leave the relative safety of the palisade.

Returning through the gate at a gallop, they head back to their comrades who are about to face the brunt of the Empire army. Jiron sees the soldiers of the Empire are forming ranks this side of the palisade as more and more stream through the gate. *Guess they're not going to wait for us to attack.*

Out in front of their force, the crossbowmen take position as they prepare to rain down a volley of death upon them. Jiron recognizes the army commander that was with the warrior priest when he and James had gone for the initial meeting before all the hostilities erupted. The man must think now would be his best chance at success seeing as how James has collapsed and one of the priests of Asran is down.

"Delia," Illan says. "Are your people ready?"

"As ready as they're ever going to be," she says. To her slingers she says, "Wait for my signal before you remove anything from your pouch!"

"Yes ma'am," Orrin's voice answers from his position down the line.

Illan turns to Ceadric and says, "They'll want to take out the catapults first. Be prepared."

"Aye sir," he says.

A hush falls over the battlefield as the final men make their way through the palisade and take position. They are outnumbered seven to one, Black Hawk's Raiders number somewhere near a thousand while the Empire's force appears to be at least seven or eight thousand strong. The initial numbers they had of the enemy may have been off.

None of the enemy cavalry has yet taken the field. Illan nods to Jiron as he retakes his position at the head of his men. "Cavalry not coming?" Jiron asks.

Illan nods to the two ends of the palisade far in the distance. "My guess would be for them to make an end run around the far side of the wall once the battle begins."

"I'll keep that in mind," he says.

Illan turns to the officer in charge of the catapults. "Give them a volley."

"Yes sir," he replies. Turning to his men he hollers, "Let em go boys!"

As one, the five catapults are loosed and their deadly projectiles are thrown toward the massed men before them. The five boulders fly through the air and come to land in the midst of the soldiers. Most are able to dodge out of the way but two are struck by the rocks after they hit the ground and begin to roll.

"Not very effective against ground troops," comments Ceadric. "Need grapeshot."

Just then, they hear a command shouted by the enemy commander and horns begin to sound.

"True," replies Illan. "Hadn't planned on using them against troops, just the walls."

The enemy crossbowmen move forward and raise their crossbows. At another command, hundreds of bolts are loosed and fly toward them. "Raise the shields," cries Jiron as he and the others raise shields to protect themselves as well as Delia and her slingers from the barrage.

As the bolts reach the apex of their arc and begin descending down toward them, the three crystals atop the staves James had planted in the ground flare. A shimmering field springs to life between them and extends above the staves at least thirty feet. Most of the bolts are deflected away. Some soar high enough to go over the top of the field but are easily brushed aside with shields.

"Way to go James!" Devin's voice rings out.

"Quiet back there!" Illan orders as the crossbowmen ready another volley. "Hedry, see if you can distract them."

"Archers!" he hollers. "Ready bows!" The line of bowmen including Errin and Aleya put bow to string and draw them back to await his command. Hedry raises his arm and then lowers it as he cries "Fire!"

A hundred arrows fly toward the enemy, some taking out crossbowmen while others fly further and find their mark among the rank of soldiers. From the walls of Lythylla behind them, a cheer erupts from the onlookers.

"Fire at will," Illan says to Hedry.

"Fire at will!" Hedry repeats to his men and as fast as bowmen can put arrow to string, they fire at the enemy.

Horns from the enemy blow and the soldiers behind the crossbowmen surge forward with a war cry. Swords gleaming in the morning sun, they rush Illan's position. "Any time, Delia," Illan tells her. Another round of bolts is loosed from the crossbowmen as they and Hedry's archers exchange fire.

"Okay my lads," Delia says as she turns to face her slingers. "Take out one from the pouch and set it into your sling. As soon as you do, launch it to the enemy. Wait five seconds then do it again."

Removing one of the special missiles James had put together, she places it within her sling. Before she finishes twirling her sling up to speed, several of the others let fly with theirs.

As the approaching soldiers see the missiles flying toward them, they pause in their charge and raise their shields. The hardened clay missiles shatter on impact and the soldiers are surprised at the crystals contained within. Each has a glow to them and after nothing happens, they resume their charge.

"What went wrong?" Illan asks Delia after the first round fails to do anything.

"I don't know," she replies as she winds up her sling to launch her second volley.

Then all of a sudden, soldiers closest to the first volley of crystals begin falling to the ground as the crystals leech power from them. A second later, orbs begin filling the air and start emitting bursts of electricity.

The momentum of the charge falters as men are struck with the lightning from the orbs. Officers order their men forward and the charge resumes as more and more men fall victim as the second volley of crystals activates.

"They're not going to get all of them," says Ceadric.

"No, they aren't," agrees Jiron.

"Be ready," Illan says as he draws forth his sword.

Behind them, the catapults fall silent as the approaching soldiers close the distance and move out of the target range. Catapults are for long range attacks, not much good for in close fighting.

The last volley of crystals soars over head, some of the slingers aiming for the remaining crossbowmen at the rear of the charging men. "There's their cavalry!" hollers one of Ceadric's men.

From his position on the walls of Lythylla, Lord Pytherian sees the hundreds of cavalrymen emerging from around both sides of the palisade. "Send forth our men," he tells Henri beside him.

Henri turns to the men waiting in the courtyard below and gives the signal. First through the gates rides the cavalry, five hundred strong. They split up on the far side of the bridge, half moving to meet the oncoming riders on the right and the other half those on the left.

Illan takes note of the riders spewing forth from Lythylla, coming to their aid. "About time," he mumbles. The lightning from the orbs is creating merry havoc with the men charging his position. Though their momentum is faltering, it isn't stopping. "Jiron! Ceadric!" he hollers as he sits his horse with sword in hand. "Hold your position! Let them come to us."

The first line of soldiers runs into the barrier between the staffs, their faces showing the startlement of hitting the unexpected barrier. Then they become squashed against it as other soldiers hit them from behind. Around the far sides of the barrier the soldiers encounter Jiron on the right and Ceadric on the left and the battle is joined.

Delia and her slingers are protected from the onslaught by the barrier and the fighters on either side. "Fire at will!" she calls out as she sets a slug to sling and begins twirling. Letting loose, she watches the slug fly through the air and strike a soldier square upon the forehead. The man stands stunned for a moment then disappears from sight as he falls to the ground and is trampled by the men coming up behind him.

At first she was worried that the barrier would prevent the slugs from going through, but James had allowed for that. You can't imagine the relief she felt when her first slug went through the barrier. Now, they rain a constant hail upon those wedged on the far side. Most of the slugs simply bounce off the soldier's armor, but a few find their mark and take them down.

Given the chance she would lead her slingers off the field of battle, this is no place for them. If the barrier were to fail, they would be cut down in no time. Out of the corner of her eye she keeps track of the fighting going on around her. Jiron and his men are devastating the line of enemy soldiers, Shorty stays closer to Delia and her bunch as his knives wouldn't be as effective in such a melee.

A group of Parvatis moves against Ceadric's position and wades into them with both swords felling men fast. "To the left!" she cries to her slingers. "Take out the Parvatis!" Turning slightly left, she winds her sling up and lets loose another slug. It flies through the air striking a Parvati in the side of the head. As he falls, more slugs and arrows from Hedry's group begin to take their toll.

The memory of the Parvati Qyrll whom she had met once while he was staying with James flashes across her mind. A good man and honorable, she dislikes having to kill his countrymen, possibly his kin. But what else can she do?

From the edges of the battlefield, the sound of horses neighing can be heard as the two cavalry forces meet. The riders from Lythylla are outnumbered but are holding them at bay while their foot soldiers rush to their aid. Still streaming from the gates of Lythylla, they race as fast as possible to join in the fray. Already, the number of allies on the field is approaching that of the Empire.

The light from the Star moves throughout the battlefield as Miko tends the wounded as only he can. He longs to join in the battle, but the need to save the lives of these men outweighs the need for glory. Moving from injured man to injured man, he ministers to them with the healing power of Morcyth.

At one point he was healing a man with a severed arm. He reattached it through the power of the Star and was about to move to another when the tide of battle shifted. The line between himself and the enemy suddenly collapses. Putting away the Star, he draws forth his sword and meets the oncoming soldiers.

With speed the likes of which few soldiers have ever encountered, he blocks the attack of one while kicking out at another. In a blinding attack, two soldiers fall away with mortal wounds while a third launches into a series of attack which Miko is able to easily counter.

From the side a sword strikes at him and leaves a long gash along his side. The pain of the wound is barely even noticeable as he strikes out at the soldier and removes his head from his shoulder.

Then, Scar and Potbelly are there and stand with him shoulder to shoulder. "Miko!" hollers Potbelly, "Stig needs you!"

"We'll hold here!" yells Scar.

Nodding, Miko takes out the man he's facing with a quick thrust through the chest and then disengages. He finds Stig a few yards away, a rapidly growing stain spreading across his front. Returning his sword to its scabbard, he hurries over.

"Miko," Stig says weakly as he approaches.

"Just relax," he tells him as he removes the Star.

Stig lays back, the pall of death upon his face as the glow from the Star shines forth. Miko has done this enough now to be able to tell if he's too late or not and with relief he realizes he's not. With the power of the Star and Morcyth, he closes the wound in Stig's stomach, repairing the severed intestines and other organs within.

When the glow disappears, Stig sighs in relief. The pain, once a flaring sun is now little more than an ache. "Thanks man," he tells him.

Miko takes his arm and helps him to his feet. With one of Stig's arms across his shoulders, he helps him back to where Delia and the slingers stand near the center of their force. "Keep an eye on him," he tells Delia as he sets Stig on the ground.

She nods her head as she begins twirling her sling yet again.

Looking around, Miko finds another in need and goes to him.

The battle has been raging now for fifteen to twenty minutes. The individual moments of valor and bravery are too many to count. When the line crumbles under the onslaught of the Empire, reinforcements move to close the gap.

Once the men from Lythylla joined the fray, Illan could see that after the effect of James' crystals, the two forces were equally numbered. When the archers from Lythylla finally made their appearance after the foot soldiers took the field, the outcome was a foregone conclusion. Their deadly barrage began mowing down the enemy in swaths.

Taking advantage of a momentary lull in the fighting, he surveys the battlefield and can see where the Empire's men are beginning to turn and flee. Now that victory for them is out of the question, most are simply interested in survival. Suddenly, the line of men close to Ceadric's force breaks off and turns to flee toward the palisade. As Ceadric moves to follow he hollers, "Hold your position!"

Ceadric glances back and sees him looking at him, covered in blood from head to toe, some friendly but the vast majority is from those he's slain this day. Nodding, he begins forming up his ranks and holds his position. A cheer rises from his men at their victory.

Then all of a sudden the entire enemy line is in retreat. The forces from Lythylla set out in pursuit as those under Illan maintain their position. They'll let Madoc's forces do the mopping up.

"Report!" he hollers.

"Lost a third of my men," Ceadric says as he comes near.

"No one got close to us," Delia tells him. Glancing at her boys she says, "They all did magnificent." Illan nods his head and then turns to Jiron.

"Would have lost half of mine if Miko hadn't been with us," he says. "Most won't be good for a day or two, but they'll live to fight another day."

"Very well," he says. Looking to the fleeing soldiers, he grins when he finds the palisade, which had so well protected them during the long siege, is now a wall barring their escape. Madoc's forces, so long desiring retribution for the rape of their country don't even offer them quarter, they simply cut them down.

The battlefield is a ghastly sight, the dead and dying cover the ground between the river and the palisade. Cries from the wounded men sing out and the light from the Star can be seen moving from one to the next as Miko does his best to save every last one of them. Even Brother Willim and the three remaining members of the Hand are out among the injured doing what they can for them.

"Ceadric!" hollers Illan. "Have some of the men get the wounded and those unable to fight back to the city." They may have beaten this force, but there's still the other force James saw in his mirror on the way.

"Delia, have your group stay with Hedry's" he hollers. The battle before the palisade is winding down, men are escaping through the gates. Madoc's men are riding in pursuit. Seeing one of Madoc's officers nearby, Illan shouts, "Kippen!"

Looking his way, Kippen brings his horse to a halt. As he does, Illan hollers, "Get your men back. There's another force on the way and we have to get into position."

"Yes sir," he replies and kicks his horse into a gallop as he races to the palisade.

"We're not going to fight another battle are we?" a voice from the slingers calls out.

Illan turns to them but can't determine who asked the question. "Yes we are. They're not expecting an attack and the element of surprise will give us an edge."

"Any of those son's of a dog we take down now will be less we'll have to face later," Ceadric adds.

As Ceadric's men begin removing the injured and recently healed, Illan starts moving toward the palisade. The remainder of his force, still over seven hundred strong, follow along behind.

Calling to the officers from the various forces to fall in, he begins marshalling the chaos around him back into an effective fighting force. Hedry and Delia's people stay to the rear this time, no need being out front.

To one officer of a cavalry unit he orders, "Send out riders and find the force coming from the south."

"Yes sir!" the officer hollers as he carries out the order. Soon, four riders are racing for the gate in the palisade.

"They may already know of the battle from those who fled," one of Ceadric's men states.

"Be that as it may, we are still going to engage while the numbers are on our side," he says.

Madoc's archers fall in behind their force as well as soldiers from many units, swelling their numbers by the minute. While not in the actual line of command for any of these forces, in the face of the Black Hawk banner, none will gainsay him. His legend awes them into compliance.

On the far side of the palisade, they find what's left of the enemy's camp. Tents, wagons and a large number of slaves who are being set free. Many can't believe their lives are once again their own. Some have never known freedom, having been born slaves and simply don't know what to do now that they are free.

Off in the distance, pockets of fighting are still going on as Madoc's men continue the annihilation of the enemy. No quarter is given as their anger and rage at the Empire has finally found an outlet.

Illan sends the cavalry off to the right to swing around the approaching force to take it from the rear once the fighting begins. As his army makes its way through the palisade's gate, he gets them into position to meet the oncoming force. At the rear are the five catapults with wagons of rocks to use for ammunition, this time filled with smaller rocks ranging from the size of a baseball to that of a watermelon. Moving along at the pace of the slowest unit, the army doesn't cover ground very fast. But then Illan would like to hold off confrontation until the cavalry has had a chance to maneuver around them.

Having sent the cavalry around to come at their rear, all he's left with is several thousand men at arms, hundreds of archers and what's left of the Black Hawk Raiders. The bearer of the Black Hawk banner takes position at the head of the force and the wind whips the flag as if to display the black hawk for the entire world to see. A scattered cheer rises up from the men.

Once the pockets of resistance have been nullified, he gathers all friendly forces together and marches down the road to meet the oncoming reinforcements of the enemy army. The brief look in James' mirror had revealed roughly five thousand strong strung along several miles.

With just plains to contend with, there's very little chance to orchestrate an ambush. They'll know they are coming and will move into a defensive posture as soon as they realize what's going on. That is if they don't already.

From the road up ahead, two of the four scouts return at a fast gallop. "What's the news?" questions Illan when they pull up to him.

"They've stopped about five miles down the road," one scout explains as he rides beside him.

"Looks as if they got word of what happened here," the other adds.

"How many?" Jiron asks.

"Five thousand foot soldiers," the first scout replies.

"No horse?" asks Illan.

Shaking his head, the scout says, "Not that we saw. We returned with the news of their whereabouts and numbers, they were still arranging themselves to defend against attack."

"Rejoin your unit," Illan says as he thinks about what they just told him. *No horse, just foot. Excellent.* If as the scout said they still only have five thousand, then the numbers will be on their side by about two thousand. With the cavalry coming up behind them as well as the riders with Ceadric, they should be able to win the day.

It isn't long before the enemy force comes into view. They've positioned themselves across the road, a massive block of heavy infantry with several hundred crossbowmen protected in the center. No matter which direction a force attacks from, the crossbowmen can easily decimate them.

When the enemy sees them on the road, they form their ranks tighter. The soldiers at the leading edge have long spears to use against any cavalry units that attack.

Stopping just out of crossbow range, Illan turns back to his men and says, "Form ranks, bows and slings to the rear." As the men begin moving into formation for attack he takes his horse to the rear where the catapults are sitting.

The officer in charge comes to attention as he approaches. "Captain," Illan says, "are we close enough to pepper them with grapeshot?"

"Yes, sir" he replies.

"Then as soon as you are ready, let them have it."

"Yes sir," replies the captain. To his men he hollers, "Get them catapults into position and bring those wagons closer! We need to soften them up a bit so our delicate soldiers can go and be heroes."

His men break into a laugh and quickly get the catapults into position. Once they're ready, the men begin filling the catapult's bucket with the grapeshot from the wagons. As soon as they are filled and ready, the Captain yells, "Let 'em go boys!"

Five arms fling their deadly projectiles into the air. All of Illan's forces hold their breath as the projectiles fly to their target and then let out a cheer as they begin ripping through the enemy soldiers. Even though most of the soldiers had lifted shields to protect themselves from the rain of death, several dozen men fall. The crossbowmen, without the benefit of the shields fall in droves.

A command is given within the enemy force and they surge forward to attack, not willing to simply stay in one position and be stoned to death. "Once more if you will captain!" Illan hollers.

The catapult crews work quickly and soon have the arms back in position and their buckets filled. "Now!" he cries as the five catapults let loose. The grapeshot flies over the heads of Illan's force and rips once again through the attackers. Men fall as stones smash heads, crush arms and legs, and just about every other portion of the body as well.

When their crossbowmen reach effective range, they stop and begin firing into the defenders. "Shields!" cries Illan and his men raise their shields to ward off the bolts. As the bolts fall, the majority are either deflected by the shields or embed themselves into them. Some manage to find their target.

"Orry!" cries out Terrance as a crossbow bolt strikes Orry in the neck. Thrown backward, Orry hits the ground. His lifeless eyes stare up at Terrance as he reaches his side.

"Leave him!" Jiron cries out as he draws his knives.

"Ready slings and bows!" Hedry's voice sounds over the roar of battle.

Terrance, angered by the loss of his friend gets to his feet and puts a slug in his sling. When the command 'Fire at will' comes, he twirls his sling and lets loose at one of the approaching attackers. Maybe it is the anger at the loss of his friend, but his slug flies true and hits the man square between the eyes. In the heat of battle, he doesn't have time to be surprised at his skill, just places another slug in the sling, twirls and fires again.

"For Madoc!" the cry rings out as the two forces meet. "For Black Hawk!" another voice screams.

Jiron braces for the impact and as the soldier directly in front of him strikes out with his sword, he meets it with his left knife. Then he strikes out with his right and the man falls to the ground as blood gushes from his neck. An instant later the dead man's spot is filled with another and the battle continues.

Hedry's archers target the enemy crossbowmen, taking them out with devastating results. Shorty again stays near the slingers, there to protect them should an enemy make it that far.

Scar and Potbelly stand shoulder to shoulder as they deflect and return attacks with the enemy. Scar with his two swords is devastating, as is Potbelly with his sword and knife. Neither ever cared much for shields, figured they were for those whose skill was insufficient to keep the enemy away.

Atop his horse, Illan lays about him with his sword as enemy after enemy falls. From out of the corner of his eye he sees the cavalry he sent behind their force materialize. The enemy doesn't even realize their peril until they are upon them.

The shock of their charge mows down the enemy and are soon in among the crossbowmen, taking them out quickly. At that point, the battle is over. Over half the enemy lies dead and dying, encircled and outnumbered, men begin throwing down their weapons.

Around him, Illan sees Madoc soldiers striking out at the unarmed men. "Enough!" he cries, his voice piercing through the noise of battle. Men pause and the fighting comes to a stop. To his right a Madoc soldier strikes out and kills an Empire soldier that has already dropped his weapon in surrender. Illan rides over and kicks the man in the head. "Next one I see kill an unarmed man will get my sword!"

He spies one of the leading officers of the Madoc force and says, "Take your men and escort the prisoners back to Lythylla."

Next he gets the attention of one of the cavalry officers and has him send scouts in all directions to see about any further enemies either in the area or on the way.

Another unit is put in charge of collecting the wounded and taking them back to the city.

From somewhere the cry goes up, "Black Hawk! Black Hawk!" The men begin joining in until the very air resonates with the cry. It finally begins to die away as the various units start returning to the city.

Illan glances over to where Jiron and Delia stand near Orry. Saddened by the loss he dismounts and joins them. "Let's take him back," he says. "He died a hero's death."

"He did, didn't he?" Terrance asks as he turns his red rimmed eyes toward him.

Illan comes over and rests his hand on his shoulder, "Yes son, he did."

Terrance, along with the others from The Ranch put Orry over a horse and begin the trip back.

Chapter   Twelve

"Our scouts have reported no other hostile forces in the immediate area," Lord Pytherian tells those assembled in the meeting room.

James and Illan, as well as Brother Willim, are among those gathered to assess the ramifications of the events earlier in the day. They had an informal meeting with Lord Pytherian shortly before where they laid forth their plans to push deeper into the Empire. Thus far, the only one other than those directly associated with James' group who knows is Lord Pytherian.

"My Lord," a grey haired officer says as he gets to his feet, "shouldn't we press our advantage? With the help of Black Hawk and his mage ally, wouldn't this be the best time to drive out the Empire?"

James notices several heads nod in agreement. For over a year these men have accomplished little to remove the Empire from their lands. Rather, they've been pushed back as town after town falls to the enemy. Brothers, sisters, mothers, all have been taken as slaves into the Empire and they feel it's high time for some good old fashioned retribution.

Lord Pytherian turns his attention to the officer and replies, "Black Hawk and his force will be leaving us in the morning."

"What?" one young officer cries.

"You can't be serious!" shouts an older soldier, a member of one of the alliance's factions from the north. A general murmur spreads throughout the conference room as they comment to those sitting next to them on what they just learned.

Lord Pytherian lets it run its course for a few moments then raises his hand, at which the room becomes silent once more. "He and his force are leaving in the morning, that's true. However, they will be forging on into the Empire. They plan to cause such mischief as to force the Empire to draw a portion of its army home to deal with them." Glancing around the room, he sees many heads nod in understanding.

"During which, we will be coordinating with our armies to the east and west," he continues. "We still have two sizeable forces, one at the base of the Silver Mountains to the west, and another to the southeast. Our success here does not mean victory until we have dealt with those."

"Wouldn't it be wiser to consolidate our forces and strike at the force at the base of the Silver Mountains in one fell swoop?" a cavalry officer asks from the back of the room.

"To do that," explains Lord Pytherian, "we would have to take all but a small force from Lythylla. We dare not risk leaving our capitol open to the enemy. If they were to get wind of it, they could come and raze Lythylla to the ground."

"So what are we to do?" comes from the side of the room.

"We let Black Hawk do his thing," he replies. "You've all heard of his exploits in the War of Barrowman's Field. He will do that once again, though this time he doesn't go alone. James the mage, as well as the brothers of Asran will accompany him."

"They'll be slaughtered!" a younger officer hollers out from the side. At that, many of the old timers who had been around during the War of Barrowman's Field give out with guffaws. "Hardly," and "Not likely," are the responses some of the other officers give to the young man. They remember what Black Hawk had accomplished before.

"We let them soften up the enemy," Lord Pytherian says when the assembled officers quiet down, "then we take the battle to them up here. No reinforcements will be on the way, they'll be too busy hunting down Black Hawk. There's no way they'll allow him to once again roam free, burning and destroying their towns."

"They have a lot of confidence in our ability," James comments to Illan who only nods in reply.

For the next several hours, plans are made, changed, then revised again detailing various strategies to be implemented once the effect of Black Hawk's push into the Empire is felt.

While the meeting is still in full swing, Illan, James, and Brother Willim leave the meeting once it's clear what is being planned will no longer include them. Brother Willim takes his leave and goes to see about the brother who Miko had healed. He tells them that he and the others will meet them in the morning before they set out.

Back at the plaza, they find the new recruits badly shaken by the death of Orry. He was a favorite, always with a smile and never complained. As they approach the plaza, Devin comes forward. James can see his eyes are red from where he's been crying over the death of his friend. "James!" he says. "They're burying the dead in a large communal grave. They came by for Orry but we wouldn't allow him to be dumped in with all the rest." He glances up to him. "He deserves better than that."

"Wrap him in blankets," Illan says. "We'll take him with us in the morning and bury him away from town."

Relieved that Orry will get a decent burial, he says, "Thank you." Turning away, he returns to the others and let's them know what they plan to do.

"Fortunes of war," Illan says after they ride over to where the horses are picketed and dismount. "There's no way the soldiers here will have time to bury each soldier who died in an individual grave."

"I understand," James tells him. "It's best to get them in the ground as fast as possible."

Ceadric appears out of one of the tents and makes his way over to them. "So what's the plan?" he asks.

"Nothing's changed," replies James.

"We leave in the morning and play merry hell with the Empire," adds Illan.

Grinning, he says, "I like that plan."

"See that everyone has a good night's sleep," Illan tells him. "We leave at first light."

"Yes sir," he replies.

Turning to James, Illan says, "You better get some rest too. You look tired."

"I am tired," he replies. "But I need to see about the others first."

"As you will," says Illan as he gives out with a yawn. "I'm for bed however."

"Good night," James says as he makes his way over to where Jiron and Delia are sharing a fire.

When he approaches, Jiron hands him a plate of food. "Thought you might be hungry," he says.

Taking the offered food, he says, "Thank you, I am." Sitting next to them, he begins eating the beef stew and Delia hands him a quarter loaf of bread to go with it. Nodding to the slingers preparing Orry's body for tomorrow, he asks, "How are they doing?"

"As well as can be expected," Delia replies. "I think before yesterday they thought this would be a grand adventure right out of a bard's tale.

Then when the reality of it hit them, especially the death of Orry…" She trails off as her eyes move to settle on the tent where they are preparing Orry's body for travel.

"They realized this is no game and war is an ugly, horrible experience," Jiron finishes for her.

"I'm sure they'll be okay," adds Delia, "it's just rough on them right now."

James sits there in silence for awhile as he finishes his stew. "We're still leaving in the morning," he tells them.

"Then you better get some sleep," Jiron states.

"I will when I'm done with this," he replies, indicating the last couple bites of food left on his plate. As he chews the last bite, he glances around the camp and finds everyone winding down, many already asleep in their bedrolls. Devin and the others exit a tent carrying a shrouded body and lay it in the bed of a wagon. When Devin glances his way, James nods.

Standing up, he says, "I better get to sleep too." To Jiron he adds, "Make sure everyone is up before dawn."

"Sure," he replies with a catch in his voice.

James turns to find him grinning at him. Remembering the last time he awakened him, he adds, "No water this time."

"If you say so," he says, his grin growing slightly wider.

Shaking his head, James makes his way over to his tent and enters. Things inside aren't in their usual place, testament to the worry and sadness on Devin's mind. He didn't come and tidy up as he usually did. Checking his bedroll on the cot, he finds it still damp so he throws it to the side as he thinks unkind things of Jiron.

Lying on just the cot, he uses a pack for a pillow and lets exhaustion claim him.

Early the next morning, the camp is quickly disassembled and packed on the pack horses. The items James brought from The Ranch were reduced by half during the raid on the catapults and the subsequent battles that followed. Still should have enough for all he plans, he hopes.

Brother Willim shows up with the rest of the Hand shortly before they are ready to leave. The brother who was injured during the battle now looks much improved, a night of sleep, not to mention the healing from Miko, has done wonders. Miko is still absent, no one has seen him since the battle. Word has it that he's still seeing to the injured, James sent Errin to find him and to have him return before they set out.

The Black Hawk standard bearer takes the lead as they move through the city streets. Near the front of the column rolls the wagon carrying Orry's body, his friends riding along beside. Behind them comes Jiron and his group, then Ceadric with the Black Hawk Raiders.

"I thought we lost many of your men during the battle?" asks James.

Illan glances behind them at the throng of men at the rear and replies, "We did. These are others who have decided to join us." He glances to James with a grin, "Seems they want to ride for glory."

"Glory!" scoffs James. "There's nothing glorified about what we're doing. They just want revenge."

"Maybe," agrees Illan. "But for whatever reason, we can use them."

James nods his head and continues riding through town.

The streets are lined with many soldiers and civilians who are there to see them off. Every once in a while, a cheer would erupt when they turn a corner and appear to those who are waiting for them.

At the gates they find Errin with a tired looking Miko. Eyes all but closed with heavy bags under them, he sits on his horse as if he's about to fall off. When he takes notice of them approaching, he perks up and rides forward with Errin beside him.

"Found him still among the wounded," she says. "Had to practically drag him away."

"Save many did you?" James asks his friend.

From behind them, Lord Pytherian replies, "Many? I would have to say there are a hundred or more who owe either their lives to him or the use of a limb." He glances to those following behind with the Raiders and adds, "I see many of the ones he saved are among your men."

"We didn't ask them to come," James says apologetically.

"It's alright," he says quietly. "You can use the help and another hundred or so here won't really make that much of a difference."

"Any reports of the enemy?" Illan asks.

"Not so far Black Hawk," he replies. "From what our scouts are reporting, the forces to the east and west of us are maintaining their positions. They may not yet know of what transpired here."

"That won't last for long," Jiron says as he comes to join them.

"Just remember you promised to build the temple," reminds James.

"We will, I assure you," Lord Pytherian states. "Good luck to you."

"Thank you," replies James. "You too."

Getting their horses moving, they ride toward the open gate. When they pass through, the men on the walls give them a cheer.

As they cross the bridge, they take note of the men still working to remove the dead from the field. The soldiers of the Empire are being heaped together in one big pile while the men of Madoc are laid out more carefully. Far away from the banks of the river, two work forces are digging out large holes for the bodies, one for the Empire and horses, and the other for the men from Madoc and the alliance. Already a stone plaque has been commissioned to memorialize the men who are to be laid to rest there.

Taking the road south, Illan sends out riders to scout ahead and to their flanks for any enemy presence. After Lythylla disappears behind them, they locate a copse of trees near the road and take a momentary break while Orry is laid to rest.

Unwilling to allow others to dig his grave, Devin, Nerrin and the others who were closest to him take shovels and find a spot beneath a large tree. James and Illan stand nearby until they have it deep enough, then watch as his body is transferred from the wagon and laid within the earth.

Once they cover him with dirt and place rocks atop the mound to prevent animals from digging him up, Brother Willim comes forth and says a few words. While he speaks of life and how death is but another path, each reflects upon how Orry enriched their lives and how he will be missed.

Those standing nearby remain quiet in respect for the dead until Brother Willim winds to a close. Then with a last goodbye, they remount and resume their journey. One of the newest additions to Black Hawk's Raiders is given the duty of taking the wagon back to Lythylla.

From the head of the line, Illan glances back at the rest of the recruits and comments quietly to James, "Wonder if any of us are going to survive this?"

"I don't know," he replies. He misses Orry as does the others, though he never really had a chance to get to know him well. Few of the recruits have had much personal dealings with him other than Devin. Glancing back at Corbin's son, he feels saddened for his loss and can see his emotions are barely kept in check.

He spies Scar and Potbelly riding not too far behind him. "Scar!" he hollers. When he has his attention, he asks, "Didn't you and Potbelly once face a band of thieves all by yourselves?"

"As a matter of fact," Scar says, "we did. It was several years ago during…" As Scar continues on with his narration, Illan glances to James and asks, "Have you heard this one before?"

Giving him a grin, he shakes his head and says, "No. But knowing those two, I figured they would have a tale of some sort to go along with it. Besides, this will give everyone something to think about other than Orry."

Nodding, Illan says, "Good thinking."

"No, no you got it wrong," Potbelly interjects. "We weren't hired by the Baron of Falsberg, it was the Duchess of Twyst."

"That's right, now that you remind me," Scar says. "We were on our way through…" For the next hour or so, they regal everyone with their tale of daring do and for a brief time, the death of their friend is forgotten.

Not to be outdone, Uther and Jorry begin a tale once they're through of how they single handedly slew some giant that had taken an entire village captive. After listening to the narrative for several minutes, James turns to Illan and asks, "Are there giants here?"

"Not that I've heard," he says. Despite the improbability of their story, it is rather entertaining.

They continue following the road for the rest of the day. The scouts would return periodically to give a report then would switch to a fresh mount and ride off again. During one such time when a scout returns, the scout tells of a caravan approaching from the south. "Looks to be supplies for the army that was at Lythylla," the scout says. "It is but an hour away."

"How many soldiers accompany it?" Illan asks.

"Three score," the scout replies.

"Keep an eye on it," Illan says. The scout salutes before changing to a fresh horse and gallops back down the road.

"Ceadric!" he hollers.

"Yes sir," Ceadric replies as he brings his horse closer.

"We have an approaching caravan," he tells him. "Three score guards. Take your riders and capture it."

"Yes sir!" he says.

Before he rides away, James says, "Don't kill the drivers."

"What about the soldiers?" he asks.

"Do what you have to," he states.

Turning to his Raiders, he says, "We got a caravan to liberate!"

A cheer erupts as he and his men break into a gallop and race down the road.

"So it begins," James says under his breath as he watches Ceadric and his Raiders disappear down the road.

"Indeed," comments Illan from beside him.

It isn't long before they arrive at the captured caravan. Off to one side, a pile of dead Empire soldiers riddled with arrows stands testament to the battle which raged here. Many of Hedry's archers still have arrows to string as they keep the drivers from attempting to escape. Several wagons are without drivers and the bloodstains on the benches show they didn't give up easily.

The wagons are filled with food, weapons and supplies needed by an army on the move. A string of horses were also captured, spare mounts for their cavalry.

Ceadric meets them as they arrive and says, "All secured. No losses."

"Good," states Illan. "Have some of the men escort the caravan back to Lythylla."

"Yes sir," he says and then begins assigning those new to their force to escort the caravan. Some grumbling arises from those who believe they'll miss out on the glory of accompanying Black Hawk, but do as they are told.

As the wagons begin rolling back to Lythylla, their force once again resumes their advance on the Empire.

Over the course of the next several days, that scene is repeated three more times as they capture caravans and send them back to Lythylla. After the first day, James was sufficiently recovered from his fight with the creatures that he could again use his mirror to locate enemy patrols. If they weren't very large, Ceadric and his riders were dispatched to take them out.

During their third day from Lythylla, James locates a force of at least five thousand men heading north, most likely to reinforce the force that used to be at Lythylla.

"Should we take them on?" Jiron asks.

Shaking his head, James says, "That's not the idea. We are to draw them after us and out of Lythylla, avoiding any direct confrontation with large forces for as long as possible."

"Besides," adds Illan, "the force remaining at Lythylla will be able to handle them."

By the fourth day, any caravans they raid are no longer sent back. Instead, what they need is transferred to their pack animals and the rest is destroyed. Axes are used to chop the wagons apart, the supplies they aren't taking are destroyed in one manner or another. Nothing is to be left that will be able to aid the Empire. Any civilians with the caravans who aren't killed in the initial assault are allowed to go free. James simply can't bring himself to slay innocents. Plus, they'll begin to spread the word of what they're doing which is precisely what he wants.

James is surprised at the lack of response from the Empire. He thought there should have been something by now. The only thing he can figure is that the word has yet to reach local officials. Those who they've left alive have been on the fringe of the Empire and communications in this world being as they are, it may take awhile before they get word to the powers that be.

On the fifth day as they approach where the old border used to be between Madoc and the Empire, patrols and troops become more frequent. Still they continue as they have, either taking out the enemy should the force prove small, evading it should it prove large. Anything they come across from this point on, if it can be used by the Empire in the war effort, gets destroyed.

During the midafternoon of the fifth day while using his mirror to find enemy patrols, James discovers a fortress to the southwest sitting along the main road running north and south.

"That has to be Al-Ziron," Illan explains when he informs him what he found. "It's been guarding the Empire's border for centuries."

"I take it that it will have a sizable garrison?" asks James.

"Perhaps," he replies. "With this no longer being the border, they may not feel it requires many men." After riding a few more moments in silence, he asks "Do you plan to take it?"

Shaking his head, James replies, "No. It would be too risky. Let Madoc's soldiers take on the enemy, we're primarily interested in the country's infrastructure and its war industry."

"Then I suggest we skirt more to the east to avoid any possible patrols which may be in the area," offers Illan.

"Good idea," he replies.

Later that day when he again checks his mirror for enemies in the surrounding countryside, he spies what looks to be a long supply caravan escorted by several hundred soldiers heading eastward. When he informs Illan, Illan says, "Most likely heading toward the army fighting with the Kirken Federation. How far away are they?"

"A couple miles," James tells him.

"One last fight before nightfall?" Illan asks.

"We do have numbers and the element of surprise on our side," replies James.

"I concur," he agrees then hollers for Ceadric. After a couple minutes for James to show them the supply caravan in his mirror and to work out the battle plan, they alter their course and move to intercept.

Ceadric and most of the riders take off to the north in an attempt to get around them while Illan, James and his people move directly toward them.

"We're finally going to get in on the fighting?" Jiron asks.

"Yes. There are too many for Ceadric and the Raiders to take by themselves."

"About time," Scar says from where he overheard his reply. "Hate just riding along while others get to have all the fun."

From up ahead one of the scouts they sent to keep an eye on the caravan appears riding quickly toward them. "They're not much further ahead," the scout reports as he comes abreast of Illan.

"Does it look like they are aware of our approach?" he asks.

Shaking his head, the scout replies, "No. They're strung out in a line over a mile long. Most of the accompanying soldiers are at the head of the column, the rest are bringing up the rear."

"Excellent," Illan states. To Delia he asks, "How are your slingers on horseback?"

"We've done some practice while mounted but they're not very accurate unless on the ground," she admits.

He nods his head and wishes he hadn't sent all of Hedry's archers with Ceadric, the only ones left are Errin and Aleya. "Who is fairly accurate?" he asks.

"Other than myself, probably Devin, Caleb and Nerrin," she replies. "The others simply can't do it."

"Alright, here's what we do…"

Jiron and his riders are riding guard on Delia and the other three slingers who are accurate on horseback as they ride quickly toward the enemy caravan. Errin and Aleya ride with them as well, as do Moyil and Terrance, each of whom is bearing a lit torch. They plan to target the center of the caravan where there are the fewest number of soldiers.

The drivers of the enemy wagons take note of their approach as soon as they appear on the horizon. Several of them draw crossbows and one sounds a horn which summons the riders on either end to their aid.

When Delia comes within sling range of the wagons, she brings the group to a halt. The four slingers wind up their slings and let fly a single oil bomb each. Simultaneously, Errin and Aleya set one of their treated arrows to string, then wait as Moyil and Terrance light them from the torches they're carrying before sending it after the oil bombs.

Just as the first oil bomb strikes one wagon, Errin's flaming arrow follows and the wagon erupts in flame. A second later another wagon is struck by Aleya's arrow and is soon being engulfed by fire. They quickly ready two more arrows and let fly at the remaining two wagons hit by the oil bombs. Crossbow bolts fly toward them but miss their mark, they just aren't that accurate over long distance.

Once the wagons are burning, Jiron hollers, "Time to go!" From either end of the caravan, riders ride hard to close with the attackers. As one, Jiron and the others turn to race back to where James and the others wait.

Not many were left behind when the raiding party set out. James, Illan, Miko, and the Hand of Asran, as well as the few slingers whose accuracy from horseback was less than desirable, were all that remained.

As they flee from the approaching riders, Jiron and the others see their comrades already in position to ward off the attackers with James and the Hand of Asran stationed in front. As he and the others race around to their rear, a greenish glow surrounds the brothers.

Hundreds of green sprouts rise from the earth before the oncoming horsemen. Growing quickly, they rise three feet or more from the ground, large thorns appear and soon a wall of thorns impedes the path of their pursuers. Some of the horses leap over the barrier, others go around, but the majority comes to an abrupt halt.

Crumph! Crumph!

The ground erupts beneath the riders swinging around the ends of the thorn wall throwing riders and horses into air. Arrows and slugs fly toward those riders who had jumped the wall, felling them rapidly.

Of the dozen or more who had jumped over the barrier, only four continue toward them. Illan and Jiron move to the fore to stop them. Suddenly, a massive apparition appears before the riders. Seven feet tall, green and looking for all the world like a man made of leaves, it spreads its arms wide and lets out with a roar.

The charging horses roll their eyes in fear and rear backward, knocking their riders to the ground. Before the riders even hit the ground, the apparition disappears and Illan and Jiron move forward to engage them.

Over their heads, arrows and slugs continue to fly into the riders moving around the barrier to attack with deadly accuracy. Jiron reaches a rider who's dazed from his fall and quickly strikes out with a knife, taking him through the throat.

As the dead man falls, he moves on to the next who is already up and in position. Next to him he hears another rider fall from the death blow Illan dealt him as he engages the rider.

The rider strikes out with his sword as Jiron approaches. Sidestepping, he allows the blade to pass next to him. Lashing out with one knife, he catches the rider along one side, leaving a six inch trail of blood across his swordarm.

Jumping back, the rider looks at Jiron in anger. With a cry, he takes his sword in both hands and hacks down with all his might. As the blade descends toward Jiron, he dodges to the side and strikes the descending blade with a knife. At the same time, he lashes out with a foot and knocks the rider off balance. Before the man has a chance to regain his balance, he thrusts with his other knife and slips it through a gap in the armor beneath the ribcage, sinking the blade to the hilt.

With a cry of pain, the rider staggers a couple of steps before dropping to his knees as blood flows from his side. His sword falls from his hand as he topples over and hits the ground where he lies still.

Retrieving his dagger from the fallen man, Jiron looks to find Illan having already dispatched his two.

Horns sound behind the attacking riders announcing the arrival of Ceadric and his bunch. With the odds so much against them, the enemy riders break off the attack and flee.

Hedry's archers fire at the fleeing riders while riding at a full gallop. Some of their arrows find their marks, but the majority go wide. He divides his men in half, sending each half after the two groups of fleeing riders.

"Wagons secured," Ceadric reports as he nears.

"Any survivors?" James asks.

"Most of the drivers and about a dozen soldiers," he replies.

James glances to Illan and nods. "Good," he says.

To Ceadric, Illan says, "Keep them at the wagons. We'll wish to interrogate them."

"Yes sir," Ceadric says as he salutes and turns around to head back to the captured wagons.

"Went pretty well," comments Jiron.

"Yeah it did," agrees James. "Let's move to the caravan and see about the prisoners. We need to get out of here before too much longer."

Illan nods as he says, "I agree."

As everyone gets under way, James glances to Brother Willim and then nods to the thorn barrier. "Is that going to last awhile?" he asks.

"Maybe," he replies. "It's real so it could thrive here if it's the will of Asran. Though I doubt it, too dry."

Working their way around the thorn hedge, James, Illan and the rest make their way across the recent field of battle to where a score of Ceadric's riders guard those who survived their assault. When they arrive, Illan directs Ceadric to have his men gather what supplies they require before destroying the wagons.

Ceadric gives him a 'Yes sir,' then orders two of his junior officers to take care of it.

"Take what rest you can," Illan announces to the others. "We leave in under an hour."

While the group from The Ranch dismounts and begins distributing rations among themselves for a quick meal Illan, Ceadric, Jiron and James go to where the prisoners are being held.

The men being guarded are a sad, dejected looking lot. A dozen civilian drivers plus over a score of soldiers sit in a group off to one side. "Sergeant!" Illan barks upon approaching.

One of the soldiers guarding the prisoners steps forward and asks, "Yes sir?"

"Release the drivers," he tells him. "Get them out of here and moving on the road north."

"Yes sir!" the sergeant replies with a salute and with the help of two other Raiders soon has the drivers free of their bonds and heading down the road. When they don't move along fast enough, some of the Raiders decide to hurry them a bit with the broad side of their swords.

Illan turns to the remaining soldiers and asks, "Who here understands me?"

The prisoners return blank expressions, all that is except one. A soldier in the center of the group hesitantly says in heavily accented northern, "I can."

"You know who I am?" he asks.

"You are the Death Hawk," he replies, venom dripping from his words.

"Death Hawk?" James asks as he turns to Illan.

"That's the name they gave me," he says then turns back to their prisoner. A look of stony defiance is set in his face as he stares back to him. "What can you tell me of the defenses at Al-Zynn?" At this time one of the two bands of riders that had set out after the fleeing riders returns.

The soldier simply stares back in silence.

The leader of the band comes to a stop before Illan, snaps him a salute then says, "Got 'em all."

"Excellent," Illan tells him. "Have your men stand down until we leave."

"Yes sir," the rider replies. He gives Illan another salute before he and his riders move to the pack horses to retrieve some food and drink.

Turning back to the prisoner, he asks, "Now, what do you know of Al-Zynn?"

"I'm not telling you anything!" the soldier states defiantly. "Though it's sure to mean my death, I will never help one who so ravaged the Empire."

"Al-Zynn?" Jiron asks Ceadric.

"Al-Zynn is a major city that holds the Empire's stockpile of weapons and supplies for its northern armies," he explains. "During our last campaign here, we planned on razing it to the ground. But before we could get close enough, the Empire brought in too many forces to defend it and we had to go elsewhere. At the time we didn't realize it but that marked the beginning of our retreat from the Empire."

Nodding over to Illan, he adds, "The fact that he wasn't able to take it has gnawed at him since then. He means to head there and take it before they're able to bring in sufficient forces to stop us."

Jiron glances over to James who nods in agreement.

At this time the second band of Raiders shows up from their pursuit of the fleeing Empire riders. The lead rider comes forward at a gallop and says, "Black Hawk! A force of over four score riders may be on the way."

"What happened?" he asks.

"We gave chase and took down all but half a score when another force appeared. Those we were chasing joined up with them so we returned as fast as we could to give you the news. There were too many for us to effectively deal with."

"Very well," he says. To Ceadric Illan says, "Get ready to ride." After a brief glance to James, he adds, "And kill the prisoners."

"Yes sir," Ceadric says then signals several soldiers to aid him as he draws a knife and begins slitting their prisoner's throats. The first one he comes to is the man who they were questioning. Taking the prisoner's

154 Shades of the Past

hair in one hand, he pulls back the head and cuts his throat before moving on to the next one.

"We're leaving!" Illan hollers, loud enough to be heard by everyone. "Mount up!"

It takes but a moment for everyone to get in the saddle and when all are ready, Illan leads them with all speed southward.

He was sure he was a dead man when his hair had been pulled back and saw the glint of the knife out of the corner of his eye. Somehow the knife failed to penetrate his throat and missed the jugular. Still bleeding from the cut encircling his throat, the soldier feigns death as Black Hawk and his men ride away.

When the sound of their horses begins to fade away in the distance, he rises to a sitting position and glances around at his comrades. None but he remains alive. Tearing a strip of cloth from the shirt of a dead friend lying nearby, he binds it around his neck to stem the flow of blood from the thankfully shallow cut.

The caravan he was escorting had been on the way to resupply those fighting the Kirkens. They will now be sorely pressed to remain effective without the much needed supplies. Getting to his feet, he stumbles among the bodies in a futile search for another survivor but only manages to reaffirm what he already knew to be true, he alone survived.

Just after he finishes checking the bodies of his comrades, the sound of approaching horses alert him that others are approaching. At first afraid that more of Black Hawk's men were nearing, he lies down and pretends to be another of the dead. But when the riders draw closer he sees they are from the Empire. Returning to his feet he waves them down.

"What happened here?" the commander in charge of the riders asks. Among those riding behind him, the soldier notices several riders who had been among those guarding the caravan.

"They slew everyone," he explains. "Somehow, the man who cut me did a poor job." He lowers the cloth to show the commander his wound.

"How many were there?" the commander asks after taking in the scene.

"Hundreds," replies the soldier. "But commander!"

The tone in the soldier's voice causes the commander to turn his attention once more upon him. "Yes?"

"They are planning to take Al-Zynn!"

"Tell me everything," he commands.

Chapter   Thirteen

———————————————

Leaving the scene of carnage behind them, they head fairly due south as fast as the horses can carry them. Illan glances over to James where he's checking his mirror and asks, "What are they doing?"

Glancing up from the mirror, he says, "They just reached the dead soldiers. The one we left alive is talking to the commander."

"Think they'll take the bait?" Jiron asks.

"We were pretty convincing," Ceadric says.

"Thought you had actually cut his throat for a moment," James tells him.

"So did I," he admits. "Then I saw him move his hand up to his throat and apply pressure to stop the blood flow while attempting to appear like he was dead."

James returns his gaze to the mirror then says, "Looks like they did." He glances to Illan and adds, "Riders are moving at breakneck speed in all directions. The majority are heading south, just to the east of us."

"Makes sense," Illan says with a nod. "That's the general direction of Al-Zynn."

"We'll have everyone after us in no time," comments Ceadric.

"That's what we wanted," states James. He hated to kill those soldiers in that fashion but as Illan explained to him, there was no one to spare to escort them back. No sense letting go soldiers who will only try to kill them later on.

"With any luck all their forces will converge on Al-Zynn," Illan says.

"Would make things easier, that's for sure," Jiron says.

While they ride, James periodically checks his mirror for any hostiles ahead of them which they may have to deal with. The area to the south is clear for the moment. Moving the image back to the force behind them, he finds several enemy scouts keeping an eye on them. Scrolling even further to the north, he sees the force that had been heading toward Al-Zynn now turned to follow them. The scouts must have reported their position and the army moved to follow.

"They've turned to follow us," he says, "and are keeping their distance."

"I would too if I were in their position," Illan states. "They don't have the numbers to take us on. We don't have much to worry about unless they are joined by another force."

"Should we attack them?" asks Jiron.

Shaking his head, Illan says, "No. They're cavalry and would just run away."

"Then what should we do?" he asks.

"Just as we are," replies Illan. "Let them follow and think we are oblivious to the fact they are there." Shrugging, he adds, "Nothing else to do I'm afraid."

None of them like the fact of enemy soldiers following them, but as Illan said, what can they do about it? James keeps a watch on the pursuing force the rest of the day, worried they may try something. But his worries are for naught as the enemy force continues to maintain a discreet distance.

The sun droops to the horizon with the coming of night and James announces that other than the force following them, there are no others close enough to pose a threat. Illan calls a halt and they set up camp.

They keep a wary eye on the force behind them and through the mirror see that they too have set up camp. Once the tents are up and the fires built, James calls a meeting of the leaders to fill them in on just what they are planning to do.

Once they've gathered together, he says, "We've done well so far." Glancing around the group, he can see their grins and nods of agreement. "Tomorrow we set a moderate pace somewhat directly toward Al-Zynn, continuing to act in the manner we have thus far, destroying caravans, attacking small forces should the opportunity present itself. Though since riders were dispatched by the force behind us and are now to the south of us, possible encounters we can win are going to disappear as word of our approach spreads."

"But if we don't set a fast pace aren't we likely to face even more forces at Al-Zynn?" asks Brother Willim.

James turns to him with a grin and says, "We're not going to Al-Zynn. We simply want them to believe that we are so they will move all their forces to its defense."

He returns James' gaze with a confused one of his own. "Then where are we going?" he asks.

"Korazan," James replies. "From the intelligence gathered by Lord Pytherian's agents, there's a large stockpile of supplies and weapons there."

"Not to mention hundreds if not thousands of possible recruits in the fight with the Empire," states Miko from where he sits by the tent flap. When Brother Willim appears to not understand he says, "The slaves."

His head nods as understanding dawns on him.

"We have never intended to face the brunt of their forces," explains James. "We are simply here to create unrest, do some damage so they will pull their forces from Madoc in an attempt to get rid of us."

"But there will be very few slaves who know how to fight," Brother Willim says.

Miko nods his head and says, "True. But you don't need much skill to wield a crossbow, the preferred weapon of slavers. You have a couple hundred bolts flying toward a mass of soldiers and no matter how inept the crossbowmen are, it's bound to be devastating."

"Korazan is a big city," Illan says, drawing every eye to him. "We aren't necessarily planning on taking it, just the slaver compound on the outskirts. If the opportunity presents itself, we may do more but that will be determined when we get there."

Delia glances from Jiron and James. "You both have been planning this since we were last there haven't you?" she asks.

"Slavery is abhorrent," James replies. "And yes, when I first thought to enter the Empire to draw their forces back to the Empire, I wanted to make a stop there to free what slaves I could."

"They deserve no mercy!" blurts out Miko who lived as a slave for a time. The horrors he witnessed during his slavery still haunt him at times.

"How can one who bears the Star say that?" questions Brother Willim. "We priests are here to serve men, not kill them."

Miko turns his attention to him and says, "Be that as it may, no slaver should ever be allowed to live and propagate their trade." He glares at Brother Willim a moment then continues. "Besides, I'm not a priest in the strictest sense of the word and I have no compunction whatsoever about the death of a slaver." Ever since he first came to possess the Star, his vocabulary has changed slightly. Words he never before used have begun to creep in.

Brother Willim gazes into his eyes a moment and then shakes his head sadly.

"I concur," adds Jiron. His sister Tersa had been a slave for a time and to him that deserves some payback.

"Where do we go after Korazan?" Delia asks.

James glances to Illan and then says, "Illan will take the slaves and his Raiders back to Madoc. The rest of us will proceed a little further into the Empire. With any luck we'll draw all the magical types after us, leaving only the ordinary soldiery for Illan to contend with."

"Where are we going?" she asks.

"I'll tell you that once we split with Illan," he says. "Too many things may happen between here and there and I wouldn't want one of us to be captured and interrogated." When he sees the worry in her eyes, he adds, "Don't worry, that isn't likely to happen."

"I hope not," she says, worried.

"The force behind us seems content merely to follow along behind us," Illan states. Then to Ceadric he says, "Be sure to post extra sentries through the night. We don't want to be taken by surprise."

"Already done," he replies.

"Good," says Illan.

The meeting breaks up and they each file out of James' tent to see about the respective men under their command. Delia hangs back, remaining inside after everyone else has left.

"Shouldn't you go and see about your people?" James asks her.

"In a moment I will," she replies. Standing there by the tent flap she can't help but notice how much James has changed from the man whom she and the others first met after the fall of the City of Light. He's so much more sure and confident of himself and his abilities.

"Are you sure going to Korazan is the smartest thing to do?" she asks.

"What?" he asks in reply.

"I mean, could this be simply a way to get back at the slavers for the part they played in the death of your friend Dave?"

Sitting down on the edge of his cot, he sighs and looks up at her. "I'd be lying if I said it didn't. Yes, I want retribution. Yes, I blame them at least in part for what happened to Dave."

Dave, his friend from back home who managed to follow him through to this world. Ravaged and tormented, soul twisted until he became the willing accomplice in the Empire's attempt to steal the Star of Morcyth when James discovered it, only to be consumed when he laid hands upon it. Anger still smolders within him at those responsible.

"But there's more to it than just that," he continues after a brief pause. "The economy of the Empire is based on the slave trade. Striking a blow at a major slave marketplace such as Korazan can only weaken it. There may be no immediate results, but the long term effect could hurt them in some way."

"I see," she tells him, still not entirely believing his rationale. "Well, see you in the morning."

"You too Delia," he says as she lifts the tent flap and leaves.

Devin pokes his head in once she's left and asks, "Anything else sir?"

"No, Devin," he replies. "I'll be fine. See you in the morning."

Nodding, Devin backs out and closes the flap.

Getting ready to sleep, James thinks about what Delia had said. Their whole society is based on the slave trade and if it were to be in jeopardy, they would have to do something or face economic ruin. With any luck, they'll recognize that.

Lying down, he goes over in his mind the plan for the days ahead and fervently hopes it will be enough to not only draw their forces out of Madoc but also to enable them to return to Madoc once it's done. Eventually though, sleep wins out and he passes into unconsciousness.

"Which one, which one?" he mumbles to himself as he glances around the midway. A single ticket is clutched in his hand and he wants to make sure he doesn't waste it. Seeing a roller coaster off to one side, he makes his mind up and heads toward it.

As he makes his way through the various stalls and rides where the carnies are shouting out their various pitches to entice him to visit whatever they are in charge of, he has the feeling that he's been here before.

"Probably resembles one I've been to back home," he reasons.

The coaster is currently moving upon the rails, traveling with incredible speed as it twists and turns first up one way then down the other. The thrill of it surges through him as he hurries to be the first in line.

Upon reaching the front of the line, he realizes he's the only one who will be riding on the next turn. Thinking this odd, he turns and glances back over the midway and realizes that except for himself, the only others there at the carnival are the carnies. Not thinking anymore about it, he stands there and waits for the coaster to finish its run.

It makes a final loop and then begins to head in to the loading dock. Before it has a chance to come to a stop, he catches a glimpse of golden hair out of the corner of his eye. Turning his head he finds a golden haired girl making her way past the roller coaster.

"Ready sir?" the carnie asks once the coaster comes to a stop.

"What?" he asks, tearing his gaze from the girl as he turns back to the carnie.

"Are you ready to ride?" the carnie asks. He stands there at the edge of the coaster and holds the restraining bar up so James can enter the car.

He makes to hand his ticket to the carnie when the sight of the golden haired girl once again draws his attention. Just as the carnie is about to take the ticket, he snatches his hand back and says, "Maybe later." Turning around, he runs back through the waiting area for the ride and moves to follow her.

She's made her way to a ride on the edge of the carnival and is getting into a boat. Before he can reach her, the boat she's in begins to move down the narrow waterway and toward the opening of the Tunnel of Love.

Again the feeling of being here before comes over him. Not knowing why he feels the need to catch the girl, only that he must, he races after her and comes to the carnie in charge of the ride. Handing the man his ticket, he takes a seat in the waiting boat and is soon on his way toward the opening.

The golden haired girl has already entered the tunnel and he can barely make her out in the darkness within. A large heart with two white lights is upon the wall just within the entrance. The light coming from the two lights within the heart is the only illumination within the tunnel. Once he passes through the entrance, his eyes grow adjusted to the gloom and he sees her riding in the boat ahead of him.

"Hello!" he hollers to her but she fails to respond. "HELLO!" he cries at the top of his lungs, but again his cry goes unheeded. "Damn!" he curses to himself as he sits in the boat as it makes its way through the ride. He thought about getting out of the boat and wading up to the girl but decided against it, might be too unsafe.

There's not much to this ride really, some soft music playing in the background, he thinks it might be some Carpenter's song without the words. Scenes begin appearing on the walls of the tunnel. One is of two people, a man and a woman sitting side by side with their heads leaning upon each other. Another is of the same couple dancing at a merry festival.

Taking his eyes off the scenes upon the walls, he looks ahead for the golden haired girl but can only see darkness ahead. Anxious not to lose sight of her, he strains his eyes but is unable to see her.

His boat moves inexorably toward the darkened area and the temperature begins to drop, his breath misting in the coldness. The music playing starts to change subtly at first then moves into a more haunting melody and the tranquility the previous portion of the ride had induced fades away.

As he reaches the darkened area, the light fades altogether and he travels in complete darkness. The darkness seems to deepen and the coldness becomes more pronounced as does his feeling of unease. Holding out his hand, a glowing orb suddenly appears and dispels the darkness.

He gasps as he sees shadows moving along the fringes of the tunnel, none seem to pay him and his glowing orb any attention. They appear to be moving in the same direction as is the ride. When his gaze falls upon the shadows a shiver of fear runs through him, he's seen them before.

With uncertain dread, he peers forward in an attempt to locate the golden haired girl but the light from his orb doesn't pierce the darkness far enough ahead for him to be able to see her.

"This boat is moving too slow," he thinks to himself. "I'll never reach her in time!" In time for what he's not sure but the feeling that time is running out rises from deep within. Taking hold of the edge of the boat, he vaults over and splashes into the water.

As it turns out, the water is only two feet deep. Glancing at the moving shadows one more time, he begins sloshing his way through the water in an attempt to reach the boat bearing the girl.

The tunnel remains dark except for the light of his orb. Off to either side he's able to make out vague outlines of the scenes which should be illuminated but are now only dark. He rounds a corner where the ride makes a sudden right turn and finds the boat that had contained the golden haired girl sitting askew on the ride. It continues to rock from side to side as the chain below it which should have been moving it along rubs against the bottom.

He looks around the darkened tunnel, but all he can see are the dark shadows continuing to move along the walls. Unwilling to risk drawing their attention by shouting, he leaves the boat behind as he quickly makes his way along the tunnel. Staying alongside the center of the ride, he occasionally brushes a leg against the chain moving under the water. Once, his legging became caught by it and only by ripping a large hole in it when he tore it off was he able to get loose.

The cold of the tunnel grows in intensity the further along he moves. From up ahead, he hears the girl, at least he thinks it's her, singing a soft melody. At last he sees a glow and within it is the golden haired girl. She's walking as he is, along the center of the tunnel and is totally oblivious to the shadows moving along the sides. Quickening his pace, he tries to close the distance to her. But no matter how fast he moves, he fails to gain any ground.

All of a sudden the tone of her melody changes, becoming more sad and tearful. Altering her course, she begins moving from the center of the waterway and makes her way toward the right side of the tunnel. The glow around her appears to keep the shadows at bay as she steps out of the water and moves upon a raised platform holding one of the ride's attractions.

As she moves onto the dais, the movement of the shadows alters and they begin converging on the platform. "Watch out!" he cries as the shadows move toward her but the girl pays him no heed.

The shadows halt at the edge of the platform and become still, malignant hate radiates from them as they stand and watch the girl. Upon the dais, the glow which seems to surround her illuminates what looks to be a man hanging by his wrists from a rope that descends out of the darkness above. His features are hard to make out, though the blood, cuts and bruises dotting his body are not. This man has been treated badly and doesn't look like he can survive very much longer.

Her song stops and sobbing can be heard as she reaches a hand out to touch the tortured man's face. As she touches his face, a tremor more felt than seen runs through the shadows watching. Whatever is going on, they don't care for it.

James comes to within ten feet of the edge of the ring of shadows and stops in the water. He feels as if he should know the man hanging at the end of the rope but recognition does not come. Unsure how to make his way through the ring of shadows, he remains there in the water.

A waft of nauseating air suddenly surges through the tunnel from the entrance and James turns his attention in that direction. Another boat is coming through the tunnel toward him. He peers intently to see if there is anyone riding within it and only when it comes closer does he see something that causes his breath to catch and his heart to practically freeze in his chest.

Riding within the car is one of the monstrosities he saw when he had been on that other plane of existence. That time when Igor had showed up and rescued him. Unlike the shadows which had traveled along the edge of the tunnel, this monstrosity sees him. Its red eyes are fixed directly upon him, steeling the will and strength from him by the second.

Suddenly, it gives out with a mammoth roar which thunders through the tunnel and makes jelly of his muscles. He begins backing away down the tunnel from the approaching nightmare. That's when he notices the shadows have begun to leave the edge of the platform and are now making their way toward him.

Fear courses its way through every nerve in his body. It's all he can do to keep his legs moving. He turns and starts running down the tunnel when his legging again becomes ensnared by the chain pulling the boats along. Losing his balance, he falls into the water and once he rights himself, frantically tries to pull his legging from the chain.

Back down the tunnel, the monstrosity is now out of the boat and coming toward him quickly. There's no way for him to escape. Out of the corner of his eye, he sees the girl turned toward him, a look of pleading upon her face. Then the shadows block the sight of her as the monstrosity draws near.

Evil, malignant evil, radiates from the creature as it reaches its hand out toward him. His heart freezes in his chest and a scream is ripped from his throat as the creature's hand draws near.

AHHHHHH!!

He starts awake and bolts upright on his cot. His breath comes in rasps as the fear continues to course its way through him.

His tent flap opens and Jiron rushes through with a knife in either hand. "What happened?" he shouts as he looks around for an attacker.

"She needs my help!" he cries as he begins to calm down. His breath continues to be labored as the fear starts to dissipate.

"Who?" he asks as others crowd the entrance to his tent to see what the commotion is about. "Who needs your help?"

"I..." he starts to say but the memory of the dream is already beginning to fade. "I... don't know." Like sand slipping through your fingers, the dream which had been so clear earlier is now all but gone. All that's left are small fragments: golden hair, fear, and a sense that something needs to be done and done soon. But just what eludes him.

"I can't remember," he tells them as he puts his face in his hands. Breathing steadily, he brings his nerves under control.

Putting his knives away, Jiron turns to the others congregating at the tent flap and says, "He's alright. It was just a dream."

From outside the tent James can hear the sound of the others muttering as they head back to their tents. He takes his head from his hands and sees Jiron, Delia and Miko there just within his tent. "I appreciate your concern," he tells them, "but I'm alright."

"You gave us quite a fright," Delia says, worry still in her eyes.

"Was it a vision?" Jiron asks.

"I don't know," he replies. "I can't recall."

"Dreams of that intensity usually are," Miko says in a tone sounding very sure of what he's saying. "Try to hang onto the memory next time, it could be important."

"I'll do that," he says. To Jiron he asks, "How far away is dawn?"

"Still a couple more hours away," he replies. "You should try to get a little more rest if you can."

Laying his head back on his cot, he glances over to them and says, "I doubt if I'll be able to right away."

"Get what you can," Delia tells him and then gestures for everyone to leave the tent.

"I'll try," he assures her as they file out through the tent flap. The last thing he sees before the tent flap closes is Devin's face gazing in at him with concern, then the flap closes.

Lying on his cot, he tries to recall the dream but is unable. After awhile, he yawns and actually returns to sleep for a little bit before the call comes for the camp to awake.

Chapter   Fourteen

Despite repeated questioning by the various members of their group, he's still unable to recall anything but a vague feeling of unease about the dream of the night before. Finally he just quits trying.

It doesn't take them long to pack everything and be on their way shortly after sunrise. James continues checking his mirror frequently for any forces which may be heading in their direction. The force behind them that had trailed them throughout the day before continues to keep a discreet distance behind them. From what the mirror shows, their number has swelled dramatically through the night. Their plan must be to crush Black Hawk between their force and those waiting for them at Al-Zynn.

James scrolls the mirror as far south as he can and finds units moving in the general direction of Al-Zynn. It appears all is going as planned, the Empire believes they intend to sack Al-Zynn and are moving every available unit there.

They keep a moderate pace, neither rushing nor being too slow. As best they can, they try to maintain a course that will take them a little west of Al-Zynn rather than directly toward it. If the Empire realizes they are not entirely on a straight heading, with any luck they will simply write if off as they don't know the exact way.

By late afternoon, James has been able to acquire Al-Zynn in his mirror. The flurry of activity surrounding the town shows that they believe an attack is imminent. Troops are moving toward it from all directions, including a sizeable force from the direction of Korazan.

"Hope that's the majority of the garrison at Korazan," Illan says when James informs him what is transpiring there.

"With any luck, they won't realize what we are up to until it's too late," replies James.

"When they do," comments Jiron, "everything at Al-Zynn will be sent after us. They aren't likely to allow us much time at Korazan for what we intend."

Nodding, Illan says, "That's why we are only hitting the slaver's compound, killing all the slavers and freeing the slaves. Those who wish to come with us we'll arm with the weapons found at the compound."

"Can't imagine anyone wishing to remain behind," states James. "They would only be made slaves once more."

"Never know," Illan replies.

All day long there are no further opportunities for attack. The caravans and patrols must have been diverted to prevent them from falling to them as they head south. By early evening, it's determined that Al-Zynn is a little over four hours away. Scouts have reached the city and reported back that breastworks are being dug between where their force now lies and the walls of Al-Zynn.

James turns to Illan and asks, "From their perspective, would it seem reasonable for us to stop here, seeing as how our scouts have returned and reported what they saw at Al-Zynn?"

"Yes it would," he replies. "Now that we 'know' what we are up against, it would be reasonable for us to stop and assess the situation."

"Very well," James says. He checks his mirror for hostiles in the area and finds more units stationed in and around the town of Al-Zynn than previous. To the east and west of their position is fairly clear, the only units he discovers are smaller bands on their way to reinforce the town. The force that's been following them remains at the same distance they've been since the chase began.

"Looks like we may be okay until the morning," he tells Illan as he puts his mirror away.

"By then it will be too late for them to do anything," Illan replies. Raising his voice, he hollers out to the rest of the riders following along behind, "Bring 'em to a halt! We stop here tonight."

As Devin begins to take his tent down from the pack horse to set it up, James tells him not to bother. "No tent tonight," he tells him. Lowering his voice he adds, "We're not going to be here all that long."

"Yes sir," he says.

They get fires going and cooks begin working on dinner. Bedrolls are laid out nearby and it isn't long before everyone has had a quick meal.

Other than the sentries and the scouts riding the perimeter, everyone turns in early, well before the setting of the sun.

Before climbing into his bedroll, James checks the status of the various forces before and behind them. The one behind has stopped and made camp as well, the forces by Al-Zynn still look to be on alert and ready. He grins as he puts the mirror away and then lies down to sleep.

It isn't long before a tired looking Devin awakens him. "Illan said it was time," he says. When he sees James stirring and then gives him a nod, he gets up and begins to prepare James' horse for travel.

With eyes longing to close after such a short rest, James sits on his bedroll as he tries to come completely awake. The camp is a flurry of activity as everyone readies themselves for travel. Despite the hustle and bustle there is relatively little noise as they ready for a quick push to the west to take the enemy by surprise. If they can get away without anyone noticing, by the time sunrise comes they'll be many miles away before the enemy realizes what happened.

Earlier, Ceadric had some of his men comb the countryside surrounding the camp in an attempt to locate any of the enemy who may be keeping an eye on them and take them out. A few men with fast horses will remain to keep the campfires lit and to give the overall appearance that they are still here.

Despite the number of men and horses being prepared for travel, the noise level remains subdued. Unless an enemy scout is close, they may not notice anything out of the ordinary. The number of campfires they usually have were reduced by two thirds to lower the light level in the camp in the hopes of keeping their move more secret.

Illan appears out of the dark and walks toward him. "We will be ready to ride shortly," he says as he comes to a stop near him.

"Any sign of enemy scouts?" James asks as he gets to his feet. Once up, Devin comes and collects his bedroll to secure it behind his saddle.

"Ceadric reported that a half dozen or so were taken out earlier," he replies. "He thinks they got them all."

"Let's hope so," James states. Glancing around the camp, he sees indistinct shadows moving about as the men make ready to ride. A horse rides close and Delia comes to a halt before him.

"Our folks are ready," she tells him then glances over to where Devin is finishing securing his bedroll. "That is, when he has your equipment stored."

"Good," he comments with a nod. Terrance appears with a plate of rations which he takes with a 'Thank you' and commences to eat. To Illan he asks, "How far is it to Korazan?"

"A day or so," he says. "Are you sure you still want to go through with your plan?"

Nodding while chewing a mouthful of food, James then swallows and says, "Yes. A nation the size of the Empire can lose soldiers and hardly bat an eye. But you mess with its economy and they'll feel it."

"As you will," replies Illan and then his attention is taken by the approach of two of Ceadric's men.

Finishing his meal, James walks over to one of the campfires set away from the tents where some of those from The Ranch are congregating while they await the order to get underway. Terrance is one of them and he hands his empty plate back to him.

Stig looks up at his approach and grins. "Is it time for a little payback?" He has his mace in one hand while absentmindedly thumping it in the palm of the other.

Of all those associated with James on this venture, only the pit fighters whom he had bought out of slavery are completely in favor of taking out the slaver compound. The indignity and abuse they endured while in their hands demands retribution.

"Shouldn't be too much longer," he replies. They stand there sharing the fire until the word comes a few short minutes later that all are ready. Devin approaches him with his horse in tow and holds the reins while he mounts. Once mounted, James begins moving toward where he knows Illan will ride at the head of the column.

He doesn't get very far before the force begins to move away from the campfires still burning in the dark without a word. James glances back to the men left behind to maintain the illusion they are still there as they walk to and fro in the fire's light. Returning his attention back to the fore, he quickly moves through the riders to join Illan and Brother Willim in the lead. The rest of the Hand of Asran rides further back in the column with the others.

As the campfires disappear further into the distance behind them, his anxiety peaks as he waits for any indication the move has been found out. But as minute after minute passes uneventfully, he begins to relax.

A force this size doesn't exactly move silently and the noise from the horse's hooves seems to reverberate throughout the night. The tack on the horses prone to jingling has been muffled with cloth to prevent it from making any sound.

They ride in silence for several hours, scouts reporting in periodically only to report that no other forces have been sighted ahead of them. When the sky begins to lighten and still no sight of the enemy has been made, James realizes they may have just pulled it off. By now, their pullout had to have been detected by the enemy. The enemy scouts that were posted around their encampment will not be reporting back in and by now others have most likely been sent to investigate. The men who were left behind to make it appear they hadn't left were to leave and race to catch up when the sky first began to lighten.

"Should be to Korazan by early tomorrow if we keep a steady pace," Illan says, breaking the silence. He glances to where James is riding beside him and asks, "Can you check for hostiles?"

"Sure, but they'll know where we are," he replies.

Shrugging, Illan says, "Doesn't matter much now. They know we didn't go north or south, east would be pointless, so they're going to send everything this way. Probably will try to crush us quickly with all they have."

"Alright," agrees James and then reaches for his mirror.

"Scouts say there's a road ahead of us a mile or two running north and south," he says as James gets his mirror into position.

Nodding, James gazes into the mirror and lets the magic flow. The image clarifies and he sees their force from a bird's eye view. Scrolling the image, he first looks to the west to see what's ahead of them. It doesn't take long to find the road that the scouts reported. "There's traffic upon it," he says to Illan. "Regular people and a few caravans." Glancing to Illan he says, "I don't think they were expecting us to move this way."

With a grin, Illan replies, "Good."

Returning his gaze to the mirror, he scrolls the image still further. As the image moves further from his position, the drain of magic increases. "Doesn't look like anything ahead of us will present much of a problem," he says. "There are a few forces on the move but nothing we can't handle."

Moving the image, he begins to scan clockwise. To the north of them rides a band of horsemen heading in their direction, looks to be two score doubtful if they would even try anything against so overwhelming an army. About an hour behind them to the east he finds those riders they left behind at the camp riding hard to catch up. Two to three hours behind them follows the force from Al-Zynn, easily twice the number of those riding with James. The force is entirely made up of cavalry, three brown robes ride with them.

"Our riders made it safely away," he tells Illan. "They're about an hour behind us."

"That's good news," he replies.

From behind him Ceadric asks, "What about the force from Al-Zynn and the one that was following us?"

"The army from Al-Zynn rides several hours behind our men, and they're twice our number with three brown robes," he says as he scrolls the image to locate the force that had been trailing them. "The others are moving to join with them."

"Three mages?" Brother Willim asks.

Nodding, James turns his gaze to him and says, "Three."

"That will make things interesting," he says.

"Where do they get them all?" James asks as he returns his gaze to the mirror to check to the south.

"They periodically test children and those who show an inclination or talent toward magic are taken to their School of the Arcane," explains Illan. "From what we understand, not many make it through the training process."

"I take it that it's not exactly a voluntary choice?" he asks. The south looks fairly clear of any immediate threat so he returns his mirror to his pack.

"Actually, most desire the prestige and honor that goes with being a mage for the Empire despite the risks involved," Ceadric adds. "I suppose a few don't want to go and they're probably the ones who fail to survive."

Just then they see ahead of them a scout returning. As he pulls up to ride beside Illan he says, "The road is just ahead."

"Are they aware of our approach?" Illan asks.

"Not yet Black Hawk," replies the scout. "People are still traveling along at a normal pace."

James gazes to the horizon ahead of them in the morning light and can just begin to make out those traveling upon the road.

Illan turns to Ceadric and says, "Take your riders and secure the road. Take out any caravans but leave the people alone. We're not here to kill innocents." He glances to James and receives an approving nod.

"Yes sir," Ceadric replies. Behind him ride two of the four men he's designated as Raider Captains, both rode with Illan in his earlier campaign. One is Nerun, a grizzled old timer who still retains his strength and wits. The other is Wylick. Six foot six with just a peppering of gray in his hair, he still gives an imposing appearance. The other two captains ride further back with their men, protecting the rear of the column.

Turning back to them he says, "Nerun, take your men to secure the road to the north. Wylick, you take the south."

"Yes sir!" Wylick says before he hollers to his men and they race to the south. Nerun and his men gallop to the north.

James watches as the two bands of riders, over two hundred strong each, near the road. The travelers soon take notice of the approaching riders, at first thinking they are forces of the Empire. But then when they finally realize they aren't, panic ensues as they begin racing for their lives.

Neither of the bands of men strike down the civilians without provocation. A few are taken out when they try to fight them off in a futile gesture. By the time Illan, James and the others reach the road, it's been cleared and secured. To the north the sound of breaking wood is heard as Nerun's men begin destroying a twenty wagon caravan.

One of Nerun's men returns down the road with one of the wagons trailing along behind him. When he reaches Illan he comes to a stop and says, "Nerun thought we might want to save this one."

"What is it?" Illan asks.

The driver of the wagon, another of Nerun's men pulls back the tarp and reveals a hundred crossbows with accompanying boxes of bolts.

"Nice," states Ceadric approvingly.

"Get them distributed among the packhorses," Illan tells them. "We can't afford to linger here."

"Yes sir," the rider says. Then he and the wagon move to the center of the column where the packhorses are kept for safety. With the help of others they begin the transference of the crossbows and bolts.

"That's going to come in handy," states Jiron. Having come up behind James while they were paused on the road, he saw the wagon load of crossbows as it headed for the packhorses.

"More is always better," agrees James.

By the time they've been transferred, the men who were left in camp finally join up with them. While waiting to resume their progress toward Korazan, James goes over to Brother Willim and the rest of the Hand.

"The force from Al-Zynn rides a few hours behind us," he says as he draws close.

Two members of the Hand nod as Brother Willim replies, "That's not going to leave you much time at Korazan."

"I know," states James. He glances from Brother Willim to the others and then his eyes settle back on Brother Willim. "I have an idea of how to slow them down."

"Oh?" says Brother Willim questioningly.

"Are you game?" he asks.

"What do you have in mind?"

Illan continues with the rest of the force while James, the Hand of Asran, and Jiron with his fighters from The Ranch stay behind to set up a few surprises. James was at first annoyed by the lack of help from the Hand when he first began to lay down what he wanted. He saw what they did against the warrior priest back at Lythylla and expected them to do something similar now.

"We do not kill men," Brother Willim states adamantly when asked if they could do something against the approaching force. "The warrior priest was an entirely different matter." But they work out a few things they could do without compromising the sanctity of life.

Now, two hours later, they wait just within visual distance of the section of the road where the caravan lies destroyed. Jiron figured the Empire's men would take a few moments to examine the wreckage before they continue the chase on the off chance someone was left alive.

"Here they come," says Stig as he returns from his lookout position by the road.

The force comes into view with the three mages riding in the lead. Coming up behind the mages is a force of cavalrymen over a thousand strong. Their foot soldiers are still hours behind, following as best they can.

When the mages take notice of the destroyed caravan and the dead bodies of those who fought back, their approach slows. Moving closer to the wagons, soldiers begin dismounting as they search for survivors.

"Any time now," whispers James under his breath. To Brother Willim he says, "When it begins, that's your cue."

"We'll be ready," he replies. He and the rest of the Hand gather together, a subtle green glow springs into being around them. James can feel the unmistakable tingling of nearby magic as the Hand readies themselves.

At that time, one of the mages suddenly sits erect in his saddle as he gazes in their direction. "One senses the magic," he tells them. "I just hope he..."

Crumph! Crumph! Crumph! Crumph!

All along the road in the vicinity of the wrecked caravan, crystals which James had secreted earlier, respond with violent explosions when they detected the mage casting a spell.

James glances over to Brother Willim and gives him a nod indicating it's time.

The green glow surrounding the Hand intensifies tenfold as they summon the power of Asran. Cries are heard from the horses as ants, millions of ants, swarm out of the ground and up their legs. Green shoots also spring out of the ground from the seeds which the brothers had sowed earlier, causing even more confusion and panic.

Horses try to run but their legs become entangled in the rapidly growing thorn bushes. Men scream as their horses rear and throw them into the carpet of ants covering the ground. No sooner does a man hit the ground then the ants are upon him, crawling inside the armor and begin biting. Nothing lethal but these are fire ants and each bite brings pain.

The dust which had been thrown into the air by the explosions begins to dissipate. One mage lies on the ground, the one who had initiated the blasts in the first place, and it doesn't look as if he's getting back up. The other mage who was near him at the time of the explosion is rolling on the ground, his hands flying fast as they try to get the ants off him.

The remaining mage was bucked off his horse when the explosion happened and managed to land without injury. He now stands safely just outside the perimeter of the ant swarm. James can feel the tingling spike as he works to counter the magic wielded by the Hand.

"How long can you keep this up?" James asks Brother Willim.

"His power is not nearly as great as ours," he replies. "As long as you require."

Jiron comes to him as he continues watching the events unfolding by the road. "Are you thinking what I think you are?" he asks.

"One mage down, another incapacitated by the ants, and the third locked in a duel with the Hand," he says and then turns his attention to his friend. "We may never have a better chance." The enemy force is in total chaos. Between the ants and the thorn bushes which continue to grow, most of the force is out of action.

Jiron gives him a grin and turns to the rest of the riders. "Mount up!" he yells.

"Yeah!" shouts Potbelly as he jumps into the saddle and draws his sword.

"We get in, take out the mages and then retreat," James says to the others when he gains his saddle. "Now ride!"

With a whoop and holler, the fighters from The Ranch break into a gallop and charge. The enemy mage is quick to take notice of their attack and halts his attempt to counter the Hand. Turning his full attention to the attackers, he raises his hands and a greenish black globular substance forms before him. Moving with incredible speed, the substance flies toward the approaching riders.

James summons the magic and forms one of his protective barriers around the airborne mass, completely encompassing it. Nudging its trajectory slightly with another burst of power, he has it hit the ground far to their left. Once the barrier encased goo comes to rest on the ground, he releases the spell and sets the goo free where it sizzles and burns upon the ground.

He feels another spike when they are halfway there and this time the ground shakes violently, their horses begin to lose their balance and footing.

"We got company!" Shorty hollers out as a force of several score enemy riders appear riding hard from the rear of the force around the edge of the ant swarm.

A memory comes to mind and rather than attempting a direct confrontation with the mage, he selects a point within the swarm of ants.

Crumph!

Letting the magic go, the earth erupts in a massive explosion sending dirt and a cloud of ants into the air. A portion of the flying mass of dirt and ants is headed directly for the mage. Just then, Scar's horse loses its battle with the shaking ground and stumbles, sending him to the ground.

When the mass of dirt and ants hit the mage, James feels the tingling stop as hundreds of ants begin crawling and biting all over the mages body. No one could possibly maintain concentration while beset by hundreds of stinging fire ants.

Their horses once again pick up speed as the ground quiets. Potbelly slows and glances back to his friend Scar who's already off the ground and has his horse's reins in hand. "You okay?" Potbelly hollers back to him.

Swinging into the saddle, Scar yells, "Of course!" Kicking the sides of his horse, he's soon caught up to Potbelly and together they ride to catch the others.

"Uther, Jorry," James yells to the pair. "You two stay with me." Then to Jiron he says, "Take out those mages, we'll slow down the riders."

"You got it," Jiron replies.

Turning to face the onrushing riders, James reaches into his pouch. Pulling forth one of the two remaining crystals, he makes a conduit from the darkly glowing crystal to himself. Feeling the power rush into him, he immediately sends it forth to a point directly before the oncoming riders.

Ka-Boom!!!

An explosion of massive proportion detonates under the leading edge of the force. Riders, horses and debris are thrown into the air, their screams and cries only silencing when they slam back into the ground.

James glances back to Jiron's force and find them already at the mages. Unable to defend themselves with magic, they fall quickly. Many of the soldiers, covered in hundreds of welts from the bites of the fire ants, have managed to disengage themselves from the thorns and are beginning to engage them.

A quick glance back to the settling dust of the massive explosion, he doesn't see anything moving. "Let's go and help our friends," he says.

With a cry, Jorry and Uther turn their horses and the three of them race back to the growing battle. More and more of the soldiers are extricating themselves and are moving to engage Jiron and the others.

All three of the mages lie still upon the ground, their heads severed from their bodies. There can be no doubt now as to whether they will pose a future threat. When James comes within shouting distance, he cries out, "Disengage! Retreat!"

As he slows down and pulls a slug from his belt, Jorry and Uther race past him. Scar and Potbelly are faced off against six opponents and they race to their aid. Seated upon their horses, they are able to keep the enemy soldiers at bay but are unable to disengage without grave risk to life and limb.

Just as Jorry and Uther reach them, a slug flies past and takes out one of the enemy soldiers. Charging through the enemy, they allow Scar and Potbelly the opportunity to disengage. Scar strikes out at his remaining opponent with his sword and severs the man's left arm.

"Let's go!" Jiron yells.

James launches three more slugs and then the rest of his men are able to break away safely. A quick count shows no one was lost, many have wounds seeping blood but nothing that looks life threatening.

"Think that will slow them down?" Yern asks with a laugh.

Behind them, the scene remains one of confusion and chaos as horses and men continue in their attempt to rid themselves of burning, biting ants.

"I would think so," laughs Shorty.

Back at where they left the Hand, they find them already in the saddle and waiting for them. The green glow that was present when they left is now gone.

"Where did all those ants come from?" Stig asks Brother Willim.

Indicating the ground he says, "In the ground beneath our feet are countless insects and animals. They are Asran's creatures and will do his bidding."

"Fascinating," remarks Jorry. Uther nods in agreement.

"Let's save this for later," Jiron announces. "We better catch up with the others before too much longer." With that, he kicks the side of his horse and breaks into a gallop. The others are quick to follow.

Behind them, the enemy riders decide not to give chase and begin giving aid to their comrades.

Chapter   Fifteen

"You're really something you know," Illan says when they finally rejoin the main force and tell him what happened.

"Actually most of the credit should go to Brother Willim and the Hand," replies James. "It was the ants that caused the mages to be unable to focus well enough to control the magic."

He barks out with laughter. "I know that to be true," he says, still chuckling. "When I was a young lad I fell asleep in an area swarming with them. I must have moved in my sleep for they started biting me. By the time I made it to the nearest pond and dove in, I had welts from head to toe. Miserable buggers."

From behind they can hear Scar and Potbelly recounting the events to the rest of the men. Of course from their version you would think they had killed the mages all by themselves, not to mention the hundred or more soldiers they had slain. James just grins and shakes his head, by this time no one really takes what they say as fact. He still wants to call them on one of their wild claims but so far hasn't been able to.

Pulling out his mirror, he checks the force behind them and discovers they are still by the road where the attack occurred. From the looks of them, it doesn't seem as if they are in any hurry to proceed. He then scans in a full circle for any enemy forces but only comes up with more desert. There are civilians traveling here and there, none likely to cross their path.

He scrolls the image as far west as he can before the drain of magic becomes too great in an attempt to find Korazan but isn't able to reach that far. "Looks like there's nothing close," he tells Illan as he replaces his mirror back in his pack.

"That's good news," he replies. "If we move fast enough, we may be able to stay ahead of the word of our approach."

Nodding, James rides in silence for awhile. Behind him, he can hear Jiron as he talks with Aleya.

"I took out one of the mages myself," he boasts. Riding along beside her, he glances out of the corner of his eye for any spark of reaction to what he just said. Nothing. She simply continues riding along, pointedly ignoring him.

He never was one to boast of his deeds before. In fact, he can't remember ever doing it before just now, at least not for the sole purpose of impressing someone. Why does this woman affect him so? He's drawn to her but it seems as if nothing he does has any effect. Back when he and James had first encountered her in the hills near Mountainside she was friendly to him. He even felt they were growing closer. Yet here they were, separated by something completely unfathomable to him. After riding along beside her for several more minutes, he sighs and then slows to drop back.

"You okay?" Delia's voice comes to him as she moves to ride alongside him.

"Yeah," he says in a voice not quite convincing.

Delia takes in the way he keeps glancing at Aleya and tries to hide the grin that is threatening to come forth. She's been watching his attempt at becoming closer to her and is pretty sure she knows what's keeping him from achieving it. But she's not quite sure how to tell him.

"I thought you and Aleya liked each other?" she asks.

"We do!" he blurts out with more force than he wanted. Face turning red, he turns his gaze to her and adds, "At least I do."

"Then what's the problem?" she asks.

"I don't know," he replies. "I try talking to her and all I get is silence. At first she and I hit it off, but then things began to cool until now it's absolutely frigid."

"What do you talk about?" she asks.

"Oh, the war. The adventures James and I have had, my time in the Pits," he tells her.

The grin she's been holding back is all but breaking through the barriers she's erected in an effort not to make him feel bad. "Do you ever talk about her?"

"What?" he asks.

"Have you ever asked her a question about her life? Her thoughts?" She pauses a moment to let that sink in. "There are many different types of women in this world," she explains. "Most of the ones you've been acquainted with probably have cooed and gone all mushy when you tell them of your exploits."

"Isn't that what women want?" he asks in all seriousness.

A soft laughter breaks through her barrier. Shaking her head she says, "Not one such as Aleya. If you want her, you need to think of her as more of an equal. She needs to feel you are interested in her as a person."

He turns to look at her, a thoughtful expression playing across his face.

"Ask her about her life, her past, what she hopes for the future," she goes on. "And for goodness sake, just listen when she talks. Don't interrupt or she will think you aren't interested in what she's saying. Your deeds gained her interest, but alone they won't gain her heart."

Nodding, he begins to see where he's gone wrong. "Thanks," he says to her.

"Just be patient. That's the most important thing a man can do where a woman is involved."

"I will," he assures her then nudges his horse to move up the line to ride next to Aleya.

"Think he'll listen?" Errin asks as she pulls up next to her.

"We'll see," states Delia.

Up ahead they watch as Jiron pulls next to her and says something. Delia holds her breath in expectation until Aleya slightly turns her head in Jiron's direction and replies. Both Delia and Errin let go their pent up breath at the same time.

"She really does like him," Errin states.

"I know," replies Delia. "We were talking about just that thing a few days ago. He only needed to be shown the way."

"Just hope he doesn't make a mess of it," says Errin.

"Of course he will, he's a man," Delia says and then turns to Errin with a grin. "They can't help themselves."

At that they break out into soft laughter at the expense of all males everywhere.

Throughout the rest of the day they continue to push on toward Korazan. James periodically checks the surrounding area for any hostiles which may be on an intercept course. But other than the odd traveler, there doesn't appear to be anyone around. Just after their midday break to give the horses a breather, he discovers that the force they ambushed back at the road is once again on the move after them, though half a day behind. Now augmented by the foot soldiers that have caught up with them from Al-Zynn, they outnumber them by more than two to one. On the plus size, in order to keep their two forces together, they have to travel at the speed of the foot soldiers which is greatly less than a horse and thus will continue to fall further behind.

"If they get too close we'll have to slow them down again," James states.

Nodding, Illan replies, "At the rate they'll be moving, it isn't likely going to be a problem."

Occasionally their scouts report forces on the move which James readily finds once he knows where to look. They're never more than a score or two and none are heading in their direction.

By the end of the day, he's able to at last see Korazan in his mirror. Still hours away, if they travel a couple more hours by nightfall, they will be within striking distance for the following morning.

At this point, Illan begins sending out groups of eight riders whose purpose is to find and detain anyone who might raise the alarm. If they can strike with surprise in the morning they'll not lose as many men.

"There's a force of men camped on the north side of town," James tells Illan.

"How many?" he asks.

He studies the image a moment then says, "A couple hundred." He glances over to him and adds, "Most are foot soldiers."

"Good," he states. Turning to where Ceadric rides just behind them, he waves him closer. "Time to send them in."

Ceadric nods and moves further back into the column. Shortly after that two riders, wearing the regular garb of those living in the Empire, detach themselves and race for Korazan. Dressed as one of them, these two men will attempt to find out strengths and deployments before the morning's attack. James felt very fortunate to discover that several of the Raiders had a working knowledge of the Empire's tongue.

When the scouts report that Korazan lies about two hours away, Illan calls a halt. Cold rations and no fires is the order this night. No chances will be taken that might alert anyone as to their whereabouts.

While waiting for Devin to bring him his dinner, James takes out his mirror and does one final check. The force pursuing them still remains far behind and isn't looking as if they are going to catch up to them any time soon. Elsewhere it still looks like nothing else is heading their way.

"You okay?" Jiron asks as he approaches.

Looking up, James sees him carrying two plates of food, he hands one to him. Taking the offered food, he says, "Just worried."

Jiron sits on the ground opposite him. "Aren't we all?" he questions as he takes a bite. "We aren't exactly in a safe environment."

"It isn't that," he explains. "Remember when we were on the way to rescue Miko, the whole area seemed to be practically teeming with soldiers." When he sees Jiron nod he adds, "Now there doesn't appear to be anyone around. It feels like they are up to something."

"Perhaps," he says through a mouthful of food. "It could also be that most of their forces are either in Madoc or over to the east taking on the Kirkens. Keep in mind too that since I met you, you've managed to reduce the numbers of their army by quite a lot."

"Still, it just doesn't feel right," he insists. They eat in silence a moment while they each mull it over.

"What are you doing here?" Delia asks as she joins them.

"What?" asks James.

"Not you," she replies and then points to Jiron, "him."

James arcs an eyebrow at him and grins. He knows what she's talking about.

"That poor girl is sitting there all alone and here you are," she says accusingly. Turning her head, she draws Jiron's gaze over to where Aleya sits by herself. Her head turns briefly in their direction when she takes notice of them looking her way, then returns to her plate of food.

"If you don't get over there right this very minute I'm going to send Scar and Potbelly over there to keep her company," she tells him.

"Don't do that," he says as he gets to his feet. "She already has enough problems without adding them to it." With a nod to James, he leaves them and makes his way over to her.

Delia sighs after he leaves them and sits in the spot he just vacated. "I don't know what I'm going to do with that boy!" Glancing over her shoulder, she sees Jiron has taken a seat next to her and is engaging her in conversation.

James can see the smile playing across her lips as she turns back to him. "Some of us take more effort than others," he says.

"You got that right," she replies. "But I think Jiron is heading in the right direction. At least he wants to do right."

"That he does," he agrees.

Just then he sees Devin approaching. "I laid out your things over there," he says, pointing to an area near the center of the encampment.

"Thanks," James replies.

Nodding his head, he excuses himself and then makes his way over to join the rest of the recruits at their meal.

He and Delia sit there and talk about inconsequential things as the light continues to fade. Before it becomes too dark, they each say goodnight and make their way to their respective bedrolls.

As James lies down upon his he thinks about what's going to happen tomorrow and prays he thought of everything. Laying his head back, he gazes up at the stars beginning to appear in the sky above and lets his mind wander. He knows part of the reason for tackling Korazan tomorrow is in retribution for the slavers' role in the death of his best friend Dave. The other part is simply that slavery is an evil blight upon the world and one which should be every good man's duty to hinder and stop.

It takes awhile, but he's able to finally subdue the thoughts running through his mind and fall asleep.

Sitting up in the dark, he looks around, unsure of what woke him. The night is peaceful, the stars overhead giving some light with which to see. Making a quick survey of the sleeping forms around him, he realizes that he is the only one awake except for the shadow of a sentry walking the perimeter. All is as it should be but here he sits, wide awake and all traces of sleep gone which is unusual.

A soft breeze blows across the slumbering forms, ruffling his hair with a gentle caress. Taking another look around, he still fails to discover anything out of the ordinary so settles back down to sleep. That's when he notices a light emerging from an old tear in the front of his tunic. The sight of the light sends a shiver down his spine and the hairs on the back of his neck stand up.

Grabbing the chain holding the medallion bearing the Star of Morcyth, he pulls it out of his shirt. Light bathes the immediate area as it clears his collar. *This is not good!* He gets to his feet and holds aloft the medallion, turning full circle as he gazes around the camp. Light only comes from the medallion in certain circumstances, so far all of which have been bad.

Continuing to cast quick glances around the camp, he quickly moves over to where Miko lays. Kneeling down beside him, he lays a hand upon his breast and shakes him. "Miko!" he whispers urgently.

"Wha...?" Miko asks groggily until he sees the light coming from the medallion. Snapping awake, he turns his eyes on James.

"I don't know," he replies. He's about to say something else when Miko suddenly grabs him and rolls to the side.

"Attack!" he yells as he rolls with James quickly. When he comes to a stop, James is behind him and the Star of Morcyth is in his hand. "Up! We're under attack!" Holding the Star high, he gets to his feet as the Light seems to enfold the shadow.

James looks around him and sees a shadow being held at bay by the light coming from the Star. Suddenly, green light flares from the side as Brother Willim and the Hand summon their power. "James!" Brother Willim shouts, "Behind you!"

Turning, he finds another shadow almost upon him. Holding up the medallion before him, he bathes the shadow in its glow. Not nearly as effective as the Star, it slows the creature but doesn't halt its progress. He sees one of Ceadric's Raiders charge it with a sword. "Stop!" he calls to the man but the man pays him no heed. Striking out with his sword, the man attacks the shadow. When the sword comes into contact with it, the man spasms violently before falling to the ground where he lies still.

"Together!" Brother Willim orders the rest of the Hand as a greenish glow surrounds the shadow before him. Stopping in its tracks, the shadow begins to shrink in on itself as the glow surrounding it becomes more pronounced.

Lights spring up around the camp as men quickly light lanterns and torches. "Ceadric!" shouts Illan as he quickly gets over his shock.

"Sir!" replies Ceadric.

"Send out men and see if an attack is imminent," he orders.

"Yes sir!" he replies. Grabbing several men standing nearby, he begins organizing scouting parties.

The shadow before Miko also begins to shrink as the light from the Star intensifies. A ring of onlookers surrounds them as Miko and the Hand battle the shadows, both are now half their original size. For a moment the shrinking halts then all of a sudden, they wink out. As they disappear, so too does the light from the Star and the medallion. The greenish glow surrounding the Hand remains as they keep vigilant.

A blazing orb springs into life above them bathing the entire area with light. A quick look reveals no other shadows in the area. The light also reveals two lines of dead bodies, each line the path taken by one of the shadows. In their passing, they killed all they touched.

"You okay?" Illan asks as he comes to James' side.

"I think so," he says. "If it weren't for Miko's quick thinking, they may have had me."

Illan casts a quick glance to Miko and says, "Good job."

"Thank you," he replies as he begins moving toward the body of the Raider who fell when he attacked the shadow. The light from the Star flares briefly but winks out a moment later. Getting up, Miko looks to them and shakes his head, then begins moving to the nearest of the unmoving men on the ground on the off chance he can still be of help.

"This wasn't an attack on us," Jiron says.

"No," agrees Illan, "it wasn't."

The two lines of dead bodies lie in an almost straight line from the edge of the encampment. It's quite obvious that they knew who they were after and where he was.

"From this point on," Illan says, "you have a guard near you while you sleep."

"My brethren and I will be honored to have that duty," Brother Willim says.

Illan gives him a nod just as Ceadric returns.

"No one else is out there," he reports.

"Keep the men out," he tells him. "I want a revolving pattern around the camp in case more are on the way."

"What should the men do if they encounter one?" Ceadric asks.

They look to James who says, "Call for help and stay away. They are helpless where these shadows are concerned."

Nodding, Ceadric turns to begin carrying out his orders.

To the rest of the camp Illan hollers out, "Get back to sleep. It's over." When the men begin returning to their bedrolls he glances to the orb shining overhead and says to James, "Don't need that anymore."

Canceling the spell, the orb winks out. Light from dozens of lanterns continue to illuminate the area. "Weren't those things the same as we saw in Willimet?" Jiron asks.

"Exactly the same," he replies.

"They could have wiped out everyone before they were noticed," Delia says from where she joins the group.

Nodding, James replies, "Definitely a good portion if that had been their goal. But they were after me." And that's what worries him. He feels a hand on his shoulder and turns to find Brother Willim there.

"Don't worry," Brother Willim says. "Now that we know what we're up against, they'll not so easily get that close to you again."

"That's right," another of the Hand offers.

"Thank you," he says.

"We still have several hours until dawn," Illan states. "I suggest we all try to get what sleep we can." He's talking to everyone but his gaze is on James.

"Wylick!" Illan hollers.

"Yes sir," comes the reply as the tall captain approaches.

"Get a party of men and bury the dead," he says.

"Yes sir," the captain replies as he begins organizing the burial detail.

Nodding, James returns to his blankets, though after such a close call he doubts if he'll be able to sleep. Captain Wylick and his men get busy carry the dead out of camp and gather them in one area. Then they begin digging a large grave for all of them.

Brother Willim and another of the Hand remain up and as the lights from the lanterns and torches wink out, a soft green glow can be seen emanating from them as they patrol the camp. The glow gives comfort, allowing the mind to rest and sleep to come.

187 Brian S. Pratt

Chapter   Sixteen

In the early light of dawn, they make ready to get underway for their assault on Korazan. James takes out his mirror and checks on the force trailing them. Still over half a day behind, they shouldn't pose a threat. Then over to the west he brings Korazan into view. The gates of the city remain shut, a line of civilians stands outside waiting to enter.

Scrolling to the south, the road there leading to Korazan has minimal traffic, none of which is military in nature. To the north he finds two riders, each trailing a mount as they ride hell bent for Korazan.

"Illan!" James exclaims.

Coming to his side, Illan looks at the image in the mirror of the two riders. "They're going to alert Korazan of our approach. How close are they?" Widening the image, James is able to determine they are less than a half hour away from the city. "No way to catch them before they get there."

"At least they'll have little warning," offers James.

Illan nods. "There is that," he says. The two men sent into Korazan the day before have yet to report back which worries him. "Ceadric, get the men moving."

"Yes sir," he replies. "Mount up!" he hollers and the men start climbing into the saddle. When everyone is mounted and ready, he turns back to Illan and says, "Ready."

"Move 'em out," Illan says as he nudges the sides of his horse to get going. James does the same and as soon as they have taken their place at the fore, Ceadric calls for the rest to follow.

They steadily pick up the pace until the entire company is galloping toward Korazan in the hopes of arriving shortly after the ones riding to warn them. A half hour into the ride, they meet up with the two men who had gone to gather information the day before. Illan calls a brief halt while they report.

"All they have is a skeletal garrison," one man reports. "Word is the rest left several days ago and headed east."

Illan nods in understanding as the second rider adds, "A couple hundred men at arms and maybe fifty crossbowmen is all we'll have to deal with."

"Any mages?" James asks.

Shaking his head, the first rider says, "Not that we heard."

"There was one there that left with the others," the second rider explains. "But word on the street is that there isn't one now."

James glances to Illan and says, "That's good news."

"Appears your plan worked," comments Jiron. "Most likely the mage they're talking about lies dead on the road behind us."

"Let's hope so," agrees James.

"Any word about reinforcements heading to Korazan?" asks Illan.

"No," the second rider replies.

"Very good," says Illan to the two spies. "Grab a quick bite to eat, we're leaving shortly." They both give him a salute and then move back toward where the pack animals are held to get some food.

Turning back to James, Illan says, "By the time we get there, they will have little time to do more than man the walls and shut the gates."

"I'm sure they will send out riders requesting reinforcements from the nearby garrisons," Ceadric adds. "Not that they will get there in time."

"Probably," agrees Illan. "It's what I would do."

James takes out his mirror again and they gather round as he brings Korazan into focus. "The riders have arrived," he says when they find the gates closed, soldiers lining the wall facing their approach and all signs of civilians outside the walls gone.

"So it would seem," breathes Illan. They take a few moments to size up the enemy's forces as well as the slaver compound just within the eastern wall. When they are through, James puts the mirror away and they get going once again. In less than an hour the walls of Korazan come into view.

When they reach about a hundred yards from the walls, James brings them to a stop. Illan arranges their forces for the coming assault while James moves back to the pack horses and finds the bag with the crystals he needs for the attack. Removing the bag, he attaches it to his belt and returns to the front line. Dismounting, he hands the reins to Devin who stands there with spear in hand, the same spear James had given him during his first time in Trendle.

"You ready?" he asks Illan as he rejoins him at the front.

Illan nods and replies, "All set." He motions for one of the Raiders standing behind him to come forward. To James he says, "Jared can speak the Empire's tongue well."

"Alright then," he replies with a nod to Jared, "let's go." With that he and Jared step forward and begin making their way to the walls, if he figured it correctly, the slaver compound should be on the other side. As they draw closer to the walls, a shimmering field springs up around the pair. "Whatever you do, stay close," says James.

"I will," Jared assures him.

Several bolts are loosed at them before a command is hollered by someone on the wall. The bolts arc toward them and are deflected by the barrier. James hears Jared sigh with relief when the bolts fail to find their mark. "Nothing can get through to us in here," he says.

"Yeah," replies Jared, "I saw that during the battle at Lythylla. It's just unnerving seeing them flying toward you."

James brings them to a halt when they are within a dozen feet of the wall. Still no tingling indicating a mage is working magic, perhaps what the spies had said was in fact true, no mage is within the walls.

Jeers reach them from those manning the walls. The men up there see the numbers arrayed against them and know that such a force will stand little chance in breaching their defenses. James glances up at them just as a wad of spittle flies toward them and hits the barrier. "What are they saying?" he asks Jared.

"That we should go away and not to waste our lives," he says, though from the redness of his face James doubts if they're using those exact words.

"Tell them this," James says as he gazes up toward the battlements. "They are to release all the slaves in the city. Send them to us and we will leave them be."

Jared's bass voice booms forth with the message to those within the city. The men atop the battlements quiet down as the words roll forth. When he's done, there's a quiet hush for a moment before the jeering continues.

A command is given and a great vat of oil empties its contents over the side and pours over the barrier, behind it falls a flaming brand. James notices Jared about to bolt when he sees the torch falling to ignite the oil. Laying a hand on his arm, he says, "We'll be alright."

Whoosh!

The oil bursts into flame and the outer edge of the barrier becomes a roaring inferno. Inside, the temperature rises abruptly and sweat begins rolling down their faces. The oil is quickly consumed and they stand there unscathed until the fire dies down. Atop the wall, the men are no longer jeering. They stare down in awe at the fact they are still alive and untouched.

"Holler back up to them, 'So be it'," he instructs Jared. Once he has done so, James tells him to walk with him. Reaching into the pouch hanging at his hip, he pulls out one of the four glowing crystals within. He wishes he would have brought more of these but he didn't think about it when back at The Ranch. Making more is easy, but you need crystals and somewhere to drain power from. He isn't about to drain the men who came with him, he has a hard enough time grappling with the morality of doing it to his enemies let alone friends.

Tossing the crystal to the base of the wall he says, "Four." Walking along the base, he tosses down the other three crystals at twenty feet intervals. "Three." "Two." "One." After the last crystal rests by the stone wall, he turns to return back to their lines.

Bolts rain down upon them now as well as stones roughly the size of a man's head, each are easily deflected by the barrier. Breaking into a run, he and Jared race back to their lines. When they leave the range of the bolts, James cancels the barrier allowing them to make even better speed.

Ke-Pow!

The magic of the four crystals is released beneath a single section of the wall, blasting it up and out.

"Dear lord!" Ceadric breathes as he watches a section of the wall easily twenty feet wide launch itself in the air.

"Watch for falling debris!" Illan shouts and the word is passed throughout the waiting men. Most of the larger chunks fall well short, some of the smaller pieces manage to reach them and men dance aside to avoid being hit. A few either weren't fast enough or not observant and are struck by the falling debris.

The concussion of the blast knock James and Jared to their knees as it rolls past them. By the time it reaches where the others wait, it isn't nearly as forceful.

"Hedry!" Illan shouts.

"Sir!" comes the reply as Hedry rides forward.

"Take your archers and kill anything that moves," he orders.

"Yes, sir," he replies. With a command to his men, they race forward, bows in hand.

Jared is the first to regain his feet and offers a hand to James. Taking it, they both resume their run back to the lines.

"Ceadric," Illan shouts. "Take your men and begin securing the interior. After that blast there shouldn't be much left, most of their men were concentrated up on the battlements."

"Yes sir," he says. Turning to his men, Ceadric cries, "For Madoc and Black Hawk!" With a deafening roar, the Raiders charge forward.

Hedry's force has already come within range of the walls and has begun picking off anything that moves. A few bolts rain down from above but the crossbowmen up there are soon taken out. By the time Ceadric and his riders arrive, bolts are no longer falling. Hedry gives him a grin and a salute as he races past.

The dust is beginning to settle and the hole that had been blasted in the wall materializes before them. *Damn!* Ceadric thinks as he sees the depth and width of the crater the blast created. He leads his men toward it. If James had the spot right, they should be at the slave compound.

Slowing their speed, Ceadric leads his men through the opening, staying as far to the side as possible to avoid the crater's center. As they pass through the wall, the slaver compound materializes before them on the other side. Off to one side several slavers are lined up with crossbows and let loose a volley.

Three of Ceadric's men are hit and go down. "Charge!" he yells as he and the others race for their attackers. With swords drawn and war cries on their lips, they are a fearful sight.

Losing their courage, the slavers throw down their crossbows and flee across the compound to the gate leading into the city. Cheers can be heard from the slave pens as the slaves held within revel in their captors' plight.

"Secure the compound," he shouts to one of his lieutenants. When Hedry and his archers move within the walls, he has them post themselves on the inner wall surrounding the compound. While normally used to keep an eye on the slaves, the walkway will afford them a view of the surrounding city.

The *whoosh* of a passing crossbow bolt flies within inches of Ceadric's face. Scanning the area, he finds the window from which the bolt was fired and directs a squad of his men to secure it. Dismounting, the score of men break in through the door to the building and the sound of fighting can be heard coming from within.

"Walls are secure," Hedry calls from his position upon the wall of the slaver compound.

"And the city?" Ceadric hollers back.

Hedry glances over the wall then turns back. "People are fleeing for their lives but no sign of any soldiers."

"Keep me posted," he shouts back.

"What about the city?" one his men asks him.

"We were told to secure the compound," he replies. "And that's all."

"Shame," comments the man.

Just then James and Illan make their way through the hole in the wall. Jiron and the others remain on the other side to patrol the area for incoming hostile forces. Ceadric rides over to them and salutes Illan. "Area is secure."

"Good," replies Illan. "Release the slaves and gather them in the compound."

"Yes sir," he replies.

James glances around at the wreckage the destruction of the wall wrought. One of the pens had been built up against it and now a good portion of it is missing. He feels saddened by the fate of the slaves who had been held within it. All around the compound the bodies of slavers and soldiers lie strewn about. Some were killed when the wall blew, but many show signs of being cut down by Ceadric's men.

Voices ring out from the walls as the men who are fluent in the Empire's tongue begin shouting for all slaves who wish for their freedom to make their way to the slaver's compound. Whether any will heed the call is the question.

"We can't stay here too long," Illan says to James. "Another couple hours and the army from Al-Zynn will be here."

"Don't worry," James assures him, "we won't be tarrying here very long."

From the surrounding buildings, slaves begin filing into the compound's courtyard. A rider comes to a stop before Illan and says, "We found their weapons cache."

"And?" Illan questions.

"Must be a couple hundred crossbows there and several thousand bolts," he replies. "Not to mention swords and other useful items."

"Very good," Illan says nodding. "Begin taking the equipment out and set up an area where it can be distributed to the slaves. Start with the crossbows and bolts."

"Yes sir," the rider says. With a quick salute, he turns his horse and races back across the courtyard.

The city around the compound is in a state of panic. Cries and screams of people reach them as they race away from the scene of the attack. By the time the slaves have been gathered together in the courtyard of the compound, the city has grown silent as it waits to see what they will do.

Atop the walkway running the length of the wall, the men continue to shout the word for slaves who wish their freedom to come. Near the compound gates leading into the city, a squad of Ceadric's men as well as half a dozen archers, stand guard. A few slaves who heard the announcement arrive and are promptly let through to join the others.

James climbs onto one of the auction platforms with Jared by his side and faces the assembled slaves, or rather, the newly freed. Gazing across them he sees hundreds of faces gazing back; men, women, and all manner of children. He gathers his thoughts as they look up to him expectantly.

Off to one side, a pile of crossbows, swords and other such equipment is being brought forth from the storehouse. The pack horses which had carried the crossbows gathered from the last caravan they sacked are brought in as well.

"Time is short so I will get to the point," he says loudly. Pausing just long enough for Jared to translate, he continues. "We mean to fight the Empire. They've taken our lands, our people, our children and it's time they paid."

He pauses as his gaze travels the breadth of the assembled people. "We came to Korazan, not to take it, but to take you from them." A murmur ripples through the crowd as Jared translates. "Slavery is hateful. I would see every slave free and every slaver put to the sword." At that, a ragged cheer goes up.

One of the men standing in the front hollers up at him, "That's all well and good, but we aren't fighters. Seems to me most of us will die if we go with you."

"True," admits James. "I'm not about to lie to you. We are an army at war in enemy territory and it's a long way back to Madoc." Scanning the crowd, he sees many nodding their heads at that. "Should some of you wish to remain here in slavery, we won't force you to come. Anyone who wishes for the chance to be a free citizen of Madoc rather than a slave, may. What I offer is the chance for freedom. You will have to fight for it and it's quite likely we all may die before we return home."

Gesturing over to the gates leading from the compound into Korazan, he says, "If you wish not to accompany us, there's the gate." He pauses a moment. Not one person makes to move toward the gate. In the quiet of the courtyard, they hear the gate opening and many turn to see another dozen slaves enter at their chance for freedom.

"Very well," he says. "An army is even now on the way here and will be here within a couple hours." Fear comes to the eyes of many, while others have the look of those ready for a little payback. "Do not fear," he assures them. "They are not so great as to destroy us."

"You mean to fight them then?" a voice cries out.

"Yes," he replies.

"Is that why you are setting us free?" one woman hollers. "To let us be the fodder for their swords?"

Shaking his head, James replies, "No. But if you want your freedom, you'll have to fight for it." He gestures to the armament laid out on the ground and says, "Any who will fight for their freedom, see the men over there and you will be given the opportunity."

Men have already been designated to aid in the distribution of the weapons. As the freed slaves begin moving to either the crossbows or the other weapons, Raiders begin handing them out. Those who choose the crossbow are given a crossbow, a brace of bolts and are being grouped into squads of thirty. The ones able to wield the other weapons such as swords and knives are grouped together in one unit.

Once the squads are formed, they are taken from the compound and through the wall where they begin learning the rudiments of wielding a crossbow. The fighters on the other hand, most already know how to wield their weapon of choice. One young lad of about thirteen stands with a short sword in hand and despite the seriousness of his expression, appears like he's never held one before.

"Think they'll do the job?" James asks Illan. They've moved off to the side away from the hustle and bustle going on in the arming process.

"We'll see," he says. "Anyone's first battle is always the toughest. We'll know after that."

While the new additions are armed, escorted out through the hole in the wall and begin practicing, Illan sends forays into the city for some much needed supplies. In the immediate vicinity of the slaver's compound are many business which yield sufficient quantities of food, equipment and other necessities that their force requires.

Wagons are also commandeered to haul the additional supplies. Many are used strictly to carry barrels of water. Seeing as how their force will be reduced to moving at the speed of the slowest person, wagons will no longer be a hindrance.

Citizens of Korazan are seen here and there as they keep an eye on the invaders, but other than watching from a window or peering around a corner, no hostile move is made. James wonders what became of all the slavers that had been at the compound. The number of dead slavers couldn't account for half of the ones he saw here during his last visit. Gone to ground most likely until they leave.

Once word comes that the pursuing army is now less than an hour away, they begin taking their force out of Korazan and getting it into position in the field. Those unable to join in the fight remain within the slaver's courtyard. To protect them, Illan has a squad of crossbowmen and the unit of newly armed fighters remain with them in the event of an attack from the city.

The ground around Korazan is fairly flat with some scrub brush and stunted trees doing their best to survive in the dry environment. With no high ground of which to speak of, Illan forms the ranks a couple hundred yards away from town. In the center stands Jiron with his fighters, Delia and her slingers are just behind. To either side of them sit Ceadric and his raiders. The newly formed squads of crossbowmen stand behind the Raiders. In their loincloths and slave garb, they are a stark contrast to the armored riders before them. If the situation wasn't so grave, it would almost be funny. But there's nothing amusing about the determination exhibited by each of the crossbowmen. Totaling over three hundred, what they lack in skill their numbers should readily make up for.

At the fore, Illan stands beside James. "Scouts say their numbers haven't increased," he says.

"That's still twice ours though," counters James.

"Not any more," he says with a nod toward the crossbowmen. "Besides, we have you."

"There is that."

To the east a dust cloud rises from the approaching army. Delia and her slingers move to stand before the others, each carries a pouch at their hip containing two crystals. They wait as the Empire's forces continue to advance.

Several hundred yards away, the enemy army comes to a halt when they see James and the others already arrayed for battle. Trumpets sound as their force moves into position for attack. Over a thousand men-at-arms, several hundred cavalry, and ten score crossbowmen make ready their assault.

After several minutes, the army before them finally gets itself into attack formation. Then the horn sounds the attack and they begin moving. "Here they come!" Potbelly announces.

"We can see that," mutters Jorry in reply.

"Yeah," states Uther, "does he think we're blind?"

James pays little heed to the good natured bickering between them. To Delia who stands before him he says, "After you send the crystals flying, fall back."

She simply nods her head in reply, all the while keeping her eyes on the advancing army. When they've covered half the distance between them, she hollers, "Ready!"

Her slingers place their free hand on the pouch containing the crystals. When they are within a hundred yards she yells, "Now!"

Each of the slingers removes a glowing crystal from their pouch and places it in the sling's pocket. Twirling the sling rapidly over their heads for a second, they let fly their crystals toward the advancing soldiers. The crystals fly through the air and land a dozen yards before the front rank of men.

"Again!" she hollers.

Once more, her slingers remove a glowing crystal from their pouch and send it flying to land near the others. As their second crystal is released, each turns and hurries back through the soldiers behind them.

After the first crystal was removed from the pouch, James began counting down from sixty. Each of the crystals has a sixty second delay before going off. The forward line of men charging toward them comes ever closer to the crystals lying on the ground. When James reaches ten, the front line races past the crystals.

"Ready bows!" Ceadric cries out, never once taking his eyes off the enemy. Hedry's archers, as well as the newly formed crossbow units, prepare to launch their deadly missiles.

Eight.

"Fire!" commands Ceadric as hundreds of deadly projectiles are loosed.

Seven.

Men fall as the hail of deadly projectiles find their marks. An answering swarm of bolts emerges from the rear of the advancing army.

Six.

"Ready shields!" Men up and down the line raise shields to ward off the attack.

Five.

The bolts fall and many are deflected by the raised shields. Two are deflected by the shimmering shield James erects around himself to ward off the attack.

Four.

"Nerun! Wylick! Now!" commands Ceadric.

Three.

Two bands of horseman charge forward, angling to bypass the advancing men. Those enemy soldiers on the fringes alter their course to intercept.

Two.

"Fire!" comes Hedry's voice as another barrage of deadly missiles is released into the charging men. A hundred or more men fall as the missiles find their targets.

One.

The leading edge of the attack men is now no more than a dozen yards away. "Make ready!" Illan hollers as he draws his sword to meet the charge.

Crumph! Crumph! Crumph! Crumph!

Explosions erupt in the mass of charging men throwing hundreds into the air only to fall back to earth lifeless. The momentum of the attackers falters as the concussion rolls through them. Two seconds later, the second volley of crystals detonates and more men are taken out.

Knowing what was going to happen, James and the others are braced for it. No sooner than the concussion rolls by than Illan hollers "Charge!" The remaining line of horses bolts forward into the now somewhat rattled army.

"For Madoc!" riders yell as they wade into the ranks of the Empire's soldiers and the fight is joined. Hack and slash, men strike out as each side tries to kill those of the other.

James takes slugs and begins peppering enemy soldiers as they become available in the churning melee. Jiron, now on foot, is a blur as his knives dance in and out. Blocking the attack of one only to turn and sink a blade into the exposed side of another.

Another rain of bolts falls from the Empire's crossbowmen before the riders of Nerun and Wylick are among them. Riding them down, the Raiders soon halt the hail of the deadly bolts.

It isn't long before the Empire's commanders realize they aren't going to win the day. Men begin throwing their weapons down in surrender only to be cut down by Raiders. Before the battle, Illan ordered that no prisoners would be taken.

198 Shades of the Past

With a slug in hand, James watches as man after man is slaughtered rather than allowed to surrender. *What are we to do with them?* Illan's question returns to him. When he first heard that none would be spared, he came to Illan to argue the point. James quickly came to realize they didn't have the manpower to supervise possibly hundreds of prisoners on their march back to Madoc. The only other choice was to let them go, but that would mean they would have to face them again. So the order was given to allow no quarter.

It doesn't take the remainder of the Empire's men long to realize surrender is not an option. Gathering his men in a tightly formed wedge formation, they set themselves to sell their lives dearly. James wonders how many more Raiders will die before the last man is slain.

A calm settles over the battlefield as the two sides face each other, one now completely surrounding the other. Easily three hundred battle hardened men now stand in a tight group as they face the inevitable. One officer stands near the center of the group, bloody sword in hand. He calls to his men, rallying their strength and attempting to keep their moral high.

Turning his back on what's about to happen, he finds Brother Willim and the rest of the Hand there behind him. "Terrible things happen when one land goes to war with another," states Brother Willim. He and the others all wear somber expressions. He turns to his brothers and says, "We have work to do."

As the Hand begins moving among the wounded, lending what aid they can, James gazes around at the fallen. A group of wounded have already begun to grow around the spot where Miko is using the Star to save what lives he can.

Behind him, the thrum of bowstrings announces the beginning of the end for the lives of many Empire soldiers. Shaking his head, he heads back to the makeshift camp on the outside of the walls and tries to ignore the cries of the dying men.

Chapter   Seventeen

During the aftermath of the fighting, Miko and the Brothers manage to save many of the fallen. The area where they healed the wounded reminded James of a scene right out of MASH as the wounded were brought to them.

Armor and weapons from the dead Empire soldiers are cleaned up as best they can be and then are given to the newly formed units of crossbowmen and fighters. By the end of the afternoon, what wounded that could be saved has been. Devin puts up James' tent so the leaders will have a place to meet to discuss their next course of action.

"What do you mean you're leaving?" exclaims a weary Miko. Exhausted and wearing a fresh clean shirt as his other had been stained beyond repair with the blood of the wounded, he gazes at James in disbelief.

"I'm taking Jiron and Jared further into the Empire while the rest of you follow Illan back to Madoc," he explains. Even though he had told them that he would be taking everyone from The Ranch with him when he split off from Illan, he came to the conclusion that a small group would travel faster without attracting as much notice.

"I'm coming too," he states very matter-of-factly.

Shaking his head, James replies, "Not this time." When he sees Miko ready to begin another tirade about coming along, he holds up his hand to forestall him. "Illan will need the Star to keep as many of his men alive before they make it back to the safety of Madoc."

"But…" he begins to say then stops.

"You are more than just the kid I found on the streets of Bearn now," James tells him as he lays a hand on his shoulders. "There are times when duty, especially duty for others, will force us to abandon our own wishes. They need you." Gazing into his eyes, James pauses a moment before adding, "I doubt if they will be able to survive to return to their families without you."

Emotions war within him from anger to helplessness as he comes to grips with what James just told him. After a prolonged silence, he at last nods his head in defeat. Patting his shoulder once again, James turns to Brother Willim who nods as well. Just before the meeting, he had explained things to the brother.

Returning his attention to the others assembled there, he says, "I've checked the surrounding countryside and it doesn't look as if any other forces are on the way. I plan on sneaking out once night has fallen when any searches done with magic will be less effective, I hope."

"Now, what's going on with Korazan itself?" he asks.

"Fairly quiet, all things considered," replies Illan. "Ceadric?" he says.

"The foraging parties we've sent into the areas surrounding the slaver compound have met little resistance," he explains. "There have been isolated incidents where bolts have been fired at us, but those are relatively few."

"Since our presence has been kept here on the east side of town, our scouts keeping an eye on the north and south road tell us that some brave souls are leaving the city and making their way to safety."

"Send Nerun and his riders to the north to halt any further people fleeing in that direction," Illan tells him. "When we leave in the morning, we'll be taking the north road. Don't want a bunch of civilians getting in our way."

"Yes sir," he says.

"Delia," James says turning to her. "There are still several dozen crystals left that you will be taking with you. Make sure no one but you touches them until it's time for their use."

"What are they?" she asks.

"Similar to the ones I used to breach the walls," he explains. To Illan he says, "You can use them to blow any bridges you come across on your way north too."

Nodding, Illan grins and says, "We'll do that."

"But won't that make it hard for you to get out of the Empire?" Miko asks, worried.

"We'll be returning another way," he replies. "With any luck we'll meet up with you by the time you reach the border."

"Still an army or two between us and Madoc," Ceadric interjects.

"True," replies Illan. "But with any luck, Lord Pytherian and the Alliance will have softened them up some before we encounter them."

"Maybe catch them between our force and his?" offers Ceadric.

"That's the plan," Illan says.

"Where are you planning on going?" Delia asks.

James looks to her for a moment and says, "Oh, just some places south of here that the Empire would hate to lose." Then to Illan he adds, "On your way north, free as many slaves as you can. They may not be able to fight well, but every bit helps."

Illan stands up and says, "We all have things to see to before we leave in the morning. I suggest we get to them." And with that the meeting breaks up. Ceadric heads out to find Nerun and have him close down the northward migration of civilians. James takes Delia to the pack horses where he separates the crystals he's planning on taking with those he's leaving for her.

Jiron on the other hand has something else on his mind. It doesn't take him long to locate Aleya, she's with other archers working to fletch arrows damaged during the battle. It took them some time but they managed to retrieve a good portion of those used.

As he approaches, the talking ceases as she and the others turn toward him. "Uh…" he begins then stops.

"Yes?" she asks when he fails to continue to talk.

"Can I see you a moment?" he asks. When she nods he adds, "In private?"

An arrow lies in her lap, the arrowhead slightly skewed from where it had struck armor. "Give me a sec," she says.

He waits patiently while she works on the arrow. Once the arrowhead is again secured firmly in the correct position, she puts it in her quiver which is propped against the pack lying next to her. As she comes to her feet, Jiron leads her away to a spot of relative privacy away from the hustle and bustle of the camp.

Coming to a halt, he turns to her and says quietly, "James and I are leaving this evening."

"What?" she asks. "I thought we were all going together?"

He takes her by the hand. "So did I," he replies. "I'm not sure exactly where James is leading us but I do know it's further into the Empire. You and the others are going to begin the journey back to Madoc."

Sadness comes to her eyes as she gazes into his. "I understand," she assures him. "You be careful."

Giving her a crooked smile he says, "I will." Pulling her close he wraps his arms around her and happily feels hers wrap around him. "I love you, you know," he whispers into her ear.

"I do know," she replies with an emotional catch in her voice. "I love you too."

Their embrace lasts for several minutes until the stillness of the moment is disturbed by James clearing his throat. They both turn to see him there a few feet away, a slightly embarrassed look upon his face. "I hate to break this up," he says, "but the sun is almost down." He glances from Aleya to Jiron and says, "We need to get ready."

Jiron nods his head. Then to Aleya he says, "Would you mind helping me?"

"Not at all," she replies. Arm in arm they walk over and begin getting Jiron's equipment ready for travel.

He, James and Jared assemble their equipment for travel and for the time being leave it inside James' tent. They will wait for the protective cover of night before they transfer their things to their horses, in case anyone is watching. Once everything is ready, they get something to eat. Jiron and Aleya go off away from the others to have some privacy while they share their meal.

"Just when things between them are improving, they are thrust apart again," comments Delia as she takes a seat on the ground near James.

"Parting is such sweet sorrow," James says dramatically.

"What?" she asks.

He grins and looks at her. "The drama club at school put on a play and that was one of the lines that sort of stuck with me."

"Oh," she says in that slightly confused manner that they all have when he talks about things from his past. Never quite understanding just what he's talking about. During the meal, he uses his mirror before it gets too dark to see if any hostile forces are on the way. Other than some patrols and scouts keeping an eye on them, there's nothing out there of any size. Illan glances at him when he's through and James gives him a shake of his head. Illan nods understanding and returns to his meal.

The sun finally sinks below the horizon before they finish their meal. Those from The Ranch gather together around the fire to have one last social time before James and the others take off. Jorry and Uther begin another of their tales. It must be the fact that James and Jiron will be heading into danger that keeps Scar and Potbelly from picking the story apart as they usually do.

When the story, which was a doozy about some underworld figure they ran afoul of and got the best of, finally ends, the stars begin to come out. "It's time," James announces as he gets to his feet.

Devin and Moyil move to help him transfer his equipment to his horse and Terrance helps Jiron. By the time they have changed into native attire and are ready, a similarly dressed Jared joins them with his horse all set for travel. James mounts and waits while Jiron says goodbye to Aleya.

A tight embrace, then a quick kiss before he swings into the saddle. "You come back to me," she tells him.

"I will," he assures her as he looks down into her eyes. "You just stay alive until I return."

"Until we meet again," Illan says as he comes forth. "Good luck."

"You too," James replies.

"Give 'em hell!" Scar says from where he and Potbelly stand with the rest of those from The Ranch.

James gives Scar a quick nod and then pats his pocket wherein two glowing crystals lie. For what he's about to do, he may need the added power. "You ready?" he asks Jiron and Jared.

Jared gives him a nod and Jiron says, "Yes."

"Alright then." Summoning the power, he casts a spell which should render him undetectable by magical means just as he had with the Fire. This was one reason that he decided to leave at night. In the event someone is keeping an eye on him, it may not be readily noticeable that he left the main force. But when they do, they will try to break through the spell shielding him, just as they had with the Fire.

He waits a moment to see if anything develops. When nothing does, he nudges his horse forward and turns to the south, Jiron and Jared follow.

"Good luck!" Delia hollers as they begin to move away from the camp.

Angling away from the walls to prevent their leaving from being noticed, they stay off the main southern road that runs along the large lake to the west. Tears of the Empress it's called and the reflection of the moon overhead off its water gives them a guide in the dark.

Jiron moves ahead of James and Jared and keeps alert for any scouts or sentries that may be in the area. James keeps just within visual range of him and slows down when he sees him come to a stop.

"What's going on?" asks Jared quietly.

"Shhh!" James says as he watches Jiron dismount from his horse. Moving further ahead, he disappears in the dark. Sitting there anxiously for several minutes, James begins to grow worried until he sees Jiron reappear in the moonlight. Mounting his horse again Jiron glances back at them, waves for them to follow, and then resumes moving ahead.

Jared glances questioningly at James but remains silent. When they reach the area just past where Jiron had stopped, they find a riderless horse standing by a motionless form on the ground. "He's good," Jared mumbles.

James nods silently in agreement as they continue to follow Jiron south. The incident with the scout isn't repeated and after little over an hour, Jiron slows down and has the others join him. "I think we're past whatever sentries and patrols were watching Korazan," he says. "Now, just where are we heading?"

"Two days to the southeast lies Ki," he replies. "According to the intelligence Lord Pytherian's agents gathered, there's a large iron mine in the mountains close to it. It's a relatively small town and doesn't have much of a garrison."

"Going to do the same thing there as you did at the island?" Jiron asks. He remembers how James had utterly destroyed the Iron Mines at Sorna when he caused a massive volcanic eruption to completely engulf the island. Intelligence gathered by Lord Pytherian said a whole chain of eruptions sprung into being and have since played merry hell with shipping in the area.

"Hardly," he says. "Going to try to collapse it, make it unusable for quite a while. If they lose the iron from there, they will only have one other mine of any size in operation or so the reports said. The other one is too far south for us to reach and have any success in making it back to Madoc again."

They ride for another hour or so before coming to where the road forks to the southeast. Skirting around the town that sits across the juncture, they move to follow the new road to the southeast.

Throughout the night, they continue to follow the road. Other than them, no one else is traveling so late in the evening. Two hours before sunup, they come across a small village straddling the road. Little more than huts with goat farms, there is at least an inn.

"We should stop here," James says when the inn comes in sight.

"Are you sure?" Jared asks. "If we're found out, it's all over."

"I doubt that will happen," Jiron says, joining the discussion.

"All you have to do is go in and get us a room," James tells Jared. "Tell them we'll send someone down in the morning to let them know when we will want breakfast sent up."

"Alright," says Jared, a trifle skeptical.

The inn has a lone lit candle in the front room. They pull up to the rail outside where James and Jiron wait while Jared goes inside. He isn't long in returning and indicates he's obtained a room. They take their horses around back to the stables. Only one horse is all there is within the stables and they have their choice of stalls. They pick three close to the entrance. Once their horses are settled in, they take all their bags with them up to their room.

As they reach the door to their room, James' orb appears. Opening the door, the light from the orb reveals a single bed. They both look at Jared. "Sorry," he says apologetically. "It was all they had."

"All they had?" responds Jiron in amazement. "The stables are nigh on empty and this place hardly seems a major stop along the road."

"It's okay," assures James as he enters through the door. Once the door shuts behind them, they stack their bags against it as an alarm.

"You take the bed," Jiron offers James.

James nods and takes a seat on the edge while the others make themselves comfortable on the floor. "It's a couple hours until dawn," he says. "When it's light enough, someone may realize I am no longer with our main force. Things could get interesting when it does."

"How will we know if they do?" Jared asks.

Jiron chuckles and says, "Believe me, we'll know."

Before getting comfortable James removes the two crystals he had in his pocket as well as another from the sack of crystals. The power stored within these three crystals will aid him to ward off detection in the event an attempt is made to locate him. Setting them on the bed next to him, he lays down.

"Good night," Jiron says from his position by the door.

"You too," replies James as the room plunges into darkness with the vanishing of the orb. Only the glow from the crystals remains.

Crack!

Jared comes awake at the noise and quickly looks around the room. The light from the rising sun is just beginning to shine through the room's window. Jiron is sitting on the bed next to James who is surrounded by a faint glow.

"What's happening?" he asks as he gets to his feet. Coming over to the bed, he discovers a glowing crystal gripped in James' right hand, another lies on the bed next to him. His other hand moves to the edge of the bed and drops a plain white crystal to the floor where it breaks into two halves.

"They're trying to locate him," whispers Jiron.

"Is he okay?"

"So long as the glow remains, he's fighting them," explains Jiron. "Keep an eye on the door, wouldn't want anyone coming in just now."

Moving to the door, Jared puts an ear to the door and listens. "No one's out there," he says.

"That's a relief," mutters Jiron.

"Why?" Jared asks as he returns to the bedside.

"You see, when mages work magic, others who are nearby can sense it," Jiron explains. Gesturing to James, he says, "This has been going on for awhile and if there had been one near, they would have been here by now."

"You mean he could attract a mage from the Empire?" he asks.

"Yes."

They watch him as he lays there and combats those seeking him. The glowing crystal in his hand gradually loses its glow until…

Crack!

…its glow completely disappears and shatters in his hand. After dropping it on the floor with the other, he takes the remaining crystal in hand and the battle continues.

"Doesn't look like much is happening," comments Jared after several more minutes.

"If they knew exactly where he was, it would be more dramatic," Jiron replies. "Now they know he's missing and are trying to punch their way through whatever deception he's got going." Turning to gaze at Jared, he continues. "Think of it like there's a pebble hidden beneath a large blanket and you have to keep poking the surface of the blanket until you discover where it is hiding. Once you locate where the pebble is, then you use all your force to tear through the blanket until you have the pebble."

"I don't understand," he says.

Jiron smiles at him and says, "I didn't either at first. But he's explained it to me often enough that I think I get what he means."

The glow from the crystal in James' hand flares as the light within begins to drop dramatically. Muscles in James' body start to twitch as he struggles against the power of those searching. His breath becomes more labored as sweat beads across his forehead.

"What should we do?" Jared asks, the sight of what's transpiring on the bed is starting to unnerve him. Battle hardened though he is, magic is an altogether different matter and has always unsettled him.

"Wait," replies Jiron as he grabs a cloth and begins dabbing the sweat from James' brow.

Suddenly, another loud *'crack'* is heard as the last crystal shatters completely. "That's not good," mutters Jiron.

Jared picks up James' sack and begins to open it thinking to get him another crystal.

"Don't!" yells Jiron as he snatches the sack from his hands. "We don't know which ones he can use. Take out the wrong ones and you could kill us both."

Gulping, Jared stares at the sack as if it contained live vipers.

A moan escapes from James and both turn their gaze to him. Sweat is now streaming down his face, breath coming in ragged gasps. It doesn't look as if he'll be able to hold on for much longer.

A cry, a massive spasming of his muscles and then he flops back down only to lie still. Whatever was going on has obviously stopped.

"Is he dead?" Jared asks in a shaky voice.

Moving closer, Jiron lays his ear to James' chest. After a brief moment, he hears the lub-dub of his heartbeat. Glancing to Jared, he says, "He's alive."

Sighing, Jared comes forward. "Thank goodness," he breathes with relief.

"Go downstairs and have them bring food and ale up to us," Jiron tells him. "When he wakes up, he'll be ravenous."

"Okay," he replies and then exits the room, closing the door behind him.

Jiron rests on the bed next to his friend, still worried about the outcome. *Did they find him or not?* Have to wait until James comes to before he finds out. Getting up, he moves to the window to keep an eye out.

High atop the Tower of the Magi, Kerith-Ayxt stops his impatient pacing as Aezyl, Mage of the Third Circle enters his tower. "Well?" he asks.

"He's nowhere to be found milord," Aezyl.

"How is that possible?" he shouts in anger.

"We do not know," the mage replies, head bowed in submission. "Twenty slaves died in the attempt, but we were unable to find him."

"Fools!" he cries as he moves across the room to the window overlooking the School of the Arcane. Not so much seeing as thinking, he tries to come to grips with Aezyl's failure. A Mage of the Third Circle is no meager practitioner of the art, but someone of great power. Few ever manage to ascend from the Second, most who try fail to survive the tests.

A rogue mage on the loose, and one who is able to counter whatever they have to throw at him. *Where did he come from?* That's an answer many would like to know. A number of Mages of the Fourth Circle have already fallen to him, and none of the others wish to challenge him.

The last three he sent to kill him were but Mages of the Second Circle, though each had great talent. They were promised ascension to the Third if they killed this mage, this was to be their test. He witnessed the battle which had taken their lives and couldn't believe the relative ease with which his mages were dealt with.

Since the disastrous battle at Lythylla when their forces were completely annihilated, he's had a mage keep a constant eye on him. It cost the life of a slave every six hours to maintain the magic necessary, but slaves he has in plenty.

Until this morning, all was going well. Then, when the sun rose over Korazan, he was gone. Black Hawk and his army were on the move along the north road, most likely heading back to Madoc. But where the mage was is anyone's guess.

"Milord?" the Mage of the Third Circle asks.

Turning back to face Aezyl, Kerith-Ayxt says, "Convene the Assembly of Masters."

"Yes milord," he says with a bow. Backing from the room, he leaves to carry out his master's command.

Once Aezyl has left the room, Kerith-Ayxt says a word of power and a wall disappears revealing a room on the other side. Moving into the room, he crosses over to the far wall where several shelves are lined with aged tomes. Removing one extremely old tome whose cover was made from the skin of a king, or so the story goes, he places it on the small table beneath the shelves.

Sitting down, he creates light with a thought and takes great care when he opens the fragile tome. Yellowed pages that have survived millenniums turn slowly under his fingers until he finds what he's looking for.

Aekion, the Seeker. A powerful being from the plane of fire that has done the bidding of the High Lord Magus in the past, though not during the reign of Kerith-Ayxt. His predecessor had told him the tale of the last time the Seeker had been summoned centuries past to deal with a grievous threat to the Empire.

The summoning of such is not without its risks and never to be undertaken except in the direst of need. While the Assembly of Masters gathers in the Great Hall, he commits to memory the words and gestures of the spell. Even the smallest slip and the summoner will be taken as Aekion returns from whence he came.

He studies the passage until the bell tolls signifying that the Assembly of Masters have gathered in the Great Hall. Closing the book, he returns it to the shelf and then leaves the room. Speaking the word of power once again, the wall materializes.

He makes his way down to the bottom of the tower and crosses the courtyard to where the Great Hall lies on the far side. The summoning of Aekion takes three days. First the Hall must be prepared to hold him. Second, the plane of fire is accessed and a way created for Aekion to pass through. Lastly, the summoning of Aekion.

Each task takes its toll from the summoner and he must rest between each. For to attempt to summon Aekion in a tired or weakened state would surely mean the death of the summoner.

Entering through the massive door, he finds the masters and those of the Fourth Circle who are about to attempt to become full masters assembled. His footsteps echo through the massive rotunda as he passes through their ranks to the center of the Hall. Coming to rest on the Sigil of Power, he turns to the assembled mages and says, "We have work to do."

Chapter   Eighteen

Regaining consciousness with one dilly of a headache, James shields his eyes from the light coming in through the window. The palm of his right hand is bandaged and aches.

"You okay?" Jiron asks as he comes forward from across the room.

James turns his head and sees him approaching. Upon the table in their room are stacked several plates of food as well as a pitcher and three mugs. "A little thirsty," he says, his voice rasping slightly.

Jared takes one of the mugs and fills it with ale from the pitcher. Bringing it over, he hands it to him.

Taking the mug, he props himself up against the wall at the head of the bed and takes a sip. "Ahhhh," he says after downing the entire mugful of ale. He hands the mug back to Jared and says, "Thanks."

"You're welcome," he replies. Filling the mug once more with ale, he hands it back to James. This time, he drinks it more slowly.

"You had us worried there for awhile," Jiron says with a grin.

"I was too," he admits. After taking another swallow of ale he adds, "I don't think they found me. I couldn't believe the power that was being used though. It was massive. If they would have narrowed their search down any further, I couldn't have held them off."

"Feel up to traveling?" Jared asks.

"Worried about being found out?" Jiron asks him.

"A little," he replies. "I've already had several people ask about you two. One person heard you moaning."

"What did you tell them?" asks James.

"That you're sick," he tells him.

"We'll need some sort of cover story that's believable," he says as he thinks about it. Getting up off the bed, he wobbles over to the table where he starts in on the food.

"Eat what you want," offers Jiron. "We already have."

"Thanks," he says through a mouthful of bread.

Jiron comes up with the idea of posing as merchants again but James shakes his head. "What would we use for wagons? Goods? Not to mention a letter of travel. No, we need something that will prevent anyone from asking any questions."

"Like what?" Jared asks.

"Like this," he says. Reaching into the pouch attached to his belt, he pulls out a necklace with a medallion attached to it. Upon the medallion are three dots forming the ends of a triangle with lines running between them, yet not touching.

Jiron recognizes the necklace James found on the body of a dead priest in the underground temple they discovered on their way back from Saragon. The symbol is that of the warrior priests who worship Dmon-Li. Nodding, he says, "That might do it."

"What does it mean?" asks Jared as he stares at the necklace hanging from James' hands.

"It means that I am a servant of Dmon-Li," he says. "On business for the temple."

"Isn't that sort of dangerous?" he says. Then pointing to the necklace he adds, "I mean, what if the wrong person should see that."

"Let's hope that doesn't happen," Jiron comments.

James swallows a bite of chicken and turns to Jared. "Go down and get the horses ready. We shouldn't tarry here too long."

Jared glances to Jiron.

"Are you going to be able to ride?" Jiron asks. He remembers the other times when James had to be tied to the saddle after a magical effort such as he just underwent.

"I'm not feeling that bad," he replies.

Jiron nods for him to go ahead and Jared leaves to get the horses ready.

Once Jared leaves, James holds up his bandaged hand and looks questioningly to Jiron.

"One of your crystals shattered in your hand," he explains. "I think at the end when you began spasming was when it was cut."

"Oh." He finishes his meal in short order and then gets to his feet. "Shall we?" he asks.

"May as well," Jiron replies.

They leave the room but not before giving it a once over to make sure they didn't leave anything behind. That's something his grandparents always instilled in him whenever they went anywhere. When the car was packed with everything from the hotel room, James was given the chore of returning one last time to check for anything left behind. Once in awhile his grandfather would leave something of James' hidden in the room just to see if he was actually looking.

They reach the stairs and are halfway down when a man who may have been the proprietor meets them halfway up and asks a question. James feigns feeling unwell and Jiron simply shrugs as they continue on past. The proprietor continues to give them a puzzled expression even after they reached the bottom of the stairs and begin heading for the door.

"Wonder what he was trying to say?" asks Jiron as they hurry across the courtyard to the stables.

"Who knows?" responds Jiron. "Maybe just asking how you were doing."

"Maybe," he agrees.

At the stables they find Jared having already saddled their horses. It takes little time to secure their packs behind the saddles. Once they're ready they waste no time in mounting and returning to the road.

When the small goat town is behind them, Jared says, "Several people asked if I had any word about what's going on at Korazan. It appears word has already spread that something is going on there."

"What did you tell them?" asks James.

"Just that we came the other way around the southern tip of the lake and didn't pass by Korazan," he explains. "And that we heard a large force had seized Korazan and were executing all the civilians."

"Why did you tell them that?" James exclaims turning on him.

"Give them something to talk about among themselves and they won't bother you anymore," he relies. "It worked too."

"Great," sighs James.

Jiron chuckles beside him. "Don't worry about it," he says. "By the time we're done the tales will be spreading far and wide, none even close to the truth."

"I suppose so," he says with a sigh. They ride on in silence for awhile. After mulling it over, he turns to Jared and says, "From now on, stick to the truth, okay?"

Shrugging, he says, "Sure. I didn't mean anything by it."

"I know. But either stick to the facts or stay quiet," he states. "I don't want any more wild rumors circulating about me and my doings than can be helped." He stares into his eyes until he nods then turns back to the road.

Just after noon, they come to a sizeable town sitting at a junction where a road running north and south crosses theirs. The town looks to be of some importance, buildings three and four stories high can be seen rising above the walls.

"Shall we go around?" Jiron asks as they approach.

"That would look suspicious," replies James. "We'll go through."

Nodding, Jiron says to Jared, "You take the lead. If anyone approaches, you deal with it and remember, we are on business of the temple."

"Right," he says as he moves ahead of the others.

Two guards are posted at the gate through which their road runs, neither one appearing to be too interested in the people passing through. They both lean against the wall as they keep an eye on the overall area, probably there more to keep order than to watch for infiltrators.

As they approach the gate area, they're forced to slow due to the number of people making their way through the gates. James' heart skips a beat when one of the guards glances directly at him, but then his eyes dart to another as they pass through to the other side.

Moving through the throng on the street, they sense a definite feeling of heightened stress and anxiety from the locals. People are a little too intense in haggling and move along the street in a more hurried manner. Here and there pockets of people are seen talking among themselves, rarely does laughter spring forth.

One thing that James notices is the relative scarcity of guards. Most towns they passed through when they played the part of merchants had many guards walking the streets. Other than the two at the gate, none other has made an appearance. *Wonder if they sent them all to deal with Illan?* If that were the case, this whole area would be a sitting duck should an army show up.

The road takes them through the heart of the city where the larger and more impressive buildings lie. Before they pass the first large structure, guards begin to appear. Here at the heart of the city is where the highest concentration of guards lies.

Many well dressed people are upon the streets in this area leading James to believe this is the city's government district. The affluent are seen coming and going from the impressive structures situated within this area.

Moving quickly but not so fast as to draw attention to themselves, they make it past the government district and reenter the city proper. Before the eastern gates are in sight, a caravan of a dozen or so wagons comes toward them from up the road.

Jiron motions for them to move to the side to give the caravan room to pass. As the first wagon comes abreast of where they have paused at the side of the road, he sees a small red flare coming from the underside of the second wagon. Casting a quick glance at James he finds him staring intently at the caravan as it passes.

Then as the last wagon rolls by, he catches sight of another flare out of the corner of his eye. *Just what is he up to?* Looking around, he searches the crowd for anyone else who may have noticed. The people on the street appear to be engrossed in whatever they are doing and none look to have taken notice. After the last wagon and guards pass, they resume their progress toward the eastern gate. Another pair of disinterested guards stands watch at the gate as they pass through.

The eastern road is much more crowded than the one on the other side, probably owing to the fact the western road leads in the general vicinity of Korazan. And with what's going on there, none wish to risk an encounter with the enemy.

Dying to ask James what he was doing but unable to do so due to the other travelers on the road, Jiron remains silent until they come to a stretch of road devoid of other travelers. Coming to ride next to his horse, Jiron asks, "What did you do back there?"

"What do you mean?" James replies innocently.

"I saw what you did with those wagons," he states.

James flashes him a grin. "Oh that. Just something I thought of back at The Ranch."

"What?" he asks.

James shakes his head and nods toward where Jared is riding. Understanding comes to Jiron that he doesn't want to talk about it in front of Jared. Nodding, he stops the questioning and turns his attention back to the road ahead.

Throughout the rest of the day whenever they ride past a caravan, whether it was going in their direction or not, Jiron would catch red flares flashing briefly beneath one, two, or sometimes even three of the wagons. He would glance to James only to receive a grin in return.

When the sun reaches the horizon and no inn has made an appearance, they decide to pull off the road and make camp. The cool of the evening is a welcoming relief from the heat of the day. Now that it's summer, the days are nigh on unbearably hot.

After they've finished eating and are sitting around the fire, the sound of a horse comes from the road. In the light from the stars overhead, they make out the silhouette of the rider coming in their direction. Jiron nods to Jared to be ready to deal with whoever is approaching.

Jared gets to his feet about the time the rider reaches the fringe of the light cast by their campfire. It's a man and doesn't look to be military in nature. He brings his horse to a halt and asks a question.

Coming forward, Jared replies to the man.

Whatever he said didn't sit too well with him, the smile that was on the man's face quickly disappears. His eyes dart to where James is sitting and then he unconsciously licks his lips in nervousness.

Jared pauses in what he was saying a moment and when nothing further is forthcoming from the man, says one final thing. Whatever he said was more than the man could take. Turning his horse around quickly, the man kicks his horse into a fast trot as he leaves their campfire.

After the man disappears in the night and the sound of his horse's hooves can no longer be heard, James asks, "What did you tell him?"

"That you were a servant of Dmon-Li," he explains with a grin. "I thought that alone would have him out of here. You see those who serve Dmon-Li are an unstable bunch to be around, never know when one will get it into his head to kill you."

"But that didn't do it?" Jiron asks.

"No." Then he chuckles as he says, "But when I told him you were on your way to give Dmon-Li a sacrifice, that was all he needed to hear."

"You know," begins Jiron. "I've been thinking."

"About what?" inquires James.

Turning to Jared, he says, "When you were talking to that rider, I began wondering what if things went bad. If it had, before you could tell us to do anything, he might have had the chance to escape and warn others."

"What are you getting at?" James asks, not sure where he's going with this.

"There may come a time when action is called for at a moment's notice," he explains. "I think it would be a good idea to come up with subtle gestures Jared could use to indicate how it is going."

"You mean like if he crosses his arm, you take out whoever it is he's talking to?" suggests James.

"Something like that, but not crossing his arms," Jiron states.

"Why?" Jared asks.

Jiron turns to him and says, "Because you cross your arms all the time, it's a habit."

Jared looks surprised, he had no idea he did it that much.

"Something else. Like say scratching your ear with your right hand."

Nodding, James says, "That would work. Maybe there would be gestures on how I should react as well. I mean, when you are talking, a stern gaze or an amused smile could give the illusion that I am understanding what's going on."

"How about my right hand for you James, left for Jiron," Jared suggests.

"Alright, but let's keep it simple." Over the next hour or so before they turn in, they work out some simple gestures Jared will use. For Jiron it's fairly simple, if he scratches behind his left ear with his left hand, he attacks and takes out who he's talking to.

For James it's a bit more complicated. A touch of the ear and he gets indignant. Running his fingers through his hair means to act amused, etc. All of these are with the right hand of course.

They practice the gestures until they turn in. Jared has the gestures down and the other two now know how to react depending on what he does.

Jiron takes the first watch with James following after for the mid watch. When he awakens James for his turn at watch, he again asks about the red flashes and the caravans.

Bringing him away from where Jared is blissfully snoring, he puts some distance between them before stopping. He casts a quick glance over to their sleeping comrade and then in a whisper says, "Back when I first began planning for this campaign, I wanted to really hurt the Empire's infrastructure. At first, I thought about taking all those from The Ranch and destroying factories, bridges, etc. But then I realized that wouldn't be feasible. There was no way the Empire would sit still and allow us to do that."

"I figured what we would be able to accomplish would be limited in nature and not do the sort of damage that I wanted. Then I started thinking about Delia and her caravan, about how they go all over. That's when I got the idea to plant seeds of destruction in the wagons of various caravans."

"What is that suppose to accomplish?" he asks. "Destroying more caravans isn't going to hurt them all that much."

"Not just the caravans, no," agrees James. "But what if those seeds of destruction would wait until they encountered certain things?"

"Like what?" Jiron questions.

"I have it so that what I planted in the wagons will continue to draw minute quantities of power from their environment and store it," he explains. "Now don't worry, the draw is so small that I seriously doubt if any passing mage would detect it. The seed will continue to grow in power until it encounters one of three things, then explode."

"The first thing is a bridge," he says, "When it detects that it's over flowing water it blows, hopefully taking out the bridge. And, when a bridge is destroyed, that avenue over the river will be gone. All caravans will have to find an alternate way across."

"And each time they do..." Jiron prompts.

"Ker-Pow!" James says dramatically. Then he glances over to the sleeping form of Jared and relaxes when another snore comes to them through the night. "Eventually, most of the ways goods are transported within the Empire will be severely handicapped."

"The second trigger will be coming into close proximity of iron, such as swords. I'm not talking about a couple hanging at the hips of guards, no. I'm talking about a company of men in armor."

"The third trigger is if the wagon comes in close proximity to live magic, or a mage who is currently working magic."

"That could take them by surprise," comments Jiron approvingly.

"I hope so," he says. "Another by product of all this is the confusion that it will bring. Bursts of power going off at different points within the Empire, none knowing just what is going on."

"Be hard to pin down exactly where you are," grins Jiron.

James grows somber as he nods. "True. The only problem I have is with the innocents that will be killed by the wagons."

"But many more will die if the Empire isn't stopped, or at least slowed down," counters Jiron. "Don't be sorrowful about what you have to do in war. Your intent is not malign in nature."

"True," replies James. "You better get some sleep. Morning isn't too far off."

"Alright," he says and then they return to the campsite where Jiron climbs into his bedroll.

James paces throughout his watch. The vision of the innocents he will kill running through his mind.

The morning dawns bright, forecasting another scorcher. They make an early start to take advantage of the coolness while they can. Far on the horizon ahead of them, mountains rise out of the desert.

"That's where we'll find Ki," states James. Looking up from a small map Lord Pytherian supplied him, he glances to Jiron. "Should be there by nightfall if we keep a steady pace."

James has felt probing attacks ever since leaving the inn as someone tries to break through and find him. It doesn't feel as if whoever is doing the probing is all that serious in finding him though. More like just checking on the off chance that the shielding cover is no longer there. The fact that they haven't tried to punch through since the first time has him a little worried.

They continue to make good time as they ride along the road. Traffic here is steady but not heavy. Whenever they encounter a caravan, James continues to plant the seeds beneath the wagon beds. By the time the sun begins its descent to the horizon, he's managed to plant more than two dozen in different caravans.

Late in the afternoon, another caravan approaches them and they move to the side of the road to let them pass. Just as he had with others, he plants a seed in the second wagon. The wagon rolls on for half a minute before he feels a minute tingling sensation. A cry comes from behind and he turns to find the wagon's bottom has broken out and iron ingots are spilling through the bottom.

Jiron glances at him and he jerks his head indicating they should get out of there fast. Moving quickly, they leave the merchants to the mystery as to what happened to their wagon.

Once they've moved far enough along, Jiron rides close and whispers so Jared will not overhear him. "What happened?"

"It was the iron in the ingots the wagon was carrying," he explains.

"But I thought you said it would explode," says Jiron.

"It did," James replies. "The spell didn't have time to gather much power. When it gathered enough to begin seeking evidence that would trigger it, it encountered the iron. So it blew. But since it didn't have time to accumulate very much power, all it managed to do was break the boards lining the bottom of the wagon."

"Not very effective," observes Jiron.

"I couldn't make it gather power any quicker or those it was gathering from would sense something not right," he explains. "Not to mention that any mage in the area would be sure to detect what was going on as well."

"I see," Jiron tells him. "Just be more selective about which caravans you do."

"Right," agrees James with a grin.

Directly ahead of them to the southeast, the mountain range that has been steadily growing all day is now rising high in the sky. Somewhere at its base lies Ki. Another hour finds them at a crossroads where their road ends at another moving north and south along the base of the mountains. Checking his map, James indicates they should take the branch to the south.

Turning onto it, they continue until the road ends at another going east and west. Here they turn to the east and it isn't long before the road winds its way to the small town of Ki.

"Let's get a room and then do a little reconnoitering," suggest Jiron.

"I'm for that," agrees Jared.

Ki, as it turns out, isn't really much of anything. On one side of town lies a complex with many smelters belching black smoke into the air. The rest is just a smattering of homes and a lone two story building sitting at the edge of town with a sign outside depicting an iron ingot.

"Is this the inn?" James asks indicating the two story structure.

No other building in town even looks close to being an inn. They have Jared go inside to see about a room while the other two wait outside. He isn't inside long before he returns with a smile on his lips. "Got the biggest room they have," he brags. "It's actually two rooms joined together and there are four beds."

"Excellent," praises James.

They make their way around back to the stables and soon have their horses settled in. A stableboy is there and produces a bucket of grain and another full of water for each. James flips him a copper as they turn to head for the inn. Their room lies on the second floor at the end of the hall.

Just as Jared said, the room is actually two. The first room off the hall contains two small beds, a table and two chairs, as well as a dresser. To one side is another door leading into a much larger room.

With two large beds, a larger table, wardrobe and dresser, it's about half again the size of the first room. The feature of the second room that perks James up is the bathtub setting near one wall.

"Alright!" he exclaims when he sees it. Suddenly his whole body begins to feel dirty and the itchiness of his scalp magnifies tenfold. "Jiron you stay in here with me," he announces. "Jared, you get the outer room all to yourself."

"Fine by me," he says, pleased.

"Go down and see about arranging for dinner to be brought up and a bath afterwards," he tells Jared as he sets his bag of crystals on the floor by his bed.

"Yes sir," he says and leaves the room.

Laying down, James sinks into luxurious comfort. "Wonder how much this is costing us?" he muses.

"Don't know," replies Jiron as he sits on the other bed. When he feels the softness, he lies down too and adds, "But it's worth it."

"Ain't it though," sighs James.

"I'm rather surprised to find a room such as this here in a town like Ki," Jiron says. "An outer room for servants and a bath here in the main room just seems odd."

Shrugging, James replies, "I don't care why, just glad it's here." They lay there for a few more minutes until Jared returns.

"They'll have it up in a few minutes," he tells them. "The proprietor said to let them know when you want the bath."

"Thanks," says James. "When the food arrives, have them bring it in here and we'll eat together. It's the only table large enough for the three of us."

"Very well," replies Jared as he returns to the outer room and leaves them alone.

Ten minutes later James is snapped awake when Jared and the servers from the inn come in with their dinner. Roast beef, tubers and two loaves of bread make a mouthwatering aroma. Getting up, he makes his way over to the table where dinner is being laid out.

As soon as the servers have everything on the table they make a hasty retreat and shut the door behind them. Jiron notices their quick exit and asks Jared, "What did you tell them?"

Gesturing to James he grins and says, "That his lordship there is a servant of Dmon-Li."

"Lordship?" asks James.

"Added that," he admits. "People act differently when they think they're dealing with royalty or someone of importance."

"Indeed," adds Jiron as he gives himself a heaping portion of the roast beef.

They eat in silence as each savors the succulent meat and the fresh baked bread. Once they are done, Jared is sent down for servers to come and retrieve the dirty dishes. He also arranges for the bath to be filled at the same time.

"You should stay here while Jared and I take a look around," suggests Jiron.

"But what if someone comes or one of the servers asks me something," he counters. "What am I to do then?"

"Don't worry," assures Jared. "I'll make sure they leave you alone."

A knock comes to them from the outer door and Jared leaves the room to answer it. Several lads are there with buckets of steaming hot water. After dumping them in the bathtub, they each take some of the dirty dishes with them as they leave. Another two lads enter after the others have left and begin doing the same, one of whom brings in a cake of soap and a couple towels.

Once they have the bath sufficiently filled, James removes his clothes and gingerly enters the steaming water. In no time at all, he's lounging back with all but his head submerged under the water. He closes his eyes and begins to feel the tension and stress melt away.

"We'll be back," whispers Jiron to him as he grabs Jared and leaves the room.

On their way down the stairs to the common room, they come across one of the servers on his way up with a bucket of water. Jared lays a hand on his arm and tells him something. The lad gives him a nod, turns around and hurries back down the stairs.

When they leave the inn, Jiron asks, "What did you say to him?"

Jared flashes him an amused grin and says, "Only that his lordship is relaxing and it would be unwise to disturb him. Also that the last one who did was invited to 'attend' a service at the temple. I doubt if anyone will so much as go near the door while we're gone."

Laughing, Jiron claps him on the back and they head down the street.

With the mountains to the west, the streets of Ki grow dark quickly. They wander from one end of town to another, finally finding a road that will take them up into the mountains. Deciding this is the most likely place for the mine to be, they follow it.

As they leave the town behind, the ground begins to rise as the road makes its way up the side of the mountain. About the time the lights from Ki disappear around a bend, the sound of a wagon is heard coming toward them from up ahead.

Moving off the road a ways, they wait in the shadows as it draws near. It's actually two wagons full of ore coming from the mine, which tells them they are on the right road. They wait until the wagons pass and are further down the mountain before returning to the road.

The road continues on and finally works its way into a box canyon. They slow when lights appear coming from up ahead. A tall wooden wall, similar in nature to what James and Jiron found surrounding the mine on the island, blocks off the canyon from one side to the other. The road continues straight toward it and passes through a gate.

The wall itself is easily twenty foot high and guards carrying crossbows can be seen walking along the top. Jiron pulls Jared to the side where they crouch and watch for several minutes.

"How are we going to get in there?" Jared asks.

"We're not," he explains. "We'll stay here a little while longer then return to let James know what we found."

They settle in and wait for over half an hour. When nothing develops, Jiron indicates it's time for them to return.

Chapter   Nineteen

Back at the inn they find James asleep in the bathtub. A single candle is all but burnt down to nothing on a nearby table. "Go ahead and get some sleep," Jiron tells Jared. "I'll take care of this."

Grinning, Jared nods his head and backs out of the room, closing the door behind him.

Coming over to James, he can't help but allow a chuckle to escape. At first he was going to startle him awake but changed his mind at the last moment. He places his hand upon James' shoulder and gives it a gentle shake. "Wake up," he says softly.

Startled out of sleep, James sits up abruptly in the tub, splashing some of the now cold water onto the floor. Looking behind him he sees Jiron standing there. "You're back!" he exclaims.

"Here," Jiron says as he hands him the towel that was sitting next to the tub.

"Thanks." Taking the towel, he gets out of the tub and proceeds to dry himself off. "So what did you find out?"

"The mines are a couple hours from town," Jiron explains. "It's situated at the end of a box canyon."

"A canyon?" he asks.

"Yeah. A wooden fence, similar to the one back on the island where we rescued Miko and Nate, blocks the entrance. There's but a single gate and guards patrol the top."

Nodding, James continues getting ready for bed. "Did you get a look inside?"

"No," he replies shaking his head. "No chance for that. We waited and watched for awhile but nothing happened, then we came back."

Finished getting ready for bed, he lies back on top of the covers and mulls over what Jiron just told him. "Tomorrow afternoon I'd like to go up there and have a look around if you think we can avoid being noticed?" he finally asks.

"The road winds through some barren hills before it reaches the box canyon," Jiron explains. "Not much in the way of concealing cover but we'll see what we can do." Going over to the burning candle he snuffs it out and then crawls into his own bed. He plans on getting a good night's sleep this night. After tomorrow things are likely to be a little lively.

Back in his tower, Kerith-Ayxt stares out at the moon rising in the distance. Exhausted from the two days of preparation, he pauses here by the window for a few minutes as he looks out over the Great Hall.

All the safeguards have been set and the way is prepared. The only thing left is the actual summoning of Aekion. When he told the Assembly of Masters his plan to summon Aekion, few knew what he was talking about. But those who did spoke out against it for they understood the risks involved with such a hazardous undertaking.

He allowed them to speak their minds then said they were to undertake this for the good of the Empire. At that they grew silent, none would speak against an action the High Lord Magus pronounced as good for the Empire. Things often happened to those who did.

During the sealing of the Great Hall, fifty slaves were drained of their life force to power the holding spells needed to contain Aekion. Once he is summoned, those holding spells will be all that will contain him until the spells of binding are put into effect.

Another hundred slaves were used in preparing the way for Aekion to pass from his plane to here. With but two of the three stages accomplished, they have less than half of their slaves remaining. He had no idea when he started that he would already have used so many already. With the most dangerous and magic consuming part before him, he prays he has enough. But once started, you can't simply stop something like this.

Moving his gaze from the Great Hall, he looks out to the north where the army that took Korazan lies. Slowly but surely it's moving inexorably toward Madoc. His mages have kept a constant eye on its progress and have reported that as they reach each town along the road, they free the town's slaves and kill the slavers. At first they thought that odd until realization set in that they were arming them with arms taken from dead Empire soldiers they defeat in battle. Now they have twice the numbers they had when they left Korazan, although most are ill equipped and lack adequate training.

Armies are currently on the move from the south to deal with them, but whether they will arrive in time to prevent them from reaching Madoc is anyone's guess. The best guess is, maybe. Not only that, but as they move they destroy every bridge they come to, no matter how small.

Still further to the north, Lord Pytherian with the help of the Alliance is beginning to push their remaining forces back toward the Empire. Some reports even state that Cardri forces have been sighted among the Alliance, though those reports have yet to be substantiated. Even if they were, the Empire is no longer in a position to do anything about it.

A month ago the Empire stood on the verge of taking the rest of Madoc. Now it's in retreat back to its border. The army at Lythylla which had contained the bulk of its northern strength has been all but destroyed, an army roams at will in its northern provinces, and a mage is loose that no one seems to be able to find.

Sighing, he turns from the window and crosses the room to his bed. Tomorrow night at midnight they will summon forth Aekion and he will require all his strength for the ordeal. Lying down, the last thing that crosses his mind is the question of where the mage is and what he's up to.

Sleeping in late, James and the others don't leave the inn until well past noon. As they make their way through the inn, James puts on a grim expression like he's mulling over some unpleasant thought. One worker doesn't see them coming until they're almost upon him. When he turns and realizes how close he is to 'his lordship', his face turns pale and makes a hasty withdrawal out of their way.

Leaving the inn, Jiron leads them through town toward the road that leads up into the mountains and to the mine. Word must have spread about his being in town for as they make their way through town, those who take notice of their party quickly put distance between them.

Before they turn onto the road that leads up to the mine, Jiron notices from the corner of his eye an officious looking man exit a building on the far side of the street. When the man moves to cross to their side and looks to be heading directly for them, Jiron quickly turns into an alley between two buildings.

"What are we doing in here?" Jared asks.

Jiron gestures with his head to the man coming up behind them. Stopping, they turn to face him.

As the man nears, Jared moves in front of the others and waits for the man to speak first.

Ignoring Jared, the man looks directly at James and says a brief sentence. From the tone of his voice it sounded like a question.

Jared attempts to respond but the man barks a command and holds up his hand. Face growing grim, he glances to Jiron and raises his left hand to scratch behind his ear.

Seeing the signal, Jiron lashes out with his fist and connects with the side of the man's head knocking him unconscious. As the man begins to fall, Jiron grabs him and quickly pulls him to the side of the alley.

James scans the alley for anyone who may have witnessed it and finds the alley empty. He then looks to Jared for an explanation.

Taking his eyes from the unconscious man on the ground, he looks at James and says, "He asked what business you had here in Ki and why he wasn't told of your coming. When I tried to respond, he stopped me. He wanted to hear it from you."

"You did the right thing," states Jiron. "Now, what are we to do with him?" He glances to James and asks, "Kill him?"

"Must we?" responds James. "After tonight they'll know where I am anyway."

"If he's discovered it's what he may do before tonight that I'm worried about," argues Jiron.

"He's right," adds Jared. "He's the enemy and I think is of some importance."

Jiron begins going through his pockets and pulls out a rolled letter secured with a piece of string. Removing the string he opens it up and after a brief glance hands it to James.

James takes the letter. Unable to decipher the writing, he scans to the bottom and to the symbol inscribed there, three dots forming a pyramid with lines running between them yet not touching them.

Sighing, he hands the letter to Jared and asks, "Can you read this?"

Taking the letter, Jared looks at it and shakes his head. "No, I can only speak the language," he replies. Then his eyes widen when he see the symbol at the bottom. Looking up at James he says, "This…"

"Is the symbol of the warrior priest," he finishes. Pointing to the man on the ground he adds, "Whoever that is either is one, or works for one."

"Most likely an agent," guesses Jiron. "Never would have taken an actual warrior priest out so easily." Pulling a knife, he looks to James. He can see the warring emotions play across his face at the thought of killing the defenseless man.

James turns his back on Jiron and begins walking down the alley away from them. He takes four steps before hearing the man grunt as Jiron's knife sinks into his chest, puncturing his heart.

Jared helps Jiron to hide the body in a trash heap further into the alley. With any luck the body won't be discovered until they have done what they came here for and are long gone. When they are satisfied it's hidden as well as they can make it, they hurry to catch up with James.

As they reach him, Jiron pats him on the shoulder. He knows how hard it is for him when something like that has to happen, even though he understands the necessity. "Let's get to the mine and have a look around," he says. James gives him a nod and then they reach the end of the alleyway. Turning onto the street, they walk a short distance before reaching the road that will take them up into the mountains.

The road is deserted. Just as Jiron had said, there isn't much more than scrub brush and small trees, nothing in which to conceal themselves should someone approach.

"It's only about two miles or so," Jared tells him. They follow the road as it winds its way through the hills until the wall of the mine complex comes into view.

On either side of the mine, the mountains rise sheer and tall. Unlikely that anyone, especially James, would be able to scale them to enter. Off to one side lies a pile of stone from where the mountain had given away at some point in the past. James points over to it and says, "Those rocks would give us some cover while we're here." Moving over to them, they settle in behind.

While Jiron keeps an eye on the gate leading into the compound, James pulls out his mirror and brings the view of the other side of the wall into focus. Guards patrol the wall as well as the inner compound. Slaves move to and fro as they go about their duties. Many buildings, similar to those found in the complex where they rescued Miko are positioned off to one side.

At the base of the mountain at the end of the box canyon lies the mine entrance. A hundred feet wide, there are two sets of ore cart tracks upon which mule drawn ore carts are brought out of the mine. From the looks of it, one is for ore carts coming out and the other is for them to return.

The contents of one ore cart are currently being transferred by slaves into a waiting wagon. Several other empty wagons wait in line for their turn. While the ore cart is being unloaded, the mules are unhitched and then rehitched to the other side. Once the cart is empty, a switch is thrown and the tracks shift allowing the mules to pull the cart to the other track, the one upon which the carts return to the mine. Once past, the switch is thrown again and the next cart waiting in line is pulled forward.

James works the image to move into the mine but is unable to see clearly due to the lack of sufficient light. Having seen all he needs to, he puts away his mirror.

"So," begins Jiron, "will we need to get in there?"

Shaking his head, James replies, "I don't think so. Give me a minute while I check out something." Jiron nods his head as James' eyes close.

"What's he doing now?" Jared whispers to Jiron.

"I don't know," he replies. "Maybe taking a look inside the mine."

Just then the gate begins to swing open and four ore filled wagons roll through. When the last wagon passes through the gate, it again swings shut. Each wagon has a driver and a guard, neither look to be too worried about attack. By the time the wagons have rolled out of sight down the road, James comes back to them.

"There are fissures all in that mountain," he tells them. "We'll come back tonight and collapse the mine."

"Why not do it now?" Jared asks.

Before James has a chance to answer, Jiron says, "Because the mine is full of slaves and they would all be killed. At night they are taken out, makes them last longer."

"Right," agrees James.

Moving quickly they return to the road and in no time are on the outskirts of Ki. Wary at first in case the dead man has been discovered, they approach the town slowly. But when they see the people moving about in a normal manner, they relax. Going directly to the inn, they are soon back in their rooms.

"We'll leave shortly before midnight," James tells them. "Get what rest you can for it may be the last for awhile." They have a quick lunch before they turn in for a nap. James sits on the side of his bed as he gazes down at the sack of crystals he brought. Within are several more of the power crystals as well as others that have a more specific purpose. He wonders if the power stored within will be enough to enable him to maintain the spell that prevents anyone from finding him magically. When the mine goes, they'll know precisely where he is and all their power will come to bear until they find him.

Dong...Dong...Dong...

The tolling of the bell announces it's time for the Assembly of Masters to gather in the Great Hall. Kerith-Ayxt sits at the table in the secret room going over for the last time the spells needed to bind Aekion to his will. A day's rest has restored much of his strength, he will need it for what is to come.

When the bell tolls for the last time he closes the book and comes to his feet. As he leaves the secret room he says the word of power and the wall once again seals shut. He dons his ceremonial robe and then leaves his room.

Aezyl, Mage of the Third Circle, awaits him outside and walks with him as he takes the stairs down to the bottom. "Everything is ready milord," he says.

"Excellent Aezyl," he replies. In the courtyard outside the Tower of the Magi, all those not included within the Assembly of Masters have gathered, even the novices who have yet to achieve the rank of the First Circle.

As he exits the tower the assembled mages part for him, creating a way to the Great Hall. A hushed murmur runs through them as he makes his way through their ranks, for though they may not know exactly what will happen, they know it's something monumental.

Upon reaching the Great Hall he begins to climb the fourteen steps to the ornate double doors at the top. Upon reaching the tenth step, two Mages of the Second Circle who are standing before the doors open them for the Lord High Magus. Once he and Aezyl pass through the doors, the Seconds close them with a resounding thud.

All the mages gathered within the Great Hall are dressed in ceremonial robes similar to his. Light from hundreds of candles illuminates the Great Hall. In the center of the rotunda lies the Great Seal of Power, upon which a pentagram glows darkly with power.

Moving to his place at the apex of the pentagram, Kerith-Ayxt readies himself. Coming to a stop, he faces the assembled mages and says, "Let us begin."

Before they set out for the mine, James takes out his map of targets within the Empire that Lord Pytherian had supplied him with. Laying it out upon the table he indicates a town to the southwest. "Here is our next target. This town is used as a supply depot for the army," he explains. "Food, goods and weapons are brought here from all over before being sent to the armies at the front. If we can take out the storehouses and goods, it could take them some time before supplies can be sent to the front."

"Those will definitely be guarded," Jared states.

"I realize that," he says. "We'll deal with that when we get there." He then moves his finger along the road leaving that town to the west. "From there we high tail it west and cross the river here at Inziala." He stops his finger over the river town. "Once across the river we work our way north until we rejoin Illan and the others."

"Shouldn't be a problem," Jiron says. Jared gives him an odd look and he only grins in reply.

"Now, let's go down to the stable and get going," he says. "Bring everything. I seriously doubt if we will be coming back here."

"You got that right," agrees Jiron.

Leaving their room, they make it down to the stables. Outside is quite dark, the sun has been down for several hours now. Despite their attempt at being quiet, the stableboy wakes up and comes to help them in getting their horses ready for travel. When all is ready, James flips the boy another copper before they mount.

They leave the inn's courtyard and make their way through town to the road leading up to the mine. The streets are dark with only the moon overhead lighting their way. Once on the road leading to the mine, they waste no time in hurrying along.

A cool wind blowing off the mountain feels good after the heat of the day. The sound of their horses' hooves reverberates in the quiet as they proceed further up the mountain.

It doesn't seem all that long before the wall enclosing the mine complex appears before them. Torches are spaced at twenty foot intervals along the top of the wall and several guards are visible in the light.

"That's dumb," comments Jiron.

"What?" James asks.

"With those torches up there they won't be able to see much of what's on the outside," he explains. "Will ruin their night vision."

"I doubt if their greatest concern is what's on the outside," James replies.

Jiron nods in agreement.

They pull off the road a ways and leave Jared with the horses while Jiron and James work their way closer to the wall. In the darkness they are able to come fairly close without fear of the guards seeing them.

"I think this will be close enough," James says as he comes to a stop. The place he stops is a dozen or so yards from the wall and twice that from the gate. He settles down on the ground and Jiron comes to stand next to him.

At his belt is the pouch containing power crystals, similar to the ones he used when the enemy tried to locate him. He takes a few deep breaths to settle his nerves and then glances up to Jiron standing next to him. "Get me out of here if things go bad," he says.

Jiron grins. He knows what he means by bad. "Don't worry, I will," he assures him. It wouldn't be the first time he's had to carry an unconscious James to safety after he expended himself doing magic. Fortunately though, those times are becoming fewer and fewer.

Closing his eyes, James brings forth the magic and sends his senses into the mine. The mine is on a single level that extends deep within the mountain. A moment's hesitation comes when he finds slaves still within the mine, but not nearly the number that would be there during the day.

Jiron hears him sigh and asks, "What's wrong?"

"There are still slaves within the mine," he tells him.

"A lot?" he asks.

"No, just about a dozen or so," he replies.

"That going to be a problem?" he asks, afraid of the answer.

James shakes his head and then returns to what he came for. He takes his time in examining the stone encompassing the mine. What he's looking for are points where he can take advantage of unstable sections of rocks to collapse the mine.

As he searches, his mind keeps returning to the slaves still within the mine. It doesn't look as if they are doing anything, might be sleeping. From what Miko had told him of his time as a mine slave, these slaves may be undergoing punishment for one thing or another and that's why they are still in there.

Then an idea comes to him. Searching for just the right spot, he begins weakening support beams and widening cracks in an area further into the mine than where the slaves are. If he creates a cave-in, they may just run out.

After a few minutes, he can feel the rock above the tunnel shift and begin to rumble. Then suddenly, rock begins falling as the ceiling caves in. Moving his senses to the slaves, he's relived to discover they are now further toward the entrance.

When Jiron initially had returned and described the box canyon, he thought about bringing the side of the mountain down to block the mine. But then when he came and saw the complex in his mirror, he realized that if he did it would bury the entire place and kill everyone. Sometimes he wishes he was a bit less concerned with the welfare of others, sure would make life easier. But he is, so now he's trying to bring it down from the inside.

They begin to hear noise coming from the other side of the wall as the cave-in is reported. He realizes he has to work fast before more slaves and workers are sent in to clear it. Again sending his senses deep within the mountain, he works on reducing the strength of the stone.

Crews begin rushing into the mountain to begin clearing the cave-in as more tremors shake the mountain. James begins to sense sections of the mine beginning to collapse as the mountain gives out with a groan. The men who had so recently entered the mine to shore it up are now running back out.

Then what he had tried to avoid happens. A massive rumble courses through the earth as the side of the mountain gives way. With a roar like a thousand giants going into battle, rocks and trees begin to slide down the side.

Recognizing the sound from the last time James had brought the mountain down on the trail back from Saragon, he grabs him by the shoulder and jerks him to his feet. "Come on!" he yells. Propelling him before him, he gets him moving quickly back to where Jared waits with the horses.

"What's going on?" Jared yells when he sees them running toward him.

"Avalanche!" James hollers over the roar. "We got to get out of here."

Mounting quickly, they turn their horses toward the road leading down the mountain and ride like their lives depend on it.

From behind them, a belch of dust envelopes them and blinds them to the road. Coughing from the dust clouding the air, they continue racing blind down the road. A sudden flare of light and James' orb appears overhead to help them keep to the road.

When the roar of the mountain falling behind them finally grinds to a halt, they slow only slightly to prevent an accidental misstep by their horses. "Go!" James yells when Jared begins slowing down even further. "We've got to get out of here, they know where I am and will be coming."

Jared nods and then picks up speed again. The dust cloud diminishes the further away from the mine they go.

Lights appear out of the darkness ahead as citizens of Ki come to investigate what happened. Hundreds of people are hurrying up the road, those on horseback leaving those on foot behind in their haste to reach the mine. James cancels his orb and plunges them back into darkness.

"Don't stop for anything," Jiron yells to the others as the riders come near. The lead rider slows down at their approach and starts speaking to them as they fly by. The man yells something but then is left behind. Moving to the edge of the road, Jiron takes the lead as they race past worried and fearful townsfolk.

As James rides past, he can't help but see the worry and fear on the faces of many women. He knows they aren't likely to find their men alive when they get there. Sadness comes over him a moment then he swallows it down and tries to concentrate solely on keeping his horse behind Jiron and not on what he just did to these people. Riding fast in the night, they soon leave Ki behind as they race westward.

Sweat streaming down his face, Kerith-Ayxt faces Aekion where he's bound within the pentagram. Twice the height of a man, Aekion towers over the High Mage. Wreathed in flame, the heat coming from him is almost to the point of being unbearable. He can feel Aekion working against the spells holding him.

Tendrils of power come to him from the other mages within the Great Hall. Several have already fainted away from the exertion despite the power being taken from the slaves. They started with a hundred and twenty two slaves, now only forty four remain with a couple dropping every minute. And the spells that are to bind Aekion to hunt for the mage have yet to be completed.

Aekion's form shifts as he stands within the pentagram. First the shape of a man aflame, then that of a wildfire and then something even more bizarre. But Aekion always returns to the humanoid form.

Kerith-Ayxt wrestles to place spell after spell upon the creature before him. Another mage sags to the floor, and then another. *This is taking more than I thought.* The errant thought comes to him, disrupting his concentration for a split second before he banishes it. Concentrating on the task at hand, he steadily works to bind the creature.

When all but the final spell has been laid upon the creature, the power coming to him begins to diminish. Casting a glance toward where the slaves are being held, he finds there are no longer any left to supply

234 Shades of the Past

power. Panic begins to ensue as he realizes he's not going to have the power to finish what he began.

Out of desperation, he yells to the mage who had been draining the slaves, "The Novices!"

Nodding understanding, the mage rushes from the Great Hall and shortly afterwards, the flow of power is restored.

Returning to the flaming creature before him, The High Magus completes the task at hand and lays the final spell of binding upon the creature. When at last it is complete, the glow of the pentagram fades and Aekion stands free before him. If any of the spells he laid this night was not done with perfection, the creature will kill him.

What would you have of me, master?

"A mage walks the Empire," he tells it. Between them a shimmering image begins to form and then solidifies into an exact replication of the rogue mage. "Find this man and kill him."

Yes master.

The flames wreathing his body suddenly flare to twice their brilliance and then Aekion is gone. Thus begins the hunt.

Chapter   Twenty

After leaving Ki behind them, they ride for several hours after taking the southwest road out of town. Wanting to put as much distance behind them as they can, they push their horses almost to the point of exhaustion before they decide to pull off the road and make camp.

Throughout the ride, James was expecting whoever tried to find him magically several days ago to attempt it again. What he did at the mines had to have been a beacon telling anyone where he is. Why they haven't yet makes him wonder. No matter the reason, he's glad he didn't have to fend off another of their probing attacks.

Jiron tells him to sleep through the rest of the night while he and Jared take turns at watch which suits him just fine. Twice during the night, riders could be heard moving in the direction of Ki. Neither time did the riders notice their camp set back off the road.

Jared was on watch when the first band of riders appeared and woke Jiron who prevented him from waking James. "I doubt if they will even know we're here," he explains. They don't have a campfire and are not very close to the road. Sure enough, the riders went on by without even slowing.

When the sound of the riders disappears in the distance, Jiron returns to his blanket. Before settling in he tells Jared to only wake him when 'Riders slow down and approach the camp'. The second set of riders passes by during Jiron's turn at watch. Keeping an eye on them in the moonlight, he watches while they race past.

Even before dawn begins to dispel the darkness, they get underway. The short rest break they had wasn't enough, but they need to put as much distance between themselves and Ki as they can. Now that it is light, they will be much more leery of anyone approaching.

James takes out his mirror and brings the mine area into focus to see what he wrought. As the image clarifies he finds the mine complex completely gone, buried under tons of stone. The whole area is crawling with people as they search for survivors, though he seriously doubts if they'll find any.

Then he scans their immediate vicinity and finds a force of a thousand men east of them approaching Ki from the south. Whether in response to what he did there or if they were already on their way, he isn't sure.

Scrolling the image, he scans the road ahead of them and finds where their road intersects with another at a sizeable walled town. There they will need to take the road moving more westward in order to reach the next and most important area to hit.

He wasn't entirely truthful with Jiron and Jared when he told them of a storehouse and stockpiles of weapons. What he plans to hit is much bigger than that and likely to prove quite dangerous. For further to the west lies the Empire's School of the Arcane. He doesn't have any grand design to take on the mages there and kill them all, it's doubtful if he could even accomplish that.

No. What he wants to destroy is their library. Of all the things he's come to understand about making magic do what you want, is that knowledge of what you are trying to accomplish is the most important thing. He believes that taking out their library and the books contained within will greatly reduce their ability to train more mages effectively. The idea of destroying aged tomes of knowledge really bothers him however. But leaving knowledge in the hands of those who will use it to the detriment of others bothers him more.

Finished with his mirror, he returns it to his pack. "The area ahead of us looks clear," he tells the other two. "By tonight, we'll be at a crossroads where we will turn more to the west. Then another day and a half will see us to our destination."

"After that we head home?" Jared asks.

James nods. "That's right," he replies. "After that we rejoin the others and get out of the Empire as fast as we can."

"Good," says Jiron. He's been thinking about Aleya and has been missing her. The memory of her in his arms makes him want to see her again.

All that day they keep a steady pace with short stops to keep up the horses' strength. It was during one such rest in the latter part of the day when James again pulls out his mirror to check for hostiles in the area.

Not finding any, he scrolls down the road to the town ahead of them that lies at the crossroads. From the looks of it, it isn't more than an hour or so away.

As he brings the image closer to the city, the image starts turning hazy. Using more magic, he tries to overcome the distortion. Suddenly, the glass of the mirror begins to warp and the metal frame which he is grasping grows red hot.

"Damn!" he cries as he quickly throws the mirror away.

"What happened?" Jiron asks. Stopping there in the road, he turns back to find out what's going on.

"I don't know," replies James.

They look to where the mirror lies in the dirt on the side of the road. Smoke tendrils begin rising from it as the mirror and metal frame both begin to turn fluid. As the metal starts to drip, a fiery glow appears within the melted glass.

Jared gasps as a form wreathed in flames seems to rise from the glass.

"Fly!" yells James as he turns his horse and flees down the road.

The other two turn and race after him as the figure behind them continues to grow.

"What is that thing?" yells Jared.

"I don't know," replies James. Bending low against the neck of his horse, he works to make it go even faster.

A deafening roar sounds behind them as the fiery creature leaves the ground and begins to soar toward them. Even from this distance they can feel the heat radiating from it.

James lashes out with magic but the spell of force which should have knocked it backward barely fazes it. "Make for the city!" he yells to the others as he reaches into the pouch hanging at his hip and pulls out one of the power crystals.

Slowing the forward momentum of his horse slightly, he turns in the saddle and holds the crystal toward the now rather close creature of flame. "Hold!" he yells and a shimmering barrier appears around the creature.

The creature slows when it becomes trapped within the barrier and begins settling to the ground. Within the barrier it's exerting massive pressure and the power of the crystal is draining rapidly.

Tossing the crystal to the ground, James kicks his horse and races after the other two who are now a hundred yards ahead of him.

Crack!

With the shattering of the crystal, the barrier vanishes and the creature once again resumes the chase.

A crackling noise sounds behind James and he glances back to see a spear of flame flying toward him with incredible speed. Responding with magic, he manages to deflect it at the last minute, causing it to veer to the left where it strikes the ground several yards away.

Other travelers on the road see the fiery creature chasing after James and scream as they run for their lives. Wagons are abandoned as people flee into the desert for their lives.

Taking another crystal, James again cries 'Hold' as another barrier springs into being surrounding the creature. Just as before, the entrapped creature begins to sink to the ground as it fights to escape. Tossing that crystal to the ground, he slows his horse to a slow walk as he hurriedly begins to untie the sack of crystals from behind his saddle. He works the knot binding it closed furiously but only manages to cinch it tighter.

Removing his belt knife, he cuts through the leather thong just as the power crystal cracks and the barrier trapping the creature disappears. Roaring to life once more, the creature springs into the air.

James opens the sack and hunts for a specific pouch of crystals, one tied with a string dyed blue. Before he finds it, crackling noise announces another of the fiery bolts coming toward him and he again responds with magic. The bolt is deflected to the right where it impacts with an abandoned wagon.

Ka-Bam!

The wagon erupts in a fiery explosion. Out of time, James takes his last power crystal from his belt pouch and again confines the creature. As it settles again to the earth, he hunts for the pouch with the blue string.

"Aha!" he cries triumphantly when he finds it. Quickly untying the string he pulls out two crystals glowing a dark crimson. These crystals are the last of the ones he created to deal with the hell hounds, those creatures of fire sent by the followers of Dmon-Li. This creature could very well come from the same place.

Crack!

The crystal maintaining the barrier shatters and the creature is again hurtling forward. Tossing both crystals toward the creature, James unleashes the magic contained within them. Immediately, a shimmering blue field springs to life surrounding the creature. Its roar of pain can be heard as the frigidly cold barrier sears into it.

James adds his own power to that of the crystals as he fights against the power of the creature to implode the barrier and kill his attacker.

Crack!

James' unbelieving eyes flick toward where one of the crystals now lays shatters on the ground and the glow of the other is diminishing rapidly. "Damn!" he cries. He isn't going to be able to do it. Even if he drains himself to the point of unconsciousness, there's little chance of stopping this creature. He continues to use his own magic to hold the creature while he turns his horse and begins putting some distance between them.

Kicking the sides of his horse, he quickly gets it back to a gallop. Half a minute later, the remaining crystal shatters. With that, the drain on his own reserves is too great and he's forced to let the spell go. When the barrier disappears the creature again roars to life, the sound similar to that of a forest fire and the chase is on.

Jiron and Jared had come to a halt while he was facing off with the creature. But when they see he lost the battle and was in flight, they again bolt down the road.

As James races down the road, he removes the remaining crystals from his sack one at a time. These crystals contain spells he so painstakingly worked to get just right. With a thought he removes the embedded spells and quickly uses them to power barriers to slow the creature. Each one only gives him a minute or two to get further down the road before they fail. *This creature is powerful!*

Behind them in the road, a wake of burning wagons which caught fire either by the fiery bolts or by just being in close proximity with the creature, sends a billowing cloud of black smoke into the air.

Soon, the walls of the city appear before them. What safety they may afford them is questionable, but it has to be better than out here in the open.

People are fleeing in through the gates to escape the inferno roaring down the road toward them. The gates begin to swing shut before Jiron and Jared even come close. By this time, James has managed to put a hundred yards between the creature and himself. His store of powered crystals is all but exhausted, only three remain.

He comes abreast of Jiron and Jared where they have stopped near the gates. Jared is pleading with the guards on the walls to open the gate but his pleas have no effect. They are not about to take the chance of the creature entering their city.

James glances behind and finds the creature has escaped the latest barrier and is on its way. "Get back!" he yells. Removing one of the three crystals, he tosses it down to the base of the gate before moving back down the road.

Crumph!

The crystal explodes and the gate is knocked from the wall. With a groan, it tips and falls inside the walls. "Move!" he yells. A quick glance behind shows the creature gaining fast.

Racing for the gate, they bowl over several guards as they pass through. Inside the gates is mass confusion as the citizens stand in awe struck wonder at the gate now lying in the road. When James and the others race through there is little reaction other than pointing and getting out of the way. But when the fiery creature roars through the open space where the gate had stood, pandemonium erupts. People scream and flee in all directions.

They are forced to slow even though they are knocking people down left and right. Fortunately the panic is behind them, most of those ahead of them are as yet unaware of what's about to make an appearance.

"James!" yells Jiron. "Where should we go?"

"I don't know!" he cries out.

"There!" yells Jared, pointing down the road. Ahead of them is a rather large and sturdy looking building made of stone. Easily four stories in height with windows only along the upper floor, the place looks like a fortress. A single wooden door stands closed with two guards standing watch.

"That will have to do," he replies.

Without hesitation Jiron bolts forward, his horse knocking down another pedestrian. Before he reaches the guards, the fiery creature enters the street behind them. The guards pay Jiron no attention as they see the figure of flame coming toward them.

Jiron rides into one as he leaps from his horse at the other. Knife flashing as he sails into the man, he quickly takes him out. Turning quickly to face the other, he finds Jared pulling his sword out of the man's chest. Replacing his knife, he makes for the door. Finding it locked, he turns to James just as James comes forward and places his hand on the door. Releasing the magic, the door explodes inward and Jiron is the first one through. Another guard is positioned just within and two quick passes with his knives leaves the man dead on the floor.

Jared slams the door shut after James enters but it's skewed off its hinges and won't close all the way.

"This way!" Jiron yells as he runs down the hallway leading from the door.

James races behind him with Jared following close. Securing the pouch with the last two powered crystals to his belt, he tries to figure out the next course of action. A well dressed man enters the hallway in front of Jiron who knocks him aside.

The man starts yelling as they race past. Then the door they entered the building through slams open. Framed in the doorway is the fiery creature, heat radiates from its body down the corridor. The stone walls on either side of the creature begin to turn black as it makes its way into the building.

A crackle announces another of the fiery bolts coming toward them. James instantly erects a barrier behind them in the hallway and the bolt rebounds off it back to the creature. When the bolt strikes the creature it gets reabsorbed and doesn't even slow it down.

The heat in the hallway is tremendous and the temperature continues to rise.

More people enter the hallway to see what the commotion is and promptly turn around to flee when they see fire racing toward them.

Jiron comes to a very sturdy wooden door. Smashing into it with his shoulder all he manages to do is bruise his shoulder. "Damn that's a sturdy door," he says to himself. Then as he places the point of a knife in the lock he yells to James, "Can you hold it off a moment?"

"I'll try," he says. Stopping in the corridor, he says to Jared, "Go help Jiron." He then turns to face the creature and lashes out with magic. The force of the blow slows the creature only slightly but doesn't stop it. Next he encloses it in a barrier which manages to halt it but at a staggering cost of magic. His reserves are being depleted at an alarming rate.

"I can't hold it much longer," he shouts back to Jiron. Sweat running down his face, he holds the barrier despite the dots dancing in front of his eyes.

"Got it!" Jiron yells as the door swings open.

"Come on!" hollers Jared as he and Jiron race into the room.

Backing up quickly, James makes it to the open doorway. Just as he begins to pass through, a man from further down the hall yells, "Not in there!" Ignoring the man, he releases the creature and then bolts inside.

Jiron slams the door shut and throws the bar across the door to hold it secure. They are plunged into complete darkness when the door shuts. Suddenly, James' orb springs to life revealing a room containing dozens of barrels stacked across the floor and against the walls. Along every wall are shelves lines with neat stacks of tubes.

"What is this?" asks Jared. "A storeroom?"

"But why would they need such a secure storeroom?" comments Jiron. "This place looks like it's more suited for a treasure room than somewhere you store your goods."

Then suddenly there's pounding on the door as the creature tries to gain entry. "That's not going to last very long," James tells the others.

"So what are we going to do?" Jiron asks. Aside from the door through which they entered, there's no other way out.

James thinks hard to come up with a solution. Then his gaze settles on the tubes. Roughly four inches in diameter and anywhere from a foot to three feet long, they look oddly familiar. Then a memory comes to him.

"Jiron," he says, a slightly nervous edge to his voice. "Do you remember that time back in Trendle when Miko thought that woman and her guards were assassins?"

"Yeah," he says. "We still kid him about..." He comes to a stop when he realizes what James is talking about. Those tubes on the shelves look an awful lot like the ones the woman had carried with her. "Do you mean...?"

"Yes I do," he replies. He suddenly feels like Yosemite Sam in an old Buggs Bunny cartoon when he tunnels into a dark room full of dynamite and lights a match to see by. Pointing to one of the barrels, he says to Jiron, "Smash that open."

Taking out his knife, he smashes into the lid with the pommel. Breaking open the top, he knocks it to the ground and black powder spills out.

"Oh my god," breathes James as he looks around at the kegs and kegs of black powder surrounding them. Then the door begins to smolder and smoke as the heat from the creature begins to set the wood of the door on fire.

"Quick!" yells James. "Jared!" he then points to the corner of the room furthest from the door. "Move those barrels out and clear us a space."

"Right," he says and hurries to carryout the order.

"Jiron!" he yells getting his attention. "Start smashing open containers, as many as you can." With that James begins lifting the smaller kegs and smashing them on the ground.

Keg after keg they smash on the ground until a dozen keg's worth of black powder is scattered across the floor. Smoke is beginning to fill the room from the door as the smoldering increases.

"That's enough!" he yells to Jiron. "Now, everyone over in the corner." As he races to the corner, James removes one of the two remaining crystals and holds it in his hand. When all three are in the corner he has them sit on the floor. Once they are in position, he uses the power of the crystal to create a shield around them. Stronger than any shield he's ever used before, he's not really sure if it will be enough.

"Close your eyes," he says with a final glance toward the door. No sooner than he shut his eyes than the door flies open and the creature enters the room.

Ka-Boom!!!

Blinding white light sears through their closed eyelids as the fire from the creature ignites the black powder. The ground beneath them rocks violently from the explosion and even within the barrier they are tossed around.

James channels more power to the shield as the force of the blast almost rips it to shreds. He has a fleeting thought, 'Captain, the shields aren't going to hold much longer' then the concussion wave rolls past and the ground calms down.

"Dear lord," Jared breaths in awe when he finally opens his eyes. The ceiling as well as the upper three stories of the building is gone. Massive sections of stone can still be seen in the air as they fall back to the ground. A gaping hole now lies where the floor of the room had been. Even the floor upon which they sat within the barrier is now two feet lower than it had been. The shield had protected them but still the force of the blow had ripped away two feet of ground below them.

Jiron comes to his feet and turns to James. "You okay?" he asks as he offers a hand to help him up.

Taking the hand, James replies, "Sort of." Getting to his feet, he hears Jared groan as he makes it up as well.

"We need to get out of here," Jiron says.

Nodding, James indicates for him to lead the way. The only problem with climbing out of the hole is the fact that the ground is still rather hot from the explosion. Thinking of the heat, he quickly glances around for the fiery creature that had been pursuing them. "Do you see it?" he asks.

The others look around as well and Jared says, "There it is!" Pointing off through the broken remains of the bottom floor, he directs their attention to a flaming, man-shaped form lying still amidst the rubble.

Taking out his remaining crystal, James begins to head toward it.

"Let's get out of here," suggests Jared.

"I need to finish this," James tells him. "Keep an eye out."

Even as he makes his way toward the creature, he sees how flames from burning pieces of wood seem to leap toward the creature and be absorbed by it. *It's regenerating!* Knowing this may be his only chance, he uses the magic of his sole remaining crystal to encase the creature in a barrier of ice before it has a chance to regain its strength.

As soon as the barrier forms, the creature responds. Fighting against the cold searing it, it lashes out with power of its own. To his surprise, James is able to hold the barrier. Augmenting the barrier with his own power, he begins to shrink it in upon the creature.

Weakened by the blast, the creature's efforts are not nearly as effective as they were before. Though it struggles, it is unable to prevent the barrier from imploding. Inch by inch, the diameter slowly grows smaller.

Pouring more and more power into the barrier as it shrinks, James can feel the opposition within the barrier diminishing. Finally, the barrier completely implodes and the creature is no more.

Sagging with exhaustion, Jared catches him before he hits the ground and puts an arm under his for support.

Jiron glances back at them and Jared gives him a nod. Beginning to make their way out of the wreckage that once had been the Illuminator's Guild, Jiron comes to a stop. Citizens surround them as well as several of the town's guards.

None look particularly threatening and he draws his knife. "Get out of our way," he says, the threat of imminent violence in his voice.

Either due to the fact they are stunned by the destruction of the building, or having watched James destroy the creature, whatever the reason they back away and clear an avenue out.

Jiron nods with his head indicating for Jared to follow. As they walk from the rubble, the people stand in silence and watch them go. They walk steadily and surely through the ring of people and down the street. He glances back once he's past the onlookers and sees they are still watching him, some have begun to poke around the rubble.

The city itself has caught fire in several districts from the flaming debris that fell back to earth after the explosion. As they make their way further from the site of the explosion, the town becomes much more of a flurry of activity as people rush to put out the fires that threaten to consume their town.

Walking with a purpose, they arrive at an inn where Jiron leads them to the stables. He and Jared saddle three horses while James sits on a barrel and rests. "You okay?" Jiron asks while cinching on one of the saddles.

"Just tired," he replies. "I'm out of crystals."

"That's not good," comments Jiron. "Still going to hit that other place before we go?"

James sits there and thinks a moment before replying. "It's on the way out of the Empire," he tells him. "Let's see how I feel when we get there. If I'm up to it we'll take it out."

"Fair enough," he says. It takes but another minute to saddle the remaining horse then he comes to help James into the saddle. He finds a stash of water bottles which he fills and attaches to their saddles. Then once they are all mounted, they leave the stables.

Smoke rises in the air from the fires. Riding quickly through the streets, they make it to the western gate and with luck find it open with no guards. They are all busy fighting the fires.

Once through the gates, Jiron takes them off the road and cuts across the desert.

Chapter   Twenty One

"Milord!" Aezyl cries as he throws open the door to his chambers and rushes in.

Snapping awake, Kerith-Ayxt's anger flares at the gross breach of decorum, not to mention the fact that he's completely exhausted from the ordeal of summoning Aekion. With a harsh reprimand on his lips he turns eyes red and full of anger on his aide.

Before he has a chance to speak, Aezyl suddenly realizes what he just did and comes to a stop. "Forgive me my lord," he cries as he drops to his knees. "But the mage has been found!"

"What?" exclaims the High Lord Magus as he sits upright in bed. "Where?"

"Just to the southeast of us milord," replies Aezyl. "In the city of Taerin-Alith."

"Taerin-Alith?" he asks.

"Yes milord," his aide replies. "And he has vanquished Aekion!"

"Impossible!" he cries out. "You must be mistaken."

"No milord," he insists. "Inyi had the duty to search for the mage and all of a sudden the mage's protection was gone."

Getting out of bed, all thoughts of reprimanding his aide gone, he says "Tell me everything."

Aezyl then proceeds to tell him of discovering the mage in a destroyed building, the subsequent destruction of Aekion, and how the citizens of Taerin-Alith seemed to simply let him go. "Of course the city was awash in flame, most likely due to the battle between the mage and Aekion," he suggests for the reason they let him go.

"Where is he now?" the High Lord Magus asks.

"In the desert," he replies. "I think he may be coming this way."

"Here?" he asks.

"Maybe not here," his aide replies. "But the direction he's going will definitely have him pass nearby."

Pacing and thinking furiously, Kerith-Ayxt begins to formulate a plan. Turning to his aide he says, "He can't have much left in him after overcoming Aekion. Which of our masters has recovered most from the summoning?"

"Inyi has milord," he replies. "He has since been keeping an eye on the rogue mage," he replies.

"Have him take a score of the more powerful from the lower Circles and destroy the mage," he explains. "Tell him the mage is weakened and to move fast before he can recover."

"Yes, milord," says Aezyl as he comes to his feet. Giving his lord a bow, he quickly leaves to carry out his lord's command.

Defeated Aekion! Unbelievable! Kerith-Ayxt paces his chambers as he tries to come to grips with the impossible.

Shortly after leaving the town behind, James realizes his protection against magical detection is no longer in operation. Bracing for opposition, he reinstates his protective shield and waits while they ride. Immediately, he feels them try to break through but the attempt is half-hearted at best, not nearly what he experienced the time before. When it finally stops, he wonders why they didn't try more. Whatever the reason he's happy about it, confused, but happy.

Riding through the desert under the hot sun, they stay just out of visual range of the road to the south. He knows the magical school isn't more than a day down the road. It's entirely likely that they will send someone to investigate what happened back at the town.

With the light beginning to fade and James being exhausted from the battle, they move even further into the desert to find a spot to camp for the night. "Maybe you could use that mirror of yours to find a place where we could water the horses," Jiron suggests.

"Can't," he replies. "It melted when the creature of fire appeared."

"Oh yeah, right," he says, a little embarrassed for having forgot.

Before the sunlight completely disappears, a stand of trees appears to the north, the kind normally found near watering holes. Relived to have stumbled upon an oasis, they alter course and make their way quickly toward it.

Other than half a dozen of the date bearing trees, the area surrounding the water is bare. The watering hole itself is barely three feet wide and not very deep. The horses eagerly approach and are allowed to drink their fill while they lay out their bedrolls.

Once settled in and they are having a bite to eat, he tells them what they are really after in the next town. As he lays it out, Jared gets a look of disbelief while Jiron just grins.

"Are you out of your mind?" exclaims Jared when he finishes laying it out. "You are but one mage and you plan to go up against dozens, maybe hundreds?"

"I don't actually plan to fight the mages themselves unless forced to," he explains. Glancing over to Jiron he sees the expectant look of impending battle. "My plan is to get in there, destroy their library and get out fast."

"And they will simply allow you to do that?" questions Jared. "How do you plan on doing that with everyone looking for you and knowing your approximate position?"

"Haven't quite worked that out yet to tell the truth," he admits. "But take it from their point of view. Here I am in hostile territory, just having gone through a draining battle." He glances to Jiron and asks, "What would be the logical thing to do?"

"Certainly not take on a group of mages," he says with a nod. "They may not realize you know the School is even there. But once you do, the smartest course you could take would be to get as far away as possible. The last thing they will expect is for you to attack, one mage against who knows how many."

"Exactly!" declares James. Turning back to Jared he adds, "They won't expect it. Piece of cake."

"You're going to get us all killed," Jared grumbles.

"Likely," he admits. "But no guts, no glory."

"Since when have you been interested in glory?" asks Jiron with a wry grin.

James laughs and says, "I'm not. It seemed an appropriate thing to say under the circumstances." They both stare at each other and then break into laughter once again. Not sure where the laughter is coming from, maybe just giddy at still being alive.

Jared just stares at them and shakes his head.

Ka-Boom!

From the southwest a light flares in the deepening gloom of night a second before the sound of a massive explosion rolls over them.

"What was that?" Jiron exclaims as they get to their feet.

James felt the distinctive tingle of magic being performed briefly with the light of the explosion. "Magic," he says.

"Should I check it out?" Jiron asks. "It couldn't have been more than a mile or two away."

"It might be a trap to draw you out," cautions Jared.

Shaking his head, James says, "I don't think so." To Jiron he nods. "Go find out what it was but be careful."

"Right." Quickly saddling his horse, it doesn't take him long before he's mounted and ready to go. He glances to Jared and asks, "Do you have a candle?"

"A couple, why?" he replies.

"Keep one burning so I can find my way back," he explains.

"Okay," he says.

James comes to Jiron and says, "Find out and come right back."

Jiron smiles and replies, "You worry too much." Kicking his horse in the flanks, he bolts from the oasis.

Where the explosion occurred is easily found, torches and lanterns light the scene. The area of destruction looks to have been where a caravan had pulled off the road and camped for the night. Destroyed wagons, dead horses and damaged goods are strewn all over. Dozens of bodies are being gathered by those still alive.

He slows down and stops before he enters the light. Watching from the darkness, he tries to understand just what happened. Then all of a sudden he sees a robed mage appear from around one of the few wagons left untouched. The mage's robe is in tatters and stained with blood. Limping and holding one arm close, it appears as if he's in a lot of pain.

That's when he realizes many of the bodies lying across the ground are robed mages. *What the hell happened?* Unable to understand the language, he watches for several more minutes as the survivors scurry around, see to the wounded and stack the dead off to the side.

Other than that one mage, it looks as if all the others were killed in the explosion. Whatever the reason, at least there are now less to deal with when they go for the library. Finally deciding he's seen all there is to see, he turns his horse back to the desert and hurriedly returns to the others.

Jared's candle is a beacon in the night and he has little trouble in finding his way back. When he arrives, he tells the others what he saw. "It makes no sense," he states. "Could there be another mage out there who's fighting them?"

James shakes his head as a grim expression spreads across his face. "I don't think so," he replies. "You said there was a caravan there?"

"That's right. Mages and wagons..." he begins then suddenly understanding comes. "The wagons!"

Nodding, James says, "The wagons. One of them must have been doing magic and got too close."

"What does wagons have to do with it?" Jared asks.

Never having explained to him what he had done and not wanting to now, James says, "It's complicated and I don't want to get into it right now."

Jared glances from Jiron to James knowing he's the only one who doesn't know what's going on. A little hurt at not being trusted, he keeps silent.

"Must have been on their way to strike at you," suggests Jiron.

"I would think so," agrees James with a nod. "How many were there?"

"I saw over a dozen lying dead on the ground," he tells him. "One survived but he was in bad shape."

James sits and considers all that Jiron has told him. The idea with the wagons is working better than he had anticipated. Only the unexpectedness of the attack could explain the death of the mages. Had they had any warning at all, there would have been fewer killed.

"Blow out the candle and let's get some sleep," he says to Jared.

"Don't you want to get out of here?" Jared asks.

Shaking his head, James says, "No. We need the rest and I don't like the idea of wandering around this close to enemies in the dark unless I have too. We'll keep a watch and make an early start."

Jiron takes the first watch. As James settles into his blankets, he hears the soft tread of Jiron as he moves around the camp. Settling down into his blanket, he tries to relax and eventually falls asleep.

In a room adjacent to the Great Hall, several mages stand around a circular table with a mirrored surface. The master in control of the Table of Sight directs the image as he scans the wreckage. Mages he has known for years, some for decades lie dead. Two, Inyi included, were accounted among the most powerful at the School. And for them to be so easily taken out didn't bode well.

The door to the room opens as the High Lord Magus enters. Turning to face him, the master wilts slightly under the burning glare of Kerith-Ayxt.

"Inyi's gone my lord," the master says with a slight tremor in his voice.

Burning with barely controlled rage, the High Lord Magus says in a voice deceptively calm, "Show me."

Moving aside, the master makes room for Kerith-Ayxt to view the image. As the master shows his lord the faces of the dead he can feel the rage mounting in him. Finally settling the image on the lone mage who survived the blast he says, "Only Nyz survived."

"Send riders to bring him back," he orders. As one of the other mages leaves the room to carry out his orders, Kerith-Ayxt turns to the master in charge of the Table. "Find the mage."

The master licks his lips in nervousness as he turns his full attention to the Table. Sending magic into the Table, he hunts for the mage but to no avail. The image of the Table shifts and ripples but fails to reveal anything. "I am unable to milord," the mage finally admits as he halts the search.

"Slaves are due here by noon," Kerith-Ayxt states. He turns to look at the mage and says, "When they are, use them to find this mage." The tone of his voice leaves little doubt of his fate should the master fail.

"Yes milord," the master replies.

Kerith-Ayxt motions for another mage, one of the Fourth Circle, to come close. "Have the First's go in search of the mage," he says.

"Milord?" questions the Fourth.

"Have them comb the area to the south and east by horse and foot until they find him," he clarifies. "If they should find this rogue mage, have them create a beacon that we can home in on. Tell them not to attempt to take the mage on their own but to wait for others. Once we know where exactly to look it should be easy to keep an eye on him."

"Yes milord," the Fourth says as he quickly leaves the room.

Turning back to the image of his dead mages, the High Lord Magus seethes with rage.

Early the next morning when the sky is just beginning to lighten with the coming of the dawn, they set out. Same as the day before, they run parallel with the road while maintaining a discreet distance.

Jiron rides point a hundred feet ahead of James and Jared. The sun no sooner begins to crest the horizon before he makes out the silhouette of a rider almost directly ahead. The rider is sitting there staring in their direction. Jiron comes to a stop and waits for the others to join him.

Indicating the rider he asks James, "What do you make of that?"

Staring through the glare of the rising sun, he sees the rider just sitting there. "I'm not sure," he replies.

"Could he be a scout?" suggests Jared.

"Seems a little young for that," replies Jiron.

"Probably a farm lad out and about early in the morning," decides James. "Pay him no attention."

"Alright," says Jiron as he gets his horse moving.

They don't travel very far before James feels the tingling sensation of magic. "He's a mage!" he exclaims. They look and find the lad with arms raised and sitting still.

"What's he doing?" Jiron asks.

"I'm not sure but we better find out," he replies. Kicking his horse into motion he races toward the boy with the other two right behind. Seeing them charging forward, the lad turns his horse and begins racing away.

They begin to gain on the boy when from the west and north, other riders make an appearance as they angle toward the fleeing rider. "Damn!" curses James. With their position now known, it's unlikely they'll be able to make an attempt on the School's library.

More tingling is felt as the riders each summon magic. "They're all mages," James tells the others. "We better get out of here before more come." Turning his horse, he heads north.

"Are they from the School?" asks Jared as he swings in to follow.

"Have to be. Since they couldn't locate me by magic, they sent riders out to find me," he speculates.

"But they still aren't going to be able to track you though, right?" Jared asks nervously.

"They don't need to track me specifically now," he explains. "They can simply watch the stretch of desert that we are on and keep track of us that way."

"So what do we do?" Jared replies.

"Wait for dark and try to lose the watchers then," he says, though with the riders keeping an eye on them that will be hard to do. With Jiron again in the lead, they race north through the desert, all thoughts of tackling the library gone. Following behind them are five riders, each able to wield magic.

"Finally!" exclaims Kerith-Ayxt as the beacon comes to them. The master in charge of the Table soon has the desert in view where the First indicated. They see the First sitting there staring off across the desert. The master scrolls the image and soon has three riders in view.

"That's them milord," the master says.

"Excellent," breathes the High Lord Magus. Staring at the three, he's able to easily pick out the mage. To a Mage of the Fourth standing there with him he says, "Gather the Circles. We're going to ride forth and take care of this mage once and for all."

"Yes milord," the Fourth says with a bow then leaves the room.

To the master in charge of the Table he says, "I shall leave you a couple Firsts and Seconds to aid you. When the slaves come, you know what to do?"

"Yes milord," the master says with a nod, never taking his eyes off the mage's party.

Kerith-Ayxt glances one last time at the image of the riders riding hard before leaving to make ready to ride. When he had been selected to be the High Lord Magus, he thought his days of battle were behind him. Relishing the thought of again being able to wield magic in battle he hurries from the room.

The five riders continue to follow. For two hours, James, Jiron and Jared have been fleeing northward and still the five riders continue to pace them. Once they tried to turn and confront them, but they simply ran away. Apparently they are only there to keep them in sight.

At one point they stop to rest their horses while James digs a shallow hole in the desert. Within the depression, he places one of his pouches and opens it as wide as it will go. Taking out one of their few remaining water bottles, he pours the contents into the pouch.

"What is he doing?" Jared asks Jiron.

"He's trying to figure out which is the best way to go," he says. "Without his mirror, he needs a flat reflective surface to do it."

Jared keeps an eye on the five riders behind them who came to a stop when they did. He's glad all they wish to do is observe.

Once the water fills the pouch, James waits a moment for the surface to stabilize then releases the magic. Aside from the five riders behind them, there aren't a whole lot of others in the area. To the west lies a road running north and south. All that's on the road is a slave caravan heading south.

"Is there a town where we could acquire fresh horses?" Jiron asks. "We could outdistance them over time if we could."

"Let me check," he says as he returns to the image upon the water. Northward lies nothing but desert. To the west along the road a little north of the caravan sits a small town. There's an inn as well as several other businesses situated along the road.

"I think I found one," he says and then relates what he saw.

"That will work," states Jiron. "How far?"

Checking the image again, he says, "Half an hour give or take ten minutes." Carefully removing the pouch, he pours as much of the water as he can back in the water bottle. Once the pouch and water bottle are again secured behind his saddle, he mounts.

Indicating in which direction the town lies, James nods for Jiron to again take the lead. Flying across the desert they make good time, all the while the five riders remain behind them. Less than a half hour later, the town appears ahead of them.

Slowing his horse, Jiron indicates their pursuers then says, "Deal with them and I'll get us some horses."

"Very well," replies James. To Jared he says, "You stick with me."

As Jiron gallops toward the town in search of fresh horses, James and Jared turn to face the oncoming horsemen. When the riders see them halting, they slow their pace.

"Come on!" yells James as he kicks his horse into a gallop. Jared follows close behind.

Upon seeing them charging, the riders turn to flee. James summons the magic and the ground near the fleeing riders erupts in explosions. One explosion erupts under a horse and throws the rider to the ground. The remaining four riders stop and return to their fallen comrade.

Removing a slug from his belt, James launches it at the nearest rider and feels the tingle of magic as it's deflected to the side. The tingling sensation increases as the riders begin summoning magic.

James throws up a barrier around himself and Jared as a ball of fire appears and arcs toward them. "Hold still!" orders James when he sees Jared try to turn to flee.

Not heeding his command, Jared kicks his horse into a gallop and smashes into the shield. His horse rears backward and crashes into James', throwing both riders to the ground.

The barrier winks out as James hits the ground. Rolling onto his back, he sees the fireball about to strike and another barrier springs into being, cocooning him a second before it strikes.

A scream of pain is ripped from Jared's throat as the fireball slams into him. James is surrounded by fire as it envelopes his cocoon, rapidly raising the temperature within.

Lashing out with magic of his own, James blasts the fire off the barrier and gets back to his feet. Next to him lies the twitching burnt body of Jared. The flame of the fireball continues to burn him, his cries of pain echo across the desert. His eyes flash open and look pleadingly to James.

Swallowing hard, James acquiesces to his request and removes a slug from his belt. With the force of magic behind it, he throws it and ends Jared's torment. Turning back to the mages, he finds three are still on horseback while the other is on the ground seeing to the fallen rider.

Another fireball is arcing toward him and he envelopes it with a barrier, dragging it to the ground. Unleashing magic of his own, the ground begins to shake. The rider's horses begin to neigh and rear from fright. Two riders are bucked off while the third hangs on for dear life as his horse takes flight across the desert.

Suddenly, the ground beneath the remaining four mages opens up. Two immediately fall in, the others grab onto the edge and hang on. The shaking of the ground continues causing one of the remaining two to lose his grip on the edge and falls.

Magic springs to life from the four as they work to counter what he's doing. But whatever they are trying is insufficient to stop him. With a clap, the two sides of the pit slam shut upon the lads inside. The one hanging onto the lip of the opening is caught as the shutting of the hole crushes his lower half. After a moment's agony, he grows still.

Stopping the flow of magic, the ground begins to settle down. The rider whose horse bolted on him pauses several hundred yards away for only a moment then turns and races away in the desert.

Beginning to feel drained from the magical endeavors, James returns to where Jared and the horses lie dead upon the ground. Everything they had on the horses is now a charred mess. He feels bad for Jared, emotions almost getting the better of him. Putting the carnage behind him, he runs toward the town.

Before he even gets halfway there, Jiron races from between two buildings on the outskirts, the reins of two other horses held in his hands. Galloping fast, he sees James and angles toward him.

James starts to wave to him when he sees a dozen other riders emerge from between the same two buildings as had Jiron. Their angered cries reach him as they chase after Jiron.

James sighs and readies himself as Jiron and his pursuers approach.

Crumph! Crumph! Crumph!

Three explosions throw dirt and sand before the charging riders causing them to come to a brief halt.

Jiron reaches James as the dirt begins falling back to the ground. Grabbing the saddle of one, James quickly mounts.

He glances back to the scene of battle. "And where's Jared?" he asks.

"Dead," replies James.

Jiron's pursuers have halted behind the blasted earth. James creates his orb and launches it toward them.

Seeing the glowing orb flying toward them after having the earth erupt and almost kill them is more than they can stand. Three horses aren't worth tangling with a mage of such power. Turning back to town, they flee for their lives.

Once they are on their way back to town, James cancels the orb. Turning their horses westward, they quickly get to a gallop and race past the town. James fills Jiron in on what happened and how Jared came to die.

Chapter   Twenty Two

"Damn!" curses James.

"What?" asks Jiron as he walks over to where James is kneeling over a small pool of water. While Jiron was watering the horses from the spring, James had dug a hole and filled it with water to use to scan for hostiles. Looking over his shoulder, he sees over fifty horsemen riding through the desert. "So?"

"Take a closer look," James says as he moves aside to allow Jiron to take his place.

The riders whom he had first thought were soldiers turn out to be mages. He glances to James and asks, "How far away?"

"Can't be more than an hour," he figures. He lets the water's surface return to normal as he says, "I don't think I can handle that many. I took a closer look and several of them have gray hair."

"Meaning we are about to be hit by mages with experience?" he asks.

Nodding, he adds "And with power I would imagine."

"What should we do?" Jiron asks.

"I don't know," he replies. "To the north I saw some old ruins but nothing there that could even begin to protect us against them I'm afraid."

Walking over to where the horses are drinking from the spring, they quickly get back in the saddle. Jiron gets a thoughtful look and asks, "Could you raise another sandstorm? Turned out to be quite effective the last time. We could ride north and take shelter in those ruins you saw."

"Maybe," he says. "It might work if the storm could be raging when they get to it. Else they may be able to stop it before it even gets started."

"Then what are we waiting for?" he asks. Kicking his horse in the flanks he bolts away from the spring with James right on his tail.

They keep a hard pace, trading off on the spare horse to maintain the horses' strength for as long as possible. Little over an hour later, the first sign of the ruins comes into view, a single broken wall jutting straight out of the sand.

"We're getting close," comments Jiron as they pass by the broken wall. Up ahead are still more jagged walls jutting out of the sand. Most rise vertically while others leave the ground at an angle.

"Strange," breathes James as he glances at the walls around them. As they progress further into the ruins of what is beginning to appear to have once been a city, the number of walls steadily grows. Again, some of the walls are vertical while others are slanted in one direction or another.

As they pass through, they hunt for a structure that will afford them some protection against the storm James intends to summon. Several minutes after passing the first broken wall, a series of more sizeable structures appears ahead of them.

"Find us a place in which to shelter," James tells him indicating the structures ahead. Dismounting, he hands his reins to Jiron and adds, "I need to begin this storm before they come any closer."

"Right," he says. Taking the reins, he leaves James to summon the storm and makes his way further into the ruins. He passes sections of walls that once had been buildings. Some of them are practically whole with but a single wall missing or a portion of the roof. The wind begins to pick up and he glances back at James who's lost in concentration. *Take your time,* he thinks as he hurries to find shelter.

Working his way through the ruins, he comes across a stone dome rising several feet from the ground. At first thinking it was resting on the ground, he's soon to realize that most of the dome is still beneath the ground with only the uppermost section visible. That gives him a better appreciation of the scale of the buildings that used to be here. He had thought the broken walls they've come across were from the first floor of the buildings. But taking into account the dome, these walls must be what remains of the upper stories. No telling just how far down the buildings actually extend.

Finally, he comes across a building with most of the walls and good portion of the ceiling still intact. Taking the horses through the hole in the wall, he walks them over to the far side. Leaving them behind, he returns to tell James what he's found.

On his way back to James, the wind begins to pick up. Sand starts flying through the air as the wind whips it up off the ground. Pulling his shirt over his head to protect his face, he hurries through the ruins.

He finds James exactly where he left him. Eyes squinting tight to ward off the flying dust, he has a hand over his nose and mouth in an attempt to keep the sand out.

"They're fighting me!" he shouts to be heard over the wind as Jiron comes to a stop before him.

"Can you hold it?" he asks.

"I doubt it," replies James. "There are too many of them working against me."

"I found some shelter," he tells him. "I left the horses there."

Nodding, James turns to look at him. "We better get them. This storm isn't going to last much longer."

Taking him by the hand, Jiron says, "This way." As he leads him through the raging storm, the winds that had begun to whip the sand violently begin to gradually subside.

Several mages lie unconscious on the floor around the Table of Sight. The master in charge has been fighting James' control of the winds until the High Lord Magus arrives. Still an hour behind him, they had begun to be affected by the winds.

The master retains visual lock on their quarry and watches as the other man leads him through the ruins of Baerustin. When they enter the building wherein their horses were left, he sees his chance to hold them until his lord arrives.

Just then, a First Circle mage comes hurrying through the door. "The caravan is here," he announces.

"Finally," exclaims the master. "I need them now! Hurry and bring the slaves to me."

"Yes sir," the First says then backs out of the room. He runs down the corridor until he reaches the courtyard outside.

On the far side of the courtyard the porters of the caravan have already begun unloading the various goods purchased by the school. The First comes up to the caravan master and says, "You're late!"

"My apologies good master," the caravan master says humbly.

The First notices the pallor of his face. "You don't look too good," he states.

"Been feeling down last couple of days," he explains. "I think the cook used bad meat or something and made us all sick."

"Where is the cook?" he asks.

"Killed him for poisoning us," the caravan master replies. "Tossed his body somewhere back along the road."

"I need the slaves now," says the First.

"Let us untie them for you," the caravan master says as he begins to signal to his men.

Shaking his head, the First says, "Never mind that." Not willing to wait the minutes his men would take, the First uses one of the first spells he ever learned. Summoning the magic, he casts a spell of breaking to free the slaves all at once. The casting of the spell triggers the seeds of destruction which James had planted in the wagon beds a week before.

Ka-Boom! Boom! Boom!

Three massive explosions of immense proportions detonate all at once. The force of it literally takes out a third of the school and collapses the room containing the Table of Sight. Taken unawares, his concentration firmly on what he was about to do to hold James, the master at the Table doesn't react in time and is crushed by the falling stone of the ceiling. The same stone which takes his life smashes through the Table, destroying it.

Stone and rock launched into the air by the blast begins to fall on the rest of the school. Massive chunks of stone rip through roofs and cause even further damage as buildings which were already weakened by the blast are struck by the falling stone and give way.

One building of particular importance, the library, had been in close proximity to the blast when it went off. Filled with tomes older than memory, the basis for which magic works and knowledge gleaned through a millennium of research, is now nothing more than a gaping hole. Along with the rocks coming back to land, myriad pieces of paper blasted from thousands of books rain down as well.

All of a sudden, the resistance to the storm disappears. "It's stopped," James tells Jiron as they enter the building where the horses were left.

"What's stopped," asks Jiron.

"It feels like whoever was working against me isn't any more," he clarifies. Sending out the magic, he begins working the storm once more into a frenzy.

Realizing James is once again planning on staying and working the storm, Jiron has them move to the back of the room where the horses are to stay. If the storm becomes as bad as the last one James created, he wants them as far away from its effects as they can. James slips back into deep concentration as he resumes intensifying the storm.

After a half hour, the storm is now raging wildly outside. The open areas of the building allow the sand to enter and even though the force of the gale is abated by the walls of the building, still the sand stings when it strikes them. When he feels the storm has reached a point where it will continue on its own, he halts the flow of magic and settles down against one wall.

"That should take care of it," he says. Taking a water bottle, he drains it completely before setting it down.

The light from the sun is greatly reduced by the time it makes its way through the swirling dust storm outside. With but faint light with which to see, Jiron takes a closer look at the building they are in. The walls are rather plain and unadorned, parts of the floor show through the mounds of sand which has built up over the years.

"Look at this," he says when he comes to a depression in the floor by the far wall.

"What?" asks James too tired from creating the storm to want to cross the room to see.

"There are stairs here," he explains. "Choked with dirt and sand." He then tells him of the dome he found and how he believes there may be more below the surface.

With scenes of movies he's seen running through his head, he wonders what could lie below the surface. Treasure? A lost city? A thousand mummies hell bent on their destruction? In this world who knows? Intrigued, he gets to his feet and goes over to investigate.

Just then he feels the tingling of nearby magic. Stopping halfway across the floor, he cocks his head to one side as he attempts to discern from which direction it's coming. He glances to Jiron and whispers, "There's magic nearby."

All thoughts of the stairs vanish as they move to the opening and look out. Shielding their eyes from the whipping sand, they search for anyone approaching. It doesn't take them long before several men appear out of the swirling storm. Each is surrounded by a dimly illuminated shield protecting them from the storm.

"Mages?" asks Jiron.

James nods his head, never taking his eyes off the men coming their way.

The prickling and tingling of working magic gradually increases as the men draw closer. Soon, more forms are seen out there among the ruins, each encased in a protective barrier. They are fanned out in a search pattern, whenever one comes to a wall or opening, they pause a moment to inspect it before continuing on.

"We've got to get out of here," James says as he makes his way to the horses.

Jiron stops him and says, "Leave them. The horses will never survive the storm outside."

James realizes he's right. Leaving the horses, he says "Stay close." A barrier suddenly appears surrounding them both.

"Won't they sense this?" Jiron asks.

"Probably," he replies. "But I'm hoping that with all the magic they are doing themselves, they may not realize it's me until it's too late."

Approving of the boldness, Jiron gives him a grin.

"Now, let's try to get through the storm before they realize we're gone," James suggests. He then moves through the wall and starts to move in the opposite direction of the searchers.

Jiron puts a hand on his shoulder and says, "Wait a second. If they're on foot, then their horses must be left behind. How about we work our way around them and steal a couple of their horses. They would have to be kept outside the worst of the storm."

He considers the idea and nods, "Alright, we'll do it."

Altering their course, they begin working their way away from the searchers. Then after putting some distance between them, they alter their course to run perpendicular to the searchers. They keep an eye out for the telltale sign of men in barriers walking in the storm. Each time one appears, they quickly move back and alter course to avoid them.

A sudden increase in the tingling sensation stops James in his tracks when out of the storm a blinding white light appears and strikes the barrier. The shock of the impact stuns James for a moment and the barrier keeping the storm at bay disappears.

Instantly they are knocked off their feet as the wind strikes them with fierce intensity. Quickly recovering, the shield again springs up around them as another blinding white light strikes from out of the storm.

Ready for it this time, James manages to keep the barrier from failing but the draw of power from him was great.

"What's happening?" yells Jiron over the roar of the storm.

Then a form appears out of the storm. An aged man easily in his fifties strides forward. Behind him appear more men encased in protective barriers.

Kerith-Ayxt expected more of a challenge from this mage. True, the mage weakened himself by building a useless storm but he still thought this fight would be more of a challenge.

Again he sends the bolt of energy hurtling toward the two men and this time he can feel the barrier drop for a second before the mage recovers. Grinning, he continues to advance.

"Run!" yells James as the effects of the third bolt dissipates. He almost lost the barrier that time but managed to bring it back. He and Jiron turn to race into the storm and away from Kerith-Ayxt.

The tingling spikes again. He grabs Jiron and they dodge to the right, barely avoiding the bolt as it flies past. Summoning the magic, James lashes out with a wave of force of his own but Kerith-Ayxt simply brushes it aside.

Then the rest of the mages arrayed against him unleash a barrage of spells. Fire, ice, waves of force, the attacks become unrelenting until all James can do is simply concentrate on maintaining the barrier. Kerith-Ayxt conserves his power while his mages throw everything they have at the pair.

"Watch out!" yells Jiron as a massive section of wall comes flying through the air toward them. Backpedaling rapidly, they barely get out of the way before the stone slab hits the ground. Slamming into the ground with a resounding thud, the impact shakes the ground like an earthquake.

All of a sudden, the ground beneath the slab gives way and it plummets down into darkness. Jiron sees the slab fall and quickly takes hold of James. "Come on!" he yells. Jumping forward, he yanks James off his feet and they both sail into the hole.

They fall briefly in darkness before James' orb springs to life. The light illuminates the buried room seconds before they hit the ground. Seeing the floor coming up fast, they brace for impact. James hits hard and feels like he may have sprained his wrist from where he tried to cushion his landing. Jiron simply tucks and rolls, coming quickly back to his feet.

Jiron then takes a fraction of a second to survey the room and finds a doorway off to one side. Lending James a hand, he helps him up just before a blast strikes the ground where James had just lain. Running for their lives, they make the doorway just as a flaming ball of fire hurtles toward them from the opening in the ceiling.

Again the barrier flashes into being just before the fireball explodes. James falls to his knees from the drain of power, Jiron helps him back up and they move into the hallway extending from the room.

At the edge of the hole, Kerith-Ayxt looks down at the doorway through which his quarry disappeared.

"Should we go after them?" asks a mage of the Fourth Circle.

Shaking his head, he says, "No." The wind has continued to die down due to several mages working to bring it to a halt until now it's barely a bother. Most of the mages have already canceled the protective barriers they used to ward off the storm. "They've entered Baerustin." At that the mage nods his head.

"Set up patrols through the ruins in case they somehow manage to make it out," the High Lord Magus says. Glancing at the hole he says, "Though I doubt that they will."

Stopping several yards from the entrance of the room they just left, Jiron eases James to the floor of the hallway. Moving back to the doorway, he glances back up to the hole in the ceiling.

"Are they coming?" James' whisper comes to him.

Turning his head back, he replies, "No. There's one looking through the opening but it doesn't appear that they mean to follow." He remains there watching for several more minutes before returning to James' side.

Jiron takes notice of the way James is favoring his right wrist. "You okay?" he asks with a nod to the wrist.

He holds it out a little bit and flexes each of the fingers. Though he grits his teeth in pain, he at least is able to move them which indicates it's not broken. "I think I sprained it when we landed," he says.

"Sorry about that," Jiron apologizes.

"Hey, don't apologize," James tells him. "That was good thinking. We wouldn't have survived up there much longer."

Jiron settles down to the floor against the wall opposite James. Sitting there across from each other in the light of the orb, their situation looks pretty hopeless.

"Any ideas?" asks Jiron after several minutes of silence.

Shaking his head, he says, "Not really. We're in a hole in the ground with at least fifty mages who collectively can kick my butt."

"At least we're alive," asserts Jiron. "Until we are dead, there is hope."

"I like your attitude," agrees James with a grin.

Jiron returns to his feet and says, "You stay here and rest while I have a look around."

"Alright," James says. Before Jiron begins moving away, another orb blossoms to life and he hands it to him. "You might need this."

Taking the orb, Jiron says, "Thanks. Be right back." Then with a grin he adds, "Don't go anywhere."

James chuckles at that then leans his head back against the wall and closes his eyes.

Again checking to be sure no one is coming through the opening in the ceiling of the adjoining room, he moves back past James then heads down the hallway. The first door he comes to opens readily and he has to jump back fast as dirt spills out into the hallway. By the time it stops, the hallway is practically choked with sand. He curses as he works his way past the newly created obstruction.

Once past, he continues down the hallway and doesn't travel far before the light from the orb reveals an open doorway on his right. He slows as he approaches it and comes to a stop. Peering through the doorway, he finds a small room no more than thirty feet by twenty. The walls and ceiling are still intact and the room is free of sand. He steps within the room and the light from the orb reveals the room is bare. Making a quick inspection, he finds no other way out but the doorway he just passed through.

Returning to the hallway, he continues down still further. Ten feet or so from the previous room, sand again appears in the hallway. A light dusting at first but the amount grows steadily the further he progresses. Suddenly the level of the sand rises dramatically just before another doorway appears on his left. As he draws close to the doorway, he discovers the hallway ends ten feet further down. The building must have collapsed at some time or the ceiling caved in for the hallway is blocked by sand.

The doorway is choked with a great deal of sand as well but checking with the orb, the room on the other side of the doorway appears to be clear. Jiron is forced to dig some of the sand out before he's able to crawl through. Holding the orb out in front of him, he wriggles through to the room on the other side.

Another empty room of modest dimension, off to one side he finds a winding staircase descending to the next level. He moves over to the top of the stairs and shines the light down. The only thing revealed by the light are the stairs as it continues its descent. Figuring he's seen enough, he climbs back through the choked doorway and returns to where he left James.

When he returns, Jiron finds him fast asleep against the wall. He moves past his sleeping friend to where the hall opens on the room with the hole in the ceiling. Peering around the corner, he gazes up and sees two figures silhouetted against the sunlight as they gaze within.

Realizing they are not going to leave anytime soon, he moves back and sits down on the hallway floor across from James. Letting him sleep a little while longer, he thinks about their situation.

In all the time since he first came to know James, this is the first situation that appears hopeless. How are they going to get out with a pack of mages watching the only opening? He'll let James get some sleep before waking him and hopefully they'll be able to figure a way out.

True, there is the flight of stairs leading down further beneath the desert. But whether that will yield a way out is anyone's guess.

Chapter Twenty Three

An hour passes while James sleeps. Figuring they need to begin working their way out of this predicament, Jiron finally gets up and nudges him awake.

Snapping awake quickly, James is at first disoriented but then realizes where they are. He looks to Jiron and asks, "Are they still watching the way we came in?"

"Yes," he says.

"And they haven't made any move to follow after us?" he asks.

"Not so far," Jiron replies.

"That's not good," mumbles James.

"Why?"

James cocks his head to the side and looks at Jiron for a moment before replying. "First ask yourself why would they pursue us all this way and then stop when they were so close to victory?"

Shrugging, Jiron says, "Maybe they feel we will have no choice but to come out the way we came in. Why would they risk it?"

"Think about it," insists James. "They could easily enough collapse this whole area and squash us like bugs. Why haven't they?"

Jiron starts to answer then stops. He remembers how readily James had been able to do similar feats in the past when the situation called for it. "I see what you mean," he finally says.

"There has to be a reason that's keeping them out and making them unwilling to destroy this place."

"Maybe it's holy?" he suggests. "Or taboo in some way?"

"Let's hope that's the reason," says James.

"Right," nods Jiron. "Could also be they're afraid to disturb this place."

"In which case, our being here is not a good thing," states James.

"Then let's get out," Jiron says. "I found some stairs further down the hallway that lead down."

"Do they go anywhere?" asks James.

"Didn't look," he explains. "But there was no sand blocking them, so maybe." Indicating the room they originally entered from he says, "It has to be better than going that way."

"Let's hope so," says James. He then works to get to his feet, his injured wrist still throbbing.

Jiron takes the lead as they head down the hallway to the stairs. Once past the doorway choked with sand, James moves to the stairs and shines the orb's light down into the opening.

The stairs are made of stone and look to have weathered the passage of time. Jiron notices his hesitation. "It's the only way," he says.

"I know," replies James. It's just that something about all this bothers him if for no other reason than the mages above have done nothing other than watch the opening since they came in here. Sighing, he says, "Lead on."

Jiron moves to the top of the stairs and begins the descent into the darkness below. With James following several steps behind, he works his way around the winding stair until it opens up onto another passage that looks to have once ran to the right and left. The left side passage has collapsed leaving them the option of taking the right or continuing to descend further.

Glancing back to James, he receives a nod to the right. Leaving the stairs Jiron begins working his way along the passage. Motion from up ahead gives him a start until he realizes it's only a scorpion scurrying across the floor. Taking a breath to calm his nerves, he continues on.

The doorways they come across are either collapsed or choked with sand. When they reach the end of the hallway, they discover the wall ahead of them broken. A jagged crack roughly two feet wide runs from the floor to the ceiling. Taking the orb, Jiron inspects the opening.

When the light shines through, it reveals a narrow open area. The area tapers to a small hole barely large enough for a man to crawl through. He moves aside and lets James look. "What do you think?" he asks. "Should we chance it?"

"I don't know," he says after looking at the small crawlspace they will have to go through. "I would hate to get trapped in something like that."

"So would I," agrees Jiron. "Better try the stairs." With an agreeing nod from James, they return to the stairs leading further beneath the desert.

As before, the stairs wind around until they come to the next level where they end. The hallway it opens out on is nearly blocked by the collapse of the ceiling. A section of the ceiling sits askew, one end braced against the floor and the other against the side of the hallway. Beneath is a small crawlspace large enough for them to pass through.

"Stay here," Jiron says as he gets down on his hands and knees. Having to practically scrape his stomach along the floor, he wriggles his way through.

James watches his feet disappear in the opening and then listens to him as he works his way through.

"I'm through," Jiron's voice finally comes back to him. "It's a crawl of about six feet before you clear the rubble."

"Okay, I'm coming through," announces James as he gets down and starts crawling through the opening. There isn't much room and he feels like his back is being scraped raw. The light from the orb Jiron's carrying reveals the other end of the blockage which gives him the impetus to continue. His wrist throbs from the struggle to crawl but he perseveres.

"It looks like this hallway continues further down," Jiron states as James' head appears from out of the crawlspace.

Making it through, he gets to his feet. "You okay?" Jiron asks.

"Does it matter?" he asks as pain radiates across his back from where the stone scraped it. "Lead on."

Jiron glances at the way he's favoring his hand then turns to continue down the hallway. They don't travel far before an opening appears on their left. When they reach it they discover a small room. A quick survey reveals nothing and they continue on.

The hallway continues for several more yards before they reach the end. Here they find a gaping hole where the end of the hallway had once been. Letting the light of the orb shine through, they see a drop of about fifteen feet.

What looks to be the side of another building rests against the one they are in no more than two feet above the jagged opening, creating an open space below. A window lies directly before them in the other wall and is packed with dirt. Again, they wonder what happened here.

"After you," Jiron says.

James again looks over the drop to the ground below. "That's quite a ways," he observes.

Jiron holds out his hand and says, "Take my hand and I'll lower you over the side. That should leave only several feet for you to drop."

Nodding, James gets down on the floor then turns and lowers his feet over the side. Before his stomach goes over the edge, he takes Jiron's hand in his good one and pushes himself over the edge.

His left hand isn't as strong as his right and continuously feels as if he's going to lose his grip. But Jiron maintains a firm grip as he lowers James down the side of the building. Once he's been lowered as far as Jiron can reach, Jiron says, "I'm going to let go, brace yourself."

James gives him a nod and then all of a sudden, Jiron lets go. He hits the uneven ground and stumbles slightly before regaining his balance. "Made it," he yells up to Jiron.

"Good," comes the reply. "Here, catch." The orb sails through the air and James grabs it before it hits the ground.

Looking up, he watches as Jiron swings his legs over the edge and lowers himself as far as he can before letting go. Landing much more gracefully than James, he's soon standing next to him.

Increasing the luminosity of the orb, they see the area beneath the wall extends in both directions. The one to the right appears slightly less rubble filled than the other. Figuring one way is as good as another, they go in that direction.

The follow the gap provided by the leaning wall, every twenty feet or so another window appears in the wall above them. Every one is clogged with dirt and has a matching mound of dirt directly below it on the ground.

Thirsty, James takes out his water bottle and discovers that he only has half a bottle left. Taking a small sip, he returns the bottle to his belt. "You have any water left?" he asks.

Checking his water bottle, Jiron replies, "Little over half. You?"

"About the same," he says. Water could be a problem if they don't get out of here soon.

After passing two more dirt clogged windows above their heads, they find one that's free of dirt. They pause beneath it as James tries to shine the light from the orb into the opening. "I think there may be a way through here," he observes.

"Looks like it," Jiron replies. He glances to where the area they've been following continues further into darkness. "Should we continue down or try the window?"

"Continue down," decides James. "If the rest of the windows have been filled with dirt, it isn't likely we'll get too far that way."

"You may be right," agrees Jiron. Casting one last look up into the opening, he turns and resumes leading the way.

Not far past the open window, large blocks of stone stand in their way from where the wall that had been their ceiling had broken. Dirt fills most of the passage, leaving only a narrow gap beneath two large stones resting against each other. The gap is large enough to allow a man to pass, barely.

"Well?" asks Jiron coming to a stop. "What do you think?"

James eyes the gap with reluctance. He moves to the edge of the gap and holds his orb so the light shines into it. "It extends further than the light will show," he says. Turning back to Jiron he adds, "Might be alright."

Jiron moves to his side and takes the orb. He then squeezes in between the two stones and begins working his way through.

Another orb springs to life on James' hand. He stands there at the opening and watches as Jiron makes his way through the gap. As he stands there, his stomach grumbles with hunger. He takes out some dried beef from his pack and chews on it while he waits.

Just before he takes his second bite, he catches the scent of fresh baked bread. The aroma makes his stomach cramp even further. *Can't be,* he thinks as he takes his second bite. As he chews he sniffs the dried beef but it just smells like dried beef. Thinking his imagination is playing with him, he continues watching Jiron's progress.

Then the smell comes again, this time with a hint of cinnamon. Holding aloft his orb he glances around, trying to figure out where the mouthwatering aroma is coming from. He finally determines it's emanating from the passage they just came down.

Curiosity getting the better of him, he begins moving back down the passage as the aroma leads him on. It gradually grows in intensity until he reaches the open window they passed under before. Once he passes by the window, the strength of the aroma begins to diminish. Retracing his steps, he realizes the mouthwatering aroma is coming from somewhere on the other side of the window. Stopping just below, he gazes up and tries to see what lies further beyond the window.

Reaching the far side of the passage, Jiron comes to an open area. Easily a hundred feet wide and two hundred long, it looks to have been the interior of some important building at one time. All four walls are still standing and each shows delicate carvings that the builder had used for embellishment.

Glancing to the roof, he finds most of that is intact except for one of the corners where the side of another building had smashed into it. The roof there had caved in revealing the wall of the building that struck it. A pile of broken stones lies below the impact site. He scans the room and discovers two doors, one to the right and one to the left. The door to the right is closed but the one on the left stands ajar.

"James!" he hollers back through the crevice. "I'm through, come on." He waits a moment but no answer is forthcoming. "James!" he shouts again. When James again fails to respond, he curses and reenters the crevice to work his way back through.

Exiting from the other side, he's dismayed to find James gone. "James!" he yells and begins running back down the passage. A knife leaps into his hand as he starts to fear the worst. He slows when he sees the light from James' orb ahead of him. Illuminated by the orb's light, he sees James standing there looking up into the window above him.

"James!" Jiron hollers. "You had me worried."

James ignores him and continues to stare up at the window.

"James?" Jiron asks. Coming closer, he looks up at the window to see what is so interesting but only sees darkness.

When he lays a hand on James' shoulder James asks, "Don't you smell it?"

"Smell what?" He definitely doesn't smell anything other than the earth around them and their own unwashed bodies.

"My grandmother's cinnamon rolls," he tells him.

"No, I don't smell anything," replies Jiron. "Come on, let's get out of here." Taking him by the shirt, he pulls James along.

"But…" begins James and the mouthwatering aroma which had been so strong quickly disappears.

"But nothing," he says as he continues dragging him along.

With stomach growling, he follows Jiron back to the crevice. "Man, that was so real," he states.

"When you're hungry, you can imagine all sorts of tasty smells," observes Jiron.

"I can believe that," he says.

"Follow me," Jiron says as he enters the opening. "It isn't far."

"Right behind you," James assures him. Once Jiron has entered the crevice and moved far enough to allow him to follow, he pauses a moment and glances back down the passage. Sighing, he enters the opening.

He works his way through until he reaches the far side. As he exits the crevice, Jiron points out the two exits. James takes a moment to inspect the delicate carvings on the walls but can't discern any sort of drawings or picture. Kind of reminds him of wallpaper you might find in a doctor's office, just something used to break up the plainness of the wall.

"Check the one on the right," James says, pointing to the one that's closed. "I'll check the other." Moving across the room to the open door, he can't get the memory of his grandmother's cinnamon rolls out of his mind. Each time he thinks of them his stomach growls again. It's been so long since he's had food from home, he didn't realize how much he misses it.

Reaching the door, he opens it further to find a hallway clear of debris extending away from it. Glancing back to where Jiron looks to be working on the lock of the other door, he decides to see where this goes while Jiron is busy.

Holding his orb high, he passes through the doorway and enters the hallway. Not far down he comes to another door on the right.

"Ahhh!"

Back in the other room, Jiron cries out in surprise then the sound of a thud echoes down the hallway. "James!" he cries out.

Racing back down the hallway, he pulls a slug out of his belt and has it ready when he runs into the room. Jiron stands with his shoulder against the door. "What's wrong?" he asks. Crossing the room quickly, he comes to his side.

"There's something on the other side of this door," he says.

Alarmed, James asks, "What is it?"

"A headless torso," he replies. "Just like one of those we encountered back in the swamp."

Not even wanting to think of the ramifications if those things are wandering around down here with them, he pulls out the medallion bearing the Star. He holds it before him and says to Jiron, "Open the door." The last time they encountered these things, the Star had blazed forth and destroyed the undead creatures. "Better to deal with this now than run the risk of it joining with others."

Nodding, Jiron takes hold of the handle of the door with one hand while he draws a knife with the other. "Ready?" he asks. When he receives an affirmative nod from James, he yanks open the door.

Braced for immediate attack, James is surprised when the door swings wide and reveals nothing but an empty corridor. He glances to the medallion in his hand which has remained quiet, no light emanates from it.

Jiron looks at the empty hallway in surprise, then bolts down it in search of the creature. "It may have moved away," he exclaims.

James follows after and keeps one eye on Jiron and another on the Star which has remained quiescent.

The hallway doesn't extend very far before they reach an area where it has collapsed and the way is impassable. "It was here!" Jiron exclaims.

"Are you sure you weren't imagining it?" asks James.

"No," insists Jiron. "I opened the door and it reached for me."

"Well, it's not here now," he says.

Jiron moves to the dirt and stone blocking the hallway and feels it to see if it's real. Finding that it is, he turns back to James with an odd look on his face.

James shrugs. "Could have been a trick of shadows," he reasons.

"Maybe," concedes Jiron.

Coming forward he pats him on the shoulder and says, "Come on. There's another hallway leading from the other door."

"Alright," says Jiron as he follows James back to the room and then over to the other door. *But it had seemed so real!*

They enter the hallway and move down to the door James found before Jiron cried out. The hallway continues further on past the door and into darkness. With Jiron's recent experience in mind, they both make ready for battle as Jiron opens the door.

Swinging open the door slowly, they brace for attack but only find a hard packed dirt wall on the other side. Shutting the door, Jiron turns and leads the way further down the hallway.

"There's got to be another way to the surface somewhere," he mutters as he moves away from the door. James nods behind him in silent agreement.

Further down they come across another door on their right. Only attached by one of its hinges, it sits askew in the middle of the hallway. Dirt that has completely filled the room beyond the door has spilled through and practically obstructs the hallway. Climbing over the mound of dirt, they discover the rest of the hallway is all but destroyed. The floor above had collapsed.

"Damn!" exclaims James from his position on the mound of dirt behind Jiron.

Holding aloft the orb, Jiron inspects the obstruction for a possible way through. "We're in luck," he says pointing to the top of the obstruction. "The cave-in opened a way up to the floor above."

"Be careful," advises James as Jiron begins working his way up the pile of stone and dirt. He starts to follow when Jiron's foot dislodges a stone which falls and almost hits him in the head. Deciding to wait until he reaches the top, James holds his position.

When Jiron hollers down that he's made it, James begins climbing up. The unstable rubble makes climbing difficult, the rocks shift under him and twice he starts sliding back down when they give way. Taking it slow, he finally makes it to the top and finds that they are in another room.

Jiron reaches down a hand and helps him the last bit until he's standing in the room. The ceiling of the room has collapsed in two places, one of which has left an opening.

Broken stone lies strewn across the floor of the room. A single closed door appears to be the only way out other than the hole in the ceiling.

James considers the hole in the ceiling while Jiron moves to investigate the door. Holding his orb high, he sees there's an open area beyond the hole in the ceiling. "If we can get up there it would bring us closer to the surface," he observes.

Jiron pauses at the door and turns to face him. Glancing from the floor to the ceiling he says, "That's a good twelve feet at least. How would we get up there?"

Shrugging, James replies, "Not sure."

Turning back to the door, Jiron pulls it open to find what used to be a stairway leading down. But the stairwell has long since collapsed and the way is no longer passable. "This way is blocked," he says as he turns back to where James is trying to figure a way up to the hole.

"Maybe we should take a short break while we work on how to continue," suggests Jiron.

Glancing at him, James nods his head. "That might not be such a bad idea."

Moving over to one side where the rubble isn't nearly so thick, they clear a space and sit down against the wall. Jiron removes two pieces of dried beef from his belt pouch and hands one to James.

"Thanks," he says. Taking the beef, he bites off a piece and gazes around the room. "You know, there're some good sized pieces of stone here," he states. "Might be possible to make a pile high enough for us to reach the edge of the opening."

Jiron nods at the idea. "Would be better than backtracking to find another route," he agrees. Then he asks, "How's your wrist?"

"Still hurts," replies James. "Don't worry, I'll still help build the pile." He feels a hand on his shoulder and turns to see Jiron looking at him.

"That's not what I was meaning," he says. "Just concerned is all."

"I know," James assures him.

They sit and rest until they've finished their dried beef and drank a small portion of their depleting water supply. "Ready?" Jiron asks. When James nods his head, they get up and begin to work on building a pile to reach the hole.

At first they work together on the larger chunks of stone to build the base. James' hand prevents them from using the largest pieces but he's at least able to assist Jiron in moving some of the medium sized ones.

Stone after stone, they move each to beneath the opening and the pile steadily rises. They even remove the door leading to the clogged stairwell and add it to the growing pile to add stability. When all but the small stones that would be of little use are gathered, Jiron climbs to the top and finds he is still four feet from the opening. The pile of stone isn't stable enough to allow him to jump that far even with the use of the door. The top stone upon which he stands continuously threatens to slip off the pile at any second.

"Maybe we can work some stones out of the wall where it's broken," suggests James.

"Good idea," replies Jiron as he works his way down from the pile.

James takes out his belt knife and walks over to the wall. Large chunks of stone are imbedded within the dirt. Using his knife, he begins working the stones out from the wall. When they are loose enough, Jiron takes them to the pile.

This process takes well over an hour before Jiron once again climbs the pile in an attempt to reach the hole in the ceiling. Once on the top, he stretches to touch the edge of the opening. His fingers are only six inches away this time. The rocks upon which he stands continue to shift and rock in a most unstable manner. Deciding to risk it, he jumps.

His hands grab the edge of the opening as the rock pile beneath him disintegrates. The force of his jump dislodges the carefully arranged pile of rocks causing half of it to slide and spill across the room's floor.

James holds his breath as he watches him hanging there in the hole. Adjusting his grip, Jiron starts to pull himself up until his feet disappear over the edge. "I made it!" he hollers back down.

"Thank goodness," breathes James with relief.

A few seconds later, the rope Jiron keeps coiled around his middle drops down through the opening. At the end of the rope he has made a loop. "Here," he says. "Put your foot in the loop and I'll pull you up."

"Okay," replies James and then he climbs the pile of stone to reach the rope. Once at the top, he takes the rope in his good hand and sets his foot in the loop. "Pull it up," he hollers when he's ready.

The rope begins to be slowly drawn upward until the slack has been taken up. Then he holds onto the rope tightly as Jiron gradually pulls him up off the disheveled rock pile and toward the hole. He can hear Jiron's grunts each time he pulls him a little bit further. When his head passes through the opening, he takes his good hand and pulls his upper body over the lip.

Jiron lets go of the rope and grabs him under the shoulders. In one strong tug, he pulls him completely over the lip and onto the next level. James cries out as the rough edge scrapes along his chest as he's being dragged out of the opening.

Rolling on his back, James uses his uninjured hand to pull up the front of his shirt. The two orbs left in the room below wink out as another springs to life next to him. Looking at his chest, he finds three long scrapes several inches in length. Two are simply red, the third is beginning to well blood.

"Sorry about that," apologizes Jiron.

James glances at him as he lowers his shirt. "They're not bad, just stings a little," he assures him.

"That's good." He takes the rope and unties the loop he made for James' foot before coiling it once again around his waist.

The light from the orb reveals they are in another hallway, the hole they climbed out from divides it in half. They can either continue down the side they are on or try to cross over the hole some way to go the other.

James sits up and takes his orb in his hand. He notices Jiron looking at him with his hand out. Suddenly, another springs to life in Jiron's hand.

"Thanks," he says. "Just stay there and rest a moment if you need to, I'll head down here and see where this leads."

"Alright," replies James from where he remains sitting with his back propped up against the wall. "Can't be too far from the surface now."

Jiron nods in agreement. "If we find a way out, let's hope the mages have left," he says. "Can you sense them?"

James concentrates for a moment then shakes his head. "Either they are far away or aren't doing anything magical."

"Good. If you can't sense them, then they shouldn't be able to sense you either." Holding up the orb, he nods to it.

James just shrugs his shoulders.

"Be back in a second," Jiron says as he proceeds down the hallway. Twenty feet from where he left James the right side of the hallway is blocked by dirt that spilled in through a window in the wall. He only pauses to examine the window for a moment then is about to move on when he feels a barely perceptible breeze.

Standing still, he works to ascertain from which direction the waft of air originated. He comes to realize it's coming from the top left corner of the window. Holding aloft his orb, he inspects it closer and discovers a small opening in the dirt through which the air is moving.

After a quick glance back to where James sits with his orb on the floor next to him, he reaches up and pushes on the dirt surrounding the opening. It doesn't take much pressure before the dirt begins falling away. He works at it until he has made an opening two feet in diameter.

Holding the orb behind him, he climbs higher on the mound of dirt and looks through. There's a definite space on the other side of the window. When he dislodges more of the dirt, he can hear it fall down the other side. Excited, he hurries back to James.

James sees him running back toward him and gets to his feet. "What?" he asks.

Indicating back down the hallway with a nod of his head, he says, "Found a window that may lead somewhere. There's a slight draft passing through from the other side."

"A draft?" asks James in excitement.

"That's right," affirms Jiron.

"Let's go check it out," says James and then follows Jiron back to the mound of dirt and the window.

"See if you can widen it further," he suggests when he sees the opening Jiron had made.

Stepping up to the window, Jiron takes a rock from the mound of dirt on the floor and begins striking the dirt packed in the window. Each strike dislodges more of the dirt. He keeps hammering at it until the left half of the window has been completely cleared.

"Toss the orb through and see what's back there," James says.

He moves to the opening and tosses the orb through. The light from the orb as it sails through shows a large open area, easily thirty feet across. As the orb strikes the far side, it begins to fall. It falls at least a hundred feet before splashing into a pool of water at the bottom.

Jiron turns from the window. "It's pretty big," he tells James. "The sides are just dirt. At the bottom lies a pool of water."

"Water?" asks James. When Jiron nods affirmative, he adds, "The water may have eroded the dirt from the bottom up." He takes his water bottle and gives it a shake. Hardly any left.

"We could use some of that water," states Jiron.

"Can we make it down?" he asks.

"I'll see," he says. "Need another orb." When one appears in his hand he again moves to the opening. Tossing it through, he watches the sides of the hole as the orb falls. A little over halfway down directly below the window is a two foot dirt ledge jutting out from the side of the wall. The hollow area grows dark again when the orb hits the water and sinks beneath its surface.

James cancels the orb as soon as he sees Jiron turn back from the window. "Well?" he asks.

"There's a narrow ledge below the window," he explains. "My rope will reach it but I'm not sure how well it will support our weight."

"Let me see." Moving to the window, he creates another orb and tosses it through. When it passes the ledge, he sees what Jiron is talking about. Though not very wide, it doesn't look as if it will support their weight.

He's about ready to move away from the window when the breeze which originally caught Jiron's attention wafts through and ruffles his hair. Air movement can only mean a way out.

"I think we should chance it," he says as he turns back from the window. "That breeze has to mean there is an opening to the surface somewhere." He sets the orb on the mound of dirt while he gets ready to climb through.

"I agree," replies Jiron. "We could wander around down here for days and not find another way." He uncoils the rope from around his waist and says, "I'll lower you down first." When James nods, he ties the loop at the end of the rope for his foot. Setting the rope on the dirt mound for a moment, he helps James through the opening.

Once his feet are dangling on the other side, he works the rope through and hooks it around James' right foot. Bracing himself, he gives James a nod and holds the rope tightly while James works his way the rest of the way through the opening. He lets out slack very slowly until he hears 'I'm set', then begins lowering steadily.

James holds the rope tightly in his good hand with the other arm wrapped around it for support. As he is lowered into the darkness an orb springs to life and settles on his shoulder. He keeps an eye out for the ledge. When he sees it coming up beneath him, he hollers, "Almost there!" From above he hears Jiron holler back, "Let me know when you reach it."

"Right!" he shouts. Looking down, he watches as the ledge gradually approaches. When he is but inches from it he hollers up to Jiron to halt. Moving carefully, he places the foot not in the rope's loop upon the ledge and tests it for stability. When the ledge proves secure, he places more of his weight upon it, never once letting go the rope.

Finally standing with his entire weight resting upon the ledge, he hollers up to Jiron, "It's holding!"

"Good," comes the reply. Then the rope is quickly drawn back up.

Back at the window, Jiron takes out one of his knives. After untying the loop, he ties the end securely around the base of the knife's hilt. He then places the knife crosswise across the corner of the window and wedges it there. While maintaining tension on the rope tied to the knife to keep it in place, he tosses the rest of the rope through the window and down to James.

Jiron!

James' scream comes to him from below. He looks through the window just as a massive flash explodes on the other side and blinds him. Holding his eyes, he shouts, "James! What's happening?"

Another inarticulate yell comes from James followed by a splash. "James!" he yells through the window. From below come two explosions and James's voice calling his name.

Crumph!

Another explosion and then he hears James again calling his name, this time sounding like he's further away.

When his eyes finally clear enough to see, he looks through the window but only sees blackness on the other side. Taking his orb, he holds it high as he leans out to look below, but the ledge is empty and there's no sign of James.

"James!"

Chapter Twenty Four

He stands on the ledge as Jiron pulls the rope up. Shifting his feet, he edges over to make room for when he comes down. Once Jiron makes it down to the ledge they'll work the rest of their way down to the bottom.

Above his head, the glow from Jiron's orb shines through the window and he can see his silhouette as he makes ready to descend. Then Jiron's hand emerges from the window holding the rope then lets it fall.

James reaches out and catches the rope to steady it during Jiron's descent. Pulling the rope tight, he holds it while he waits for Jiron to pass through the window. Just then from below, he catches a glimpse of movement out of the corner of his eye. Looking down, his eyes widen in amazement as a gigantic serpentine head atop a long neck rises out of the water below.

The scaly head rises quickly, its red eyes fixed squarely upon him. Frozen with fear, he watches as it draws ever closer. Suddenly, its mouth opens revealing two rows of razor sharp teeth. Giving out a roar, the head strikes at James where he's standing exposed upon the wall.

"Jiron!" he screams and then throws the orb. Dodging to the side, he closes his eyes as he sends a burst of magic causing the orb to explode in a blinding flash.

The scaly head strikes the wall where he had been but a second before. James is struck by the side of the monster's head and gets knocked from the wall. "Jiron!" he yells again as he plummets toward the water below.

"James!" he hears Jiron shout from above. "What's happening?"

He reaches out and grabs hold of the neck of the monster to slow his fall. Even with that he hits the water hard, his breath knocked out of him. Kicking his feet, he moves out of the way just as the head hits the water.

The impact of the head causes him to be propelled by the surge of water toward the side of the underground lake. Kicking and swimming furiously, he makes the edge and pulls himself up onto the ground. Turning onto his back, he sees the creature's head silhouetted by the light coming through the window from above, rearing up for another strike. Rolling to the right, he barely avoids being caught by the razor sharp teeth.

Getting to his feet, he quickly creates another orb and finds that the shore of the small lake extends further around the water. Running, he flees the monstrous creature and lets out with magic…

Crumph! Crumph!

…and the ground explodes upward in front of the creature.

Rearing backward and letting out with another bone rattling roar, the creature halts for a brief moment allowing James to flee further along the shore.

"Jiron!" he cries out as he races along the water's edge. The ground trembles as the creature leaves the water to pursue him. A massive body with four strong legs and a long tail trailing behind, it looks just like a dinosaur.

Crumph!

Letting out with another explosion, he slows the creature down. Looking ahead desperately for a way out, he finds the water continues until it reaches the edge of a building. As the building becomes more illuminated by the orb's light he discovers the shoreline, and thus his avenue of escape, ends at the side of the building.

Glancing back, he sees the creature again pressing forward to attack. Desperate for a way out, he edges closer to the water. Scanning the area once again for any sign of a way out, he notices the water lapping at the edge of the building and that the ground beneath the wall has been eroded away by the water.

With no time to determine if the eroded area extends very far, he runs and dives into the water. Swimming quickly, he reaches the building's edge. Just then, the water swells when the creature enters after him. Praying he's right, he takes a breath and dives again under the water.

Using his hand for a guide, he swims under the stone of the building. The stone above him extends for what seems like a long distance before his hand comes to the end of the stone. Kicking to the surface, his head breaks through to open air and he takes a ragged breath.

Heart pumping, he creates another orb and finds that he's in the corner of a large room. Over time, the water had eroded the ground out beneath the foundation causing the floor to fall away and drop below the surface. Reaching out a hand, he takes hold of the edge of the floor and quickly leaves the water.

Once out, he moves away from the edge and watches to see if the creature will follow. The opening isn't very large so he hopes it will decide against it. When all remains quiet for several minutes, he sighs with relief that the creature isn't going to follow.

Then it hits him. He's all alone. How will Jiron follow and catch up with him while that creature is out there? Even Jiron's prowess with the knives will be of little use against such a massive creature.

He sits there a moment and takes stock of the situation. They're both still alive and will both be working to get out of here. He seriously doubts if Jiron will even think about trying to follow the way he went.

The room he's in is rather large, the ceiling rises up at least two stories. As all other rooms they've come across, this one is bare of any furniture or anything else that would indicate what its purpose once was. On the far side of the room lies a closed door, the only way to go other than the one he used to enter. He hopes Jiron can either find him or a way to the surface.

Crossing the room to the door he takes the handle and pulls. He has to exert a lot of pressure to get it to swing open into the room. Beyond lies a hallway leading further into the building.

James takes the orb in hand and passes through the door, holding it high to better see what lies ahead. He moves down the hallway until he the light from the orb reveals a door ahead that's slightly ajar. As he nears the door he stops when it appears as if a faint, dark light is coming through from the other side. Canceling his orb he sees that there is indeed a dark light coming through the doorway, and it's pulsating.

Stepping softly, he moves to the opening and peers around the door. "Unbelievable," he says under his breath. "I know this place." In one of the campaigns he designed for role playing, he devised a room almost identical to this one.

In the center of the room is a pulsating purple sphere of light that's twice the height of a man. Lightning crackles through it from one side to the other. Empty cages line the side of the room to the right and to the left stands an altar.

Sitting on top of the altar is a four armed, twisted, humanoid creature which in the campaign he designed was the representation of the cult's god. No one appears to be in the room. He stands there and watches for a minute to be sure the room is empty. A doorway lies on the wall between two of the empty cages with another across the room from where he stands in the hallway, both are closed. When no one makes an appearance, he opens the door further and walks in.

The pulsating sphere gives off a malevolent aura and if it's like the one he made, will lead to the plane where the god rules. Not wishing to test that particular theory, he gives the sphere a wide berth as he walks around it toward the altar where the god's statue sits.

Curiosity getting the better of him, he wonders if there's a hidden compartment in the belly of the statue same as the one in his campaign. If there is, you pull the top left and bottom right arms down at the same time to open it. He realizes it's sheer folly to tempt fate but he just has to know.

Stepping to the altar he takes hold of the two arms and pulls them both down at the same time. They both rotate down smoothly and the belly of the statue pops open. Within lies a ring. Now in his campaign, this had been a ring of three greater wishes and was guarded by a deadly trap. If everything has been the same so far, so must the trap.

Taking the statue in both hands, he rotates it upon the altar clockwise until it has come full circle. Once it rests in the same position again, he rotates the two arms back to their original position. Now, the trap should be nullified. If he's wrong, he's dead.

Hesitantly reaching out for the ring, he lays one finger on it and braces himself. Nothing happens. Breathing a sigh of relief, he takes out the ring and holds it up. Grinning in satisfaction, he contemplates whether he should use it. Of course there's no guarantee that it will do the same thing as the ring in his campaign. Also, he remembers how he used to try to come up with the worst possible results when people wished for things. If they misspoke, disastrous things would happen.

One time when Dave had found a ring, he wished for a million gold pieces. So of course he had a million gold pieces appear, only problem was that they were fused together. Too heavy to carry, he was forced to leave all that gold behind. Grinning at the memory, he grows sad that Dave is gone. Dave had always been a good friend.

Suddenly, his attention is drawn to the sphere as pulsation increases in intensity. Static electricity crackles and a bolt of lightning surges out of the altar, narrowly missing him as it flies past. Striking the pulsating sphere, a deafening boom resonates within the room and then a figure steps from the sphere.

Slipping the ring into his belt pouch, he moves to the edge of the altar and hunches down, hoping against hope that he won't be discovered. It's too far to make a dash unobserved to one of the doors.

As the first figure leaves the sphere, another emerges behind him, then one more after that. The first figure is an exact replication of the idol on the altar except it only has two arms. It's wearing a robe and has the bearing of a priest. The second figure is a human male and has his arms tied behind his back. The third figure is another of the priests and is holding a tether tied to the human's throat.

They walk across the room to the cells and the first one produces a key. Unlocking one of the cell doors, he steps aside while the man's bonds are removed and is then pushed inside. When the cell door clangs shut, the man turns to grip the bars of the cell door and rests his forehead against them.

James' heart freezes within his chest when the man turns around. His mind has a hard time crediting what his eyes are showing him. There in the cell stands his friend Dave. Looking the worse for wear, he's still wearing the same clothes he last saw him in on that fateful trek from Ironhold.

The two priests turn to move toward the altar. Rage billows forth and James lashes out with a massive magical attack. Realizing their danger too late, the priests fail to react quickly enough and feel the full force of the blow. Picked up off the ground, they're slammed into the wall. Falling to the ground, they hit the floor and remain motionless.

"James!" cries out Dave as the two priests hit the wall.

Rushing over to his friend, James states, "I thought you were dead."

Dave stares into his eyes and asks, "Is that what Jiron told you?"

Shaking his head, he replies, "No. We interrogated one of the enemy soldiers and he told us what happened."

"Whatever he told you was a lie," he says.

"Obviously," states James. Moving over to the dead priests, he searches their robes until he locates the key to the cell. Returning to the cell, he unlocks the door.

"Is Jiron with you?" Dave asks.

"He was. We got separated," explains James. "Why?"

286 Shades of the Past

Dave remains silent for a moment before replying. "He's one of them," he finally says.

"What?" exclaims James. "That's impossible. He's saved my life on more than one occasion."

"I know it may have appeared that way," his friend says. "But when I left the cave with the Star, he came too. I saw him talking with the mage before returning to you and the others."

"No," argues James. Shaking his head, he says, "I can't believe that." Too many times has Jiron been there for him. For him to be an agent of the Empire is too mind-boggling for him to come to grips with.

"Believe it!" he says. "Look, I know you're a very trusting person, but think about it. How do you think the enemy always knew where you were? Remember those times you said that while Jiron was away you got captured?"

James nods his head, "But he rescued me."

"He's the one who told them where you were!" Dave hollers. "He only rescued you to gain your undying trust."

"Why would he do that?" James asks. Doubt begins to gnaw at him, as he begins to see the logic behind Dave's words.

"There's something you must do," he explains. "I didn't find out what but did hear them talking about it. He's there to see to it that you are in the right place at the right time."

"But…" he stammers as his foundation of what he thought to be true begins to erode away. Jiron the enemy? Though he fights the idea, things begin to fall into place. Then he says, "The Fire!"

"They already have that," he replies. "They had it shortly after you and the others hid it under the mountain. He told them where it was and how you protected it."

Anger begins to grow. Anger at being betrayed! Anger at being used! "I'll kill that traitor!" he shouts as rage gets the better of him. Never has he wanted to kill someone like he does now. If Jiron were here in front of him, he'd kill him on the spot.

From behind them, the sphere pulsates again as another bolt of lightning strikes it from the altar. Then just as before, a figure emerges. Removing a slug from his belt, he throws it with magic behind it and strikes the creature before it takes two steps.

Striking it in the chest, the slug blasts through and out the other side. The creature staggers backward into the pulsating sphere. As soon as the creature comes in contact with the sphere, it begins to pulsate erratically.

The static charges within it become more frequent and the hair on the back of James' neck rises.

Taking Dave by the arm, he says, "We better get out of here." Dave nods and they make for the door between the cells as it's the closest. Static charges begin erupting from the sphere as they reach the door. Throwing it open, they hear the sphere begin to crackle loudly.

"Move!" screams James as he propels Dave through the door. He follows and slams the door shut. He no sooner puts his shoulder against the door before the sphere detonates with an immense explosion.

The concussion of the blast hits the door and knocks it off into the hallway. James is thrown backward several yards where he hits the floor hard. Getting to his feet, he turns back toward the doorway and sees electrical bolts crisscrossing the room. One enters through the doorway and ricochets down the hallway toward them.

Unable to move in time, he's struck full force in the chest by the bolt. A moment's searing pain and then he blacks out.

"James!" Jiron yells from the shore of the underground lake. Can't really call it a lake, it's not that big. He listens but no sound is forthcoming.

It took some doing but he made it down from the window. The rope is again coiled around his middle and he holds the orb high as he tries to figure out which way James went.

He sees the holes in the ground James had blasted and his footprints in the dirt. As for what he was running from, there's no indication of anything. Moving quickly, he follows the footprints in the dirt until he comes to where the shoreline ends at a stone wall. The footprints seem to end here.

James is alive, of that he's sure. Had he been dead, the orb would have gone out. As long as the orb exists then James has to be alive. But where is he?

"James!" he hollers again. "Where are you?"

Examining the water's edge, he speculates James could have gone into the water. But why? Didn't make any sense. The surface of the water is placid, only a few residuals ripples from when he left the water after descending from the ledge under the window work their way across.

He didn't swim past me on my way here. So he had to go somewhere else. The only shore adjacent to the water is that which he is standing on now. Which leaves the stone wall he's standing next to.

Remembering the secret doors James found in the past, he begins working his fingers along the cracks and grooves. Pushing here, pressing there, he tries to find a hidden opening trigger. After a quarter hour he gives up, if James managed to find and use one he can't duplicate the feat.

He sits on the shore near the water as he tries to figure out what to do next. While he sits there, his mind drifts back to a time when he and Tinok had gone to recover a broach stolen from Tersa.

It was made of silver and the only thing of any value she owned. They had tracked the thief to one of the old buildings on the waterfront. The front door was barred from within and no other way was available to get in.

As it happened, one of their friends from the fight pits walked by while they were thinking of their next move. When he learned what they were up to he suggested going into the water and try to come up underneath the building. Said some buildings in the area have openings in their floor where they can access the water without leaving their homes. Taking them around to the side of the building, he showed them how it was built up to the water line.

Sure enough, when they dove under the water and swam beneath the building, they found an open section. They soon had the broach in hand and had thoroughly taught the hoodlum a lesson to within an inch of his life.

Returning to the present, Jiron looks at the way the water goes to the edge of the building and how the stone wall runs along the water a good fifteen feet. Seeing as how James' footprints end at the water's edge there, he takes the orb in hand and wades into the water to see if he could have gone under the wall.

Seven feet out, the water is now up to his waist. Two more steps and the ground beneath him comes to a drop. Thinking this might be the place, he dives under the water. Feeling with his free hand, he finds where the wall ends and begins working his way under the building. When his hand encounters the end of the stone above, he kicks up and breaks through the surface.

Holding the orb high, he sees where the stone is wet from where James had left the water. Tossing the orb onto the floor of the room, he pulls himself out of the water. Feeling mighty pleased with himself, he picks up the orb and follows James' wet footprints to the door leading from the room.

Peering through the open door, he finds a hallway extending directly away from the door. James' footprints are clearly visible indicating he had passed this way. Moving through the doorway, he follows the footprints down the hallway.

The footprints continue until they come to an open door on the left. It looks like James paused here for some time before finally entering the room. Jiron looks around the door and finds another empty room with a door on the far side of the room and another on the right. The one on the right is open.

Just before he passes through, he hears a groaning coming from further down the hallway. Glancing into the darkness, he holds up the light but it doesn't reveal anything. "James?" he hollers as he quickly moves down the hallway toward the source of the sound. Again the groaning comes from further down the hallway.

Quickening his speed, he runs toward the sound. A light begins to be seen ahead and he's soon to realize it's coming from behind a door at the end of the hallway. It's slightly ajar and the groaning is coming from whatever lies beyond.

Putting the orb inside his shirt, Jiron slowly moves to the opening and peers around the door. On the other side is a room right out of some torturer's dream. A man is using a hot iron on a form lying bound upon one of the tables within. Another table sits closer to the door and Jiron sees what looks to be a dead body lying upon it.

The man laughs as he again presses the hot glowing metal to the man's side. When the hot iron hits flesh, the man upon the table groans as smoke rises from his skin. Wracked with pain, the man on the table thrashes about. In his thrashing, the man turns his face toward the door where Jiron is standing.

Jiron gasps in startlement as he recognizes the form upon the table. Without thought, he throws open the door and rushes into the room. The man on the table cries out, "Jiron!" before passing out.

Knives in hand, Jiron closes on the torturer and in two lightning quick passes leaves him dead on the ground. "Tinok!" he cries as he turns to his lifelong friend. Seeing him lying there unconscious, he looks at what's left of his friend. One hand is missing three fingers, scars and burns cover most of his body. Emaciated and thin, he looks like he hasn't eaten anything for days.

Untying him from the table, he picks him up in his arms not caring that Tinok's blood soaks into the front of his shirt. Surprised at how thin

290 Shades of the Past

he is, he carries him over to where a bucket of water sits on a small table. Propping him against the wall, he pats his face to wake him.

Tinok stirs groggily, not entirely aware of his surroundings. Jiron ladles out some of the water and puts it to his lips. The feel of the water trickling into his mouth brings him closer to wakefulness and he begins to swallow. After he drinks two full ladlefuls of water, Jiron puts it back in the bucket.

"Glad to see you," Tinok says.

Jiron can barely contain the emotions running through him. Alternating between rage and sorrow, he replies, "So am I. What happened to you?"

"After James made me leave, I got captured by the Empire..." he begins.

"Wait a minute," Jiron says, interrupting him. "Did you say that James made you leave?"

Nodding his head, Tinok says, "That's right. That night after Cassie died, he came to me and told me to leave."

"Why in god's name?" he asks incredulously. Such a thought had never even crossed his mind.

"He didn't give me a reason," says Tinok weakly. "Told me to get out or he would kill us both. Said he needed you but that I was a liability."

All this time, he had thought Tinok left because of his grief over the loss of his beloved Cassie. The rage he felt at the sight of Tinok lying upon the table intensifies tenfold.

Why?! James had always treated him so fairly and nice. All the while he sent away his best friend only to be tortured and maimed. He looks at the hand missing three fingers. Never again will it hold a knife.

"Jiron," breathes Tinok weakly. "I'm glad you found me. I want to go home."

"You will my friend," he assures him. "You will."

Then Tinok's head lolls to his chest and he begins to topple over. "Tinok!" cries out Jiron. Catching his friend, he knows the truth but doesn't want to face it. Tinok is dead.

"NO!"

With rage nearly consuming him, all he can think of is to find James and make him pay for the death of his friend. Getting to his feet, he casts one last glance to Tinok then draws one of his knives as he leaves the room of pain behind. Running down the hallway, he returns to the doorway where James' footprints pass through.

Racing through the door, he pauses as he takes in the jumbled mess of footprints that crisscross the empty room. Finally realizing they exit through the open door, he runs over to it and discovers the hallway leading away on the other side.

Running down the hallway, he finds a wet spot where it looks like James had lain at one time. The footprints grow more distinct as they lead further down the hallway.

James sent me away.

The words of Tinok fuel the rage already burning within him. The sight of his friend lying broken and wasted on the table continues to run through his mind.

Betrayer! Murderer! His vision becomes tinged with red as his rage mounts to even further heights.

The footprints lead him to another open door further down the hallway. Swinging it wide, he quickly scans the room and sees his quarry on the far side approaching another door.

With knife in hand, he races across the room as silently as a cat. He must strike first before the betrayer has a chance to use his magic. Ten feet from the murderer of his friend, his prey turns and sees him attacking. A wave of force hits him and sends him flying twenty feet backward where he lands on his back.

"Traitor!" James yells as he removes a slug from his belt.

"Murderer!" screams Jiron. Getting back to his feet he draws his other knife. With both knives in hand, he charges forward. He sees James' eyes flick toward the ground just in front of him and dives to the side just as…

Crumph!

…the floor explodes upward where he would have been.

Rolling to a stop, he catches James' arm movement as he cocks back his arm to launch his slug. Jumping to the right he hears the slug strike the wall behind him.

A rumble shakes the floor as the section surrounding the area James' magic exploded falls into the room below. Staggering, Jiron again hurtles himself forward. "I'll kill you for what you did to Tinok!" he yells as he closes fast.

Crumph!

The floor under him explodes outwards. Thrown through the air, he lands within several feet of James. Picking up a loose stone deposited on the floor by one of the blasts, he throws it and connects with the side of James' head.

Knocked backward, James staggers in a daze as Jiron closes fast. Unable to concentrate sufficiently to use his magic, he tries to flee. Tripping over the loose rubble the blasts strew across the floor, he falls to his knees. Then from behind, one of Jiron's knives catches him across the back, opening up a six inch long cut. He dodges to the left and immediately turns onto his back and tries to scoot away.

"Oh no you don't," Jiron says as he follows, "you'll not get away that easily." Grabbing his foot, Jiron stops him and says, "I'm going to do to you what you did to Tinok."

James tries to get away but Jiron grabs his hand and says, "First, I'll start with the fingers." He puts a knee on James' chest to prevent him from getting away.

"I didn't do anything to Tinok!" he cries out. "It was you who betrayed me! Traitor!" Taking a large piece of rubble, he tries to strike Jiron in the side of the head. Jiron sees the blow coming and lashes out with his hand. The blow causes the stone to fly out of James' hand.

"Lies!" he screams. "Nothing but lies have I had from you, one I called friend." Pulling James forefinger to an exposed position, he brings his knife to it. "This is for Tinok!"

Crack!

The floor beneath them, weakened by the blasts, is no longer able to support their weight. With a loud crack, it gives way.

Jiron loses his grip on James as they both plummet to the floor below. They fall for what seems like a long ways before they land on the floor of the room below. Hitting hard, the breath is knocked out of Jiron. James is dazed and the orb that he carries falls from his hand and rolls across the floor.

It takes a minute before they are able to move again, James is the first to get to his feet. He tries to summon the magic but due to the blow to his head, is unable to concentrate sufficiently. Moving away from where Jiron is working to get back to his feet, he hurries around a raised dais sitting in the middle of the room, to the door on the far side.

A noise behind him causes him to glance back and sees that Jiron is almost upon him. He turns to face him as the knife falls and grabs the descending arm with both hands.

"Now, let's finish this!" Jiron says as he brings his other knife in position to strike

Crack!

From above, another section of the ceiling directly above them gives way and falls. Still locked together, they both jump to the right to avoid the falling stone and land on the dais. A flash of light and then they're plunged into darkness.

"Milord?"

Roused from his slumber, Kerith-Ayxt finds his aide Aezyl standing at his tent flap. "Yes?" he asks. Sitting up on the edge of his cot, he motions for his aide to enter.

Aezyl enters the dark tent as a candle flares to light on the lone small table. Coming to stand before his lord he says, "It's over."

"They're dead then?" he asks.

"It would appear so," his aide informs him. "We detected magic being used and then nothing. When we looked for them all we found was darkness."

"Excellent," he says. "Continue keeping an eye on their last known position just in case."

"By the way milord," Aezyl says as he hands the High Lord Magus a courier pouch. "This arrived an hour ago," he explains. "When the messenger arrived at the School, they sent him up here."

Taking the pouch he sees the seal of the Emperor emblazoned on the side. Sighing, he says to his aide, "Thank you. Keep me informed if there is any indication they are still alive."

"Yes sir," he says and then turns to leave the tent.

He sets the pouch on his cot as gets up to pour himself a glass of wine. Not the recommended drink for those who work with magic, but as he's the High Lord Magus, no one will gainsay him about it.

After filling his glass with wine, he replaces the wine bottle in the travel pack. Picking up the courier pouch he moves over to the table where the candle burns. He takes his seat and places his glass of wine on the table. Opening the pouch, he pulls out a single letter.

It bears the seal of Lord Cytok and reads as follows:

Lord Magus,

> *You are to take as many mages as are able and set out forthwith to intercept the invading army before it leaves Empire controlled territory. Speed is of the essence. Leave no survivors.*

Lord Cytok

Kerith-Ayxt puts the letter down and takes a moment to savor the last of his wine before leaving his tent. Outside he finds his aide Aezyl standing by the fire with a mage of the First Circle.

"...Baerustin and other places like it are the reason the School was founded in the first place," Aezyl says to the First. "When you achieve the Second Circle you will learn in more detail the events that turned this once thriving city into what you see today."

"You mean a mage destroyed Baerustin?" the First asks.

"In a way yes," replies Aezyl. "An experiment gone wrong in a time when mages worked blind, trying to discover ever more powerful spells and enchantments. Many of the rules and laws that you have already been taught were just speculations at the time. Magic was unleashed here, magic of a most fearsome sort. Before the citizens understood the danger they were in, many of them were killed."

Kerith-Ayxt listens as his aide relates the tale of Baerustin to the First.

"Brother beset brother, father turned on sons," he continues. "None now recall just what the mage who unleashed this upon Baerustin was attempting to accomplish. But the magic is still active, even after a millennium." He turns to gaze directly in the First's eyes and says, "It turns you mad if you are exposed to it for any length of time."

"Then, we are to go mad?" he asks in apprehension.

Shaking his head Aezyl says, "No. Here above the sand we are safe."

Kerith-Ayxt clears his throat.

Aezyl turns and sees his lord standing there. "Yes milord?" he asks. The First bows to him and then moves away.

"We are moving north at first light," the High Lord Magus states. "The Emperor wishes us to deal with the invading army before it can reach friendly territory."

"Then we are to destroy it milord?" he asks.

Nodding, Kerith-Ayxt replies, "Yes. To the last man."

Chapter   Twenty Five

The sudden plunge into darkness disorients Jiron just enough for James to wriggle free. "Come back here murderer!" he hears Jiron saying not too far from him.

"I didn't murder anyone," replies James as he gets off the dais and moves quickly around it. He can hear Jiron's breathing as he follows.

The room has grown cold, very cold. He tries to formulate a spell to use against Jiron but he simply can't concentrate well enough. The blow to his head still has him unable to summon the magic. *The ring!* Reaching into his pouch, he searches for the ring all the while continuing to back away from Jiron. He steps lightly so as not to announce his exact location. His fingers search the pouch but fail to find the ring.

"Tinok told me of how you sent him away the night Cassie died," he says.

Tinok? Tinok was here too? A feeling that something's definitely not right comes over him. *Dave and Tinok being here at the same time? Unlikely.* His mind begins to throw off the anger and rage as cool logic asserts itself.

Vague outlines begin to appear as his eyes adjust to the darkness. "Jiron," he says. "When did you talk to Tinok?"

"After you fell in the water," he replies. "I followed you and found him."

"You followed me?" he asks. Suddenly, his orb springs to life in the palm of his hand. It's a strain to hold even that much magic, his head is throbbing so badly. Seeing the knife rise to strike, he says, "Wait!"

The knife pauses. "Why should I, murderer?" Jiron asks.

"How did you get past the monster in the water?" he asks.

"There was no monster," he says. "I did find where the Empire was holding Tinok. He was mutilated!" His eyes still show the intensity of emotion at what was done to his friend.

James sees the knife begin to move and hollers as fast as he can, "If the Empire controlled this area, then why didn't the mages follow?" He closes his eyes and braces for the knife to strike. When the attack doesn't come, he opens his eyes to see the knife but inches from his throat. Jiron stares at him with a thoughtful look on his face. He can see the rage beginning to melt away.

Then it all clicks together. The smell of his grandmother's cinnamon rolls; Jiron seeing the headless torso; finding a room right out of one of his campaigns. "It wasn't real," he says to him. "None of it was."

"But..." he stammers and then looks down at the front of his shirt. The blood that had stained it from when he held Tinok is no longer there. "I held him in my arms," he says as the hand holding the knife drops back to his side.

"I know," James says laying a hand on his shoulder. "I found Dave. He told me you were an agent of the Empire and had handed him over to them at Ironhold."

Jiron's head comes up. "I did no such thing," he asserts.

"Just as I did not send Tinok away," he states with conviction.

"Then what happened?" he asks.

"I don't know," he admits. "Maybe this place is cursed in some way, turns people against each other."

Jiron sheathes his knife. "I'm sorry," he says. The rage which so threatened to consume him has now completely left him.

"So am I," replies James with a sad grin. "What do you say we get out of here before anything else happens?"

"Yeah," agrees Jiron. "Let's get out of here."

The light from the orb reveals that they are no longer in the room they landed in when they fell through the floor. This one is much smaller. A raised dais sits prominently in the center of the room, the room itself is only two feet wider than the dais. It's what's depicted upon the dais that concerns James.

"Jiron look," he says as he draws Jiron's attention to the symbol of three dots forming a triangle with lines running between them.

"That's not good," he says. "But why would they have a temple here in a place that's cursed?"

James glances around the small room. A shudder runs through him from the cold that's leeching the warmth from his body. "I'm not even sure we are in the same place." Looking down at himself, he finds the front of his shirt no longer shows where the lightning bolt had struck him. He touches it to reassure himself it was never really there.

Turning back to Jiron he starts to say something when a small creature suddenly appears in the air behind Jiron's left shoulder. "Jiron!" he whispers as he points to the creature hovering just beyond his shoulder. Barely a foot in height, the scaly creature is roughly man-like. Hunched over as if it's carrying too much weight, it stares at them from its gnarled head with glowing red eyes.

When Jiron turns and sees the creature, he quickly takes two steps backward. "What is it?" he asks. The creature stays there but a moment before disappearing.

"I don't know what that was," replies James. "But we better get out of here fast." A sense of foreboding comes over him and the room all of a sudden feels smaller.

"I'm with you there," agrees Jiron. A single corridor extends away from the room. With knife in hand, he takes the lead. He doesn't make it far before another of those creatures appears between them.

This time, the creature reacts animatedly and chitters at them before disappearing. Jiron glances back at James who shrugs. Turning back, he continues down the corridor.

James' feeling of foreboding begins to grow into one of impending doom with every step he takes. Just then, the tingling that warns of magic being worked comes to him. Strong and powerful, the feeling is more intense than anything he's ever felt before.

"Jiron," he whispers urgently. "Magic!"

Stopping, Jiron glances back and sees the pallor of James' face. "Close?" he asks.

"It has to be," he replies.

Then Jiron's eyes widen. "James!" he says pointing to his chest. "The medallion."

Looking down, he sees light coming from his beneath his shirt. Pulling out the medallion, the Star upon it bursts into brilliant light.

A frigid wind sweeps down the corridor from further ahead bringing despair and sapping the will. James looks down the corridor to find a figure standing there. Suddenly, the air around them is filled with dozens of the tiny creatures. Chittering and shrieking, the creatures avoid close proximity to the light as they move to strike at them with their tiny claws.

Jiron draws forth both knives and begins fighting back. The creatures move so quickly he is having little effect. A shimmer forms around them as James creates his barrier to keep the creatures at bay. But it does little good, the creatures begin appearing within the barrier.

Jiron finally manages to impale one on his knife. The creature lets out a high pitched squeal then disappears. "James, do something!" he yells as his knives continue to dance, keeping the creatures away.

You have come, mage.

The light coming from the medallion keeps the creatures away from him, the effects of contact with it appears to hurt them. James stands transfixed by the figure at the other end of the corridor until one of the creatures braves the light from the medallion and scores on his right arm. Three lines of red, each several inches long burn like acid as blood begins to well. Then another scores on his leg, ripping the pant leg and baring the flesh beneath.

The tingling sensation spikes and he throws up a barrier to seal off the corridor between themselves and the figure in the hallway. Energy, massive energy strikes the barrier and shatters it. Then all of a sudden the air is free of the little creatures as they disappear all at once.

Jiron grabs him by the arm and hollers, "Come on!" Dragging him back down the corridor, they flee.

James glances back and sees two other cowled figures in the corridor next to the first one. Moving around the stationary figure, they make their way down the corridor toward the fleeing pair.

Running fast they return to the room with the raised dais. "Now what?" asks Jiron. From his position at the entrance to the corridor, he sees the cowled figures coming closer. The original one they encountered is now lost in the darkness.

"I don't know," admits James. Searching the walls, he prays to find a secret door or any other way in which to escape.

"How did we get here?" asks Jiron. "Think fast we don't have much time."

"Uh, we were fighting," he says as he tries to recall just what happened. "We were struggling and then the ceiling fell in. Then suddenly we were here."

"How!" yells Jiron.

"How..." mumbles James as he tries to figure it out. From his position in the room, he can see the two figures coming closer. Glancing around the room, his eyes settle on the dais. The dais?

His skin crawls as the tingling sensation spikes. "Away from the opening," he yells to Jiron.

Jumping backward behind the wall, he narrowly misses being struck by a flash of light which strikes the far wall with a sizzle. When it's gone, they see the surface of the wall where the light hit now has a hole, six inches wide and three deep, eaten out of it.

"They're almost here!" he cries.

James feels another spike in the tingling sensation and hollers, "Watch out!"

Jiron jumps to the side again but no attack materializes.

"Just what is going on here?" a deep male voice asks from behind them.

They both turn to see the armored figure of a warrior priest standing upon the dais. *That's it!* Lashing out with a wave of magic, he catches the warrior priest completely by surprise. As the warrior priest is thrown backward off the dais to smash into the wall, James grabs Jiron.

"Now!" he yells. "Dive for the dais!"

They both jump and land on the dais at the same time. A momentary feeling of disorientation then they find themselves upon an identical dais sitting in a different, larger room. James immediately recognizes this place. They are in the underground temple they found on their way back from Saragon last year. But why did they come here of all places?

The room is large with two rows of three wide columns, each extending all the way to the ceiling. Between the two rows of columns lies an open area where four braziers form the points of a square. Fire burns in each giving ample light with which to see. The dais they find themselves upon sits in the middle of the square formed by the braziers.

"How is this possible?" Jiron asks as they get down from the dais.

"I have an idea," says James. "But I'll tell you as we go. They may be able to track us to here."

No sooner do they get off the dais than one of the cowled figures appears upon it. James lashes out immediately with magic as Jiron moves to attack.

The cowled figure is thrown backward off the dais and lands on its back. A flash of light shoots toward James only to be absorbed by the medallion, causing it to burst forth with light.

By this time, Jiron has closed with the figure on the floor and strikes out with a knife. The blade sinks into the robes striking the flesh underneath. One hand of the cowled figure touches his shoulder and he rears back in pain. His arm goes numb and lets go of the knife still embedded in the cowled figure.

Out of the corner of his eye, Jiron sees another cowled figure appear upon the dais. "James!" he shouts as he points to the second one. Turning back to the one on the floor, he lashes out with his foot and connects with the side of its head. The force of the blow knocks its head to the side and causes the hood to fall away.

The sight of what's revealed elicits a gasp of surprise from Jiron. He steps back two feet as the skeletal face turns its lifeless gaze upon him. "They're dead!" he exclaims.

James, now turned to face the new arrival, lashes out with a wave of force which picks up the creature and throws it across the room. His head is clearing from the earlier blow Jiron dealt him but it's still an effort to summon the magic. He glances over to the other one on the floor and sees the skeletal head and empty eye sockets. A spike in the tingling sensation and the creature on the floor hits Jiron square in the chest with a flash of light. Knocked backward through the air, Jiron lands on his back a dozen feet away. Rolling, he quickly regains his feet.

"Jiron!" he cries as he rushes over to him.

"We can't win this," Jiron tells him, the front of his shirt smoking.

"Maybe," asserts James. "You okay?"

"Not really," replies Jiron. The front of his shirt has been burnt away and the skin of his chest is an angry red. "My left arm is numb too."

James turns to face the two attackers and summons the magic, encasing each within a barrier. One of the creatures reaches out and touches the barrier with its hand. Upon contact, James cries out and sinks to his knees. His head feels as if it's about ready to explode. Releasing the power maintaining the barriers, the pain eases and then finally disappears.

Holding aloft the medallion, its light blazing forth, he gets back to his feet and faces the approaching creatures. One sends another flash toward him but is absorbed by the medallion. Lashing out with his own magic, he knocks them off their feet. One took the brunt of the wave of force and is thrown backward several yards. It hits one of the large stone braziers before sinking to the ground.

An idea forms quickly and James removes a slug from his belt and throws it with the force of magic behind it. The slug flies through the air and impacts with the side of the brazier directly over the creature. When the slug hits, the side of the brazier cracks open and the oil contained within pours out upon the creature. As the oil flows from the opening, James tweaks the flame burning atop with magic to ignite the oil.

When the burning oil lands on the creature, it bursts into flames. A scream that is felt rather than heard rips through their minds like a red hot knife. It thrashes about for a minute before it finally lies still and the scream stops.

Another flash of light from the remaining creature and the medallion flares into blinding brilliance as it again absorbs the attack.

With one taken out of action, James can now concentrate on the other. The creature approaching still has Jiron's knife sticking out of its ribs. Removing another slug, he sends it flying toward the creature. The creature makes no attempt to avoid it and the slug rips through its stomach and exits out the back.

Not even slowing, it continues to approach. Suddenly, the flames burning over the remaining braziers roar to life. A ball of flame shoots out of each toward the dais. Meeting in the air, the balls explode as they collide. When James' eyes recover from the brilliant explosion, he sees one of the hell hounds standing upon the dais.

Behind him, he hears Jiron get to his feet. A brief glance back shows him that Jiron has his remaining knife in hand and is preparing to sell his life dearly. Tuning back, he throws a confining barrier around the hell hound while at the same time lashing out with another wave of force to push the cowled figure backward.

"Jiron, get me out of here if I fall," he says.

"Do the best I can," he replies. Though how effective he will be with a numb arm and a chest that's throbbing horrendously with pain, he's not sure.

The hell hound fights the barrier. James has to funnel more of his reserves to simply maintain the barrier while he deals with the undead creature before him. Behind the approaching creature, the oil continues to spill forth from the broken brazier, creating an ever widening area of flame.

Lashing out again with a blast of force, he knocks the creature backward into the pool of flame. The fire instantly ignites the creature's robes. Their heads are again hit by the mind tearing scream as the fire consumes the creature, which almost causes the barrier surrounding the hell hound to fail. Falling over into the pool of fire, the creature thrashes around for a moment before lying still.

When the scream tearing through his brain stops, James is again able to focus his attention back to the hell hound and the barrier encasing it.

As he's done several times before, he turns the barrier cold and begins to shrink it in upon the creature.

Struggle as it will, the barrier continues to shrink until the creature's struggles cease and all resistance to the closing of the barrier vanishes. With a pop, the barrier implodes completely.

James sags and almost falls to the floor before Jiron catches him with one hand. On the verge of passing out he says, "Help me up. We have to get out of here."

As he helps James to his feet, he glances over at what's left of the two bodies burning in the pool of fire on the floor. "What were those things?" he asks.

"I don't know," he replies. The memory of the warrior priest that he slammed with his magic before they came here is very much on his mind. Why he hasn't made an appearance yet baffles him. "You remember the way out?"

"Yeah," replies Jiron. "Let's go." He puts James' arm around his shoulder for support before moving toward the double doors they had passed through during their previous visit. Kicking one of the doors open, he and James pass through to the corridor on the other side. James' orb springs to life as they leave the light of the braziers behind them.

Turning down to the right, they walk quickly. Coming to the end they arrive at another corridor that runs perpendicular to theirs. Without hesitation they turn and follow it to the right. They soon come to the winding flight of stairs leading down.

On their previous visit, they had come up this way after crawling through a drainage pipe found in the side of the mountain. At the time they were being pursued by soldiers of the Empire and were just looking for a place to hide.

"Not that way," says James as they come to the stairs. "Better leave the same way as last time."

Jiron nods at that and continues down the corridor. They pass by another corridor extending into darkness on their right and shortly after that arrive at a small room. Standing in the room are two pedestals, upon each sits a statue of a demonic creature. They give them but a cursory glance as they pass through the room to the corridor on the right. Hurrying along, they pass three more corridors branching off to the right before entering the room at the end. So far there has been no telltale indication that the warrior priest has appeared on the dais.

Just as they remembered, they find the stairway leading to the room above them. The only exit from the room is an opening in the right wall where a corridor begins. At the top, James pauses and says, "Let's rest a moment."

"You sure?" asks Jiron. "There could be more of them coming."

"I know, but I need to." James leans against the wall by the stairwell and sags to the floor. "Just for a minute or two," he tells him.

Seeing just how tired his friend is, Jiron nods and takes position at the top of the stairs to keep an eye out for anyone approaching from below. He's not doing too great either. His chest throbs from where that dead creature blasted him, not to mention the multiple strikes of those small flying creatures that burn him like acid. Nothing would please him more right now than to lie down and fall asleep.

He turns his attention from the stairs to James and says, "You know, those dead creatures really weren't that hard to defeat."

"I know," James replies. "I don't know if you noticed, but a warrior priest appeared on the dais before we left."

"I saw something but didn't realize it was a warrior priest," he admits. Getting a confused look on his face he asks, "Then why didn't he come after us?"

"I don't know." Shrugging, James leans his head against the wall and adds, "I suppose we shouldn't question our good fortune."

Grinning, Jiron returns his attention to the stairs. "I suppose not," he agrees. He absentmindedly rubs the arm that fell numb when the creature touched it.

"Arm okay?" James asks.

"The feeling is beginning to come back," he says. "What would cause something like that to happen?"

Shrugging, James contemplates what happened a second before answering. "One of the theories that were kicked around back home was that the energy needed to keep a dead body 'alive' would have a detrimental effect on the living," he explains. "When it touched you, the energy suffusing it entered your body and 'shorted out' your nervous system."

"Shorted out?" he asks perplexed.

James gives him a grin. "Sorry, it's a term from my world. It simply means it stopped your arm from communicating with your brain. If the contact had lasted for any length of time, the damage probably would have been permanent if it didn't kill you outright." He indicates the arm that's numb and adds, "Since the feeling is coming back, it stands to reason nothing permanent was done."

"That's good to know," he says.

Closing his eyes, James tries to relax a moment to quiet the headache that throbs painfully behind his eyes. His restless mind continues trying to make sense of the last few hours. *First, Jiron and I are in a city buried by sand and are about to kill each other. Then we wind up in that other place where the little demonic flying creatures were trying to kill us. If the dais is some kind of magical transport device, why did we end up here? It makes no sense! It can't be a random transporter, that would be useless to the warrior priests. There has to be a way to control it.*

Okay, suppose there is a rhyme or reason to it. How did Jiron and I trigger it the first time? Could it be set up to trigger for anyone who does magic? That wouldn't make a whole lot of sense. The warrior priests have made many enemies over the years who can wield magic. They surely wouldn't want anyone other than themselves to take advantage of their teleportation system. So the trigger must be something that has to do with them and that only they and their agents would have. Maybe some ability they posses or an aura or something?

"James?" questions Jiron softly.

Eyes opening he glances to where Jiron is still keeping an eye on the stairs. "Someone coming?" he asks.

Shaking his head he says, "No. I was thinking we might want to get out of here." Grinning he adds, "Seeing as how you are awake and all."

The headache has subsided to a dull throb. He feels a little bit rested and able to continue, though the thought of using magic makes his headache throb even more. "Doubt if I could do anything if we were to be attacked," he says. Getting to his feet, he says, "But I am fit enough to walk without your support."

"Good," he says as he comes to him. "Then let's get out of here." He moves past James and crosses over to the corridor. There he pauses and glances back to make sure James is following before leaving the room.

He proceeds down the corridor until he comes to where another corridor crosses the one they're in. Remembering the way from last time, he takes the corridor to the right. They don't go far before coming to the three skeletons of the dead priests lying on the floor. The whole area of the corridor has been blackened as if by fire.

Jiron steps over the skeletons and continues down the corridor. He stops when he realizes James isn't following him. Looking back he finds him standing before the skeletons, staring at them. He starts back toward him when he hears James exclaim, "I got it!"

"What?" Jiron asks as he rejoins him by the skeletons.

Reaching into his pouch, he removes the amulet he acquired here the last time. Emblazoned with the symbol of the warrior priest, he holds it up and shows it to Jiron.

"So?" he asks. Puzzled as to why James is standing there with a wide grin, he waits.

"Don't you see," he says as he shakes the amulet slightly, "this is the key!" He looks to Jiron as if that should explain it all. When Jiron shrugs that he isn't following him, he adds, "The dais. This is what triggered the teleportation."

"Still not sure I'm following you," admits Jiron.

"Do you remember me telling you about my time in the City of Light before it fell?" he asks. When he sees Jiron nod he continues. "Ol' One Eye was sure interested in this when he found it in my possession, said it 'changed things'. I didn't understand it at the time but it makes sense now."

"Also, back in Mountainside when we were taken into the jail back when Tinok and Cassie were still with us, the officer there was mighty interested in it as well. I think it's no small coincidence that the dais sent us here. After all, this is where it belonged."

"So…" Jiron begins as he tries to work this out. Shaking his head he says, "I still don't understand."

Holding the amulet up before him he says, "This is a portal key! It activates the magic in the dais. That's why we ended up here, it's keyed to the dais below. When we jumped on the dais back in that other place, it sensed this key and sent us here."

"But, why didn't we come here first then?" he asks.

"I don't know," he admits. There his reasoning breaks down. He considers it for a minute then says, "But the fact that I found the amulet here and that we were ultimately sent here has to be connected in some way. It could be that each key is set for a specific temple and will always return the wearer to that temple."

He can see the doubt in Jiron's eyes. "Of course," he tells him, "the only way to test the theory is to take another ride through the portal."

Jiron laughs at that. "I don't think so," he says shaking his head.

"I agree," James states.

"Can we go now?" asks Jiron.

With a nod of his head, James indicates for him to lead on. As he follows Jiron, a memory of what he told Aleya during their last visit when she had asked about the amulet: *"Maybe it was only given to a priest once they achieved a certain level of the temple hierarchy,"* he *had suggested. "Simply having one may have afforded them some privilege or it could've been a sign of rank or trust as well."* If that is the case, then only the higher ranking priests would have access to the portal, which would make sense.

Jiron continues to lead until they come to where another corridor converges with the one they're in. James shines the light of the orb down the left to reveal the cave-in they ran across last time. Knowing they are on the right path, Jiron continues straight ahead.

Twenty feet or so they come to another cave-in. A space just large enough for a man to crawl through has been cleared at the top of the obstruction. The last time they were here, they had crawled through that hole and found themselves out among the trees on the mountainside. Taking a look at the ground on this side of the cave-in, they find impressions in the dirt from where they previously rested until it had grown dark outside.

Jiron immediately goes to the opening and crawls a short way through before stopping. He pauses a moment before coming back inside. "It's dark," he says.

"That's fortunate," comments James and indicates for Jiron to continue on through to the other side.

He cancels the orb before he follows Jiron through the hole. It takes his eyes a moment to adjust to the darkness before he's able to see the moonlight filtering in through the opening. Making his way through he finds the half moon to be high overhead. Jiron offers him a hand as he crawls out and helps him to his feet.

"Now," he says, "let's see about finding our way back to the others.

Brian S. Pratt   307

Chapter   Twenty Six

They work their way along the mountainside toward the south. Somewhere ahead of them in the dark lies the road running along the southern edge of the mountains which will take them toward Madoc. The last time they came this way, there was a sizeable presence of the enemy along the road.

It doesn't take them long to reach the road leading down from the summit, appearing in the moonlight ahead of them. Carefully looking in both directions, they determine the road is empty. With Jiron in the lead they move onto the road.

Traveling upon the road affords them much better speed than forging their way through the forest. "We need to find a couple of horses," James whispers.

"I know," comes the all but silent reply.

The road takes them quickly down the mountainside. It isn't long before the lights from the encampment of the Empire's soldiers at the base of the mountain come into view. The number of campfires indicates there isn't nearly the number of men there were the last time they passed this way. "Maybe they don't feel a large presence is warranted here," suggests Jiron.

"Could be," agrees James. "Or they could have sent most of their force to deal with Illan and the others."

"That would make sense," he says with a nod.

They continue following the road until it begins to approach the perimeter of the enemy camp before moving into the shelter of the trees. Working their way through the hills at the base of the mountain, they make their way closer to the enemy lines. Pausing a moment upon the top of a hill overlooking the enemy camp, they have a commanding view of its layout. Off to their right they see where they have their horses kept.

A series of stables have been built to keep their steeds out of the elements. Six structures with corrals adjacent to each stand in an area to the rear of their lines. In the corrals, horses are visible in the moonlight.

They wait several minutes before descending the hill. Jiron points out four sentries as they make their way through toward the stable area. Two remain in and around the stables while the other two continue on toward the main camp. He waits for the two continuing on toward the camp to leave the area before making his move. When only one of the two remaining sentries is close, Jiron motions for James to stay on the hill. Receiving James' nod, he makes his way down the hill and toward where the sentry is patrolling.

James watches as the shadow that is Jiron moves toward the closest sentry, covering the distance quickly. He gets in behind the sentry and is within a dozen yards of him when the man suddenly turns in his patrol and begins heading back in Jiron's direction. Ducking behind a tree, Jiron waits for his approach. A glint of moonlight flashes from the knife in Jiron's hand.

The sentry continues to approach, oblivious to the danger poising to strike behind the tree. His path doesn't take him directly past the tree, rather five feet to one side. When the sentry draws even with the tree, Jiron slips around to the other side until he's behind him once again. Moving fast, he closes the distance silently. Grabbing the sentry from behind, he strikes with his knife and then lowers the dying man to the ground, the whole incident happening without a sound.

Jiron wipes his knife off on the man's clothes and then moves toward the second sentry. The nearest stable is twenty feet away with an open area easily twenty feet wide. Running quickly and silently, Jiron makes the side of the stable and then presses his back against it. Listening for the other sentry's position, he hears the man's footsteps approaching from the right side of the stable. Moving quietly, he works his way to the right.

The remaining sentry calls to the other as he nears the edge of the stable. Despite the fact the man is speaking in the Empire's language, Jiron can tell by the inflection in his voice that he's asking a question. As Jiron reaches the edge of the stable, the sentry again asks the question with a slight edge in his voice.

Quickening his steps, the sentry reaches the edge of the stable. Just after he passes, Jiron jumps him from behind. Clamping his hand over the man's mouth to prevent him from alerting the rest of the camp, he runs the edge of his knife across the man's throat. Tossing the dying man to the ground, he turns toward the hill where James waits and waves. A minute later James joins him.

"Let's hurry," urges James. Jiron gives him a nod.

Jiron moves around the edge of the stable to the entrance and peers through the doorway. When he finds it empty, he signals James to follow as he enters. A light springs to life as James' orb appears on his hand. Not nearly as bright as it usually is, it's just bright enough for them to find the tack and saddle for two horses.

Along the back wall they find all the items they need stacked on shelves. While Jiron gathers the tack, James removes two fine looking stallions from their stalls. One snickers and snorts as he brings them forth. "Easy boy," he says reassuringly as he pats the nervous one's neck.

Working quickly, they soon have the horses saddled. James swings into the saddle while Jiron moves to the gate. He opens it a crack and looks out to be sure no other sentry is approaching. When he finds all is quiet, he swings the stable's gate open and returns to the horses. Taking his horse's reins, he leads him through the gate. Once James has left the stable, Jiron closes the gate and throws the bar to keep it closed. He then swings into the saddle. Unless someone stumbles upon the dead sentries, it's unlikely anyone will realize something has happened before dawn. James cancels his orb before heading out.

Moving quickly away from the buildings, they head southeast. Angling through the hills, they keep their distance from the enemy camp while they make for the road that will take them toward Madoc.

When at last the road appears before them, Jiron dismounts and leaves his horse with James while he moves to the edge of the road. Last time there had been hidden sentries along this road, but then again, the last time the Empire had known they were on the way. He comes to a stop within the edge of the forest and gazes up and down the road. Scanning both directions for several minutes for any movement he is at last satisfied the road is deserted. He then returns back to his horse and mounts. "The road looks deserted," he says in a whisper.

"Then let's get going," replies James just as quietly.

Jiron gets his horse moving and they're soon out of the forest. They turn eastwards once they are on the road and quickly get their horses up to a canter. James casts glances back to the enemy camp in the distance as they ride but no shout arises or any other indication that they have been discovered. After awhile, the lights of the enemy's encampment disappear in the dark.

They ride for an hour or two before the sky begins to lighten with dawn's approach. So far they haven't encountered anyone else traveling upon the road and with any luck they won't for some time.

When the sun begins to peek over the horizon, Jiron examines the road closely. "I think horses passed this way recently," he observes. When James glances to him he indicates the surface of the road.

Even James' untrained eye can see that hundreds of horses passed this way recently. The piles of dung the horses dropped when they passed don't look more than two or three days old. His time of being around horses has given him plenty of experience to figure that out.

"Then they have sent men to engage Illan," James states.

"Looks like it," agrees Jiron. He points out several different tracks of wagon wheels as well as the footprints of foot soldiers. "Could be a sizeable force."

"If this is the only one, Illan should have little trouble," observes James. "Two days..." Picturing the map of the area in his mind he tries to estimate the position of Illan and the rest of their friends. If this army passed through here only two days ago, they may not have had the time to reach them yet.

Glancing to Jiron he sees he's come to the same conclusion. They kick the sides of their horses and break into a gallop. Illan needs to be warned of this new threat.

Riding hard through the morning, they come to where the road ends at Bindles just after noon. Another road passes through the town going north and south. During their earlier sojourn on their way to find Miko, they had passed through here in the guise of merchants. Delia had even managed to secure additional cargo bound for Korazan to give them more legitimacy.

When the town appears before them, they slow down to look for any forces in the area. Not finding any, they continue to follow the road into town. Out of water and short on supplies they stop at the trader they visited on their last trip, the one Delia had acquired the cargo from. A sign hangs above the door depicting three barrels.

Dismounting, they head for the front door. Just as before, the people on the streets barely give them more than a cursory look. Jiron reaches the door first and opens it. Upon entering they find the same merchant they dealt with the time before.

Brian S. Pratt 311

The merchant looks up from where he was going over a ledger and sees them enter. "Good day to you sirs," he says with a grin. Closing the ledger he comes over to them and asks, "How may I help you?"

James was worried that he would recognize them but looking into his eyes can tell he doesn't. "Additional water bottles and several days' worth of travel rations," he tells him.

"And a mirror if you have one," adds Jiron. Glancing at James he gets a nod of approval. He hadn't thought to purchase a replacement for the one lost on the road.

"Very good," the merchant replies. He then goes over to a table with water bottles. "How many would you require?"

"Two bottles each," he says.

The merchant picks up four bottles and takes them over to the counter. He then moves to another table containing packages of dried beef and cheese. Picking up an armful, he brings them over to the counter. "Will this be sufficient?" he asks as he places the packages next to the water bottles. "I'm sorry I don't have much of a selection to offer, the soldiers bought almost everything and the caravan carrying my goods is overdue.

Nodding, James says, "Yes, thank you." He gives Jiron a knowing glance. The caravan in question may very well be one of the ones he secreted the explosive seeds in. The merchant may be waiting a long time before he sees his goods.

The merchant moves behind his counter and produces three mirrors of varying sizes. James selects one that is only six inches by three and has a plain bronze frame. The merchant replaces the other mirrors and then adds the one selected to the rest of their items.

"I heard that an army passed through here a day or two ago," Jiron suddenly says.

"That's right," the merchant replies. "There's a rumor going around that Black Hawk has returned. But that is hardly possible." Finishing bundling the items together he quotes a price to James who then hands over the required coins.

"Oh?" asks James. "Why is that?"

"He and his men were slaughtered years ago," he states.

Jiron casts a quick look to James who asks, "Are you sure?"

"Well, I wasn't there of course but that was the story going around at the time," he explains. "Supposedly his men were destroyed by the Empire's armies after some battle or other."

"Oh," Jiron says with a barely concealed grin. "So what about the soldiers who passed through here?"

"Well like I said, a rumor had been going around town for some time that Black Hawk had returned. I never gave it much credence, rumors seldom being reliable and all. But when the men who had been stationed at Kern passed through, they said the same thing. Apparently they are on their way to take out whoever this is. Probably someone stirring up trouble and using Black Hawk as a rallying cry or some other such nonsense."

"Yeah," agrees James. Taking his newly bought goods from the counter, he turns for the door. "You wouldn't happen to know which road they took out of town would you?"

"Why?" the merchant asks.

"We're heading east and if there's a battle about to be fought, we don't want to be anywhere nearby when it does."

Nodding, the merchant says, "They took the south road."

"Thanks," James says as he starts moving for the door. Jiron reaches the door first and opens it for him.

"May your travels be safe ones," offers the merchant.

"Thank you," Jiron replies. Stepping aside, he lets James leave the chandlery and then follows him out.

They secure the rations behind their saddles and James puts the new mirror into one of his belt pouches. Then taking the water bottles over to the rain barrel sitting against the building, they fill them up.

James says, "So they are indeed going after Illan."

"Hope he's faring all right," replies Jiron. Worries for his sister and friends have been a constant companion since he and James left them.

"With Miko and the Hand of Asran to take care of any magical foes," James says, "it would take a large force indeed to cause him any real problems."

Topping off his last bottle, Jiron secures the stopper in the bottle's neck. James finishes with his and they return to their horses to pack the extra bottles away. Mounting once more, they turn south to follow the road through town.

Once past the last building, they break into a fast gallop as they race down the road. Seeing as how the force of soldiers ahead of them has wagons traveling with them, they may be able to catch them before they attack Illan. Alternating between a fast gallop and at times dismounting to give the horses a break, they put many miles behind them. As they ride they keep an eye on the tracks of those they are pursuing to make sure the soldiers don't turn off the road unexpectedly.

By time they reach the town of Arakan, the sun has begun its descent to the horizon. Having bought sufficient supplies back in Bindles, they decide against stopping. Instead they hurry their way through town.

As they enter the outskirts, James eyes the building that the officer who had stopped and checked their papers exited from during their last visit. Since neither one of them can speak the language, any confrontation can only lead to disaster. Coming abreast of the building, he quickens the pace of his horse slightly and moves past. He breathes a sigh of relief when no one makes an appearance.

"Take it easy," Jiron says to him softly. James gives him a nod and brings his horse back to a normal gait. The last thing they want to do is attract attention. Continuously scanning the people on the streets for any potential problems, they make their way through town.

One thing James notices is the lack of guards or soldiers. Since entering Arakan, he's only seen one guard. Glancing to Jiron he sees that he's noticed that fact too. Last time they had more of a presence. Perhaps when the soldiers passed through here they took most of the guards with them.

If that is the case, James is both elated and worried. Elated in that if they are forced to strip town garrisons and city guards to bolster their army, then they must be hurting for men. On the other hand, he's worried because that would mean more to face should there be a battle.

They reach the far side of town and leave the last building behind them without incident. Not far past the town they come across an area that looks like it could have been the bivouac area the army they're following used the night before. Piles of horse dung dot the area and there's evidence of over a dozen fire pits spaced evenly throughout.

"We're gaining on them," Jiron says after examining a pile of horse dung.

"I hope so," replies James.

They push on for a couple more hours until the sun drops below the horizon and twilight has almost turned into full night. Pulling several hundred feet off the road, they make camp without a fire. Rolling out their bedrolls, they have a quick meal then James takes first watch while Jiron turns in. A little after midnight, James wakes Jiron for his turn at watch and then sleeps peacefully until dawn.

Up before first light, they're back on the road and put a mile behind them before the sun breaks over the horizon. Using the same alternating pace as the day before, they eat up the miles quickly.

Two hours before noon, date bearing trees appear ahead of them. It's the oasis where they rescued Jiron from the Commander of Ten when he was captured in that ill-fated mission to retrieve James' backpack from Mountainside. A caravan is currently watering their horses at the oasis' pool, ten wagons along with an accompanying guard of twenty.

"Better not get too close," cautions Jiron.

"I agree," replies James.

The road passes alongside the oasis and it would be very suspicious if they were to leave the road and pass in the desert. Rather than raise their suspicions, they stay as far away from those at the oasis as the road will allow them without appearing to do so on purpose. They pick up their pace as they hurry past.

One of the guards offers them what sounds like a greeting in the Empire's tongue. Ignoring him, they continue on. When the guard realizes they aren't going to answer he shouts at them, obviously offended. James glances back and sees the guards staring at them with an expression of indignation. They lock eyes for a moment before the guard turns back to the others.

"I hate not understanding their language," comments James after the oasis has disappeared behind them.

"I know what you mean," agrees Jiron. "Would make life easier. Is there anything you can do with magic that might help?"

"Possibly," he replies, "though I'm not sure how to go about it. Foreign languages were never my forte."

Picking up speed, they once again race to catch the force ahead of them. It isn't long before the road begins turning to a more southerly direction. All of a sudden, Jiron stops in the middle of the road.

"What's the matter?" asks James coming to a stop as well.

Jiron is studying the ground intently. "I think they left the road already," he explains. The telltale signs of their passing which have been evident since Bindles are no longer present.

"I think you're right," concurs James. Turning back to the north, they watch the road closely as they travel for the spot where the force turned off. A mile back, just after the road turned to the south, they find where the force moved eastward into the desert. Turning to follow, they break into a gallop.

An hour into the desert, they see the dust rising from the marching feet of thousands of soldiers. They slow when they come within visual range of the soldiers. At least seven thousand strong, they look to mainly consist of foot soldiers. Only a fraction are cavalry, maybe less than five hundred.

"Do you sense a mage?" Jiron asks.

Shaking his head, he says, "No. I haven't felt any other doing magic since before Kern." Pulling out his mirror, he brings his horse to a halt.

"Do you think that's wise?" asks Jiron. "If there is a mage with them it could get dicey."

"I realize that," he states. Glancing at his friend he adds, "But we need to know the situation. Where are Illan and the others? Are there any other forces converging with this one?"

"Alright, I understand," concedes Jiron.

Summoning the magic, James has the mirror show an overhead view of the army ahead of them. He scrutinizes the leading edge of the force and finds no sign of a mage among them. Holding the image, he waits for a moment to see if the tingling of magic comes to him. When it fails to materialize, he scrolls the image further east.

Ten miles further ahead of the army lies a river running north and south. Just to the east of the river lies a major road running alongside of it. The road is packed with people. Whole families riding in wagons, pulling wagons, or even carrying their belongings on their backs are in an exodus to the north.

"Illan's to the south," he concludes. When Jiron comes closer he shows him the image of the fleeing people.

"That means this force is moving to work ahead of him and cut him off from Madoc," Jiron reasons.

"Looks that way," agrees James. He scrolls along the road to the south and it isn't far before they find what's left of a bridge. The center span is gone. James smiles when he sees more evidence that the seeds he planted within caravans have worked. He scrolls as far as he can and still the road is packed with people. Before he reaches the point where the draw of magic is too great, he discovers another bridge destroyed.

Scrolling back north, he continues to scan the road and finds a bridge that is still standing. "That's where this force is going," he says as he shows Jiron the image in the mirror. "All the other bridges south are destroyed and this is the only way for them to get across."

"So if that bridge wasn't there they would have to move even further north in order to cross," reasons Jiron. Glancing to James with a grin he says, "That would delay their encounter with Illan."

Nodding, James says, "We need to work our way around this force quickly. Their advance units may already be closing on it." Turning back to the mirror, he scans the area between here and the bridge and discovers a score of riders making for the bridge. He then scrolls across the bridge and to the east.

"Oh, man" he says as a force of over two thousand foot soldiers appears coming from the north. "Another force is on the way from the north. Looks as if they plan to meet the ones ahead of us at the bridge."

"Then launch an attack at Illan and the others," concludes Jiron.

Putting the mirror away, James says, "We can't let that happen."

Kicking their horses in the sides, they break into an all out gallop as they angle to the north. Staying just out of visual range, they work their way around the northern flank of the enemy.

Ta-too! Ta-too!

Off to their right an enemy scout spots them and alerts the rest of the army. No longer worrying about avoiding detection, they aim their horses directly toward where they believe the bridge to be.

Another horn sounds ahead of them and the force of twenty riders James had spied in his mirror earlier appear. The riders are coming straight for them with the undeniable intention of attacking.

Crumph! Crumph! Crumph!

The ground erupts under the leading edge of the riders. Horses and men are thrown into the air as the charge falters. When the dust clears, only six riders are continuing the attack.

James slows his horse while removing a slug from his belt. Glancing southward to the other force, he sees their horsemen coming fast. Turning back to the six ahead of him, he looses the magic as he throws the slug. Moving at the speed of a bullet, it strikes the lead rider and knocks him from his horse. Removing another slug, he again drops a rider to the ground.

Crumph!

Letting loose the magic once more, three of the remaining horsemen are thrown into the air. The last man still astride his horse manages to keep his steed from faltering. With sword in hand the rider rides directly at them.

Jiron moves to intercept before the rider has a chance to engage James. With knives out, he closes with the rider. The enemy horseman strikes out at Jiron as he passes him on the left. Jiron blocks the blow with the knife in his right hand as he strikes out at the rear of the rider's horse with the left. Opening a deep gash along its hind quarters, the horse rears up in pain.

The rider manages to remain in the saddle as he works to steady his mount. Jiron quickly moves in and closes with the rider. Lashing out with a knife, he almost connects with the man's side before his sword blocks the attack.

Again, Jiron lashes out at the horse and scores another deep wound, this time in its flank. The blow severs several muscles and the horse cries out again in pain as it collapses. Vaulting from his horse, Jiron hits the ground and moves to finish the rider who has one leg caught under his horse.

Working to extricate himself from the fallen horse, the soldier tries to defend himself when Jiron closes for the attack. His sword easily blocks one knife but the other finds an opening and sinks into his side, puncturing a lung. Moving away from the trapped, dying man, Jiron catches a flash out of the corner of his eye. Turning to look, he realizes the flash was another of James' slugs on its way to take out a horseless rider that had survived the earlier explosions.

"Come on!" shouts James. He indicates the riders closing rapidly behind them.

Moving to his horse, Jiron leaps into the saddle and they again race for the bridge. Still several miles away, their horses are quickly becoming fatigued. The hard pace of the last two days has definitely taken its toll.

Staying low in the saddle, they keep the pace quick. The riders behind them gradually close the gap, their fresher horses able to maintain a quicker speed. When the riders have closed the distance to within fifty yards, they begin to see people moving across the horizon. *It's the road to the bridge!*

"Not much further now," Jiron shouts. In minutes they've reached the road and race alongside, the refugees fleeing the approach of Black Hawk line the road so thickly, James and Jiron are unable to use it. When the people who are on the edge of the road see them coming fast, they quickly get out of the way.

Behind them, the riders continue to close the gap, now only thirty yards away. Fortunately they are as hampered by the ebb and flow of the refugees as James and Jiron are so are unable to gain any faster.

Then all of a sudden the river appears ahead of them. James looks with horror at the jam packed bridge crossing over the river full of women, children and the elderly.

Jiron sees it too and yells, "You have no choice!" When he sees James hesitating, he shouts, "Do it!"

No! Focusing on the ground to either side of the bridge, he lets the magic flow...

Crumph! Crumph!

...the earth erupts in two massive explosions. The refugees scream in fear as they flee. Tweaking the dust from the eruptions, he forms it into a humanoid figure twice the size of a man and has it begin to stalk toward the bridge. That's enough for even the bravest of those still upon the bridge. At the sight of the twelve foot tall creature walking toward them, they turn tail and race for the other side.

By the time James and Jiron reach the bridge, the area is in total chaos. The creature has reached the edge of the bridge and is beginning to walk across. James aims for the bridge and races right through the dust formed creature. As he exits through the creature and begins to cross the bridge, he cancels the spell. Hooves thundering, they race across to the other side. A gathering of people has formed a little ways from the beginning of the bridge and he has to slow in order not to run them down. With Jiron right behind, he clears the bridge and turns to the right.

Behind them, the enemy riders have already gained the bridge and are crossing fast.

Crumph! Crumph! Crumph!

Three explosions rip through the center span of the bridge. The people cry out in fear as horses, riders and stone erupt into the air. James slows as he gazes back. With a crack, the center span of the bridge collapses into the river below. On the far side of the river, the enemy riders who had yet to begin crossing over come to a quick halt. None made it to the other side.

"James!" Jiron cries out when he sees several of the riders on the other side of the river remove crossbows from behind their saddles. Turning their fatigued horses from the river, they break into a gallop and head for the open desert. The people on the road part quickly to avoid being run over. Soon, they are out of crossbow range and the river is disappearing quickly behind them.

Chapter   Twenty Seven

Since leaving Korazan behind, Illan has led the Black Hawk Raiders along the road north. With a wagon train stretching out over a half mile, not to mention the freed slaves that he's brought with him, they have moved at a crawl.

From the weapon stores of the slavers and the dead bodies of the enemy soldiers, they were able to equip most of the freed men with armor and weapons. Those who had never wielded a weapon before were given crossbows and formed into squads. The women, children, and the few elderly stayed within the center of the column as it marched northward toward Madoc.

Among the freed slaves, jubilation reigns. When before all they had to look forward to was a life of misery and servitude, now they are free with the hopes of remaining that way. Surely if anyone can bring them forth out of the Empire alive and well, Black Hawk can.

The rest accompanying him have a more realistic appreciation of the situation. They know there are still forces that yet lie between them and Madoc. None of them believe they'll simply be allowed to walk to safety. It's simply a matter of time before sufficient forces gather to strike.

Scouts are out in every direction and so far haven't reported sighting any other sizeable force. When a patrol or caravan comes within striking distance, Ceadric takes several hundred Raiders and takes them out. Whenever the enemy is destroyed, they strip the dead of their armor and weapons. They then take them back and arm what freed slaves that are still without.

During their trek northward, the towns they encounter are quickly taken. Soldiers are killed, slaves are freed and given the opportunity to join them, and the shops are raided for much needed supplies. A force this large goes through food quickly. Illan gave the order that civilians are not to be accosted under any circumstances. Any who give them problems were to be brought to him for judgment.

So far the process has worked fairly well. The first town they raided after Korazan, a couple of the new, younger raiders took advantage of a young woman. When brought before Illan, the young men pleaded their innocence but too many had witnessed them taking her into the building. Illan pronounced them guilty and left their bodies hanging from the eaves of the building where the woman was attacked as an example to the rest. Since them, there have been no reports of any molestation of civilians by any of his men.

Another item the scouts were on a lookout for were bridges. The sack of crystals containing the explosive ones James had left him is now all but empty. Only two crystals remain. Whenever a bridge was sighted, he sent Ceadric with the sack of crystals to take out the bridge. He and his men would ride up to the bridge where he would toss a crystal onto the center span. Ten seconds later the crystal would explode leaving a large hole in the center. A few were made more sturdily and required two of the crystals to destroy it.

Earlier this morning while they were on the move, scouts reported the fortress of Al-Ziron was but two days ahead of them. A force of over a thousand men was estimated to be garrisoned there. Unwilling to tackle a fortified fortress, he makes the decision to leave the road and head cross country to the northeast. With any luck he and his men will be too large for them to attack, and those soldiers will remain where they are, allowing them to pass by.

The wagons rolling along behind him are filled to brimming with water and food for the horses and people. It's unlikely they will be able to forage for anything else from here on out. No more towns lie between where they are and Madoc. Any that used to be here were destroyed when the Empire came through last year.

Riding behind his banner are still over five hundred Raiders, those are all that's left from the many battles fought since they first entered the Empire. The slaves number close to a thousand; three hundred crossbowmen, five hundred bearing weapons of one type or another, and the rest is made up of the women, children and elderly. The elderly are suffering the trip the most. So far he's had to leave close to a dozen on the side of the road in a shallow grave after they died from the exertion of the trip.

His mind wanders while he rides, wondering where James is and if he's even still alive. Did this crazy plan work? Are Madoc's forces even now pushing the Empire out? But what's most on his mind is the threat of attack. They've been extremely lucky so far. How long is that going to last though? The closer they come to the border, the more likely that they will be hit and hit hard!

"Sir!" a scout cries as he rides up from the south.

"Report," Illan says as the man draws near.

"A score of riders comes from the south," reports the scout. "They don't look like soldiers, rather civilians."

From where Miko rides next to Illan he asks, "What were they wearing?"

"Most had on robes of one kind or another," he replies.

Illan glances to Miko, he understands the significance of that. "How far away are they?"

"A day, maybe more. They are moving only slightly faster than we are," he explains.

"Very well," replies Illan. "Return and keep an eye on them. If they should begin moving faster, return to let us know immediately."

Giving a smart salute, the scout says, "Yes, sir." Then he turns his horse and gallops back to the south.

"Mages you think?" Miko asks though he already knows the answer.

"Would think so," Illan states. "Moving slow though, that bothers me."

"Why?" questions Miko.

Illan glances to him and says, "It most likely means they're pacing us until other forces arrive then all will attack together." After a moment he adds, "Tell Ceadric and Delia I want to talk to them. Oh, and have Brother Willim come too."

Miko gives him a nod and then goes to find them.

Ceadric is the first to make his appearance. "What's up?" he asks.

"Tell you when the others join us," replies Illan.

They wait for several more minutes before first Delia joins them then Miko returns with Brother Willim in tow.

Continuing to ride, Illan has them move ahead of the column so he won't be overheard. "Scouts have reported a score of mages approaching from the rear," he tells them.

"A score?" asks Ceadric in surprise. "They've never committed that many at one time."

"You must be causing them difficulties for them to commit so many," suggests Brother Willim.

"Indeed," replies Illan.

"Are they close?" Delia asks.

"Right now they're about a day behind and are pacing us," he replies.

"We think they may be waiting for reinforcements before attacking," pipes up Miko.

Illan nods. "That's right." To Ceadric he says, "Send scouts further out. We need to know what's on the way. The scouts currently behind us are keeping an eye on them and will let us know if they make a move to quicken their pace."

"That would mean whatever they are planning is about to happen," comments Ceadric.

Illan nods to Ceadric who moves to get the scouts underway then turns to Miko and Brother Willim. "Can you handle them in the event of an attack?"

"Twenty?" considers Brother Willim. "I don't think so. It would depend on how strong they are."

"I'm not sure what I can do against magic," admits Miko. "The Star works well against otherworldly creatures, but flesh and blood?" He pauses a second before continuing, "I just don't know."

"Whether or not we can readily defeat them is immaterial," states Brother Willim. "If we wait for other reinforcements to arrive the situation will only get worse. I say we turn back and deal with them now while our chances are the highest."

"I agree," says Delia. "The longer we wait the worse it will become."

Glancing to the sky, Illan says, "It's still an hour before noon. Let's wait a couple hours to see if Ceadric's scouts find anything. If not, we'll turn around and attack."

"And if they do?" asks Miko.

"Then we'll adjust our plans accordingly," he replies. "Return to your people and be ready."

They break up and return to the column. Illan resumes his place at the head while the others rejoin their groups to inform them of what's going on.

With a possible attack imminent, Illan has the column tighten up and posts Raiders on either end. They stop at noon for a brief rest and lunch break, can't afford to have everyone tired and hungry if the battle should begin soon.

They no sooner come to a stop and begin handing out rations than a rider comes galloping from the northwest. At the sight of the fast approaching rider, Illan and the other leaders move to greet him.

"Milord!" the rider cries out as he comes to a stop before Illan. "There's a force of foot and cavalry on the other side of the river to the west. They were about to cross over a bridge when it suddenly exploded and collapsed!"

"James!" cries Miko in jubilation. "It has to be."

"Did you see three riders racing away from the bridge on this side?" Illan asks.

Shaking his head the scout replies, "No. The whole area was so packed with refugees fleeing your approach that I didn't notice, we weren't that close. I left Gouric to keep an eye on the army across the river. When they could no longer use the bridge, they began moving north."

"This changes things," observes Miko.

Nodding, Illan says to the scout, "Return and let us know when and where that army makes it to this side of the river."

Giving Illan a salute, the scout turns and races back the way he came.

"Ceadric, send out scouts to see if they can find James and let him know where we are," he says.

"Yes sir," replies Ceadric who immediately moves to comply.

"Could that have been the force those mages are waiting for?" asks Miko.

"Possibly," states Illan. "But I'm not willing to bet on it. However, I think before we begin any attack on the mages we should wait until James rejoins us."

"That would be a good idea," states Miko.

As a dozen men race off to the north to hunt for James, Illan keeps the column moving ever closer to Madoc.

Ever since they crossed the river, James and Jiron have holed up in an abandoned farmhouse. Their horses were all but collapsing after the grueling race they ran to the river. Outside, the moon has risen and its light casts shadows across night's landscape.

Before darkness set in he used his mirror and found Illan and the others already setting up camp for the night. Still several hours to the south, he and Jiron had decided to rest through the night to give their horses a chance to recover their strength before rejoining the others.

The force they left on the far side of the river had reached a bridge two hours before dusk and crossed over. They then moved south a couple more miles before stopping. When they crossed the river, a rider was dispatched to the fort. Shortly after his arrival forces from the fortress began moving to join the others. Now together, the two forces number close to ten thousand men.

As if that wasn't bad enough, another force was sighted moving toward Illan from the east. Composed of cavalry, they numbered in excess of two thousand. The good news is that there didn't look like a mage was traveling with either force. It would be bad enough with just that many men, but throw a mage into the mix and James isn't sure how well it would go.

His supply of crystals is now gone. Whatever is left with Delia and Illan is all that remains from the supply he brought from The Ranch. He fervently hopes they didn't use all of it, they'll need it when they encounter the forces moving to intercept them.

The farmhouse they are using has been long abandoned. The roof has collapsed on one side and the walls look like they will collapse at any time. The door that once stood in the doorway has long since disappeared. Jiron stands at one of the two windows and gazes out into the night. James lies back on his blanket and stares at the stars shining through one of the many gaps in the ceiling.

"They're going to attack tomorrow," Jiron says. Worry for his sister and friends gnaws at him.

"Our horses should be sufficiently rested by morning," James tells him. "We'll rejoin them before the battle."

"I hope so," he stresses.

"If we get through this battle, we're home free," says James encouragingly.

"I just wish Tersa had remained with Roland," Jiron sighs as he turns from the window to glance at James. "What was she thinking?"

Turning his head to look at his friend, James grins. "Who knows what girls think?" he wonders. "She's a strong woman, in lots of way like her brother."

"Headstrong and stubborn?" grins Jiron back.

"Something like that," he replies with a chuckle.

From outside, the sound of a lone horse is heard approaching the farmhouse. James immediately cancels his orb as he gets to his feet.

"Stay here," Jiron whispers as he pulls a knife and moves to the open doorway. Gazing out, he sees a horseman silhouetted by the moonlight.

The man has come to a stop and is staring at the house, probably trying to figure out why the light went out. His hands remain free of weapons as he continues to scrutinize the house.

Moving along the inside wall of the farmhouse, Jiron makes his way over to the window on the opposite side. Slipping through, he lands on the ground outside silently and makes his way back around to the front. When he gets to the corner he peers around to find the man still sitting there.

Suddenly, an orb flashes into being above the man's head, startling him. He draws his sword and makes to flee.

"Wait!" cries out Jiron as he places his knife back in its sheath. The man is obviously from the north.

James realizes the same thing and comes out from the house. "We're friends!" he hollers a second behind Jiron. The orb above the man's head winks out as another appears over James' shoulder.

"James?" the man asks.

Stepping forward, James nods his head.

Sighing in relief, the man says, "You scared me out of ten year's growth."

"Sorry," he apologizes.

"No harm done," the man replies. "We've had riders out looking for you ever since you blew the bridge earlier today."

"Are you from Black Hawk?" Jiron asks.

"That's right," the man says. "Was supposed to let you know where he is."

"We already know," explains James. "Tell him our horses are exhausted and we will be there in the morning. Also, there's a sizeable force a half a day away to the north. Another one is closing on him from the east, at least two thousand riders strong."

"With the mages coming from the south this could get bad," the rider comments.

"Mages?" asks James. "What mages?" He glances to Jiron and sees the worry in his eyes.

"Heard from another scout that had come from the south that there are a score of them," he explains.

"How close were they?" Jiron asks.

"Last I heard they were a day away," he tells him. "But that was this morning and at the time they weren't making any effort to catch us, just keeping pace."

James thinks for a minute then says, "Tell Illan to stay where he is and prepare for attack. We'll get there as soon as it's light. Hopefully no attack will come before then."

"Yes sir," the scout says then turns his horse around and gallops away into the night.

Jiron hears a sigh escape James. Glancing over to him he arcs an eyebrow questioningly.

"A score of mages," he says. "How am I going to best a score of mages?"

"Remember what you did at the City of Light?" he asks.

"Yes I do," he replies with a nod. "But if I do that, I'll end up killing us all. That much power would surely create an explosion of epic proportions. Our people would never get away in time to escape the blast."

"You always say that if you have time to prepare, you can do anything," Jiron states.

"I never said I could do anything, just that it is easier on me," he corrects.

Jiron looks at him with an expression that says 'stop nitpicking'. "What I mean is, you have all night," he clarifies. "Can't you come up with something?"

His mind is frozen with the thought of having to face twenty mages. He simply can't get around that fact. Back before they bolted into the buried city, the mages were kicking his butt badly. These are most likely the very same mages. What has changed other than he's more tired now and has fewer reserves with which to draw upon?

Shaking his head, he says, "I'm sorry. Maybe it's just that I'm exhausted." He can see the disappointment in his eyes.

Jiron stares at him for a moment. Finally breaking the silence, he says, "Then you get some sleep. I'll keep watch."

James lays back on his blanket with the knowledge he's let his friend down. *I'm only a man!* That's the problem with always coming up with clever strategies, everyone keeps expecting you to be able to do it again, time after time. *Maybe a little rest will clear my mind.*

Before falling asleep, he glances over to see Jiron by the window staring out into the night. Closing his eyes, he relaxes and let's sleep claim him.

"Wake up!"

Fighting the fog of sleep, James opens his eyes. It's still dark outside and Jiron is shaking his shoulder.

"We got company," he whispers in his ear when James stirs.

Coming awake quickly James abruptly sits up. The sound of many horses fast approaching comes to him. All vestiges of sleep leave him as he gets to his feet. He follows Jiron to the window overlooking the direction from which the riders are approaching. Pulling a slug from his belt, he gazes out the window but only sees blackness.

"Who are they?" he asks.

"Don't know," replies Jiron.

As the riders draw closer, they emerge from the dark as indistinct shadows in the false dawn of morning. The shadows are heading in the general direction of the abandoned farmhouse and will pass by close. James holds his breath as they near.

"Think we'll get there in time?" they hear one rider ask.

"If we don't, there'll be hell to pay," another replies.

They speak northern! Must be members of the Alliance come to the aid of Black Hawk. James moves to the door and rushes outside. "Friends!" he yells as he exits the farmhouse.

"James, no!" hollers Jiron in a hushed voice.

The riders, over a hundred strong, come to an abrupt stop at the sound of his greeting. They then turn back to the farmhouse.

"We don't know they're friends," Jiron says as he comes to stand beside him.

"Who are you?" asks one of the riders. His voice is rather gruff and when he stops before James the smell coming from him is almost overpowering. He smells like a man who's never seen the inside of a bathtub in his life.

James begins to realize his mistake. The men are wearing a hodgepodge of uniforms, all are extremely dirty. One man who stops next to the one who asked the question has a necklace slung around his neck that looks like it has fingers and ears attached to it rather than beads.

"Uh," he says then stops.

"We're travelers," Jiron pipes up. His right hand rests on the hilt of a knife.

"Travelers eh?" the man with the necklace asks. Several of the others laugh.

"We don't have time for this," the first man says. "Kill them."

328 Shades of the Past

"Eyes!" he yells to Jiron a fraction of a second before a massive starburst explodes just above James' head. The suddenness of the explosion startles the men and momentarily blinds them.

Jiron wastes no time. Jumping for the leader, he strikes with a knife and pulls him from his horse. When the leader hits the ground the man with the necklace is struck with a slug, sending him flying off his horse.

Swinging into the leader's saddle, Jiron takes the reins and lays about him with his knives. The men, still half blinded by the flash of light are unable to fend off his attacks. "Come on man," he yells to James.

Grabbing the empty saddle that once held the man with the necklace, he pulls himself up. Another man cries out as Jiron deals him a lethal blow. Reaching down to grab the reins, he feels the blade of a sword pass where his head had just been. Lashing out with magic, he sends a wave of force toward his attacker which knocks him backward off his horse.

Once he has the reins, he kicks his horse in the sides and bolts through the ring of half blind attackers. Jiron plunges his knife in the throat of one last attacker before he follows. Knocking men and horses aside, they race away from the farmhouse.

Crumph! Crumph! Crumph!

Three explosions rip through the group of horsemen.

Flying across the ground in the predawn light, they quickly leave the scene of the attack behind. Heading southwest, they make for Illan's last known position.

"Don't ever do that again!" criticizes Jiron. "Just because someone speaks your language does not make them an ally."

"Sorry," replies James.

As the light gradually brightens, they're able to tell the men from the farmhouse haven't followed after. Slowing their horses to a canter, James removes his mirror from his belt pouch and scans behind them. The men, only about two dozen now, are still at the farmhouse.

With pursuit not an immediate threat, he scrolls the image to the west and south to find Illan. When he finally locates him, his breath catches in his throat as he sees them lined up for battle.

Soldiers of the Empire, both foot and horse are arrayed in an arc to the north. "They must have continued through the night in order to reach them so fast," he says.

Jiron moves closer to look at the image. "At least they haven't attacked yet," he says hopefully.

James shifts the image south of Illan's position to locate the party of approaching mages. It doesn't take him long to find them, now less than an hour away from Illan and the others.

"We're out of time!" cries Jiron as he kicks his horse up to a full gallop. He may kill it, but he plans to reach his sister before the attack commences. James puts his mirror back in his pouch and follows along behind.

Literally flying over the ground, the only thing on Jiron's mind is his sister.

Chapter   Twenty Eight

Shortly after leaving Baerustin, Kerith-Ayxt received word of the destruction wrought at the School. His mind at first was unable to come to grips with what the mage who brought him word was actually telling him. When the mage finished relating the tale, all the other mages who were traveling with the High Lord Magus stood in stunned silence.

Loss of the library? ***Unthinkable!***

Twice he had the mage restate the message until the facts finally sank in. Many of the mages with him thought he would erupt in a fit of rage, but all he felt was unimaginable loss. The library had held the works of some of history's greatest minds. Leaps in the workings of magic that propelled generations onward to greater understanding are now lost.

Despite the edict given by Lord Cytok, he sent all but a score of his mages back to the school with a most insurmountable task. To write down their knowledge before it too becomes lost. Even with that, it may take centuries before the School is once again able to train the caliber of mages they have now.

Finally, anger begins to set in. He's not sure how, but this has to be the work of that rogue mage who has caused the Empire such troubles the last year. Even from beneath the sands at Baerustin, still he is able to accomplish such destruction.

His anger requires an outlet, someone upon whom he can vent the anger and sorrow that seeks to consume him. The mage may lie dead beneath Baerustin, but he can seek vengeance on those who traveled with him. Black Hawk and those who ride with him shall know the wrath of the High Lord Magus.

Maintaining a harsh pace, he finally comes to within a day of Black Hawk's forces. His rage, which once was a white hot sun demanding action, has now calmed into a calculating anger. One doesn't become the High Lord Magus by allowing one's emotions to get the better of them.

To the north he locates by magical means a force of soldiers heading to the river in an attempt to cut off Black Hawk's retreat from the Empire. Keeping a steady pace, he maintains the gap between his mages and the Death Hawk. He plans to keep this pace until he can hit him at the same time as the other attacking force.

When the bridge blew and the army was forced to proceed further north to find a bridge to cross the river, his rage almost got the better of him once more. But logic won out and he continued as he had been and simply kept pace with Black Hawk.

Finally, once the army made it across to the eastern shore, he knew it was time. Quickening his pace, he moved to close the gap for the attack.

Their horses on the verge of collapsing, James and Jiron see the cloud of dust that hangs over the battlefield. Too late to join their comrades before the onslaught, they arrive shortly after it's begun.

From the ranks of the defenders, a flight of crossbow bolts is launched through the air and lands with devastating effect among the Empire's charging cavalry. They see Illan marshalling his forces and repulsing the initial attack of the enemy. The recently freed crossbowmen send another volley toward the Empire's cavalry and more riders fall.

The bulk of Black Hawk's Raiders face off against the foot and cavalry to the north. On their southern flank, the Hand of Asran work to counter the magical attacks from mages. James' skin crawls from the amount of magic being used down there. When before he sensed magic it was a mere tingling or prickling, this time it's like bugs crawling over and under his skin. A light flares brilliantly followed by the roar of an explosion a moment later.

"The Hand is holding its own," observes Jiron. The flash of a startling white light tells them Miko is there with them.

Illan's force is completely surrounded except on the side where the mages are hammering away at the Hand. James removes a piece of rope and secures himself to the saddle. Scanning the battlefield quickly, he finds what he's looking for then turns to Jiron and says, "Follow me." Kicking his already tired horse, he races across the desert.

Rather than riding toward the mages like Jiron thought he was going to do, James angles toward the rear of the enemy soldier's line. They're almost upon them before the enemy even realizes it. Shields spring to life as James encases them both in protective barriers.

Crumph! Crumph! Crumph!

Explosions rip through the ranks of enemy soldiers, clearing a path for the charging steeds.

Crumph! Crumph! Crumph!

Dozens of men and horses are thrown into the air as the ground erupts beneath them. *Crumph!* Again and again, James unleashes the power of magic to clear a path to the beleaguered men in the center.

"James!" Scar calls out after the first explosion.

"It's Jiron!" cries Stig as his mace pulps the soldier's face that he's locked in combat with. Using his shield, he pushes another man aside as he strikes out at yet a third, crushing the man's shoulder with a thunderous blow.

Crumph! Crumph!

Suddenly, Jiron's horse collapses and he's thrown free. The shield surrounding him winks out as he lands amidst enemy soldiers. He comes to his feet quickly with knives at the ready and begins laying into them with amazing speed. As packed in as the enemy soldiers are, their own numbers hamper their ability to use their swords. Knives flash and men fall before they're able to defend themselves.

Oblivious to Jiron's predicament, James continues on toward their line. *Crumph!* All of a sudden, the way is clear to the defenders within the ring of attackers. Kicking his horse, he races for the opening. Jorry and Uther are there and stand aside as he jumps over the ring of dead before them.

"James!" they cry as he lands among them.

"To Jiron!" they cry once James is past and the fighters from The Ranch wade into the enemy in an attempt to come to his aid.

Off to his right he sees Delia and the other slingers loosing slugs as fast as they can. Next to them, Hedry and his archers target the enemy crossbowmen that stand further back. Many within the defender's circle lie dead with bolts protruding from their bodies.

"Glad you could make it," Illan shouts as he comes toward him. All of a sudden there's solid bang as a crossbow bolt strikes Illan's helm. Leaving a dent, it gets deflected away. Several other fresh dents show upon his helm as well.

"Didn't want to miss the fun," he says. Glancing back, he sees Scar and Potbelly reaching Jiron's side. Scar's double swords take the enemy out as Potbelly rushes through the opening. Using his knife to deflect a sword's thrust, he follows through with his sword and drives it to the hilt in the soldier's chest. Side by side with Jiron, they begin to fall back to their line.

Jerking his thumb to where the Hand is battling the mages, Illan says, "They really need you."

"On the way." Untying himself from the saddle, he dismounts quickly and works his way through the defenders to where the Hand and Miko are battling the mages. One of the brothers lies unmoving on the ground, Brother Willim and the other three face the mages with green glows surrounding them.

As fast as green shoots begin to leave the earth, a mage burns them with fire. Bugs appear and are quickly destroyed. Another brother cries out as his chest cracks open. Falling to the ground he soon lies still.

James runs forward, his shield shimmering around him. Summoning the magic, he lashes out…

Crumph! Crumph! Crumph!

…but has little effect other than throwing dirt in the air to create a smokescreen to obscure their vision. The mages themselves remain untouched.

He comes to a stop between Brother Willim and Miko. With Star raised high and shining brilliantly, Miko turns to him. "Knew you would come," he says.

"We can't hold them much longer," says Brother Willim as he throws another seed in the air. Moving forward rapidly, it grows into a ball of tangled vines and lands near the leading edge of mages. The vines move rapidly upon the ground and entangle the feet of two of them. Yanking them to the ground, the vines begin to squeeze and tighten, constricting like a giant snake.

Then another mage comes to their rescue and the vines literally explode off of the two trapped men.

"I've already lost two brothers," Brother Willim states. "You're the Gardener, do something."

Gardener?

Turning back to the mages, he lets the magic surge forth and the ground begins to rumble. Suddenly, the earth cracks open but then slams shut again as opposing magic works against him.

A cloud of birds swoops down from the sky toward the mages. Bolts of energy fly from the assembled mages and begin taking them out

334   Shades of the Past

before they can close. Explosions of fire light up the sky as whole groups of birds are incinerated in massive fireballs.

James reaches to the clouds to pull them in but magic again works against him and his effort goes to naught. The dust from when the ground exploded is beginning to settle and he looks across to see one of the mages, an older one, staring at him. It almost seems as if time pauses as the two stare at each other. Then the mage raises his hand and the onslaught begins.

When the ground erupted, Kerith-Ayxt felt it was slightly different than the magic of those he faced when the attack first began. Then when he stared across the battlefield and saw the mage he couldn't believe his eyes. Never has anyone succeeded in escaping Baerustin.

It must have been he who had attempted to crack open the earth beneath them and to summon a storm. The High Lord Magus had easily countered such basic magics. He is amazed at the lack of finesse this mage has in what he tries to accomplish.

Now to finish it. Raising his hands above his head, he summons the magic. And with the knowledge of centuries of mages behind it, lets it loose.

The tingling sensation flares worse than ever as the mage raises his hands. Pouring more of his reserve power into the barrier, he extends it to encompass Miko and the rest of the Hand. When the full force of the mage's magic strikes the barrier, James is literally knocked backward a step and the shield collapses. Reinstating the shield again, his mind boggles at the amount of magic that was just used against him.

Miko and the Hand continue to counter what the rest of the mages are throwing at them; fireballs, lightning, and many other types of destructive magic. All they're able to do is simply keep them at bay without any opportunity of using offensive magic of their own.

Again the mage sends a wave of magic toward the barrier. A blinding light flares when it connects and James is momentarily blinded as the barrier again falls. His nerve endings tingle and he staggers back again. Miko catches him with the hand not holding the Star.

It's a struggle to replace the barrier once more. Another attack like the last one and he may not have anything left in him, it's taken the rest of his reserves to bring it back up this third time, he doubts if he'll be able to do it for a fourth.

Miko glances to his friend and sees the strain showing on his face. "You okay?" he asks though he already knows the answer.

"I'm about wiped out," he admits.

"We can't win this can we?" Miko asks.

Shaking his head James says, "After the mage's next attack, I'll be used up if not dead." He nods to the Star blazing in his Miko's hand and adds, "Then it will all rest on you."

Miko glances to the Star. An incredible source of power, but in his inexperienced hands it isn't being used to its fullest potential. If only James could use it, his experience augmented by the power of the Star would be formidable. Only problem is, if James touches it, he dies for only those born upon this world can touch it and live. James' friend Dave learned that at the cost of his life.

Then suddenly, the mage lets loose the most massive attack of magic yet…

Around them, the cries of battle rage as the Empire's soldiers batter at the defenders. The crossbows from the former slaves continue sending wave after wave of bolts into the attackers. But for every enemy they take down, two take his place.

Illan has joined the fighting now that the defenders have suffered losses. Rallying his men to greater valor, he uses his sword with devastating effect.

Scar and Potbelly are suddenly surrounded by enemy soldiers and all seems lost until Jorry and Uther come to their aid. The two pairs, so at odds when telling their tales, stand shoulder to shoulder as each saves the lives of the others. Bodies begin piling up as they kill all who come.

Atop one of the wagons, Shorty stands next to a case of knives liberated from one of the towns they passed through. One after another, his knives fly over the heads of the defenders to take out soldier after soldier.

Aaaah!!

James staggers back as the full force of the magic strikes the barrier, shattering it. Momentarily disoriented, he soon returns to his senses.

Miko could feel the effect of the magic as it struck the barrier. It almost seemed as if a shockwave went through James to him from where he had his arm around his friend, helping to keep him standing. Then suddenly, a memory surfaces of an earlier battle after they just met.

They had gone with Rylin to rescue Sheila and her mother from the bandits after they destroyed their caravan. During the battle, he had lent James his strength so he could vanquish the bandit leader. Glancing at the Star, he wonders if they could do the same thing here.

"James!" he hollers. "Use the Star!"

"I can't!" he yells back. "It'll kill me."

"No," Miko counters. "Use it," he looks James in the eyes, "through me."

Could it work? he wonders.

Miko stretches out his hand but James shakes his head. "Call forth the magic of the Star." As Miko connects with the magic within the Star, James creates a leech line between himself and Miko. Immediately, the power of the Star flows into him. Such power. Such raw, primal power suffuses him.

This magic is different than that which he had always used. Perhaps it's the difference between priest magic which comes from the gods and regular magic found in the world around you.

Gathering new strength from the flow of magic coming from Miko, he disengages from him and moves forward. A spike in the tingling foretells the release of the magic as the mage again sends a devastating attack. Using the magic from the Star, he erects a barrier stronger than any he's been able to accomplish before. When the magic strikes it, an enormous, blinding flash of light explodes. Unlike the previous times, James hardly feels any effect. He looks across the battlefield at the surprised look on the mage's face.

Sure to have destroyed him, Kerith-Ayxt stares in shocked wonder at James standing there unfazed then quickly comes to a decision. "Aezyl!" he shouts over the roar of battle.

"Yes milord," his aide replies coming to his side.

"Form the Lattice of Power," he says.

Aezyl's eyes widen. "Yes my lord," he finally replies then turns to the other mages and makes ready.

The Lattice of Power is a means through which many mages link in order to supply a single mage with their collective magical reserves. The First Circle mages are linked to the Second who are in turn linked to the Third and so forth. It's very similar to what they do with slaves during spells requiring more than the usual amounts of magic. The only problem is that once the Lattice is formed, it can only be undone by the one at the Lattice's focal point, either by a conscious will or his death.

Before the Lattice is readied, James unleashes a wave of force toward Kerith-Ayxt. Countering the blast, the High Lord Magus gasps at the sheer power of the attack. Behind him he hears, "Ready my lord."

Casting the spell to bring the Lattice to life, Kerith-Ayxt is suddenly suffused with power as conduits merge with him, channeling the power of the most powerful mages in the Empire. The power now at his beck and call is incredible, almost makes him feel like a god. With a grin, he unleashes a devastating attack of fire and air at James. The battle is joined…

Between Delia's slingers and the enemy stands a line of Raiders mixed in with recently armed freed slaves. The Raiders are faring well but the slaves are dropping fast. Delia has her slingers target the enemy as they appear in gaps of the lines to aid the fighters but there are simply too many.

Taking one of the four crystals from the last remaining sack of crystals in their possession, she sets it to sling and sends it far over the heads of the enemy. A minute later, men drop as spheres appear among them. Bolts of electricity flash as the orbs begin discharging the magic that they drew from the soldiers now lying still on the ground.

After sending more slugs into the enemy, she removes another crystal and sends it flying. Again, men drop and spheres appear firing bolts of electricity. Dozens of men are dropped by the initial leeching of their magic by the crystal and scores more are dropped by the subsequent discharges of electricity.

She continues to do that. While waiting for the men to again group closely together, she sends slugs to fell the attackers. Once a sufficient number are together, she sends another of the crystals flying into their midst.

When the last sphere of the last crystal has disappeared, she looks on at the still overpowering numbers of the enemy. Feeling hopelessness sapping her will, she continues felling men with slugs.

Unfortunately, the rest of the slingers aren't doing nearly as well as she. Terrance is hitting men primarily on parts of their body covered in armor. A dull thud and a dent is all he's managing to accomplish.

The others are doing a trifle better, some are connecting. Perhaps not killing blows, but enough to injure which slows down their defenses, enabling Raiders to get within their guard better.

Off to one side, the line buckles. The Raiders who were holding are suddenly inundated by a two score of Parvatis and they go down fast.

Their dual swords opening up a swath twenty feet wide, they are soon among the crossbowmen.

The crossbowmen fall back fast, loosing bolts as they retreat. They take down over half the Parvatis before Illan, Ceadric and other Raiders move to engage them. By the time they take out the last of the Parvatis and reestablished the line, two score crossbowmen lay dead as well as half a score of Raiders.

Ceadric and Illan hold the line while others move to assist. The defender's line is slowly shrinking in on itself as more and more of the defenders fall.

Ka-Boom!

A gigantic cloud of smoke and flame reaches to the sky from where James is battling Kerith-Ayxt. He, Miko and the three remaining members of the Hand of Asran stare in awe at the flame burning on the other side of the protective barrier. Using the power of the Star, James extinguishes the flames and then concentrates on the ground before the mages.

A rumbling begins and the earth cracks open. Suddenly, a gigantic rock hand emerges as Rocky begins climbing out of the ground. Eight feet high and made of stone, Rocky turns on the mages and lurches forward.

Brother Willim and the other two members of the Hand work to keep the soldiers at bay. Large patches of thorny vines impede their way while others actually grasp them, constricting until they're dead. The death of any man is a hard blow to the Brothers even though it is in defense of their lives.

Miko sits cross-legged on the ground with the Star in his lap clasped between both hands. The funneling of power to James is taking its toll. His system is simply not used to having so much power passing through it for so long. Breathing has become labored and he's soaked in sweat, sort of reminds him of how James gets now and then when he does too much.

Kerith-Ayxt lashes out with power and Rocky explodes sending a myriad of rocks flying in all directions.

Just what James was hoping for, he sends out the power and takes hold of the flying debris. Stopping it in midair, he then sends it flying back toward the mages. A shield springs to life to protect the mages from the barrage. It manages to deflect all but a couple which had already passed beyond the edge of the shield. One of the rocks manages to strike a mage in the side of the head. Staggering backward, the mage's legs collapse and he hits the ground hard where he remains unmoving.

A slight drop in the power coming to Kerith-Ayxt tells him the mage that was hit is dead. Putting the fallen mage out of his mind, he brings his hands together then opens them up to reveal a shimmering ball. Launching from his hands, the ball flies toward James.

Using the power of the Star, he strikes the ball before it has a chance to close the distance and...

Ke-Pow!

...an intense explosion knocks him backward. A backlash of magic rips through him like a hot knife and for a moment, all his defenses are down.

"James!" yells Brother Willim. Rushing to his side, he grabs him as he teeters on the brink of falling.

His mind reeling, he takes hold of Brother Willim's shoulder and rights himself just as another shimmering ball flies toward him. Summoning the magic, he attacks the ball.

Ke-Pow!

Again the ball explodes sending another backlash of power burning through him. His legs buckle and if it weren't for Brother Willim, he would have hit the ground. He's not sure if he'll be able to survive another attack like that. Realizing that even with the Star, he isn't going to win this battle, he mumbles something to Brother Willim.

"What?" Brother Willim asks.

"Tell your brethren to halt all magic, now," he says with more strength.

"But we'll be killed," he states.

Shaking his head James shouts, "Just do it!" Pushing away from Brother Willim, he makes his way to Miko.

"Shut it down!" he yells to be heard over the roar of the battle. "Shut it down now!"

Miko is so caught in maintaining the flow that he isn't paying any attention to him. Stepping back, James kicks the Star out of his hands. When the Star leaves his hands, Miko collapses into an unconscious heap.

Another shimmering ball flies toward him, the mage grinning in triumph. Sending out his magic, he explodes the ball and once more he's hit by what must be a backlash of power which sends him to his knees.

Turning back toward the mages, James gazes at the mage standing there. The look on the mage's face says he's sure of victory as another of the shimmering spheres appears between his hands. Using the last vestiges of power, he casts one final spell. A shimmering bubble leaves his hand and floats its way toward Kerith-Ayxt. As his sight fades to blackness James sees the look of victory again on the face of the High Lord Magus, then passes out.

"Is that the best you can do?" Kerith-Ayxt asks.

With a thought, he sends the sphere to destroy the bubble. Instead of being destroyed, the sphere appears to be absorbed by the bubble. Then suddenly something latches onto the flow of magic coming from him and begins drawing magic.

The High Lord Magus tries to cancel the flow but realizes in panic that he is unable to. Growing in intensity, the bubble begins drawing more and more power from him. Behind Kerith-Ayxt, mages fall as the Lattice pulls ever more magic from them to replenish his reserves that are being drained by the bubble.

Sparkles begin dancing within the bubble from the accumulation of magic stored within. Brother Willim and the two remaining followers of Asran watch in awe as the bubble glows with growing intensity, the sparks within it increasing in number and intensity.

From across the battlefield, Jiron blocks a soldier's downward hack with the crossed blades of his knives and kicks him backward. Momentarily free of attackers, he glances around the battlefield and sees the light coming from where the bubble is growing. Suddenly, another soldier appears before him and thrusts with his sword.

Deflecting the blade to the right, he lashes out with his other knife and takes him in the side of the neck. As the man falls, his eyes are again drawn to the now blindingly white light. "Oh no," he breathes as recognition comes.

"What?" asks Stig from where he's parrying a series of attacks.

"We're all dead," he says with finality. Memories of the explosion that rocked the night when they escaped the City of Light play through his mind. Casting one more glance to the growing doom behind him, he turns back to the battle at hand.

The High Lord Magus, the most powerful mage in the Empire, is on his knees as magic continues to flow from him. Unable to stop it, he watches as the bubble before him grows ever larger. At one point, the light coming from it robs him of his sight as the brightness burns his retinas away.

As he falls to the ground he can feel his skin beginning to shrivel itself upon his bones as his life leaves him. Sadness grips him. Sadness of the loss of magical advances. Sadness over the loss of the many friends already dead behind him. But most of all, he's sad for what the future may hold. The School of the Arcane helped control and direct those who practiced magic so the world wouldn't have to endure atrocities. Now, without their influence, how many more Baerustin's will there be?

His lungs quit working and finally, his heart grinds to a stop. Kerith-Ayxt, High Lord of all the Magi, dies.

The bubble, now brighter than the sun reaches critical mass. The magic within it too great for it to last much longer. When at last the bubble gives out…

Schtk!

…and time suddenly freezes just as the magic was about to explode outward.

Men stand frozen across the battlefield. Poised to attack, their swords remain stationary in the air. Arrows are halted in midair on their way to their targets. A surreal quiet settles over the battlefield as all sound is stilled.

Moving across the field of battle, a man winds his way through the men frozen in combat. On one side he sees a Raider with the point of a sword protruding from his back from the thrust of an enemy. On the other a head that was shorn from a nearby headless torso hovers two feet from the ground, waiting for time to start again before finishing its fall.

The man reaches where the Star of Morcyth lies upon the ground, still pulsating with light as if in defiance of the stoppage of time. Next he comes to Miko and pauses. Bending down, he runs his hand along the side of his face, caressing it as a father would his beloved child.

Standing up again, he continues along until coming to James. Glancing over to the bubble, frozen at the moment of detonation, the man shakes his head. "Why did you have to do that James?" he asks. "Couldn't you see another way?" Gazing at the unconscious James, a tear wells from his eye.

Of all the probably outcomes of bringing James to this world, this was one of the ones they feared the most. The only one they had feared more was his death before he finished what he was brought here to do. Now, the world stands upon the brink. Time, once a friend has become the enemy.

Returning his gaze to the man in whom the hope of the world had been placed, he just shakes his head sadly. Raising his hands, he creates a protective barrier around James and the rest of the defenders, a shield against the blast. That much he is allowed to do, no more. What happens from this point on rests in James' hands.

Once the shield is in place, the man straightens his blue vest and pushes back his felt hat. "Good luck James," he says then vanishes. Once the man is gone, the passing of time resumes.

Booooooom!

Chapter Twenty Nine

The sky turns red as fire burns across the top of the barrier in the blink of an eye. Many soldiers of the Empire are caught on the other side of the barrier and are incinerated in an instant. The ground leaps and ripples causing everyone to lose their balance and hit the ground.

Heat from the fire burning on the far side of the barrier passes through and is incredibly hot. Even with the protection the barrier affords, hair smokes and those caught at the edges suffer great burns.

A full minute does the ground move until finally settling down. Illan is the first to return to his feet. Staring up at the blaze which is covering the top of the dome, he asks under his breath, "James, what did you do?" In every direction, the fire burns. How are they even alive?

"What happened?" comes a voice behind him.

Illan turns to find Ceadric approaching, his head turning this way and that as he looks at the fire.

"I don't know," Illan replies. The smell of burnt hair comes to him and he looks to where the edge of the barrier touches ground and the dead men lying next to it have begun to smolder. "Get everyone away from the edges," he says. "Everyone to the center."

Ceadric nods and begins gathering men. "Up you dogs!" he yells to those still on the ground. "Pull the injured to the center. Away from the flame's edge!"

Jiron and Scar help Potbelly to the center. During the fighting, he had suffered a severe wound to the leg. A tourniquet is tied securely around his upper thigh to stop the flow of blood. "Can't take him anywhere," Scar comments to Jiron.

"Shut up," says Potbelly weakly. "Don't need any help."

Jiron sees Stig and shouts to him, "Get Miko! Potbelly needs him."

"Right," replies Stig and then hurries over to where Miko was last seen. He finds Delia there with the slingers helping Brother Willim and the rest of the Hand to organize the wounded. Miko lies there with the rest of them, unconscious.

"Is he alright?" he asks her. "Potbelly needs him."

"I don't know," she replies and then nods to where the Star has been returned to his hand. "If that can't help him nothing can."

Stig turns back to Scar and Jiron. "Over here!" he yells and they begin making their way over to them.

"Is the entire world burning?" he asks to no one in particular.

"I don't know," replies a soldier bringing a wounded comrade to the brothers for healing, "maybe."

The barrier had encompassed less than a hundred soldiers of the Empire. Hedry took it upon himself to round them up with the help of other Raiders and bring them to a central area where they could be kept under surveillance. The enemy soldiers who were too badly wounded were given a quick end.

Less than half their force remains. All the recently armed freed slaves perished in the fighting and most of the crossbowmen as well. Of the Raiders, only three hundred are left. Illan is amazed there are even that many left. Coming to where James is laid out, he asks Delia, "Is he alive?"

"Barely," she tells him. "His skin is hot to the touch and he trembles every now and then." She looks up at him and says, "I'm not sure if he'll survive."

"Can't you do anything?" Illan asks, turning to Brother Willim.

"He was the first one we saw to," he explains. "What's happening to him is beyond what we can do." Nodding to where Miko lies unconscious he adds, "Maybe with the Star Miko could do more, but until he awakens there's nothing more that can be done."

To Delia he says, "Let me know if his condition changes."

"I will," she replies.

As the fire rages across the barrier, the temperature within continues to rise. Men begin shedding their armor and soon all are wearing nothing more than their small clothes.

Half an hour later, blue sky filled with billowing black clouds begins to be seen through the top of the barrier as the fire starts subsiding. Shortly after that, Miko regains consciousness. Groaning, he opens his eyes then snaps them closed again as light stabs them like hot knives.

"He's awake," he hears a female voice say, "get Illan."

A hand touches his chest and gives a little shake. "Miko," he hears the voice say again and then realizes that it's Delia who is talking to him.

"Water," he croaks. A moment later his head is raised slightly and the neck of a water flask is put to his lips. He takes several small swallows before the water flask is taken away.

"Miko," Delia says again. "James needs you."

Coming fuller awake, he shades his eyes and then opens them a crack. The pain knifes into him again as he's helped to a sitting position. Looking around, he sees James lying next to him.

With fingers trembling from fatigue he picks up the Star from off his lap, then with Delia's help he scoots over to where James is lying. Head swimming and spots appearing before his eyes, he tries to concentrate and bring forth the magic of the Star. The trembling in the hand holding the Star increases as what little strength he's recovered leaves him. Suddenly, the Star falls from his fingers and only the quick reflexes of Jiron prevents it from falling upon James' chest. Swooning, Miko collapses.

"Damn!" curses Illan.

"At least the fire seems to be letting up," offers Shorty.

Looking up at the barrier's apex, Illan finds the fire has continued to subside even further. "That is something," he admits. Looking down at James, Illan hopes he comes out of it soon.

In no time at all, the fire upon the barrier has completely subsided. When no more flames are touching the barrier, it winks out. Cool desert air washes over them despite the fact it's the middle of the afternoon. After being in the sweltering heat contained within the barrier, even the hot summer air feels cool.

Looking around, they see an area of devastation beginning where the barrier had ended. Flat and grey, the ground looks to have been burnt clean by the blast, there are still pockets of fire scattered here and there. Of the enemy soldiers caught outside the barrier there's no sign, not even bones.

"Get the wounded in the wagons," Illan says as he begins barking out orders. "We still have a ways to go before we reach the safety of Madoc." He pauses a moment and waves Jiron over to him. "See that James and Miko are put in the same wagon," he tells him. "And post a guard."

Jiron nods and goes to see that it's done.

Potbelly is put into one of the wagons, his wound healed by the brothers. Alive and cranky he gives his friend Scar no end of trouble as he works to get him into a wagon. Jiron grins, if he's got strength enough to complain, he's likely going to make it.

It takes them an hour to be ready to roll. A couple of the wounded that the brothers said were beyond even their skill had to be put out of their misery. Brother Willim sits on the wagon carrying James and Miko as they get underway.

Illan takes the lead when they leave the untouched area where they were sheltered from the blast. His horse's hooves kick up the grey dust which soon clings to everything. They travel for an hour before the ground shows any sign of improvement. From there it gradually returns to its former state. By the time they leave the grey area behind them, everyone is coated with the grey dust. Looking back at the column behind him, Illan can't help but think they look like ghosts passing through the desert.

When night falls, they keep going. None wish to remain any longer in the Empire than they have to, especially seeing as how close they are to Madoc. During the night, Miko stirs a couple times and by morning he awakens completely. James on the other hand continues as he has been, feverish and bothered by tremors every once in a while.

Sitting up in the bed of the wagon, he looks around in the predawn light. Not entirely sure what's going on, he sees Brother Willim sitting on the seat next to the driver.

"Where are we?" he asks.

Turning to him, Brother Willim says, "A long way from where the battle was fought."

"We won?" he asks.

Grinning, he replies, "Yes we won. How do you feel?"

"Tired," he says with a yawn. Then he notices James lying next to him. Casting a worried look to Brother Willim he asks, "Is he okay?"

"We don't know," he explains. "He's been that way ever since the end of the battle."

Miko moves closer to his friend and places his hand on his chest. Sighing in relief, he feels the heart still beating.

"Hey man," Jiron says as he rides closer to the wagon. "Glad you're awake."

Miko glances to him and can see the lines of worry marring his face. He looks around himself for a moment before Brother Willim says, "It's in your belt pouch."

Taking hold of the pouch, he feels the Star within. Opening the pouch, he pulls forth the Star and taps its magic. Mouthing words silently, he kneels next to James and lets the glow from the Star envelope them both.

Jiron sends a rider to fetch Illan who arrives a few short minutes later. They ride next to the wagon in silence as Miko continues what he's doing. Finally, the glow disappears and he sits back against the side of the wagon.

"The fever's gone," he announces. "But his mind is…" then trails off as if he's trying to come up with the right words.

"What?" asks Illan.

Glancing to him, Miko says, "I'm not sure how to explain it. But he seems to be…elsewhere."

"What does that mean?" demands Jiron.

"I don't know," he replies. "It just is."

"How can we get him back?" asks Illan.

"I don't know," he admits. He looks from each in turn and they can see the worry in his eyes.

Then a rider comes thundering toward them from the head of the column. When he pulls up before Illan he says, "Riders coming, lot of 'em."

"Where?" Illan asks.

"From the north," the rider replies.

To Ceadric and Jiron he says, "To your men gentlemen."

Jiron gives him a nod as Ceadric says, "Yes sir."

"Keep an eye on him," Illan tells Miko.

"Count on it," he replies.

Turning his horse toward the head of the column, he kicks it in the sides and rushes forward. He reaches the front just before Ceadric and Jiron come with their men. Halting the column, they begin forming up for battle.

"They're ours!" cries a Raider when the riders come closer.

Sure enough, the approaching riders turn out to be over five hundred of Madoc's cavalry led by Captain Kurk.

"Am I glad to see you," Illan tells the captain as he draws close.

"Black Hawk," the captain replies with a nod. He takes in the bedraggled look of the men before him and the number of non military personal further back. "Heard there was some kind of disturbance in the area and was on our way to investigate."

"Escort us back to your camp and I'll tell you all about it," he says. "How far are we from our lines?"

"You're standing on them," he explains. "A week after you left Lythylla, Lord Pytherian and the Alliance went on the offensive. They've steadily pushed them back and have almost managed to reach the old border between Madoc and the Empire. Still some heavy fighting to the west, but the east is falling fast. The Kirkens have joined the fight and together we're giving them what for."

"Excellent," breathes Illan.

As the word spreads to the rear of the column, a cheer goes up. 'Black Hawk' and 'Madoc' resound as the people celebrate the fact that they are now safe. They did it. Not only have they passed from the Empire but it's on the verge of being forced out of Madoc.

Captain Kurk says, "Our camp is several hours away." He dispatches a rider back with word that Black Hawk is on the way. The rest of his men move to take charge of the prisoners.

"Lead on," Illan says and with a command, the column begins to move. Glancing back to a wagon riding near the center, he wonders what's going on inside James' head.

Smoke chokes him as he tries to outrun the fire. The hills behind him are aflame and the fire is coming fast. Winds fan the approaching inferno, spreading the blaze even faster. Running, he dodges around trees as he moves over first one hill then another.

His mind has begun to play tricks on him. Out of the corner of his eye he catches movement within the flames but that can't be possible. Nothing could survive within the inferno.

Pausing a moment to catch his breath, he leans against the bole of a tree. Burning embers fly about him, burning when they land upon his skin. He takes out a cloth and puts it over his mouth in an attempt to draw in a good, clean breath. His eyes water and sting from the smoke and his body is wracked with another coughing fit. When it's over, he pushes himself away from the tree and once again attempts to outrun the fire.

The wind suddenly changes direction and begins blowing from his right. With any luck, it will keep the blaze from following him quickly. Continuing to race straight ahead, he keeps the wind on his right.

After cresting the next hill, he looks back and sees with relief that he has managed to put some distance between himself and the fire. Taking another short breather to recover his strength, he pauses there atop the hill. A flash of color at the base of the hill catches his eye and he sees something pink and brown rolling along the ground.

Glancing back at the fire, he hurries to the bottom and finds the object to be a wadded piece of cotton candy, matted with dirt and twigs. Something in the back of his mind sparks a memory.

Suddenly filled with the need to reach where the cotton candy originated, he turns into the wind and races between the hills. As he runs, another bit of pink fluff is blown toward him upon the breeze. Quickening his pace, he races forward.

The hollow between the hills comes to a stream which he jumps across without even pausing. Landing on the other side, he begins climbing the next hill. When he reaches the top, he sees a valley on the far side. Within the valley is a carnival, or what used to be one. It looks like a tornado ripped through there recently. Buildings are shattered, the Ferris wheel is lying on its side, and the whole place looks deserted.

From somewhere in the back of his mind, a memory of golden hair comes to him. Then it all comes back; the dreams, the golden haired girl and the Tunnel of Love. Scanning the carnival, he sees the Tunnel of Love ride situated over on one side of the midway. Moving quickly, he makes for it.

As he enters the valley, the fire appears on the top of the hill to his right and begins making its way down toward the carnival. Moving as fast as his legs will carry him, he races to the ride.

No carnies are present here this time, all the rides stand deserted and broken. The roller coaster track is broken and one of the coasters sits smashed on the ground below. He hunts for the golden haired girl but she's nowhere to be seen. Ahead of him stands the Tunnel of Love and inside must be where the golden haired girl will be.

Approaching the ride, he sees the channel that once contained the water the boats floated upon is empty and dry, the chain which pulled the boats along sitting exposed and still. Hopping over the rail, he lands within the channel and races for the opening. Boats sit askew in the channel and he has to dodge around them to continue.

At the entrance, he pauses a moment and glances back to the fire. It has crept further down the side of the valley and is now threatening the edge of the carnival. Not sure how much time he has before it reaches him, he moves into the Tunnel of Love.

On the side of the wall, the large heart containing the two points of light is now dimmed. One light is all but out and the other is only half the brilliance it was before. Racing past he moves further into the darkened enclosure. With a thought his orb flares to life and he continues on.

A haze of smoke fills the tunnel giving it an eerie feel. He remembers the shadows that had moved along the walls the last time but so far none have made an appearance. Slowing his pace, he moves along with caution.

Then out of the smoke before him, a shadow appears. Moving quickly, the shadow closes the distance and reaches out to grab him. Backing up fast, he removes the medallion from within his shirt and its light blazes forth.

A shriek of pain more felt than heard erupts from the shadow as it falls back. Behind it, he sees another moving. The tunnel begins to fill with shadows and they form a circle around him staying away from the light being emitted by the medallion.

Moving forward, he holds the medallion up high and forces the shadows back. Step by step he presses onward, the shadows falling back to avoid the light. As he works his way through, the number of shadows surrounding him increases until dozens circle the edge of the medallion's light.

Continuing down, a light appears from up ahead. Moving closer, he sees again the golden haired girl standing upon the dais. Next to her hangs a man by his wrists from a rope that descends out of the darkness above. She's singing the man a song, a sad song filled with loss.

As he moves ever closer to the dais, the girl stops her song and turns to look at him. For the first time, recognition comes as their eyes meet. "Cassie?" he asks in bewilderment. It can't be, she's been dead for over a year. If that is Cassie, then the man hanging next to her must be...Tinok.

A ripple seems to flow through the shadows as he works his way closer to the dais. They fear to go into the light coming from the dais as much as that of the medallion and move aside. He finally reaches the edge of the dais and sees that the man hanging there is indeed Tinok. Bruised, cut and looking to have been tortured, he hangs there limp.

Cassie moves to the edge of the dais and stands there before him. "You haven't much time," she tells him.

"Time?" he asks. "Time for what?"

Turing to glance back at Tinok she says, "My love is almost lost to me." She begins to sing again her lament for her beloved.

"What do you mean?" he says interrupting her. "How will he be lost to you?"

Growing quiet she turns back to him. "You've killed him," she accuses.

"Me?" he asks aghast.

"When the Shroud of Killian blinds the giant's eye a second time, the knife will fall," she says. Then she tilts her head back and begins wailing.

"What knife?" he asks but she turns her back to him and again moves to her beloved's side.

Suddenly, a wall of the Tunnel of Love collapses as fire rages through. The shadows which had surrounded him vanish as the fire spreads rapidly. A crack sounds from above and the ceiling collapses over the dais.

"Cassie!" he cries but both Cassie and Tinok are lost amid the flames. Turning away from the dais, James finds the shadows have now completely disappeared. Running for the entrance, he flees for his life.

Around him, smoke billows down the tunnel from the fire raging behind him. The walls on either side flare as fire consumes them. He rounds a corner and sees the entrance, the fire has already begun to consume it. Doubling his speed, he bolts for freedom. Just as he reaches the opening the ceiling collapses and he dives through barely in time.

The carnival is on fire. Looking around, he can't find anyway through. Pulling his shirt over his head to provide some protection, he moves to the rail and vaults over. Racing through the carnival, he tries to escape.

Eyes watering from the smoke, he runs through the midway practically blind. Then as he passes the side of the fun house, the wall gives way and the flaming structure crashes down upon him. Trapped beneath the burning wall, he tries to escape but the fire reaches him and begins to burn.

"Ahhh!"

Screaming, he bolts upright in the back of the wagon. Hands flailing as he tries to extinguish the flames, he hits Miko in the side of the head.

"Calm down James!" Miko cries out as he grabs James' flailing arms.

Eyes snapping open, he sees Miko staring at him with deep concern. "What?" he asks.

"Thank goodness you woke up," Miko tells him. "You had us worried."

James looks down at himself and sees his clothes untouched by the fire. He puts his hand on his shirt to make sure it's real and pain erupts from his chest. Pulling up his shirt, he sees that his entire chest is covered in burns.

Then it comes back to him. The fire in his dream had burned him in the real world. "Cassie!" he cries out. Looking around he sees Jiron riding closer with a grin on his face.

"Cassie?" Jiron asks then looks to Miko who shrugs.

'When the Shroud of Killian blinds the giant's eye a second time, the knife will fall,' she had said.

"What did you say?" Brother Willim asks from his seat next to the driver.

Not realizing he had spoken aloud he glances to the brother. "When the Shroud of Killian blinds the giant's eye a second time, the knife will fall," he repeats. Glancing around at the others he can see they think him mad. Just then, Illan rides up. Before he has a chance to say anything James holds up his hand ands says, "Listen!"

The dream is already beginning to fade but parts of it still remain crystal clear. He tells them of finding Cassie and Tinok and of what she said.

"It wasn't just a dream either," he states. Lifting up his shirt he shows them the burns upon his chest.

They look to Miko who says, "There were no burns on him earlier."

"But what does it mean?" asks Jiron.

"The Shroud of Killian blinding the giant's eye refers to the time in the moon's cycle when it turns black," Illan explains. "It's an old tale that my grandmother told me when I was younger."

"She said that I didn't have much time," he says.

"The moon turns dark in three days," Brother Willim says. "The second time will be a month after that."

"Then in a little over a month," he says, "the knife will fall."

Made in the USA
Lexington, KY
21 November 2009